COLD, COLD HEART

A Selection of Recent Titles by A.J. Cross

The Dr Kate Hanson Mysteries

GONE IN SECONDS
ART OF DECEPTION
A LITTLE DEATH *
SOMETHING EVIL COMES *
COLD, COLD HEART *

* *available from Severn House*

COLD, COLD HEART

A.J. Cross

This first world edition published 2018
in Great Britain and the USA by
SEVERN HOUSE PUBLISHERS LTD of
Eardley House, 4 Uxbridge Street, London W8 7SY
Trade paperback edition first published
in Great Britain and the USA 2018 by
SEVERN HOUSE PUBLISHERS LTD

British Library Cataloguing in Publication Data
A CIP catalogue record for this title is available from the British Library.

ISBN-13: 978-0-7278-8822-8 (cased)
ISBN-13: 978-1-84751-946-7 (trade paper)
ISBN-13: 978-1-78010-999-2 (e-book)

All Severn House titles are printed on acid-free paper.

Severn House Publishers support the Forest Stewardship Council™ [FSC™],
the leading international forest certification organisation. All our titles that
are printed on FSC certified paper carry the FSC logo.

Typeset by Palimpsest Book Production Ltd.,
Falkirk, Stirlingshire, Scotland.
Printed and bound in Great Britain by
TJ International, Padstow, Cornwall.

There are crimes of passion and there are crimes of logic. The boundary between them is not clearly defined.

Albert Camus

Two quiet knocks brought Della Harrington across her tiny apartment to the front door. She opened it and turned away. 'I thought I'd made it clear that you and I have nothing to discuss.'

He followed her inside. 'Listen to me. Hear me out. I've told you what I want, what I'm prepared to do for—'

'And I've told *you*, I don't trust you anymore.'

He stared into her face. 'How can you *say* that? I want nothing more than to help you and to do that, I have to have it, Della, now.'

'You're not having it. I'm not interested, so if you don't mind—'

His hand shot towards her, grasping her throat, colour flooding his face. 'In that case, I'm taking it.'

She lashed out, sending a small table and a heavy metal lamp crashing to the floor. 'I said, *no*.'

'Your call, Della. Now it has to be my way.'

'*Don't*. Get out! Get—'

The impact of steel on bone stopped her words. He stood back, watched her stagger and fall. He gazed down at her, then lowered himself to her side, waved his hand close to her half-open eyes. They fluttered, stilled. He stayed at her side for several seconds, watched them glaze.

'Time to give me what I asked you so nicely for, Della,' he whispered.

ONE

D avid Lockman was here to get back his life. It was the final day of the hearing. His last chance. His eyes drifted over the dark wood and vaulted ceiling, then on to his legal team, taut as hunting dogs, listening to the lead judge's summing up.

'This court has heard, and it is a matter of record, what befell Della Harrington inside her apartment on Thursday, the ninth of November, 2006. She was subjected to a ferocious, sadistic and sexually motivated attack. David Lockman was arrested, charged and subsequently given a life sentence for her murder. As a prisoner protesting his innocence from the beginning of his sentence, and wishing to appeal against his conviction, he was allowed all of the documentation in the case, plus crime scene photographs, to enable him and his legal team to prepare his appeal.'

Lockman stared down at his hands to avoid the condemnatory looks he anticipated coming his way. The atmosphere around him tightened. He felt the floor beneath him tilt. The vast courtroom began to waver and yaw. He closed his eyes, pulled air into his chest, the judge's voice now coming to him from miles away.

'. . . the prosecution case against David Lockman relied primarily on two types of evidence. The first was provided by two eye-witnesses who stated that in the late afternoon or early evening they saw a man they later identified as David Lockman close to the apartment building which was the scene of the murder. A third witness, a resident of that same apartment building, also identified David Lockman as being there earlier that same day. This court recognizes significant problems with that witness testimony which was confused in nature, plus the advancing years of the witness herself at that time. The second type of evidence was forensic in nature, specifically David Lockman's fingerprints at the entrance to the building and also inside Della Harrington's apartment.'

Hearing this, David Lockman hung his head, chill sweat collecting on his forehead. This court was about to reaffirm his conviction. He looked across at his legal team. One of them turned, looked at him, gave a ghost of a smile. He looked away, reached up to his overly-big shirt collar, his finger brushing the puckered scar on the side of his neck. A permanent reminder that as a prisoner convicted of the brutal killing of a woman, he was regarded by most other inmates as the lowest of the low, along with those who harmed children. The judge was speaking again.

'West Midlands Police struggled to make speedy investigative progress on this case, but after several months their interest settled on David Lockman as a suspect, despite his having no previous convictions of any kind. The officer in charge of that investigation could not be questioned during this appeal. He has been deceased for some years. However, the case files provide extensive detail of that investigation. Having considered the forensic evidence I referred to earlier, I concur that it is unsatisfactory. Two of those items of evidence were readily available to anyone, not specifically David Lockman.' The atmosphere within the courtroom was drum-tight. The judge broke the silence. 'This court has considered two alternative propositions: that Mr Lockman is the man who killed Ms Harrington, or that Mr Lockman had no involvement in it.' He paused, the silence absolute. 'Bearing in mind the unsatisfactory nature of the forensic evidence, the largely circumstantial or unconvincing nature of other evidence presented against David Lockman by West Midlands Police ten years ago, this court deems the original verdict against David Lockman to be unsafe. His conviction is therefore quashed.'

He watched the judges stand, turn and follow each other along the bench, down some steps, through a door which opened to receive them, and disappear from view. The courtroom filled with voices. He looked at his legal team. They were jubilant as they came to him. He felt himself being raised to his feet, the soft voice of one of his lawyers in his ear.

'We won, David. You're *free*.'

Outside in the January cold of the bright London morning he closed his eyes, made dizzy by the astounding expanse of high winter sky and the bedlam of traffic. He tensed at sudden activity from behind railings as reporters waved and clamoured, cameras and iPhones raised, his head besieged by one-word shouts, 'David! David! *David*!' After a decade of rarely hearing his first name, he was anxious, disorientated. One of his defence team seized his arm and raised it high, causing renewed shouts. He slowly formed his raised hand into a fist. He was led forward. The din quietened as he spoke, his voice unsteady.

'I know there is no perfect justice system . . . but I was badly served by ours. My mother believed in me. She did all she could to get me released.' His voice wavered again. 'I wish . . . she could have been here today.' He struggled to regain control. The din returned, more shouts, more clicks as multiple images of him were captured. He felt supportive hands at his shoulders, on his arms. 'I want to express my deepest sympathy for the Harrington family. My nightmare is over. Theirs continues. I sincerely hope for their sake that this case is reopened and that they get some closure.' Exhaustion was pressing down on him. 'I need time and peace to try and get my life back . . . Thank you.'

He tensed again as two black cabs separated themselves from the surging mass of traffic and swooped to a halt at the kerb. He felt himself being borne towards them and helped inside where he sat, pale and spent.

TWO

Professor Kate Hanson was on her way to headquarters in response to a phone call late the previous evening from Detective Sergeant Bernard Watts, officer in charge of the Unsolved Crime Unit. UCU now had the Harrington murder as its next case. Her psychological expertise was required. He'd sounded upbeat. In the four-plus years since she had first agreed to give time and expertise to the unit, Watts' resistance to her and what she was offering had changed to a grudging appreciation of the value she brought to investigations. She'd learned that beneath the big, fifty-plus officer's gruff façade was a willingness to listen and an ability to learn. Which was just as well. As the senior officer in UCU, he had to show he was no dinosaur in a force now dominated by young graduates. Her thoughts turned to the case itself and what she remembered of it. Not much. The press had been uncharacteristically measured in its reporting on details of the murder which had increased the tension of the city's female population. Ten years was a long time. She shook her head. Maisie, her daughter, had been just four years old. Turning into Rose Road, she looked ahead, reducing her speed. Watts had warned her of a likely press presence. Here it was, limited at this hour, but sufficiently motivated to stand around in the cold, early morning. Picking up speed again, she drove on, went past them, made a quick left turn between the high faux-Victorian pillars into the car park and on to a space close to the main entrance. Head down, she retrieved her briefcase from the boot, ignoring the buzz of low conversation and the click of phones from beyond headquarters' railings, and went inside.

Reaching the long corridor leading to UCU, Hanson took out her phone, selected a contact and listened to her call ring out. Maisie, now almost fourteen, should have left the house and be on her way to the school bus. Her call went straight to voicemail. She listened to Maisie and her friend Chelsey, singing in unison: *'Hi, there, how ya' doin'? Sorry you can't get thro – ough . . .'*

Hanson cut the call and sent a quick text, ending it with two words: 'Call me'.

Coming inside the Unsolved Crime Unit, she was halted by two full-colour images on the massive, wall-mounted Smartboard. Eyes fixed on them, she let her bag drop to the floor and went closer. One was a head-and-shoulders photograph of Della Harrington. She gazed up at the other picture. A woman, the same woman, lying on a floor, framed by a doorway, nude from the waist down.

'Doc?' She turned to the voice, saw Watts' broad face then on to Lieutenant Joseph Corrigan who raised his hand to her, their facial expressions probably a mirror of her own. Barely eight a.m. and they looked like they'd been here some hours, particularly Watts. 'All right, doc?'

'Yes,' she said, her eyes back on the images.

'Thanks for coming in this early. Get any hassle from that lot outside?'

'No.'

'Good. Grab a seat and I'll bring you up to speed.'

She took the chair next to Corrigan, on secondment from the Boston Police Department, headquarters' firearms trainer and also UCU investigator, her eyes on Watts' broad back as he approached the screen. Her attention went again to the head-and-shoulders photograph: a young woman, her large brown eyes thickly lashed, her dark hair worn long onto her shoulders. Della Harrington.

'You and me recall this case, doc, but Corrigan wasn't in the UK back then so I'm about to give him an overview.' He pointed. 'Della Harrington, thirty years old, unmarried, call centre supervisor. At the time of her murder she was living alone in an apartment at Marlow Gardens in Birmingham's Jewellery Quarter. Liked by her neighbours, who described her as friendly but tending to keep to herself. Apart from work, she was known to jog regularly in the area. She was also an amateur opera singer. When interviewed, residents of the apartment building described it as a safe place to live. No record of incidents of criminal activity in or around it at the time which contradicts that view. Ditto the immediate neighbourhood.' He dragged two more images onto the screen: a photograph of an exterior door, plus another of a metal plate to one side of it. 'Access to Marlow Gardens Apartments was via this main door which had a security code system for residents. Visitors without a code had to ring one of the bells at the entrance to the building and be let in by whoever they were visiting.' Hands propped either side of his wide waist, he stepped back, surveying the screen's information. 'According to Harrington's immediate neighbours on the first floor, she had very few visitors. Any questions so far?'

'What do we know about the day she died?' asked Hanson.

'Harrington's call centre work had a shift pattern. The day of the murder was her day off. A couple of witnesses saw her jogging in the late morning. That evening she had a rehearsal with an operatic group she belonged to at the Old Rep Theatre in the city centre. The group was due to give a charity performance there a week later. Another member of the group had arranged to pick up Harrington.' Watts pointed to a name. 'Him. Steffan Coultard, thirty-five years old at the time, married, accountant. He arrived at the apartment building that evening at around six thirty, texted Harrington, then waited outside for her in his car. When she didn't appear, he went into the building and up to her apartment. He found her body and called the police.'

'Coultard was in possession of the security code to the main door,' said Hanson.

'Well spotted.'

'Why didn't he go directly to her apartment when he arrived?'

'Good question, doc. One that nobody thought to ask him at the time, but we will.'

He came to the table, opened a manila folder and searched papers inside, pulling out a single sheet. The door swung open. They looked up to see Chief Superintendent Maurice Gander's bulk filling the doorway. Watts held up the sheet.

'Just about to share your email with Professor Hanson, sir.' He passed it to her. She read it. One of its lines was in bold, underlined: 'No contact with David Lockman by any member of this force, either direct or by phone, email or any other means.' As Hanson handed it back, the door closed on the chief.

'Not a word from your leader,' she observed. 'Would I be right in thinking he's rattled?'

'Putting it mildly. He and the brass know that David Lockman's defence team is getting tooled up for a compensation fight. He and the chief constable are busy, looking down the back of the sofa, hoping to find a few quid.'

Corrigan looked from Watts to Hanson. 'Who exactly is this Lockman guy?'

Hanson turned to him. 'David Lockman was quite a celebrity at the time he was caught up in the Harrington investigation. He was a novelist.' She got the full force of the blue eyes.

'*That* David Lockman? I've seen his books in airports and bookstores.'

Hanson gave her phone a series of quick taps and held it towards him so he could view the photographs. She leant closer, breathing in the familiar soap and cologne as she read out the accompanying information: 'Biographical information on David Lockman: thirty-five at the time of his arrest . . . married . . . two children aged five and four. Some months prior to the Harrington murder his fourth novel was published. It went stratospheric.' She pointed. 'See? On the bestseller list for twenty-four weeks and made into a film.' She read the novel's synopsis: '"A touchingly realistic account of an adolescent boy's journey to adulthood and his struggles with being different".'

'One of them misery memoirs,' sniffed Watts.

Hanson eyed him. 'It's fiction.'

He shrugged. 'Beyond me why anybody makes up stuff like that. Isn't the real enough for 'em?'

'Looks like good fortune smiled on the guy, then turned its back,' said Corrigan. 'Lucky for him he got the Court of Appeal on side.'

'It was third time lucky,' said Watts. 'There was a good case against him. He was identified as in the area on the day of the murder, but it was his fingerprints at the entrance to the building and inside Harrington's apartment that clinched it for the jury and got him his life sentence.'

Hanson's brows rose. 'Am I hearing a degree of reluctance to accept the Court of Appeal verdict?'

'What you're hearing is police reluctance to criticize other officers' decisions. "There, but for the grace of God" and all that. I know Lockman's innocent. I also know that hindsight is twenty-twenty.'

Corrigan turned to her. 'Has he told you he's now detective inspector?'

'*No.*' She looked up at Watts. 'Congratulations. That's great, and overdue. You deserve it.'

'Yeah, and look at what we've been handed, soon as I get it. One of them poisoned chalice things.' She knew that Watts wasn't the kind to accept anything positive without first giving it a thorough going over. If there was a cloud lurking behind any rainbow that came his way, he could be relied on to spot it.

'That's not the half of it,' said Corrigan. 'The chief's shorts are full of hornets because of press interest and intrusion.'

Hanson stood, went to the board, her eyes on the photograph of Della Harrington in life. 'Was she in a relationship?'

'Not according to the original investigation,' said Watts.

'She and this Steffan Coultard who found her body weren't an item?'

'Not according to the original investigation,' he repeated. 'No romantic or other connection identified between them, beyond his giving her lifts to this singing group they both belonged to. Like I said, he was married. Not that that makes a difference.'

Hanson's eyes moved over Harrington's soft face, the full-lipped, generous mouth, then on to the upper body and the deep cleavage just visible between the edges of her shirt. She returned to the table and Watts pushed two thick files towards her.

'All yours, doc. A little light bedtime reading for you, *and*—' he slid a thick envelope towards her – 'your set of crime scene photos. You've already seen one of them on the board.' She nodded, not looking at it. 'Don't leave them around where the brainbox might see 'em.'

Hanson got the oblique reference to her daughter's mathematical prowess, which since the age of twelve had taken her across the road from her school to the university where Hanson lectured, to the School of Mathematics where she joined students six-plus years her senior. Watts knew that, due to the demands of her university commitments, Hanson routinely took UCU data home, much of it extreme in nature. This case looked to be no exception. 'I don't need reminding. What's your plan, detective inspector?' she asked.

He pointed to the board. 'By the end of tomorrow, I want

names up there of anybody who we think might have relevant information about the case, including witnesses who were interviewed as part of the original investigation. What we're looking for is anything, any lead, any possibility which was missed or not followed up once the focus was on Lockman and he became a suspect. The clock's ticking on this. We need progress and we need to get it right. Our honeymoon's going to be short. The press will soon start with the criticism, piling on the pressure.' He looked at Hanson. 'You've got clearance from the university to give us some hours?'

'The chief has already been on to the VC, who's arranging it right now.' She looked down at the details of the case she had noted so far. 'Della Harrington worked at a call centre. What did her role as supervisor involve?'

'She was in charge of a team of call handlers taking inquiries from people about issues to do with car insurance . . . you know, renewals, accident claims, that kind of thing.'

'Sorting out issues like that with a call centre can be stressful,' she said.

'Sounds like experience talking to me, doc.'

'It is. That kind of work involves engaging with a large volume of people, a proportion of whom are already stressed and potentially challenging. Was there ever an indication of such stress being expressed towards operators at the centre she worked at? Did the original investigation check for instances of anger or threat specifically aimed at Harrington?'

Watts shook his head. 'From what I've read, it was never considered an issue by investigators because of Harrington's supervisory role, but I'll request the company's records for six months prior to her murder. That's if they've still got them.'

The door opened and a youthful-looking figure came inside carrying papers and a small box: Julian Devenish, one of Hanson's PhD students who assisted UCU with data searches. Watts' eyes lingered on his sweatshirt. 'What you got for us, Superman?'

'All the forensic evidence for the Harrington case, such as it is. I've done a complete data sweep. During the original investigation a search was requested of Harrington's phone calls, plus those of David Lockman, plus a guy named Fenton and a Leonard Dobbs, but no indication of any results.' He handed the box and some stapled sheets to Watts. 'There's a copy for each of you showing all the forensic details, plus an overview of the case.'

Watts took them and read the single page of details. 'Blimey, that *it*?' He caught Hanson's sharp look. 'Thanks, lad. Not your fault there's sod-all.'

She rolled her eyes. At twenty-three, the 'lad' was nearing completion of his PhD. She tried to imagine a situation in which Watts might refer to him some day as 'Dr' Devenish. She shook her head. Never going to happen. She checked the time on her phone. 'I need to get going. My work flexibility starts tomorrow. Today I've got a full day of lectures.' Her eyes strayed to the image of Della Harrington in death. She looked away, reached for the folders and photographs. Corrigan was there first.

'Easy, Red. I got 'em.'

They reached her car as press attention was occupied with vehicles arriving at the main entrance. She clicked open the boot lid and he placed the folders inside. Closing it, he looked down at her. Some months before he'd told her he was interested in her. She had already known. Partly because it had becoming increasingly evident over the last three years or so. Partly because it was mutual. It hadn't progressed. It wouldn't. They were colleagues. She didn't want or need those kinds of complications. She looked away from him. 'Don't,' she said quietly. He leant towards her. She tensed.

'Just wanted to say, I'm glad we're working together again, is all. Leave by the back way. Less press there.'

THREE

Hanson carried bowls and plates to the table where Maisie was engrossed in a phone conversation, squeals and laughter far outweighing the words. Ending the call, Maisie said, 'That was Lissy.'

'I gathered.'

'She and Chel have had this *massive* row. They're *really* mad at each other.'

Sidestepping the minefield that is teenage girl friendships, Hanson said, 'I rang you this morning. It went straight to voicemail.'

'Soz. I was probably upstairs and didn't hear it ring.'

Hanson's eyes went to the heart-shaped face and thick, dark-red curls, a mirror image of her own. 'Maisie, we both know that wherever you go, so goes your phone. I also texted you. You didn't respond to that either. We have an agreement, remember? When I ring or text you, it's because I need to ask you something or I want to know where you are. I expect a response from you as soon as possible.' She went to the stove, suppressing a niggling thought that she was being overly cautious. Safeguarding Maisie was a priority. Given her forensic training, plus the work she did for UCU, that's how it had to be. Maisie had to live with it. Which meant sticking to the rules.

'Yeah, OK,' said Maisie with a contrite look which disappeared almost as soon as it arrived. 'Hey, I just remembered. Daddy's picking me up on Saturday morning to take me to the Technology Rocks! exhibition at the NEC.'

'You'll enjoy that. Can you make a start on chopping those vegetables, please?'

Hanson carefully measured oil into the large wok then fetched other stir-fry ingredients to the counter, most of her head still occupied with UCU's new case, intermittently picking up Maisie's words.

'. . . and when she told us she's *pregnant*, we couldn't *believe* it . . . Chelsey and me have made a pact . . . no kids, *ever*. No way, Jose.'

Hanson dropped chicken pieces into the hot wok, squinted against the sizzle of hot oil and gave them a vigorous stir, registering a couple of words buried within the soliloquy. 'Who's pregnant? What's that got to do with Chelsey and you?'

Maisie and the chopped vegetables arrived at her side. 'Mom, you go on about me not listening. Ms *Grant*, one of our geography teachers. She's up the—'

'Can you put forks on the table, please?'

Maisie went to the cutlery drawer. 'This pact me and Chel have got should please you and her mom. It means you and Candice can go on for years pretending you're still young.'

'Thanks for the thought.' Hanson added vegetables to the wok. 'By the way, how is Candice coping with her builders?'

'She's not.' Maisie took forks to the table. 'She's on about dust being everywhere so she's like constantly on Chel's case about closing doors and stuff. The builders are also doing her head in. She says their normal conversation involves standing nose-to-nose while they shout at each other.'

'Oh dear.'

'No, Mom, they're not, like angry. It's just how they communicate with each other. I've seen it. It's hilarious.'

Hanson brought the stir-fry to the table and they sat. Maisie eyed it. 'Where's the salad cream and the ketchup?'

'In the cupboard where they belong.' She sighed as Maisie went to fetch them. 'I think I'll ring Candice after dinner and suggest that Chelsey stays here for a few nights, just to lighten the load a little. You'd like that, wouldn't you?'

'She can't.'

'Oh? Why not?'

'Because of Grandpa . . .' Hanson saw Maisie's eyes drift away from hers.

'What about Grandpa?'

'I forgot to tell you. He rang earlier.'

'What did he say?'

'He's coming to stay for a few days.'

'When?'

'Dunno.' The doorbell sounded. 'Like, tonight?'

'Oh, *for* . . .!'

Watching her mother jump up and head for the hall, Maisie gave the salad cream a brisk shake. 'Grandpa touching down at Trauma Towers.'

Hanson was in her study, having read Julian's summary of key investigative events. It began with the discovery of Della Harrington's body and ended with the arrest of David Lockman. Turning back the pages, she re-read them, highlighting what looked to be potential key items. Closing the file, she let her eyes drift over what she had written. The original investigative information seemed satisfactory as far as it went but she hadn't found the psychological angle she was looking for.

Reaching into her briefcase for the envelope of crime scene photographs, she smiled as she picked up the sound of the television and Maisie and Charlie's laughter. She slid the prints from their envelope, quickly spread them out on the desk, losing the smile. Twelve large, between-the-eyes, sharp focused, full colour frozen moments of Della Harrington in death. One in particular claimed her attention. She reached for it, looked down at Della Harrington lying on her back on a rug inside her bedroom, very close to the open door. Her long hair was loose, spread like a dark halo around her head, its tousled mass merging with heavy blood loss coming from somewhere beneath it. The eyes were heavy-lidded, half-closed. Hanson reached up and adjusted the desk lamp, bringing additional light to all of the photographs. Her attention went to an area of faint bruising now evident at the front of Della Harrington's neck. Her eyes moved slowly downwards to Harrington's grey-and-white long-sleeved top and the white sports bra, both pushed up, exposing her upper body. An inconsequential thought slid into Hanson's head: *Della Harrington had lovely breasts.* She recognized the thought for what it was: her mind's way of providing emotional distance whilst she adjusted to the grim reality of the scene. It made no difference how many cases she'd worked on, nor the number of scene photographs she'd looked at over the years. Every case had its own particular, distressing and disturbing features which had to be thoroughly examined. It was the only way to fully understand what had happened to the victim and why. It never got easier. The day she found that it had would be the day she stopped doing this work.

Taking a deep breath, she looked at more details within the photograph. Lying to the right of Harrington, at a distance of 128 centimetres, according to the scene measure, were grey jogging trousers, a pair of white pants entangled within them. Harrington's arms were flung wide, her watch still on her wrist. Hanson pulled the image closer, focusing on a series of small red ellipses along the pale insides of each arm, tiny, bloodless, gaping mouths in the soft-looking skin. Putting down the photograph, she picked up another, this one a close-up of Della Harrington's wristwatch. She read the label placed beside it in the photograph: 'Victim's watch showing correct time (7.32 p.m.) whilst scene under process'. Hanson knew that time of death hadn't been established, except for a wide estimate of between one and six p.m. She had been hoping the watch was damaged, giving an indication of the likely time Harrington had been attacked. She shook her head. Was life ever that accommodating?

She reached for another photograph, this one taken from directly above the body. It was shocking. Both Harrington's legs were extended wide, leaving her lower half fully exposed and vulnerable. Her left leg was raised, the foot supported on a small white wicker stool. The right leg was also extended, the foot resting on the floor. There was something about the position which chimed with Hanson. Her eyes moved slowly over the photograph and stopped at a chair standing near to the body and just to the left of the open door. It looked like it belonged in a dining room. She skimmed the case summary description of the small apartment: hallway, sitting room, bedroom, kitchen. No dining room. A similar photograph taken from a different vantage point snagged her attention. In this one, the photographer had stood close to Harrington's head, the camera lens pointing towards her feet with their neat pink toenails. Beyond them was a sitting room and beyond that a small hallway and a front door.

Looking back along the body, Hanson saw a detail she hadn't noted previously: a small pink-and-white cushion had been placed beneath Harrington's hips. One hand supporting her chin, Hanson studied the cushion. The obvious assumption was that its function was to raise Harrington's hips. She frowned at what she was seeing. Given the placing of the legs, was this a bizarre attempt to mimic a gynaecological position? The words of Hanson's beloved, elderly PhD supervisor from several years before wisped into her head. *Steady, Kate. Never assume. Let the evidence lead you.*

Her eyes slowly tracked the body again, from the dark hair of the head to the delicate pink nails of the feet, back to the face and its lazy, 'just-woken' eyes, then back to the body and its flagrant position. Sexual, rather than gynaecological? She added her observations to her notebook then sat back from the photographs and looked towards the darkened study window. Already she needed emotional distance from what she'd seen so far, knowing that there wouldn't be any as long as she and her colleagues worked the case. She looked down at the pages of her notebook, rereading what she had written. The murderer's modus operandi had involved striking Harrington on the head, possibly followed by strangulation. Possibly the other way around? He'd done much more. It was evident that Della Harrington had not fallen to the floor in the position depicted in the photographs. Her killer had moved her. He had created a deliberate scene using her body. He had left her displayed for the world to see. Or, more specifically, those who had entered her apartment through the front door after he had left. She came back to the photographs, gazed at the body. Was the intention to shock? Was the killer so proud of what he had done that he wanted people to see it? Admire it?

Reaching for the file Watts had given her, she quickly turned the first few pages. She found the name she'd heard in UCU: Steffan Coultard. The first person to enter the apartment after the killer had left. She breathed, rotated her shoulders, her eyes moving over the photographs, searching for every possible indication of the intention underlying this killer's actions. She quickly listed his apparent actions. Removal of clothing. Small cuts to inner arms. Display of body. Objectification. She absently ran her fingers through her hair. All that she was seeing screamed this killer's primary intent and confirmed the opinion of the original investigation. This was undoubtedly sexual homicide.

She left her desk and went to a nearby bookcase to locate a

file, brought it back to the desk. Opening it, she gazed down at details of the FBI training course on sexual homicide investigation she'd attended in London two years before. Among other things, it had introduced her to the term 'Lust Murder'. She read quickly through detailed notes she'd made at the time, looked back to the photographs in front of her. Lust murder fitted with what she was seeing. As an American police officer, Corrigan might well bring additional insight to the scene. She would ask him when she next saw him.

Closing the file, she returned it to its shelf. The first photograph she'd examined was demanding her attention again. She reached for it and looked down at the scattered items around the body: an open purse-wallet, a mix of loose coins, lip gloss, hair brush. *Was this a case of sexual murder followed by opportunistic theft? Or was it a theft which Della Harrington had interrupted and which then morphed into a sexual attack by someone with a rich fantasy life to guide him?* She shook her head. It was impossible to say which came first but it was clear that Della Harrington's killer had to have arrived at that apartment with those fantasies inside his head and readily available to guide his actions. Whoever he was, she suspected he had a keen interest in violent pornography.

She moved the photographs around and found one taken during Della Harrington's post-mortem. Her eyes moved slowly over the detail: a latex-covered hand supporting Harrington's head, an index finger pointing to an area of significant damage to the skull within the damp, parted hair, deep fissures radiating from it. Even without the deadly dimensions indicated by the plastic measure propped against it, it seemed unlikely that Harrington would have survived it beyond a few minutes. She wrote herself a quick reminder to check this out with Connie Chong, headquarters' in-house pathologist. It might be important. If Harrington had had some minutes of survival time she might have been able to shout. If that was the case, the proximity of neighbours could be key. *If . . . if . . . if.*

Reaching for the two photographs of Harrington's inner arms, Hanson looked from one to the other, her focus on the stark, neat lines of tiny incisions on the pale skin. Her gaze unfocused, she pictured the sharp metal point which had made them, absently mimicking the quick, purposeful piercings with her fingertip on her desk. *Tchk-tchk-tchk* . . . What had happened to the knife? She quickly re-examined the photographs, including those showing the scatter of items on the floor around the body. No knife. Something else to check tomorrow.

She now had the basics of the case inside her head along with details of the killer's behaviour towards Della Harrington. Her UCU colleagues would soon be wanting her views on those details. Based on the scene photographs, she had some observations to offer but it was too soon to go beyond them. She would stick with observations for now, which would irritate the hell out of Watts. She absently ran her fingers through her hair, eyeing the photographs. She wouldn't be pushed to go beyond the evidence of this killer's behaviour to the kind of person he was, regardless of Watts pushing for a character outline. It's what he routinely did. He wouldn't thank her for her reticence. He had his promotion and he'd been handed this high-profile case. His neck was on the line. More reasons for her to be cautious. She pressed her hands over her eyes, shutting out the details of Della Harrington's death. What she needed was a complete psychological understanding of what had been done to her. Without it, she wouldn't get to the *why* of this case, the reason for the cruelty towards Della Harrington. All she and her colleagues had right now were two-dimensional, quasi-pornographic renditions of a deceased woman. Hanson recalled hearing a brief reference to Della Harrington having a sister. One thing was certain. Both Della and her family deserved better.

She turned her attention to the few photographs of forensic evidence. One showed a narrow cream-coloured belt with a blue stripe along each edge, a small silver-coloured buckle at one end. Clearly a woman's. She had seen it in one of the scene photographs. She searched for it. The belt was lying on the floor close to the oddly placed dining chair and Harrington's left leg. Hanson stared at it. Had her killer intended to use the belt to secure her to the chair? 'If so, why didn't you?' she mused aloud. 'Were you interrupted?'

She turned to a photograph of a paper coffee cup, its distinctive blue-black brand colours identifying it as having come from a high street chain. Scenes-of-crime officers had located it on a low shelf inside Della Harrington's wardrobe. Hanson frowned. Why would a used, take-out cup be inside a wardrobe? On one or two occasions Hanson had bought coffee-to-go and the cups had occasionally found their way into her kitchen, but no further. She gazed at it, positioned between two handbags. Her eyes moved slowly over the bags, estimating that one of them at least would have cost Della Harrington, a call centre worker on a modest salary, in excess of one thousand pounds. That is, if it had been Della who bought it. A second photograph showed the same cup against a plain white background, its exterior marked by red circles indicating fingerprint locations.

She turned her attention to another photograph showing an oblong, metal plate mounted on a plastered, external wall, bell pushes set into it. She had seen it on UCU's Smartboard earlier that day. It also bore the same red markings. She read the forensic report on them. It confirmed that the prints on both coffee cup and metal plate belonged to David Anthony Lockman. Those prints would have been hugely instrumental in sending him to prison for life.

She checked the time on her phone. Almost ten o'clock. Gathering the photographs into a neat stack, she retrieved the last one from where it had slid beneath the case files. It showed the final piece of forensic evidence: a small bookmark, both of its sides depicted. One side bore David Lockman's name, his website address and a list of his published novels, the other a handwritten message: 'To Della. Do your own thing. David.' followed by a signature. A third nail in the coffin of David Lockman's freedom. Adding it to the other photographs, she replaced them in their envelope. Quickly listing names she'd seen in the files, she slid notebook and envelope into her briefcase, fastened it and stowed it beneath her desk. She checked the desk. Nothing for Maisie to see, inadvertently or otherwise.

Activating the desktop, she typed in Lockman's website address and looked at the details filling the screen. Her eyes drifted over pictures of him: dark haired, fairly well-built. Almost unrecognisable from those she had seen in the media as he left the Court of Appeal a few days before. The scene photographs had raised questions. What she and her colleagues needed were answers.

Switching off the computer she went into the hall, massaging her neck and shoulders and on to the sitting room. 'Time for bed, Maisie.' As Maisie grumped her way to the door Hanson took her warm place on the sofa and grinned across at Charlie. 'You were a very nice surprise this evening.'

'Not too much of one, I hope?'

'Maisie did forget to tell me you were coming but it's not a problem. I'm glad you're here. We both are. I'm only sorry I had to work this evening.'

'I know your situation, Kate, and I'm here for a few days . . . if that's OK?'

'More than OK, you know that.' She studied him, trying to decide if her impression that he'd lost weight since she last saw him was reliable. 'How are you?'

'Fine, fine.' He nodded. 'No problems.'

Charlie was not her biological father but he'd been there from her earliest days. Following several years of estrangement after he left her and her mother when Hanson was fifteen, they had reconciled last year. Some months later he had stayed here whilst he recovered from a serious chest infection. For Hanson, that time had been very special, and for Maisie too, who adored her grandpa. When he'd regained his fitness, they hadn't wanted him to leave. Now he often stayed for weekends, but Hanson had a plan. She wanted Charlie living here as a permanent arrangement. As a first step towards this goal, she had gone into his bedroom the previous weekend, checked one of its internal walls and decided that it could easily be extended into the adjoining smaller room to create a bathroom for him. He could use the remaining extra space for any belongings he might want to bring here. She intended to raise this with him in the next day or two. She would emphasize the benefit to him of keeping on his house in Worcester so he could return to it for periods of time whenever it suited him. She smiled to herself. She'd ring Candice sometime this week and ask her how busy her builders were.

'Would you like a drink, Charlie?'

He got up from the sofa. 'I'll make it. What would you like? Tea? Hot chocolate?'

'Chocolate, please.' She followed him into the kitchen. 'Make some for Maisie and I'll take it up to her.' She went to the wide doors and looked out on darkness, her own reflection gazing back at her. Now was as good a time as any. 'Charlie?'

'Yes, Kate?'

'What would you say if I suggested that you come to live with Maisie and me permanently?' She waited. Not getting a response, she turned. He was assembling their drinks, not looking at her.

'I'd say it's a really kind offer, but a big step for both of us,' he said quietly.

'It's not kind, Charlie. It's practical. You were very ill last winter and your GP said that there was some lung damage, remember?'

He looked up and smiled at her. 'He's been my doctor for years so I know him. He tends towards a dark view of things, which doesn't appear to include the couple of extra stones he's carrying around his middle. I'm fitter than he is, trust me.' She said nothing, reluctant to drop the issue but unsure how to continue. He turned, holding Maisie's old Care-Bear mug filled with hot chocolate towards her.

'Here you go.'

She took it from him and went upstairs. Placing it beside Maisie's bed and emphasizing the need for all technology to be 'switched off or else', Hanson gave her a hug then came downstairs. She'd decided not to continue the conversation with Charlie. Better to let him think about it. Get used to the idea. There would be other opportunities for discussion of the details during the next few days and weeks.

FOUR

Coming into UCU the next morning Hanson found Watts in full flow. 'Yes, they got the wrong man, but after looking at the course of that investigation, I can tell you, Corrigan, it was by-the-book.'

'Maybe the book needs rewriting,' she said.

He turned to her. 'That your take on the original investigation?'

'You really want my opinion?'

He frowned. 'Yes, or I wouldn't be asking.'

'I think it was narrow.'

Watts glanced at Corrigan, watched as she unloaded her briefcase onto the table. 'Narrow, because?'

'Because there was zero psychological perspective in it.'

'Such as, exactly?'

'That, I can't say. So far, I know the case from file information and photographs, which give useful but potentially simplistic information. We haven't met any of the people involved.'

Watts huffed. 'That investigation was evidence-based, exactly as it should have been. The DI in charge back then had the forensic evidence, the scene-of-crime photographs and he identified it as a sexual homicide.' He paused, his eyes on her. 'Don't tell me you don't agree with *that*.'

'I wouldn't dream of it, but we know that the way he followed that evidence led him to the wrong conclusion.' She caught the 'Gotcha!' grin on Corrigan's face.

'Yeah, well maybe there's a simple reason why there's no reference in the files to a "psychological perspective". There wasn't one.'

After working with Watts on various cases, Hanson knew that as a police officer he favoured hard evidence above all else. His acceptance of her psychological input was genuine. But that did not mean he was 'psychologically minded'.

'That being the case, I might as well dismiss myself and head to the university.'

'Settle down, doc. There's work to do here, but first . . .' She watched him reach for a large paper bag sitting on the table and remove two buns encased in clear plastic packaging. 'Breakfast's on me, Corrigan.'

She saw Corrigan look at them, shake his head. 'I'm good, thanks.'

'Suit yourself. I suppose you had eggs-over-easy, whatever that is and a protein shake. I tell you, Corrigan, you could do worse than get yourself round one of these of a morning.'

Corrigan grinned up at Hanson, showing white, even teeth. 'Like I said, I'm good.'

Watts looked down at his own breakfast of choice, his fingers wriggling in anticipation.

Hanson éyed the two buns nestling side-by-side, round, white-iced, each with a bright glacé cherry at its centre. She and Corrigan exchanged quick glances. She leant forward, her eyes on Watts. 'You need to trust me on this. There's *always* psychology. In every utterance, choice and decision we make. It didn't feature in the original investigation because no one was looking for it.'

He gazed at her for a few seconds, his eyes drifting to the buns, then to Corrigan whose attention was fixed on case data, a trace of a smile on his mouth. He looked back at her. 'Right, Clever Clogs, have a look at the names I've put up.' He pointed to a list on the wall-mounted Smartboard.

She recognized the four names she herself had noted in the files the previous evening: Steffan Coultard, Della Harrington's chauffeur to operatic rehearsals; Archie Fenton, maintenance man for the Marlow Gardens Apartments; Esther Collins, resident of the building whose eyewitness evidence was rejected by the Court of Appeal; and Andrea Jones, sister of Della Harrington.

Watts came to the board, looked up at the names. 'Harrington's estimated time of death is wide: between one and six p.m. In my book, that makes everybody who crops up in our investiga-tion a potential person of interest.' He pointed at the names. 'These are what you might call our starter POIs, either because of where they were at the time Harrington was found dead or, in Esther Collins' case, the part she played in getting David Lockman sent down. There's a couple of neighbours to speak to as well, once we delve into the files, get their names and find out where they and these four are now. Julian's already onto it.'

Hanson opened her notebook. 'I noted that Fenton, the maintenance man, had a passkey to apartments in the building.'

Watts tapped the board, pulling up more information. 'He did, but more to the point, he's known.'

Hanson eyed him. 'I didn't see any reference to his having a criminal record.'

'He hasn't but Julian's found a rape-robbery case where Fenton's name cropped up. This was a couple of years after the Harrington murder. He was questioned.'

'Is that sufficient for him to be classed as "known"?' she asked.

'Given the nature of that case and Harrington's, it does it for me. Like I said, these four names are a starting point. We'll talk to each of them. Get a feel for their lives back then. The sister should be able to give us a lot of detail about Della Harrington's history and her life. For the others, it's a case of exploring the relationship they had with her, what they knew about her at the time she was killed. Do they know anything different now? They're our way into Marlow Gardens and Della Harrington's life while she lived there.' He paused. 'Have either of you worked a ten-year-old cold case?' Hanson and Corrigan looked at each other, shook their heads. 'Me neither,' he said.

Hanson glanced at the brief notes she'd made the previous evening. 'Do we know anything about the knife which inflicted the series of small cuts to Harrington's arms?'

'It was her own. From her kitchen,' said Corrigan.

She made a quick note. 'I also noticed items scattered on the floor around the body. Are we investigating this as a combination sexual-homicide-theft case?' she asked.

'Looks that way,' said Watts. 'The sister identified Harrington's laptop and phone as missing, neither of them top-of-the-range, plus bits of jewellery, none of it pricey.'

'Whoever killed her didn't take her watch,' she said.

'It wasn't expensive.'

'Neither was her jewellery but he still took it.' Hanson looked at the board. 'I want to see the actual forensic evidence. Have we got it yet?'

Corrigan stood. She watched him lift the cardboard box onto

the table, aware of Watts eyeing her, a faint grin on his wide face. Pointedly ignoring him, she waited as Corrigan took out the items of evidence she had seen only in photographs. He placed them on the table. She looked at the belt, the coffee cup, the metal plate with its entrance bells, the bookmark, each swathed in plastic. Corrigan moved them closer to where Hanson was sitting and sat next to her.

'You've examined these already, Corrigan?' she asked.

'Yep, but it never hurts to take another look, which I guess will be one of many before we're through with the case.'

Hanson gazed at each of the items in turn. 'What was David Lockman's explanation for the bookmark with his name and the coffee cup with his prints being inside Harrington's apartment?'

'He didn't offer one. He said he couldn't recall ever having met her.' He reached for the bookmark. 'He said that many authors who do literary festivals and talks to groups provide bookmarks like this one as give-aways. He admitted it was his signature but said he had no recollection of Harrington herself. The original investigation was never able to prove otherwise.' He put it down, reached for the paper coffee cup. 'The judge at the recent appeal hearing wasn't impressed with Lockman's prints being on this. He rejected it as unreliable evidence on the basis that it was a movable item from a public place, which means anybody could have taken it, including Harrington herself, given that it was found inside her apartment. He took a similar view of the bookmark.'

'Were there any other prints found at the scene?' she asked.

'A few,' said Watts. 'Some belonged to Fenton, the maintenance bloke.'

'Where were they?'

'On an area of wall around an electric socket. Maintenance records confirmed he replaced it a couple of weeks before the murder. There was also a single print on the inside of the front door of the apartment which was identified as Steffan Coultard's. The only others found which didn't belong to Harrington were two on the inside of her bedroom door. They were data-checked but no match was found. Whoever they belonged to had no record.'

'Have they been checked since?' she asked.

'Yeah. Still no match. Looks like whoever he is, he's still behaving himself.'

Hanson thought over what he'd said. 'Two unidentified prints found in her bedroom, yet the picture that's emerged of Della Harrington so far is that she had no social media presence and that her private life was extremely quiet.'

Watts huffed. 'I know what that's like and I can tell you it's . . .'

'Too much information.' She reached for the belt, examined its length, then placed it around her own waist, aware of increasing interest from Corrigan's direction. She pulled the ends of the belt together, managing to get the keeper into the last hole. It felt tight. 'This didn't belong to Della Harrington.'

'How can you say that?' asked Watts.

She pointed at the board. 'Because Della Harrington was five-seven and statuesque. I'm five-three at a push, a ten when I breathe in and this belt is on the small side for me. 'See?' She pointed to it, removed it, placed it on the table and turned to Corrigan. 'If I said "lust murder", what would you say?'

'I'd say, a homicide in which a sadistic killer gets sexual gratification through mutilation or any number of other activities prior to the victim's death. The sexual crime itself is the equivalent of coitus.'

'*Aye-up,*' murmured Watts.

'Ignore it,' she said to Corrigan, 'it's one of his many verbal tics.'

Corrigan continued, 'Far as I recall, a sexual factor must be clearly apparent, possibly indicating underlying sexual conflict. Primary goal: to kill the victim as part of a motivated attack via the enactment of some type of fantasy that has preoccupied the killer for a while.'

Hanson absorbed his words. Despite the vague sense of dissatisfaction she'd felt when looking at the crime scene photographs the previous evening, what Corrigan had said echoed what she had seen of Harrington's body and confirmed much of what the crime scene told her. *You're overthinking it,* she told herself.

Watts brought his big hands together. 'Right. We've got ourselves a sexual homicide.' He turned to her. 'Got any ideas for a first action? Psychologically speaking, of course.'

Hearing Corrigan's quiet laugh, she said, 'I want to see the apartment where the murder took place.'

Watts looked gratified. 'Three great minds, doc. That's exactly what we want and we're in luck. I was on to the letting agent this morning to fix up a visit. That apartment's empty, waiting for new tenants who are moving in on Monday.' He reached for the phone. 'I'll give him a bell. Tell him to meet us at Marlow Gardens Apartments in an hour.'

FIVE

They drove into the apartment building's car park beneath an overcast sky, unaware that they were being watched. The watcher was here on the off-chance, as he'd often been since the news of the new police investigation broke. It had great personal relevance for him. He stood, ignoring the melee rushing past, hailing taxis, running for buses or disappearing inside nearby bars and cafes, his eyes fixed on the three people now getting out of the Range Rover, two males, one tall, heavily built, the other equally tall but athletic-looking. His eyes settled on the woman with them. Striking. Not that it was relevant. He was here for information. Intelligence. One of the best ways to get that was to watch people.

'Detective Inspector Watts!'

The letting agent hurried across the car park, his heavy overcoat swirled by a stiff wind carrying a hint of ice and a threat of rain. He raised his hand in a quick, beckoning gesture. 'Leonard Dobbs. This way. Follow me.'

They did, to the main entrance of Marlow Gardens Apartments where Dobbs halted, reached into an inside pocket and took out a small plastic card. 'Cold, isn't it? Let's get you inside, shall we?' He tapped several numbered buttons set into the metal plate beside the main door. The door opened with a sharp click.

'How's that work, exactly?' asked Watts.

'Each resident gets a security code specific to them when they move in. If you're a visitor and don't have the code, you press the numbered bell of whoever you're here to see and they let you in if they're home.'

'Was it the same ten years back?'

'Yes.'

'Pretty secure, then?' said Corrigan.

Dobbs shook his head. 'Hardly Fort Knox. Residents give their security codes to delivery people and all sorts of other random callers, or they forget them, which means I have to dig through the files to find them.'

Corrigan absorbed what he'd said. 'The codes give access only to the block, not the actual apartments.'

'Obviously, not.'

Watts looked at him. 'But *you* can come to the rescue of a resident because you know all the numbers, right?'

Dobbs hesitated, gave a brief laugh. 'I'd have to be here, wouldn't I? I'm on strict nine-to-five-thirty availability. Follow me.' He led them inside the entrance hall of the apartments, gave Hanson a quick up-down glance then approached Watts. He stood close, his voice low. 'Detective inspector, I need an urgent word with you.' Watts eyed the light brown, elaborately blow-dried hair which the wind had barely shifted, then on to the camel coat, the expensive-looking driving gloves and shiny black loafers.

'We've got a lot on, Mr Dobbs. What particular word might that be?'

'Of course, of course,' said Dobbs, missing Watts' tone. 'So have I. I've got a very important business meeting to get to.' He lowered his voice, leaning close to Watts who kept his eyes fixed straight ahead. 'The thing *is,* there's a bit of a lull in the lettings market right now. Just a short-term blip. Always happens before spring kicks in, but this apartment you want to see has been empty for a few weeks and—' he shot quick glances to right and left, lowering his voice further despite there being no one else around – 'I'm rather hoping that this will be a one-off visit by the police. If you take my meaning?'

'No. And it might not be. What's your problem?'

Dobbs' face heated up, his words coming in an urgent hiss. 'Surely, it's obvious? It's all over the news. About the animal who murdered that woman being let out of prison. These new tenants I've got lined up for that apartment are young. The boyfriend looks to be in his early twenties. They probably don't have a clue what happened here and so what, anyway? Who cares? It's all history. Because they're young, I'm banking on them not being into the news, but if they do get to hear about it, it might be . . . a bit awkward.'

'You haven't considered telling them?'

Dobbs looked horrified. 'Of course not. What would be the point of that? I'm not about to hand them a reason to have second thoughts. Actually, I'm not too bothered about the boyfriend.

He strikes me as a practical type, but the girlfriend's a different kettle of fish from what I've seen. Pretty little thing. Quiet. Looks very young. If she finds out what happened in that apartment, even though it was years ago, I'm betting she'll refuse to go anywhere near it. They could turn up here any time between now and Monday to have a look around the area. New tenants do that kind of thing, you know. They like to get a coffee or a bite to eat, soak up the atmosphere of the area. I'd rather they didn't see it crawling with police . . .' Watts moved his eyes to Dobbs' face. Dobbs gave a quick nod. 'Of course, I appreciate that like me you've got your job to do.'

His eyes still fixed on him, Watts said, 'Nobody here would have reason to think we're police officers.' Dobbs gave both tall men a doubtful look, glanced down at Watts' large, outstretched hand. 'The apartment *key*?'

Dobbs turned away from him to the stairs. 'I'll show you up to the first floor and let you in. All part of our service.'

Watts and Corrigan followed him. Hanson lingered, absorbing what was visible in the entrance hall: three sleek bicycles, another of the folded variety, all secured in a metal frame, a row of fuse boxes under the stairs, an array of six locked and numbered mailboxes attached to the opposite wall. Facing the stairs her colleagues were now going up, there was what looked to be a single apartment door. She frowned at it. No number. Dobbs' unctuous voice drifted down the stairs to her. 'This whole building is a little . . . bijou, compared to what's going up in this area now. Just three apartments per floor on floors one and two.' Hanson looked again at the unnumbered door then followed her colleagues up the stairs.

Dobbs was standing at the middle of three doors, inserting a key into the lock. He turned it. The door remained resolutely shut. Tutting, he jiggled the key, placed his shoulder against the door and gave it a few shoves. After further resistance, the key turned, the door yielded with a creak and swung slowly open. Dobbs stood aside with an obsequious bow, his hand outstretched to the interior of the apartment.

Hanson followed her colleagues inside then turned to Dobbs. 'There's an unmarked door on the ground floor.' He displayed his teeth to her. 'That's the maintenance office.'

'How long have the current tenants lived here?'

'The longest period right now is a year-plus. Shall we?' He held out his arm again for her to enter the apartment.

Going inside, she and her two colleagues filled the small space that had been Della Harrington's tiny hallway. Immediately facing them was the sitting room and beyond that the bedroom. The whole place was deeply shadowed, silent. Hanson's eyes drifted slowly over what she could see of the ceiling, the walls, wondering if any children lived in this building. Unlikely, she thought, given this apartment's small dimensions. They moved further inside. Hanson felt chill air drifting across the wood floor towards her, felt it waft around her feet, creep onto her ankles, insinuate itself beneath her long skirt and moving upwards . . .

'I'm going to tell Dobbs he can sling his hook,' said Watts. She tracked his broad back through the front door and out to the landing where Dobbs was hovering. Watts held out his hand. With grudging reluctance Dobbs surrendered the apartment key into it. 'We might be a while,' said Watts. 'You can wait out here.'

Dobbs quickly turned away. 'I'll wait in the car park. When you've finished, lock the door and bring that key to me. My car's the midnight-blue BMW convertible in the first tenant parking spot. You probably noticed it when you arrived.'

'No,' said Watts, his voice flat. He had. He'd noted the number plate: LD2. The sound of Dobbs' retreating footsteps drifted inside the apartment as Watts came back in. 'I'm adding *him* to our list of people to talk to.'

'Because he was the letting agent at the time of the murder?' said Hanson.

'No. Because he's a *git*. See his hair? I never saw anything like that on a bloke. It's probably got its own postcode.' Watts' eyes drifted around the small space where Della Harrington had lived and died. 'Right. Let's have a look round. Shouldn't take long from where I'm standing.'

Hanson was in silent agreement. Not only was the apartment small, it was empty of all the features which brought softness to a living space and made it a home. In their absence there was the abandoned, melancholy air of a space without function, now filled with stillness and cold air. She'd come here hoping for insight into what had occurred a decade before. Looking at it now she could see how it was that Della Harrington's killer had been able to take control of her and the situation. The small dimensions of this apartment would surely have helped. There was scarcely anywhere to run.

Watts reappeared through a door off the sitting room. 'A swing-a-cat kitchenette and a bathroom through there.' He and Corrigan walked across the sitting room to the wide window and looked out. Hanson remained where she was, still at the sitting-room threshold, staring straight ahead. More chill air crept towards her and circled around her legs. The half-open bedroom door directly ahead moved slightly. She stared at it, hearing its tiny, plaintive creak. When Della Harrington was found that door had been wide open, the doorway framing her, her feet towards where Hanson was standing. It would have been a shockingly intimate sight for whoever saw it upon first coming across the body.

A few steps across the sitting room and she was standing with her colleagues at the window. It faced onto the street. She looked across at the lights of nearby buildings much taller than the one they were inside, then down to cars and pedestrians moving to and fro. Anyone looking up here that dull November day on which Harrington was murdered would have seen lights indicating that she was home. For Hanson, it potentially widened the scope of their investigation. Harrington's killer could have been a complete stranger to her but also someone constantly searching for an opportunity to enact violence. Glancing up at the ceiling, she pointed. 'Listen.' The low-level sound of a television or radio was just audible. Hanson picked up more of the sound which had attracted her attention: a muted, scuffing as if something was being moved across the floor in the apartment above, followed by a couple of footsteps and a low, muffled thump, possibly from one of the apartments on either side. Elsewhere in the building a door slammed. 'Noise carries in this building. Do we know if any residents at the time indicated hearing sounds from Della Harrington's apartment on the day she died?'

'No confirmation of it,' said Watts.

She went closer to the window, looked down at the thronged street. 'And we don't have any of them to ask.'

'Not yet. When I spoke to Dobbs on the phone, he described these as "starter apartments" intended for "single person occupancy" or young couples who generally move on after a couple of years.' He looked around with a grimace. 'A starter for claustrophobia, if you ask me.'

She stood with Corrigan at the wide window, recalling her reading of the file data the previous evening. She'd noted that for several days prior to Harrington's murder a team of painters had worked from scaffolding on the building's exterior. They had been questioned along with the residents but there was no indication that any of them had been of help or of specific interest to the original investigation. The theory investigators had worked to was that Harrington's killer had come into this apartment by invitation via the front door, that he was someone she knew. They had based this supposition on the lack of damage to the door of the apartment and the absence of any report of disturbance. Hanson stared out, her head full of questions. How long were the painters here? Had Della Harrington gotten used to seeing them around? Was she careful to draw her curtains or blinds as darkness fell? Or was she so used to living one floor above ground, seemingly protected by a coded door, that she'd become blasé? Had she allowed someone unknown, maybe someone only vaguely familiar yet personable into this apartment? She shook her head. *I don't know because I don't yet know you, Della.*

She turned to face the front door through which she and her colleagues had entered this compact living space. Ten years ago, a man with sexual violence inside his head had come through it. She took a few steps from the window, hearing the sound of her own footsteps, her eyes fixed on the half-open bedroom door directly ahead. The detail, the vividness of the scene captured in photographs rushed into her head: Harrington nude from the waist down, fully visible to whoever entered the apartment after her killer had left. Steffan Coultard had found her. Archie Fenton was inside the building. She recalled the unnumbered apartment door she'd seen one floor below. Had the police asked Fenton if he had seen or heard anything from this apartment directly above his office? Had he seen or heard anyone pass his door? So many questions on which the case files provided no clarity. She thought of those who had entered the apartment following the discovery of the body. Those police officers and forensic workers whose professional business it was to examine scenes of chaos and destruction would have filled this small space, in all likelihood most of them male and all of them privy to the intimate detail of Harrington's body. Connie Chong, headquarters' in-house pathologist would have been a female presence with the professional gravitas to discourage the kind of repartee Hanson knew was common to such situations, a protective device against horror and mayhem. Except that ten years ago, it wouldn't have been Chong.

Pulling her overcoat around herself, Hanson started at Watts' voice close to her ear. 'Blimey, it's cold in here. It was cold the day Harrington died, yet Steffan Coultard, this mate of hers who gave her lifts, didn't come up here when he arrived. He stayed in his car, waiting for her to come down, listening to a CD of this opera they were doing. Or so he said. I want to know more about him.' He held up a photograph. 'This was in the file. It belongs to her sister. Have a look.' In it Hanson saw this room as it had looked with its furnishings. He pointed. 'See her stereo set up? Good quality. Pricey. Coultard could have played his CD up here, in the warm. Why was he hanging about outside?'

She shook her head, watching Corrigan move from the window and walk slowly around the room, arms folded high on his chest. Hanson guessed that whatever he was looking for, he wasn't finding it. 'I don't know. Whoever talks to him should ask.'

'How about you do it, doc?'

'OK. I'll phone Coultard and arrange it with him.'

'What's this *Cosy* opera about, that he and Harrington were both in?' he asked.

'*Così fan tutte*. It's Mozart.' She saw the deepening frown. 'Very loosely translated, it means "that's what women are like". It's about two young women who are upset when their boyfriends leave them, but the boyfriends return in disguise and . . .'

Watts was on the move. 'That's more than enough, ta. Sounds like one of them Shakespeare plays.'

She watched him go, thinking of Coultard's reason for coming here that evening. She recalled the photographs showing Harrington's jogging clothes pushed aside, wrenched from her. Why hadn't she showered and changed in expectation of his arrival? She reminded herself that the time of death was a wide estimate, due to the high temperature inside this apartment when the body was discovered. The original investigation had decided that death had to have occurred within the latter part of that estimate. It fitted with David Lockman's known presence in the area. She took a couple of steps in the direction of the bedroom and stopped, eyes widening. The bedroom door was on the move. She watched as it gathered momentum, saw it hit its frame, flinched at the ear-ringing bang.

Corrigan reached it first, throwing it wide, his dark head turning this way and that as he looked around the room, then continuing on to the window where he reached up and pulled its narrow top section shut. He came back to the sitting room looking unsettled. 'Don't know about you, but there's something about this place that's getting to me.'

Hanson nodded. Glancing at Watts' grim face, she recalled her words to him a couple of minutes earlier: 'that's what women are like.' Was that what this killer had intended when he displayed Harrington in the way he did? Did he want to demonstrate to whoever came after him what he believed was the essence of 'female'? 'Here! Take a look! This is *exactly* what women are like.' Had he wanted to shock, repel even, because this was how he himself felt about females? She thought back to Corrigan's definition of lust murder and the reference to underlying sexual conflict. It was what they had here: a killer fixated on, yet fearful and repelled by, female sexual parts. She looked up as Corrigan arrived at her side.

'Any ideas on the kind of guy we're looking for?' he asked.

'Some. Most of it conjecture: sexually repressed, frustrated, hater of females in general, driven to reduce Harrington to a stand-in, a vehicle to express the sexual conflict you mentioned.' She shook her head as Watts joined them. 'Right now, he's a work in progress as far as I'm concerned, but one thing is clear. If Della Harrington knew her killer, he was sufficiently skilful to conceal his true nature and present himself to her as someone without threat. That she let him in suggests she was totally unaware of the frustration and rage within him. It's highly possible that he was someone unknown to her who was able to present an engaging façade, sufficient to get him inside here.' She paused.

'How wrong she was about him.' She followed her colleagues out of the apartment and down the stairs, thinking over what she'd just said to her colleagues. Whatever the situation had been, a frustrated, raging killer was exactly what the physical evidence was indicating.

Dobbs had evidently been waiting for them because he was out of his car as soon as they reached Watts' vehicle. Seeing him approach, Watts caught the appraising glance he directed at Hanson as she climbed inside. He dropped the apartment key into Dobbs' outstretched hand. 'Thanks. When we need another look, I'll ring you.'

Dobbs stared at him. 'Just a minute. I thought we agreed that this was a one-off visit.'

'I don't recall any agreement. As you're here, you can tell me how long Della Harrington rented that apartment.'

'Around eighteen months and she didn't rent,' he snapped. 'She owned it.'

'Did you arrange all that for her personally?'

Dobbs narrowed his eyes. 'Meaning?'

'The finance for her to buy it.'

Dobbs stared at him then away. 'She didn't need finance. She already had the money up front.'

'Oh, yeah? How much?' asked Watts.

'I'd have to look at my records . . .'

'An approximate figure.'

Dobbs shrugged. 'Around sixty grand.'

Watts gave a low whistle. 'You don't say. That would have been even more impressive, ten years ago.'

'You wouldn't catch me living here then or now,' sniffed Dobbs. 'Too urban. I like space. I've got a little place in the country and . . .'

Watts left him standing, got into the Range Rover and started the engine. Hanson had watched the brief exchange. 'What was that about?' She listened to the scant details Dobbs had provided of Harrington's purchase of her apartment, recalling what she'd seen in photographs of the costly audio equipment, the expensive items inside her wardrobe. She frowned at him via the rear-view mirror. 'Harrington had to have earned more than I thought from her call centre job.'

'That's something we'll check. I told Dobbs we'd be seeing him again, just to give him something to worry about.'

They exited the car park. Dobbs had already left. His car was some distance ahead of them. Hanson watched the BMW's tail lights glow as it made a quick left turn. 'I thought he looked like he had something specific on his mind when you spoke to him.'

From the front passenger seat, Corrigan turned to look at her. 'We'll catch up with him, Red. Get anything from seeing the apartment?'

'Beyond what I said earlier, claustrophobia, and possibly pneumonia.' She stared out of the window at the lights of central Birmingham moving past. She was glad to be away from Marlow Gardens. The visit had left her dissatisfied. 'Della Harrington had neighbours above and on either side of her, but there's nothing which indicates they heard or saw anything on the day she was murdered. In fact, all of the witness statements seem very sketchy and lacking in detail to me.' She looked up, aware of Watts' eyes on her via the mirror. 'Come on, Watts. That's an observation, not a criticism. Any noises coming from that apartment would be relevant to the case because it might establish time of death. If no one in that building heard a sound and given the smallness of the apartment itself, I'm confident that her killer had full control of her as soon as he entered it and he never lost it. Which has got me wondering if they knew each other.'

'If that building was home to other single women, it's likely that they would be at work during the day,' said Corrigan.

'Mm . . . that's a possibility.' She wouldn't mention her vague dissatisfaction with the crime scene and its meaning which she'd had when she'd read through the files. They were approaching the end of the week and Watts was grumpy as well as tired.

He eyed her through his mirror. 'What does that say about him, this taking control you just mentioned?'

'It suggests he's watchful, that he might have had the apartment building and possibly Della Harrington herself under some level of surveillance. Which in turn suggests he's a planner. When it comes to action, he's likely to be quick-moving, strong . . .' She paused. 'My overall impression is that he was a very organized killer.'

SIX

Early on Saturday morning Hanson was eyeing the toaster. 'Maisie, I know you're disappointed but there's no point complaining about it. Your father has a big case coming up and he has to work on it.' She pictured her lawyer ex-husband at his chambers, immersed in court documents. *Possibly. Maybe. Who knows? Kevin Osborne has more secrets than MI6.*

'But it's *Saturday* and it's totally unfair,' said Maisie, face mutinous above her cereal bowl. 'He promised, Mom. You're always going on about the importance of promises. You should tell *him.*'

Aware that Maisie had a point, she sidestepped the issue. 'You've got Grandpa here for company and I'll be back at around half-eleven.'

Maisie came to the sink, rinsed her bowl and dumped it inside the dishwasher. 'I'll ask him if he'll take me.'

Hanson grabbed toast as it shot into the air. 'I'd rather you didn't. Your grandpa's probably still tired from his drive here yesterday.'

Maisie rolled her eyes. 'Come on, Mom. He's been asleep all *night.* Why do you always look for reasons why things can't happen?'

'It's a key clause in my Bad Mother script. Here.' Hanson handed her the plate of buttered toast and watched her plod to the table as Charlie came into the kitchen.

Maisie opened her eyes wide and give him a quick smile. 'Hi, Grandpa. How are you?'

He smiled at her, planting a kiss on top of the curls, grinning across at Hanson. 'I'm fine. How are you?'

'Great. Guess what. There's a fantastic technology exhibition at the NEC today.'

'Sounds interesting,' he said, getting the warning look Hanson was sending him.

'How about you come with me?' asked Maisie.

'Sounds too good to miss. Are you driving?'

Maisie sent a triumphant look to Hanson. '*Cool.* Can we leave at around ten?' Charlie nodded and she jumped up, heading for the door, toast in hand.

Hanson tracked her, waited until she was out of earshot. 'Are you sure? I would have taken her but I need to see someone involved in UCU's case who was very reluctant to meet me on a weekday.'

'Of course, I'm sure. My pleasure.' He rubbed his hands together. 'For breakfast I'm going to make a full English with fried bread. What do you think?' He laughed at the expression on her face and gave her a quick hug. 'Ease up, Kate. I'll go with the healthy option as always.'

He was halfway through his muesli when the door opened and Maisie reappeared. He stopped mid-spoonful, his eyes moving to Hanson who was pointing in the direction of the hall. 'Back upstairs and tone down the cosmetics.'

'Aggh!' *You* are so unfair . . .'

'That blusher is making you look as though you've got a high fever, and whilst you're about it, change the top. It's too low-cut. I should know. It's mine.'

'But I'm meeting Lissy at the park straight after Grandpa brings me back here and . . .'

'What for?' Maisie looked away. Hanson shook her head. 'We've had this conversation before. You are not going to the park on a winter's afternoon when there's nothing particular happening there.'

Maisie stared at her. 'What's wrong with the *park*?'

'What's wrong with it is that you and Lissy want to hang out there. I've told you, it's not going to happen, Maisie.'

'*Wha?* In a couple of weeks, I'll be *fourteen* . . .'

'Thanks for making my case for me.'

Hanson watched her stomp towards the stairs, followed by a bedroom door closing with some force. She turned to find Charlie looking startled. 'Ignore that. Our head-to-heads are increasing with her age. Or is it mine? Like she said, she's almost fourteen but in a lot of ways she's still naïve, which is why I don't allow her to do half of what she wants.' She smiled at him. 'Take my advice, Charlie, don't let her manipulate you. She's good at it. She gets lots of practice when she stays with Kevin.'

*   *   *

Hanson slid her car to a halt halfway down the wide, tree-lined residential road and looked through heavy tree-cover at what was visible of the large house to her left, one of several in this quiet enclave of spacious, 1970s houses. It looked unoccupied except for the grey Ford parked on the drive. 'Having given up my Saturday morning, that better be Steffan Coultard's car.' Collecting her bag, she headed up the drive to the door and rang the bell, listened to it reverberating in the silent house. Frowning, she rang again, turned to gaze through the trees to the scarcely visible houses opposite, some with lights still showing here and there on this grey morning. Hearing the front door open she turned to the man now standing there. 'Mr Steffan Coultard?' He nodded. 'Kate Hanson. We spoke on the phone yesterday.' He opened the door further. She stepped inside.

'Go through to the door at the end,' he said softly. Hearing the front door close quietly behind her, she followed his directions into a large square kitchen.

'Is this suitable?' he asked, coming inside and giving her a tense look through large glasses. He indicated the round table in its centre. 'We can sit there.'

'This is absolutely fine, Mr Coultard.'

She took a seat and accepted his offer of tea. Taking notebook and pen from her bag, her eyes went quickly over the neat, mouse-brown hair, the brown cord trousers, the beige and pale green check shirt buttoned to the neck, the dark grey cardigan. He walked silently from her, his feet in soft brown leather slippers. She waited as he busied himself with tea preparations. The click of the kettle switching off sounded like a whip-crack in the silence. To Hanson, even the air in the kitchen felt dead. She looked around it at tiles and beige-painted cabinets which looked hardly used. Opening her notebook, she let her eyes drift over the questions she had brought with her. Sensing movement, she looked up and smiled as he placed a cup of tea in front of her and sat opposite. 'Thank you, Mr Coultard. I've never been to this area before. Your road is very quiet. Very peaceful.'

'I like privacy.'

'When we spoke on the phone, I explained my involvement in the reinvestigation of Della Harrington's murder.' He nodded, saying nothing. 'I have some questions I need to ask you.'

He tugged the edges of his cardigan together. She was still wearing her coat but aware now of the coldness of the house she decided she'd keep it on. She paused to give him an opportunity to speak. He didn't. 'Shall we make a start?' She got a quick nod. Thinking he might be nervous, she made her first questions factual ones unrelated to the Harrington murder and to which she already knew the answers. 'You work in Birmingham city centre?'

'Yes.'

'What do you do for a living, Mr Coultard?'

'I'm an accountant. I've been with the firm eleven years.' She nodded encouragingly at the volunteered information. 'You like working there.' She saw him hesitate.

'When I started with the firm, I was in an open-plan office. Too noisy. Too much talk. It was hard to concentrate. I've got my own office now. I like the work.'

'You were a friend of Della Harrington's.' She saw a shadow cross his face.

'. . . I wouldn't say we were friends, exactly.'

'What would you say you were?' Another tug at the cardigan.

'We were members of the same operatic group.'

'Tell me about the arrangement you had to provide her with lifts to rehearsal and how that came about.'

He stared at her. 'I don't know what you mean by "arrangement".'

'I understand it was something you regularly did for her.' Hanson prompted, picking up the subtle tick of the nearby wall clock.

'I can't actually remember how it arose,' he said, his voice barely above a whisper. 'We just . . . agreed.'

'Tell me what Della was like.'

He pushed up his glasses, shrugged. 'She was pleasant, you know. She had a good voice.'

'According to photographs I've seen, she was a very attractive woman.' She watched his eyes drift away from hers.

'I suppose. It wasn't something I particularly noticed.'

Hanson changed direction to one she hoped might draw him out. 'Which role did you have in that production of *Così fan tutte*?'

'Ferrando.' His tone was firmer. 'I was one of only three tenors in the company at that time.' Seeing a glimmer of something approaching animation in his face, Hanson nodded encourage-ment. 'Della was soprano. She played . . . would have played Despina.' In the following silence, Hanson recalled that the production, scheduled for the week after Della Harrington's death, had been cancelled. Time to move the conversation on.

'I need to ask you about the evening Della was found dead.'

He looked away from her to the window. She suspected that if there had been any significant colour in his face it would have drained. 'The whole thing was . . . awful,' he whispered. 'Really upsetting.'

'I'm sure it was, Mr Coultard. To see someone whom you knew like that.' She paused, waiting. 'Can you talk a little about it, from when you arrived at the apartment?' She prompted. He looked at her then down to the table. She waited some more, the nearby kitchen clock confirming that her Saturday was fast eroding. If Coultard didn't begin to engage soon, she would make an excuse, wind up her visit and tell Watts on Monday that they needed to get him into headquarters.

His soft monotone came again, 'I got there at about six thirty and parked my car in the residents' car park. I stayed there, listening to my CD of *Così fan tutte*. It was a really important rehearsal we were going to, so it was a good use of the time. After a while, when Della hadn't appeared I decided to go up to her apartment. I rang the bell. There was no reply although I was sure she was in because I'd seen her car in the car park. I went to the next-door apartment. Rang that bell. I got no reply, so I went down to the maintenance man's office . . .'

'Why did you go to his office?'

He looked up at her then away. 'I knew he had a pass key, but he didn't come to the door either so I came back upstairs.'

'You didn't consider that maybe Della was out, perhaps somewhere nearby, or that she'd forgotten the time?'

He shook his head. 'She wouldn't have done that. She wanted to go to that rehearsal. She knew how important it was. I . . . wondered if something was wrong. I went to the next-door apartment again. That time the woman who lived there opened the door.'

'And she gave you the key,' prompted Hanson.

His mouth became a thin line. 'Finally.'

'You say you wondered if there was something wrong.'

He shrugged. 'Not exactly. I didn't know what to think.'

'Was it cold, waiting in your car for Della to come down?'

He looked startled at the change of direction. 'No. And anyway, it's what I always did. Like I said, I listened to the music. I enjoyed the peace and quiet.'

'How long were you outside, Mr Coultard?'

'I'm not sure.'

'Roughly?'

'. . . About twenty minutes.'

'It was a cold evening.' She knew this. She'd checked.

'I wasn't cold. I was fully immersed in the music. It was a first-class recording. I choose the recordings I buy very, very carefully.'

'You had the code for the main entrance door to the apartments?'

His eyes slid from hers. 'Yes, but as I said, I always waited outside for Della.'

'Was there a particular reason why you did that?'

Another shrug. 'No.'

'OK. So, at some point you've returned to the next-door neighbour's apartment and you have the key to Miss Harrington's door. What did you do then?'

Pushing at his glasses, he looked down at his hands. 'I went and unlocked Della's door. The maintenance man had come up the stairs. We went inside together.' He folded his arms, his eyes drifting to the kitchen window.

Hanson looked at him. 'I need you to tell me what you saw, Mr Coultard.'

He licked his lips, his voice dropping to a whisper. 'It was . . . the heat inside was unbearable. Like a wall.' He put his hand to his mouth. 'It made me feel ill.'

'What did you do?'

'Do?' He frowned. 'I . . . got a raincoat or something from a peg in the hall to put over her.'

'Why did you do that?'

He looked away. 'To cover . . . it, but I didn't actually do it because the maintenance man said not to.'

'Why do you think he said that?'

Coultard shrugged, not looking at her. 'He said something about spoiling evidence. I was concerned about being criticized by the police, so I didn't.'

Hanson finished note-taking and glanced at his hands. No ring. 'Are you married, Mr Coultard?'

'Yes?'

'Is your wife here?'

'No.' Seconds slid by. 'She's visiting her parents.'

'Do they live nearby?'

He frowned again. 'Why is my private life relevant? She never knew Della.'

'Your wife isn't a member of the operatic group?'

'. . . My wife doesn't sing.'

Hanson was trying to imagine this soft-looking, nondescript man delivering an expressive operatic performance. Giving up the effort, she closed her notebook and smiled across at him. 'I could never sing in public. Is it difficult?'

'Oh, no. You don't just learn the music, you learn the role. You immerse yourself. You inhabit that role . . .' The animation left his face. His voice faded to nothing. She stood. He did the same.

'Thank you for your time, Mr Coultard. I'll see myself out.' She took a few steps then stopped and turned to find him immediately behind her. Looking startled, he pulled at his cardigan. 'There's something else,' she said. 'Your fingerprint was found inside Della Harrington's apartment.'

His eyes darted. 'So? I was there, wasn't I? The police at the time told me they were satisfied that it wasn't relevant to what happened. They didn't think anything of it then so I can't see why it's a problem now.'

'Nobody has said it is a problem, Mr Coultard. I'm asking because I need to know when that print was left by you.'

He stared at her. 'I just told you. That day.'

'Thank you.' She turned and headed for the door, aware of his soft footfalls behind her. She stepped outside and heard the door close quietly. Inside her car, she clicked her iPhone into its holder. Starting the car, she glanced through trees at what was visible of the house, noting a fleeting movement at a large downstairs window. Approaching the end of the road she tapped Watts' number, then slipped into a space in the oncoming traffic. 'I've just left Steffan Coultard's house.'

'What's he like?'

'I'd say "literally and emotionally buttoned up" about covers it.'

'Meaning?'

'My overall impression is that he's introverted, highly anxious and hyper-alert to what others think of him.'

'What else has he told you about himself?'

'Not much. He wasn't keen to talk about what he saw inside the Harrington apartment.'

'Understandable.'

She smiled, raised her brows. 'Since when have you done "understandable"?'

'Ha-ha. Anything else?'

'He avoided giving an explanation for how he came to have the main door code for the building. Neither did he explain why he didn't use it on arrival but waited outside in the cold for twenty minutes.' She halted at a large, busy intersection. 'And something else. He suggested that he hadn't been aware of Harrington's physical attractiveness.'

She heard the disbelief in Watts' response. 'Yeah, right.'

'Exactly. It's the kind of response that makes any psychologist think, "Oh-Oh, someone's ly-ing".'

'You are the disbelieving type, doc.'

She laughed. 'Takes one to know one. Plus, I got the impression he didn't like Harrington's next-door neighbour, the one who held her spare key.'

'Did he say why?'

'I didn't ask,' said Hanson. 'Getting the small amount of information which I did was like pulling teeth. To get any more, I would have had to be insistent and I can tell you, Mr Steffan Coultard would not have handled that very well.'

'The stroppy type, is he?'

'Far from it.' She joined the traffic, leaving it at the first exit. 'Still there?'

'Yeah. This neighbour with the key was a woman by the name of Karen Tyler.' Like herself, Watts had the sort of mind which absorbed case file information and readily recalled the small detail.

She nodded. 'That's the one.'

'If Coultard didn't like her, I'd like to know why. There's nothing about it in the files but whatever it was, it might tell us something more about him.'

'Agreed, plus he requires another visit. Whoever does that should ask him about his wife. He was evasive about her.' She picked up traffic noise from her phone. 'Where are you?'

'Me and Corrigan are on our way to see Fenton, the maintenance bloke to find out what he's got to say about Della Harrington, plus how he came to police attention two years later. Enjoy what's left of your Saturday, doc.'

She came onto her drive. Charlie's car wasn't there. She'd been inside the house barely ten minutes when she heard the front door open. 'Hi, Mom!' was followed by the sounds of feet rushing towards the kitchen. Maisie came inside, her face flushed. She reached into a small carrier bag and lifted out a pink iPad case patterned with red hearts. 'Look what I've got, *and* a matching phone case. Grandpa bought them for me.'

'They're really nice. Are you hungry?'

'No. We had burgers 'n' chunky chips.' The doorbell sounded. 'That'll be Chel.' She ran from the kitchen, passing Charlie on his way in.

'You've been spoiling her.' She kissed his cool cheek.

'I have. There's some years of spoiling I need to catch up on.'

She switched on the kettle and reached for the cafetière, wondering if she might resurrect the conversation she'd had with Charlie about his coming to live here. *No. Let it rest. There'll be other opportunities.*

SEVEN

'Give it another thump, Corrigan.'

Turning his back on the scruffy front door, Watts surveyed the miniscule garden, most of it taken up by weeds and recycling bins in a pungent line against the low wall, lids half-raised exposing mostly take-away food containers. Hearing the door being dragged open he turned, anticipating the clean-shaven, dark-haired individual they had seen in a press photograph taken at the time of the Harrington murder. Standing in the doorway was a fifty-something scruffy bloke, his crop of grey whiskers glinting in the low sun. Watts' first thought was that if this was Fenton, the last decade had done him no favours. 'Archie Fenton?'

'Yeah. What do you two want?'

Those few words told both officers that Archie Fenton, one-time maintenance man at Della Harrington's apartment building, had identified them as police. Watts took out official identification and held it up. 'Glad you hadn't popped down to Waitrose, Mr Fenton. We want a word or three. Let us in.'

Fenton bridled. 'I don't have to talk to you. I've got nothing to say and I'm busy.' The door was already on its journey to its frame. It was stopped by Corrigan's prompt hand, plus his strategically-placed boot.

'Whoa. Hang on there, sir. We need to speak with you as a witness in the murder of Della Harrington ten years back.'

Fenton's face reddened. 'I never witnessed no murder.'

'Nobody said you did,' snapped Watts. 'I've got better things I could be doing with my Saturday morning, so let us in. It's cold enough to freeze a witch's whatsits out here.'

Fenton moved from the door, muttering under his breath as Corrigan gave it a shove. They walked into the narrow, dingy hallway. If Fenton was still into maintenance work, he was doing it elsewhere. They followed him into a high-ceilinged room, its one easy chair and ratty-looking carpet hinting that it might be a lounge. Fenton turned to them, face closed, arms folded. 'Get on with it. Like I said, I've got stuff to do.'

Watts reached inside his coat and brought out his notebook, eyeing a stepladder against one wall, paint tins and a drop cloth on the floor beneath it. 'Going for some interior décor, are we?'

Fenton's eyes narrowed. 'That's the landlord's answer to my complaints about this rat-trap. I'm expected to do it myself, with my health the way it is. What's it to you?'

'Nothing at all,' said Watts genially. 'What has got our interest is who murdered Della Harrington.' Fenton merely stared at him. 'We're hoping you can tell us something about it.'

Fenton's eyes flicked to Corrigan who was staring down at him, arms folded high on his chest. 'That was years ago,' said Fenton. 'I don't remember nothing about it.'

Watts strolled away from him to a dusty rear window to peer out on dull concrete and weeds. He turned, voice upbeat. 'Don't sell yourself short, Archie. I'd say you were one of the star witnesses in that investigation. You were living and working on the job. Speaking of which, we've been to Marlow Gardens Apartments. We've seen what was your office, back then.'

Fenton's eyes were busy avoiding Watts' direct look. 'So? What of it?'

'We're wondering if you heard anything from Della Harrington's apartment that day.'

'Like what?'

Eyes fixed on the stained carpet, Watts walked slowly back to Fenton, where he stopped and prodded his chest with a thick forefinger. 'That office of yours was close to the main entrance and beneath Harrington's apartment. I'll ask you again. Did you hear anything?'

'Such as?'

Watts glared at him. 'You're getting right on my whatsits now, you are. Get thinking before you open your mouth again, because if I don't like what you say you'll be coming to headquarters with us.' Fenton gave him a surly glance, his mouth firmly closed. 'Did you hear anybody come through the main door? Did you hear anybody go up the stairs? Did you hear anything from Harrington's apartment? Want me to repeat any of that?'

'No,' said Fenton, now sulky. 'I never heard nothing.'

'Glad we got that sorted,' said Watts. 'Moving swiftly on, now that your brain's in gear, I bet you can tell us a lot about Della Harrington.'

'No, I can't.'

'Give it a try. Start with when you found her dead body.'

Colour rushed Fenton's face again. 'You want to get your facts straight, you do. I didn't find her.'

'Interesting you should say that, Archie, because the information we've got is none too clear on that score. From what we know, you were right on the spot and so was a visitor to her apartment.'

'Her boyfriend. You should ask him. It was him who found her, not me.'

Watts looked at him then glanced at Corrigan. 'Well, well,' he said softly. 'Did you hear that, lieutenant? Did we know that Della Harrington had a boyfriend?'

'Never did,' said Corrigan with a slow headshake, his eyes not leaving Fenton's face. Watts looked back at Fenton, whose eyes skittered between the two officers. 'We've found no mention of a man in Della Harrington's life around the time she was killed, but it sounds like you know different.' They waited out the lengthy silence. Fenton's eyes were now fixed on the floor, faint colour still evident in places on his grey face. Corrigan took a step closer. 'Mr Fenton, we could sure use your assistance here. Tell us all you recall about Della Harrington.'

Fenton gazed up at the tall officer now standing very close. 'I can't tell you nothing about her. I worked at that place. I never fraternized.'

'Ever notice visitors to her apartment?' asked Watts.

'I didn't have time to watch comings and goings. I was rushed off my feet at that place.' Seeing Watts' attention fixed on him, he added, 'All I remember is the boyfriend that I just mentioned.'

Watts glanced at Corrigan, then back. 'Right. Tell us about him. Start with his name.'

Fenton shrugged. 'Search me. All I know, he was in some choir she belonged to.'

'How'd you know that?'

'Dunno. Somebody must have mentioned it. Maybe I overheard it.'

Watts slow-nodded. 'Maybe. Carry on.'

'He used to call for her. Go up to her apartment. Then I didn't see him no more.'

'And?'

'I happened to notice he'd started waiting outside in his car for her.'

'Why?' asked Watts.

'How the bloody hell should I know?' Watts stared at him. Fenton got fidgety. 'I think somebody mentioned that they'd had a row or something.'

'And, of course you've got no idea who that somebody was,' said Watts.

'No. Like I said, I was—'

'Rushed off your feet. Yeah, you said. Anything else?'

'That's it.'

'You never heard Harrington and this boyfriend talking? Arguing?'

Fenton looked dismissive. 'No. I had better things to do than listen to people nattering.'

'Let's get back to the day Della Harrington died,' said Watts. 'You were there. Tell us.'

'Tell you what? I gave a statement. Read that.'

'We have. It places you right there when her body was found.'

'Yes, but it wasn't me that found her. That was *him*. The boyfriend.'

Watts sighed, transferred his gaze to Corrigan. 'This is one of the problems with the Job, lieutenant. People don't want to get involved, they don't want to talk detail. All they're interested in is minimizing their involvement, hoping we'll go away.' He looked at Fenton. 'Which we won't.' Fenton's eyes were anywhere but on Watts and Corrigan. 'Come on, Archie. Tell us exactly what you were up to that day and I mean *all* of it.'

Fenton's gaze shifted. 'I was in my office on the ground floor, minding my own business and watching the tele.'

Watts slow-nodded. 'Sounds like you had all the mod cons of home there.'

Fenton sent him a venomous look. 'I wasn't living there, if that's what you're thinking. I was doing alright then. Had my own place. I kept an airbed and a sleeping bag at Marlow Gardens for when I was on a late shift, like that day.'

Watts gave him an encouraging nod. 'Well remembered, Archie. Tell us how you first knew something was going on there.'

'First thing I knew, there was a commotion coming from the first floor.'

Watts' face darkened. 'You just got through telling us you never heard anything!'

Fenton looked away. 'I thought you meant quiet stuff, like somebody coming in and creeping about, going up the stairs.' He closed his mouth.

Watts frowned at him. 'Take my advice and stop the thinking. Tell us about the "commotion".'

'It was just some raised voices.'

Getting an exasperated look from Watts, Corrigan asked, 'Once you heard that, what did you do, sir?'

Fenton's head spun to him. '*Nothing.* I ignored it. I was maintenance. What residents got up to in that building was their own affair.'

'Get to what you *did*, once you stopped ignoring it,' snapped Watts.

'OK, give us a chance.' Fenton assumed an air of concentration. 'The voices got louder. A man's voice. And a woman's. One belonged to that boyfriend. Harrington's boyfriend. I opened my door, had a look out. He was having a go at the woman who lived in the apartment next door.'

'Know anything about her?' asked Watts.

'Not a lot.' Fenton looked dismissive. 'Don't ask me her name because I can't tell you. All I remember is that she used to go on about this stuck-up arse she was living with, that he was a doctor at that kids' hospital in town. He was God's gift, according to her. For all I know he was probably a bloody nurse.'

'Keep going, Archie. What were the boyfriend and the neighbour saying?'

'I heard the boyfriend say, "Give it here!", or something like that and she was giving him back some lip and then he walked away. The neighbour he'd argued with wasn't happy about none of it, I can tell you.'

'Why not?'

'What am I, a bloody mind reader?'

'*Think* about it,' invited Watts, his face darkening.

'I dunno. She was going on about some key or other.'

Watts stared down at him. 'You're no joined-up thinker, are you, Archie? I'd have thought that in a situation like that, a resident might have asked you for help. You being management, sort of.'

'No, they never.'

'What then?'

'I was pissed off with both of 'em. The next-door neighbour was still shouting. I came out of my office. By the time I was halfway up the stairs I saw Harrington's apartment door open and the boyfriend was already inside.'

'What was he doing?'

'I couldn't see him from where I was.'

'Hanging back as you came up the stairs, were you?' asked Watts.

'*No.* I just thought, if he's so bloody keen to get in there, best leave him to it.' He paused. '. . . After I saw her I wished I hadn't gone in at all.' He rubbed his grimy hand over his whiskers. 'I've seen some stuff in my time, I can tell you. I was in the army back in the Eighties . . .'

'What did you see inside that apartment?'

Fenton looked at him then away. 'I saw her. In her bedroom. Lying on the floor, her feet towards the front door. You couldn't miss her.' He swallowed. 'I haven't thought about this in ages but you've brought it all back. She was in a right state, I can tell you. Blood all over the floor, her clothes ripped off her and her legs apart so you could see . . . everything, you know.' His eyes drifted away. 'Nobody wants to see a woman like that, do they?'

The two officers exchanged quick glances. 'When you say her clothes were "ripped off her", what do you mean exactly?' asked Corrigan.

'You know. All ripped apart, like some animal had had a go at her then flung them onto the floor. I was all for covering her up but that idiot of a boyfriend started acting like he was in charge. He said no. Cool as you like, he was, and it was that hot in there. Made me feel sick, it did.'

'What makes you so sure he was Della Harrington's boyfriend?' asked Watts.

Fenton's eyes slid away. 'Like I told you, he was there quite regular.'

Watts' eyes were still on him. 'Made it your business to watch comings and goings, did you?'

Fenton's face darkened. 'I don't know what you're getting at. I had a job to do there. I didn't have time to . . .'

'Yeah, you've said.' Watts took two sheets of paper from Corrigan, unfolded them then raised his eyes to Fenton. 'Your statement from that night.'

'. . . Yeah, so? I told you about that.'

Watts took a couple of steps closer, tapping it lightly against Fenton's chest in time with his words. '*So*, it's *very*, *very* interesting just how little detail there is in it.' He held the single sheet close to Fenton's face. 'Have a look. "Heard noises, went out to see what was happening, saw two people on the first floor, a neighbour of Harrington's arguing with a male known to the victim. Saw Della Harrington's dead body. Knew nothing about her." That's what you said ten years ago.' He glanced at Corrigan. 'You know, lieutenant, it sounds to me like Archie here recalls the scene inside that apartment better now than he did when he gave this statement. Is it just me, or does that seem weird to you?'

'A tad unusual,' said Corrigan. 'Makes me wonder if he was holding out, back then. *Or* maybe he's thought a lot about how Della Harrington looked when he saw her that day? What do you say, sir?'

Fenton's face was now brick-coloured. 'Look, I don't know what you're trying to pull here . . .'

'Why didn't you mention in your statement that this man you've told us about was Della Harrington's boyfriend?' asked Watts.

'I dunno! I was in shock, like. I just said what I said to get it over with. One of the cops asked me what I'd seen. I told him. He wrote it down and I signed it. He never asked me anything. I didn't want to get involved with who was having it off with who. That was his job. I wanted to keep out of it.' Watts looked at a second sheet he was now holding, his eyes skimming the printed lines.

'Dear, oh dear,' he said quietly, his eyes settling on Fenton's twitching face. 'You read this, lieutenant?'

'Sure, did.'

'What do you make of it?'

'Real interesting. Mr Fenton is known in respect of a sexual felony.'

Fenton stared at them, his face a mix of fear and rage. 'That was years ago and I never . . .'

'2008, to be precise,' snapped Watts. 'Your name came up during the course of a rape inquiry. You were questioned.'

Fenton's head swivelled from him to Corrigan and back. 'I was one of loads of blokes who got dragged into that because I lived local to where it happened. Nothing come of it.'

'You also worked in a building where Della Harrington was murdered,' said Corrigan. 'Are you saying that both of those events were a case of "wrong place, wrong time" for you?'

'They *were*.'

Watts walked away from Fenton then turned. 'Back to Della Harrington. What were you up to earlier that day?'

'What day . . .?'

'You *know* bloody well what day!'

'OK, OK. Keep your hair on.' Avoiding both officers' eyes, Fenton appeared to consider the question. 'Best I can recall I would have been at my own place. I had a nice housing association flat off Broad Street back then. I tell you, since then my life's gone down the—'

'Tell somebody who cares,' snapped Watts. 'What were you doing and what happened next? Come on!'

'I got up around nine, had a wash.' Watts looked unconvinced. 'I probably watched the tele until it was time to leave for work. Got a bus to the Jewellery Quarter. Came on duty at Marlow Gardens at around three that afternoon. Went to my office as I usually did, checked if any of the residents had left a message about a problem. None of 'em had, so, like I told you, I settled down to watch the tele.'

'You've told us you stayed the night at Marlow Gardens when you were on late shift. Why, exactly?'

Fenton shrugged. 'One or two of the residents were getting on a bit. They couldn't manage to change light bulbs, things like that but if I was there I'd do it for them.'

'Very noble, Archie. Our information is that only one of the residents at that time was an older female. The rest were young women.'

'Yeah, so? They sometimes asked me to sort out problems.'

'Such as?' demanded Watts.

'Stuff like water leaks under the sink or from a radiator. If I was there I was able to sort it. Stop any potential damage to the floor underneath. It helped them and it saved me work.'

'I could do with somebody like you on tap, so to speak, at my house.' Watts paused. 'I've just had a thought about maintenance, Archie. Tell us about the odd-jobbing you did in Della Harrington's apartment.'

'. . . I never. I don't remember ever doing anything there.'

Watts walked towards him, stopping just short of actual physical contact. 'Know what I've learned about you in the last half hour, Archie? You lie like a bloody rug. Let's have another try, shall we? Between arriving at the apartment building at three and the time you heard this commotion, what were you doing during those three or four hours?'

'I told you. I was watching the tele. Had a sandwich, made myself a cup o' tea and then all that crap started kicking off upstairs. I couldn't hear my . . . programme. I stuck my head out the door just to have a look. I was a bystander. Don't try pinning nothing on me.'

The two officers walked the dim, frigid hallway to the front door. Watts turned, causing Fenton to flinch. 'We're interested in people like you who were around Marlow Gardens that day. While you were watching the tele, drinking tea and God knows what else, think back. Do you recall seeing or hearing anything?'

'I don't know what you mean.' Fenton's eyes drifted from the big officer.

'What I mean is, while you were prowling about, maybe looking out your window, did you see anything interesting, or odd or unusual, that made you think, "Oohh, 'ello. Who's that?" or "What's going on here, then?"'

'No, I didn't.'

Watts stared at him. 'We're going through this case like a hot knife through butter and guess what?' He jabbed his thick index finger at Fenton's face. 'I've got a feeling we'll be seeing you again.' Watts' eyes drifted down to a narrow, scruffy-looking woven strip around one of Fenton's wrists. 'Got yourself a friend, have you, Archie?'

'My daughter made me a few of 'em when she was in the hospital.'

Watts waited. 'OK, is she?'

'No. She died.'

'We're sorry to hear that, sir,' said Corrigan.

Fenton looked away from them. 'Yeah, course you are. Now you can both get lost. I've got things to do.'

They walked to Corrigan's Volvo and got inside. 'If I'd been part of the original investigation, I'd have given him a lot more attention than he got back then. Just look how riffy he is.' He saw uncertainty on Corrigan's face. 'Scruffy. Dirty. The doc's got plenty of theory on people's needs and their keenness to get 'em satisfied.' He jerked a thumb at the house they'd just left. 'Can you imagine a queue of females wanting to meet him? No. Neither can I. But there he was, at Marlow Gardens Apartments, watching what he'd probably think of as classy female residents coming and going. That wouldn't have done anything to reduce his "needs" would it?' He paused. 'He's a mess now, compared to press photos of him at the time.'

Corrigan nodded as he eased the Volvo from the kerb. 'Given what he just told us, it looks like Fenton's life hit the skids during the last decade but I hear what you say about the original investigators. My opinion is they focused on David Lockman way too soon.'

Fenton peered through a gap in the ill-fitting curtains and watched them leave. He didn't like the police. Had no time for them. Forcing their way in here, throwing their weight about. Sneering and accusing. *Bastards.* He didn't give a sod how hard they were working on that woman's murder. He didn't care about her. His eyes narrowed as the shiny, black Volvo drew away. No buses for them. Instead, a load of taxpayers' money for doing sod-all. Well, they wouldn't get anything out of him. And he had something, alright. Things he'd heard. Things he'd seen that day at Marlow Gardens when he was under the stairs, working on one of the fuse boxes: feet moving upwards, door opening, voices, door closing. More noises. He'd crept back to his office, left the door open a crack, watched some more. Oh, yes. He'd seen things. He'd gone outside. Seen the car and its number plate. All of it meant one thing: big money. It hadn't worked out before, but now he was going to have some of it. It was time. *His* time.

He let the curtain drop, shutting out the day. Turning from the window, his heart leapt into his throat at the sight of the laptop leaning against the wall in the corner. He stared at it, sweat oozing onto his scalp. Had they noticed it? Surely, they had. It was right *there.* He told himself to get a grip. If they had, they would have been onto it, like dogs on a bone, particularly the sarcastic, fat bastard. His heart was banging inside his chest. He couldn't deal with stress. He needed to get calm. Think of something else. His eyes went to the laptop again. Those two thought they were smart, thought they knew everything. How smart were they if they'd missed it? Anxious, restless, what he needed now was distraction. Relief. He went to the laptop, picked it up. He'd got sod-all else to do, so why not? Opening it, he took what was lying on the keys and headed for the squalid kitchen. He'd have a cup of tea. Let time do its work.

EIGHT

Early Monday morning, Hanson read through the information on the board which her colleagues had obtained from Archie Fenton, then added the basic facts she'd managed to get from Steffan Coultard. 'There are some obvious anomalies. Coultard said he entered that apartment with Fenton. According to Fenton, Coultard was already inside whilst he was coming up the stairs. He described Coultard being in a hurry to get in there, which doesn't fit with what Coultard said to me. Plus, they each have similar but diverging accounts about their thinking and behaviour, once they were inside. Coultard told me he wanted to cover Harrington's body but was told by Fenton not to. According to Fenton it was *he* who wanted to cover her and Coultard said no.'

Her two colleagues eyed the screen. 'We'll follow it up,' said Watts, 'but playing devil's advocate, my view of Fenton is he's a weasel. I'd think twice before accepting anything he says.'

Hanson's eyes moved over the screen. 'I get that from what you've told me about him. My impression is that he presents as highly defensive about himself.' She shook her head. 'What I don't get is why he would misrepresent or exaggerate what Coultard did?'

Corrigan glanced down at her. 'He wouldn't, is my guess, but like Watts I question Fenton's reliability.'

'There's something else about Coultard that's bothering me.' She slid her finger over the board, summoning up previously gathered facts. 'According to him, his relationship with Della Harrington was one of convenience. She needed lifts to rehearsals which he was willing to provide. He says he routinely waited in his car for her yet we know that at some point she gave him the code to let himself into the building. That suggests that she was OK with him doing exactly that. So, why does he wait in the car park on that cold evening? Or any evening, for that matter?'

Watts looked unconvinced. 'Remember what Dobbs told us

about residents giving out their codes to anybody? We don't know it was Harrington who gave it to him.'

Hanson paced, her eyes on the board. 'True, but if Della Harrington did give him that code at some point, what changed between them which led to his waiting outside?'

'That's a lot of questions you've got there, doc.'

She came to the table, searched her notes. 'I expect I'll have more as we get further into the case. Coultard told me that on the evening of the murder he knew she was home because he saw her car parked nearby.' She looked up. 'That's a point. Why did Harrington need a lift if she had her own car?' She went back to the board. 'Whichever of us sees Coultard again needs to ask him and also why the arrangement between him and Harrington changed. There might be perfectly good explanations. If there are, we need to hear them.'

Corrigan studied the written facts, pointed to another name. 'From what Fenton told us, Harrington's next-door neighbour, Karen Tyler looks like our go-to for answers. Tyler had Harrington's spare key. She might have something to tell us about the nature of the relationship which existed between Coultard and Harrington.'

'I phoned earlier and left a message that we want to talk to her,' said Watts.

Hanson reached for her coat. 'When I get back to the university I'll ring Coultard and arrange to see him again. Unless one of you wants to talk to him?'

'From what you've said about him, it's probably best if you do it,' said Watts. 'All the messing about you described when you talked to him would just get me on a line.'

'Got any more ideas as to Coultard's personality, Red?' asked Corrigan.

'I'm thinking that he has an avoidant personality. It fits with his social inhibition and his ultra-sensitivity to criticism. When I see him again, I'll check that what I've already seen of him is the way he consistently operates. He comes across as very socially isolated, yet he's married.' She paused. 'His responses to questions about his wife were very vague so a second meeting would be a good opportunity to follow that up, too.' She gazed at what she'd written. 'You know, that whole house felt scarcely lived in. When Coultard was questioned during the original investigation, did they visit him at home?'

'No, they went to his workplace. Why?' asked Watts.

'I thought it possible they met his wife.'

The phone rang and Watts reached for it. Dropping belongings into her briefcase, checking her phone, she looked at Corrigan. 'What have you got planned today?'

'Armed response training, but I've fixed up for Harrington's sister, Andrea Jones, to come into headquarters later in the week. I'll talk to her.'

Watts put down the phone. 'That was Karen Tyler, the neighbour who had Harrington's spare key, returning my call. The one Coultard had the row with. I've arranged to see her at twelve thirty today. How about it, doc? It might be interesting for you to hear somebody else's take on Coultard.'

She nodded, hefting the briefcase. 'My lecture finishes at eleven thirty so I can do that.'

'I'll pick you up.'

Hanson was preoccupied with the case and with thoughts of Charlie as Watts started the Range Rover and began tapping the address into his satnav. 'By the way, she's not Karen Tyler anymore,' he said. 'She's Mrs Forster now.'

They left the campus, Watts following the satnav's instructions. Scarcely two minutes later the robotic female voice directed him to the slip road for the motorway. He glared at its source, his face and tone incredulous. 'You *are* joking, love. It's a bloody 'mare this time of day.' Hanson sighed, looked out of the window as he pulled on the steering wheel in a swift change of direction. She had long experience of Watts' initial willingness to engage with the technology, invariably followed at some point by a refusal to comply. They continued on, the voice regularly advising an immediate U-turn. Watts ignored it. Fifteen minutes later, having left Birmingham's suburbs, he slowed the vehicle and turned into a country lane. Another five minutes and the voice informed them that they had reached their destination. He stopped and they looked through glass at a cottage-style house beyond a five-bar gate. 'I'll start with the intros, doc, then we'll work it as a duo. Feel free to chip in with anything you want.'

They left the vehicle and went through the gate, the only sounds other than their muffled footsteps a few bird calls. Watts rang the bell. The door was opened by a dark-haired, heavily pregnant woman who looked to be in her late thirties. She led them through the house into an extensive, pleasantly warm conservatory at the rear. Beyond it was a vista of fields and horses, their breath hanging cloudy on the cold air. Watts made introductions, declined drinks and explained the purpose of their visit. Karen Forster settled carefully onto a hardwood chair.

'It's easier for me to get up from here. I wasn't surprised when you rang and said you wanted to talk to me about Della. I'd seen the news about the case being reopened. Well, you can't miss it, can you?'

Watts got straight to it. 'Mrs Forster, we'd like you to tell us whatever you remember about Della Harrington and Marlow Gardens Apartments at the time you lived there.' He and Hanson waited as Forster gazed through the window at the chill fields.

'It seems such a long time ago. Another life. Right there in the middle of the city. We rented that apartment for about twelve months. It was very convenient for both of us. Matthew, my partner at the time was a junior doctor at the children's hospital and I worked as a physiotherapist at a nearby clinic.' She looked down at herself then up at Hanson and smiled. 'I'm hoping to go back to it but I'm finding it hard to believe I'll ever get within touching distance of a patient on a treatment table.' Her face became serious. 'We left Marlow Gardens not long after Della was murdered. Matthew had got a job at another hospital so we moved out, bought this place and got married eight years ago. Let's see . . . what do I remember about Della?' She rhythmically stroked her mid-section. 'She was a nice woman, Della. Not that I knew her that well. She wasn't an effusive kind of person. A little reserved, I'd say, but once we got talking I found her really likeable.'

'Are you able to add any detail to that, Mrs Forster?' asked Hanson.

Forster gave it some thought. 'Della didn't volunteer much about herself. We jogged together sometimes and that's how I got to know something about her. We chatted to distract ourselves. I picked up that she was bookish, that she read a lot. And she was creative. She sang and knew a lot about music. The few times I went inside her apartment for coffee she played me some of her CDs and explained the emotions behind the music. I'm as thick as a plank about things like that,' she said cheerfully, 'but I enjoyed listening to her and when I heard the music, I got it. We didn't see that much of each other because she worked odd hours, sometimes from early in the morning, and at other times starting later. I was working too, of course. She told me she worked in a call centre which surprised me.'

'Why was that?' asked Hanson.

Karen shrugged. 'I could more easily have pictured Della working in a museum, say or an art gallery, something like that.' Hanson's memory was firing at what Forster had said about Della being bookish. A photograph of the interior of the Harrington apartment and its furnishings at the time of the murder came into her head. No books. No shelves on which to put them. Harrington's laptop and phone had been stolen. And with them her e-books?

'What kinds of books did Della read?' she asked.

'Mostly biographies of composers, from what she showed me on her phone,' said Forster. 'I'd told her I was in a book group and she recommended one or two of them but I didn't think they'd go down well with the group I was in. Like I said, she and I didn't see each other that often. When Matthew and I weren't working, we would take any opportunity to go out to local restaurants and bars. It was a great area for that kind of thing.'

Picking up wistfulness in Forster's tone, she said, 'It sounds as though you really liked living there.'

'We did. The apartment was very small but it suited us. We enjoyed our time there.' She looked away. 'That was before what happened to Della, of course. Afterwards, it was a nightmare.' She looked back at them. 'I'm not exaggerating when I say that. We're all used to news of people being murdered and thinking how sad or awful it is, but when it happens very close to where you're living, it's totally different. It's horrible.' She glanced at Watts. 'There were loads of police in the area, of course. They were everywhere, inside Della's apartment and outside, plus news people virtually camped at the main entrance to the apartments. There was no escaping them. Marlow Gardens had a self-locking rear door from which residents accessed the car park but every time we went out that way the press was waiting for us. That went on for two, three weeks. I hated every minute of it.'

Hanson paused in her note-taking. 'This rear door. Was it ever left open?'

Forster shook her head. 'No. It closed automatically. In fact, Matthew complained once that the mechanism was too strong. He used the door one morning, carrying books and notes for his work and it closed on him, bruising his arm. He wasn't pleased about it.'

'Was anything done about the door?'

'No, despite his putting his complaint in writing to the letting agent.'

'How did other residents cope with the police and media presence?' asked Watts.

'Like us, they kept their heads down, said nothing and tried to ignore it. There was one man who seemed to quite like talking to the press, but he wasn't a resident. He was the one I just mentioned. The letting agent for the building. He was probably keen to get the press on side, you know, encourage them to say positive things about the area and Marlow Gardens. I guessed he was worried about the impact of Della's murder on the value of the apartments.'

'Did you have any direct dealings with him?' he asked.

'Only when we signed our lease, although we saw him fairly often because he was always around the area. His business premises were just up the hill from Marlow Gardens. I think he handled a lot of apartments in the vicinity, not just our building, so he was usually around.'

'Anything else you remember about him?'

Forster shrugged. 'Not that I recall.'

Watts made a note of what she had said about Dobbs. 'What can you tell us about the other residents at Marlow Gardens whilst you lived there?'

She sighed. 'Again, not that much. We were both busy with work so we didn't get to know any of them that well. There were only six apartments as far as I recall. There was an older lady on the floor above us. Collins, I think her name was.' She smiled. 'A real character. Very feisty. On our floor, on the other side of

Della there was a single woman whose name I don't recall, sorry. She was really nice. She invited me in a couple of times, showed me the plants she was growing on her windowsill. She gave me one of them when we left. An orchid. I think she worked as a librarian somewhere, but it was Della I was mainly friendly with.'

Watts looked up at her. 'What about the other two apartments on the floor above yours?'

'Mm . . . a single woman lived in one of them. If I saw her once in all the time we lived there, that was about it. All I can say about her is that she was young. Around eighteen, I'd say.'

'What about the other apartment?' asked Hanson.

'A man rented it as a base during the week. He told Matthew he worked long hours in the city, but he moved out weeks before Della was murdered.' She grinned. 'On the day he went he came down and asked me if I wanted some unopened items from his fridge. I said yes and he gave us a bottle of Chardonnay, some pâté and some sushi.' Hanson saw Watts' grimace. 'He said he was leaving because his company wanted him based in London.'

'Did he mention the name of this company?'

'No. As far as I recall after he left the apartment stayed empty until we moved out.'

'Is there anything you can tell us about Della Harrington's private life?' asked Watts, moving the conversation to a key reason for their being here.

Forster looked uncertain. 'Not really. Della wasn't the type for girl-talk. Neither am I.'

'We understand she entrusted you with her spare key,' said Hanson.

Forster looked at each of them. 'You want to know about Steffan Coultard, don't you?' She grimaced, shifted position. 'Sorry, cramp.' She gazed from them to the view beyond the windows. 'It all started with some flowers being delivered to Della's apartment. She was at work so the delivery man rang our bell. I accepted them and when she arrived home I took them round to her. She asked me in. There was a small card in an envelope with the flowers. She took it out, read it, picked up the flowers, carried them into the kitchen and dropped them into the bin. They were from him. Coultard.'

'When was this?' asked Watts with a glance at Hanson.

'Mm . . . At a guess, I'd say about six months before the murder.'

'Della told you he'd sent the flowers?' asked Hanson.

'No. The envelope wasn't sealed and the flowers were so lovely, really expensive, I couldn't resist having a look. The card said something about making wonderful music together.' She wrinkled her nose. 'I thought that sounded really tacky, to be honest.'

'Did Della say any more about Steffan Coultard, either then or at any other time?' asked Hanson.

'She told me they sang opera together, that he gave her lifts to rehearsals, which I knew because I'd seen him waiting for her. She said he was a bit pushy.'

Pen poised, Watts looked at her. 'What did you think she meant by that?'

'I assumed she meant that he was interested in making the relationship between them more personal, more intimate. The flowers seemed to confirm it. A week or so after they were delivered she brought round her spare key. She said she often bought stuff online and asked if I'd accept deliveries. I said I would if I was in. She also said that I wasn't to release the key to anyone.'

'Did Della say any more about that?' asked Hanson.

'No, and I didn't ask. It seemed a reasonable thing to say.'

'Did she seem at all nervous or upset when she said this to you?'

'Not at all. She was totally matter-of-fact about it. I saw no indication that she was worried about Coultard.' Forster looked from Hanson to Watts. 'Are you thinking he had something to do with what happened to her?'

'We're exploring all angles,' he said. 'You're sure she never mentioned Coultard specifically in relation to that key?'

Forster frowned in an apparent effort to recall. 'No, I don't think so, but I assumed she didn't want him letting himself in when she wasn't there. Of course, he already had the code to the main door but he never approached me asking for the key until that day. The day it happened. The day Della was murdered.'

'Tell us all you remember about that day,' he said.

'I got home at around four o'clock. Matthew was working

late, so I used the time to tidy up the apartment, make myself a snack.' She shrugged. 'It was just a normal, quiet afternoon. It was around seven in the evening when it started. I heard a doorbell ringing nearby, then someone knocking. It sounded like it was coming from Della's apartment. Then, the knocking started on our door. Because I was on my own I was reluctant to open it. When whoever it was started shouting I was even less keen. I didn't recognize Steffan Coultard's voice. Actually, I'd hardly heard him speak, up to that time. Anyway, the noise stopped and I thought whoever it was had gone away. Then it started up again. That's when I opened the door. I thought that there might be some kind of emergency and that whoever was outside was after Matthew. It was Steffan Coultard. Straight away he demanded I give him Della's key. I couldn't believe how angry he became when I refused. *Really* angry. I tried to explain that I was following Della's instructions, but he wouldn't listen.'

Hanson thought back to her visit to Coultard's house and her impression of him as someone who would go to considerable lengths to avoid confrontation. 'How did his behaviour make you feel?'

'Very uneasy, until I saw the maintenance man at the bottom of the stairs. His being there made me feel less nervous, I suppose.'

'What about Coultard? What was he doing?'

'Oh, he was going on that he *had* to get into Della's apartment. That he wanted some property of his that Della was refusing to give him. I didn't have a clue what he was talking about. I got a bit stroppy with him but it was obvious he wasn't going to go away, no matter what I said, so I gave him the key. He went straight to Della's door, opened it and went inside. The maintenance man had arrived on our floor by then. He asked me in passing if I was OK, then followed Coultard into Della's apartment. He soon came out. The maintenance man, I mean. He looked dreadful. I thought he was going to be ill. After a couple of minutes or so, Coultard came out. He was on his phone and from what I could hear, I guessed he was calling the police.'

Hanson scanned the questions she'd brought with her. 'Did Della have friends visit her?'

'I only know of one. Della had invited me in for coffee and

as I left our apartment for hers I saw this woman coming out. I assumed she was a friend.'

'What did she look like?' asked Watts. Seeing Forster hesitate he said, 'Older, young? Fat? Light build?'

Forster grinned at him. 'The woman I saw looked as though she'd stepped out of a magazine: tall, blonde. *Really* attractive.'

'Did Della mention this friend's name to you?' asked Hanson.

Forster looked at her and gave a slow headshake. 'She did but I'm not sure I got it right. It sounded like "Rommy".'

'*Rommy*?' repeated Watts.

'That's what I thought she said.'

'Were you aware of any males calling at her apartment?' asked Hanson.

'Apart from Coultard, no.'

'You made a statement to the police following the murder,' said Watts. 'There's no mention of any of what you've just told us.'

Forster shrugged. 'The officer who came asked me to tell him what had happened that day. I told him about Steffan Coultard coming to my apartment for the key and that I gave it to him and he seemed satisfied with that. He said it confirmed what Mr Coultard had told them.' The sound of the front door opening filtered through to where they were sitting.

'*Karen*? Somebody's left a bloody Range Rover parked across the drive.'

Forster gave an embarrassed smile. 'That's Matthew.' She raised her voice. 'In here, darling. I'm talking to the police.'

Matthew Forster come into the conservatory, looking irritated. 'What's happened? Who are these people?' He went to his wife. 'Are you alright?'

'I'm fine. This is Detective Inspector Watts and Professor Hanson. They're here to talk about Della's murder.'

He frowned at them. 'I thought that was all sorted years back. Some writer killed her.'

'You haven't heard the news . . .?' said Watts.

'No. I haven't had the time.'

Watts gave him a direct look. 'Della Harrington's case has been reopened. I'm leading the new investigation.'

Matthew Forster looked at his watch. 'I don't see how we can help and I'm in a rush, so if you'll excuse us . . .?'

Watts had stood as Forster came into the conservatory. Now he regarded him with a genial smile which did not fool Hanson. 'What can you tell us about that day? Or the days leading up to it?'

'Nothing. We were hardly in that apartment when we lived there. We were both working. We were there barely twelve months.'

'Did you know Della Harrington?' asked Watts.

Forster stared at him. 'Know her? Of course, I didn't. I was a junior doc, which meant I was spending up to eighteen hours a day at the hospital.' He nodded at his wife. 'Karen was home more than I was. She's more likely to have known the woman.'

She looked up at him. 'As Della lived next door, it's under-standable that the police would want to talk to us now.'

He gave them an impatient glance. 'I'm sorry, but I can't tell you anything about her, or anybody else who lived there. Like I said, I was working long hours.' He headed for the door, speaking over his shoulder. 'I'm back at the hospital in a couple of hours. I need to shower and change.'

She watched him leave then looked at them. 'He still works very long hours and he's under a lot of pressure. He was out of this house at six this morning. Would you like to wait? He won't be long.'

Watts stood again. 'No. If we want to speak to your husband again, I'll ring you.'

'What do you think?' asked Watts when they were inside the Range Rover.

Hanson turned pages of notes. 'Karen Forster has confirmed that Coultard went into the apartment alone and stayed there for a couple of minutes. Most people in that situation would have been out of there in seconds. I want to know why he hung around inside and what he was doing.'

'She said Coultard mentioned Della having some property of his.' He eyed her. 'You've met Coultard. Did he strike you as the type who'd be able to ignore a dead woman spread-eagled on her bedroom floor just feet away?'

'I've known a few people over the years who could do that, but I wouldn't have put Steffan Coultard in that category. But then, I've met him only once.' She gave him a sideways glance. 'The witness statements which the police took at the time. I'm wondering why investigating officers didn't ask more questions.' She heard his heavy sigh. Watts' default position was one of loyalty to other officers. 'You're not wondering the same?' she asked.

'Maybe.' He started the engine. 'What do you make of what Karen Forster said about Coultard having a thing for Harrington?'

'He didn't strike me as the romantic type but the expensive flowers suggest otherwise. The indication is that he liked Della Harrington a lot . . .'

'Yeah, and he was – is – a married man.'

Hanson looked at him. 'What Forster told us suggests that not only did he believe Della would be receptive to his flowers, but that she would also be wanting to move their relationship on to something intimate. On learning that he'd misread the situation, he showed that he has a capacity for anger.'

Watts stared straight ahead. 'I'm telling you, doc, if he removed so much as a pin from that apartment on the day she died, we'll have him and it won't bother me how many years ago it was.'

'What about what Karen Forster said about Dobbs, the agent and his attitude to the press at the time?'

He huffed. 'Par for the course from my experience of him. I can just see him, all blow-dried hair and camel overcoat, standing there feeding the journos a line to protect his business interests, the git.'

She grinned. 'No change there, then?' They joined the traffic on the Bristol Road, the university coming into view. 'What do you make of Karen Forster's husband?' she asked.

'He came across as the centre of his own "I'm-a-doctor" universe. Does he think he's the only one who works long hours? I was at headquarters at half-six this morning. So was Corrigan.'

She smiled out of the window. 'Don't tell me. You're adding Matthew Forster to your Git List.'

'What was your take on him?' he asked.

Hanson shrugged. 'We saw him for barely five minutes. Maybe he's having a bad day.'

'Yeah, and maybe he was at home once in a while, when the wife was working, and got pally with Harrington.'

She looked at him. 'Are you serious?'

It was Watts' turn to shrug. 'The answer is, "a" I don't know and "b" it won't hurt to do some digging. What I *do* know is that if there's so much as a whisper about him during this investigation, no matter how trivial it might seem, I'll be back here.' They came onto the campus. 'Mark my words, doc. This case has got sex, needs and wants written all over it.'

NINE

C orrigan came into the busy headquarters' reception and headed for the tall, dark-haired woman the officer on the desk had just phoned him about. 'Mrs Andrea Jones?' He held out his hand to her. 'Lieutenant Corrigan. Thanks for coming in. Is it OK with you if we talk in that room over there?' She nodded, unsmiling and followed him inside, where she stood waiting. 'Please take a seat,' he said quietly, aware of something in her demeanour he was struggling to identify. 'Can I get you some tea, coffee?'

'No. I'm fine. I just want this over with,' she said, not looking at him, her words clipped.

He sat opposite her. 'My colleague Detective Inspector Watts has been in touch to let you know that we're investigating your sister's death.'

'He phoned shortly before I saw the news of Lockman being released.' She clenched her hands together.

He waited. When he spoke he kept his voice low. 'Is there a problem here, ma'am?'

She stared at him, then looked away. He realized that she was angry. Not just angry. Furious. 'Yes. A *big* problem for my family and for me. When we realized that that . . . *individual* was being freed, we couldn't believe it. Our parents don't understand it. Neither do I. For the last ten years, we've carried on with our lives, thinking that that whole business was over. Done with.' She looked at him. 'And now *this*. It will never be over for us. It's all wrong. Do you understand what I'm saying?'

Corrigan wasn't about to be drawn into a debate about justice, particularly with a member of a family who evidently trusted the original verdict and wanted the man a court had said was guilty to stay in prison and continue paying for a death he had now been absolved from causing. There were no winners and losers in that kind of debate. As difficult as this might be for Andrea Jones, who probably viewed merely being here as collusion with a legal decision she opposed, they needed her help. 'I hear what you're saying and I understand, ma'am, but we would still value any assistance you can give us.' He paused to allow her to speak. When she didn't, he said, 'This is a completely new investigation. We're very keen to talk to as many people as we can about your sister and her life.'

He saw her head come up. 'I hope that doesn't include our parents.'

'We understand this situation must be very difficult for them but we need to know about your sister's life so, yes, we'll need to talk to them at some stage.' He saw her tense. 'We know your sister had a job, which means she had colleagues. We're assuming she had a social life, friends. Those are the kinds of details we need from you or your family if you're able to give them.' He saw her look down at the floor. 'Mrs Jones, it's not our intention to cause you or your family additional heartache. It might help if you tell me what's worrying you.'

She looked up at him. 'It should be obvious. We don't want all of this raked up again. I don't understand why you want to know about Della's life.'

'If we can construct as full a picture of your sister as possible, it could help us find whoever killed her.'

'The police would have done that in 2006.' She gave him a quick, evaluative look. 'Do you know what this "full picture" you've mentioned says to me? It says that you're looking for something in the way my sister lived her life so you can say that she somehow *invited* what happened to her or that she was in some way to blame.'

He gave her a direct look. 'Ma'am, that's not mine nor my colleagues' intention. Like I said, we need facts, information about your sister which could help us identify who killed her and get her some justice.'

Andrea Jones looked away from him, saying nothing. He was about to speak when she said, 'My sister was good to our parents. Visited them regularly. I saw her every other week or so. She worked hard at her job. She had one or two friends at the call centre, but none that she was close to, as far as I was aware. When she wasn't working, she used her time to practise her singing.' She looked up at Corrigan. 'You do know her voice was operatic in quality?'

'Yes, we do.'

'She belonged to an operatic group. They performed for charity.' She gave him a challenging look. 'That's it. *That* was my sister's life. She didn't drink. She didn't go out to clubs. She didn't cause trouble for anybody. She was hardworking, respectable, kind and very talented.' Her voice was unsteady. 'And after ten years I still miss her.'

Corrigan was about to ask this woman one of the questions at the forefront of his thinking, knowing that there was no easy way to raise it. 'Mrs Jones, are you able to tell me about your sister's financial situation?' He waited out the heavy silence.

She stared at him. 'I don't know what you mean. Della didn't have a "financial situation". She had what she earned from her job, which was reasonable although I don't exactly know the details.'

'Our understanding is that your sister's annual salary would have been around twenty thousand pounds.'

'So?'

'Would you describe your sister's lifestyle as comfortable?'

Jones looked irritated. 'I don't know what you're getting at.'

'The apartment your sister owned was pleasant, well furnished.' He didn't add that some of the items inside it, including in her wardrobe, were high-end purchases.

Jones was now regarding him with disbelief. 'I thought the police were supposed to get their facts straight! My sister didn't own her apartment. She rented.'

'That's not our understanding, ma'am. The information we have is that your sister not only purchased her apartment for sixty thousand pounds but she did so by a single cash transaction.'

Jones stared at him. She laughed. 'This is *madness*. My sister didn't have that kind of money.' Corrigan was wondering how long it would take for her to pick up on the possible implications of what she'd just been told. He watched her face. Not very long at all. She was on her feet, heading for the door. She stopped, turned. 'Are you suggesting that somebody, a *man* was giving money to my sister? That he was keeping her?'

'I'm not suggesting anything, ma'am. We have to explore all anomalies we find in the information we have.' He'd remained seated to avoid escalating her anger. She walked back to the table and sat, her eyes fixed on his. 'Well, Lieutenant Corrigan, let me tell you, my sister *would* not, *did* not take money from any man.'

'Is it at all possible that your sister chose not to divulge something like that to you?'

She was clearly holding onto her temper. '*No*. It isn't.'

'I'm not suggesting that your sister did anything wrong here but if there was someone in her life who provided money for her to buy that apartment, it's real important that we have that confirmed. Even if you don't know his name.'

'There wasn't any *man*.' She glared at him. Seconds of silence slid by. 'My sister was gay.'

It was Corrigan's turn to stare. 'That aspect of your sister's life wasn't known to the original investigators.'

'Of *course*, it wasn't.' She glared at him. 'I didn't tell them. Do you want to know why? Because our parents didn't know about Della. They still don't. Don't you *dare* tell them.'

Aware that whatever he said wouldn't placate her, he still chose his words. 'Ma'am, it's possible that if the original investigation had been aware of that aspect of your sister's life, it might have opened up new avenues of inquiry.'

'You don't know that for a fact.' She gave him a challenging look. 'I did not disapprove of my sister and her life in any way. I didn't tell the police at the time because I was protecting our parents. It would have been in the newspapers. They wouldn't have understood.' She paused. 'I can't tell you anything else about that aspect of her life because Della never confided in me about her relationships and I never asked. She told me she was friendly with her neighbours either side of her. She got on with members of the operatic group she belonged to. That's all I know.'

'Did she mention anyone in that group in particular?' he asked.

'Only the man who gave her lifts to rehearsals. I can't tell you anything about him.'

'Why did your sister need lifts?' he asked. 'She had her own car.'

'She hated driving in the middle of the city. When she moved to that apartment it wasn't a problem because she headed out of the city to get to work. She needed a lift to rehearsals because they were held right in the city centre, sometimes at a rehearsal room in the new library or at the Old Rep theatre . . . Della was a really nervous driver.'

Corrigan gave her a quick glance, saw that her anger was dispersing. 'You're not able to say anything at all about this man who gave your sister those lifts to rehearsal?'

'No. Not even his name.'

'Della never made the odd comment about him in passing?'

She appeared to consider this. 'Once. She mentioned that he was very quiet. Della was quiet. I remember thinking those lifts she was getting from him were probably journeys of very few words.'

'Your sister never intimated to you that she was uncomfortable with this man at all?'

She gave a definitive headshake. 'Not at all.' He looked down at what he'd written, thinking how best to proceed. He looked up to find Jones' eyes on him. 'I can't tell you anything about the relationships she had because Della never confided in me and I didn't ask her. My sister was a strong, kind and, as I said, a very talented woman. Whoever killed her deserves . . .' She glanced through the window of the small interview room to the still busy reception and shook her head.

'Did Della ever indicate to you that she had experienced difficulties with callers to the centre where she worked?' he asked.

'Meaning?'

'People who ring call centres can get impatient, angry . . .'

'Oh, I see what you mean. No. Della wasn't involved in that side of the business. It was her job to advise and support her team of call operators. Della had a light touch which suited that kind of work. She never mentioned any problems to me.'

Corrigan stood, held out his hand. 'Thank you for coming in today and for your help, ma'am. We appreciate it.'

She took his hand, looked into his eyes. 'I apologize for getting heated earlier. Please. Just find who did this to Della.'

Hanson and Maisie were watching a recorded TV programme. 'Wait for it, Mom. *Look*! It's going . . . it's going . . .!' The tall, intricate cake was on the move. They both squealed, hands at their mouths as Charlie came into the sitting room.

'I don't usually get that kind of reception when I arrive with an offer of hot drinks.'

Hanson laughed up at him. 'We're watching a cake self-destruct. Maisie? Do you want a drink?'

'No, thanks. Actually, I've got an hour of homework still to do and then I'll have a bath. Grandpa's bought me some bubble stuff.'

Hanson watched her go to the door then looked at Charlie. 'Everything OK?'

'No, Kate. It isn't.'

She sat up. 'What is it? Are you feeling unwell?'

'No. Nothing like that. We need to talk about what you said a couple of days ago. About my moving here permanently.'

'And still keeping your house so you'll be independent and—'

'Kate, I can't live here. My life, my friends are in Worcester.'

'I know that, Charlie,' she said softly. 'I understand. Your friends are more than welcome to come here. Plus, you'll be free to come and go as you want. I won't have any expectations about how you live here. You'll see them whenever you choose to stay over in Worcester. I've got plans for your room. You'll have your own bathroom.' He wasn't meeting her eyes. Something clutched at her chest. 'What is it?'

He came and sat beside her, took her hand. 'Since we got to know each other again after all those years apart, it's been wonderful to have you and Maisie in my life again. Really, it has. I'll always feel guilty for leaving you with your mother. Having you back again gives me the chance to make it up to you. This isn't about houses and bathrooms. It's about people.' Hanson opened her mouth to speak. 'Actually, Kate, it's about one person.' She stared at him, plans crashing and falling inside her head. He squeezed her hand, gave her a direct look. 'Her name is Grace.'

She looked at the still-dark hair, the bone structure of his face, the slim build. Her father had a woman. Of course, he had. 'I see.' She slipped her hand from his and stood, feeling disoriented. 'I . . . I . . . understand. I just wasn't thinking.' She headed for the door as he got to his feet.

'Kate?'

She looked back, gave him a quick smile. 'It's OK, Charlie. Really it is. I just feel stupid that I didn't at least think there might be someone. You have to do whatever feels right for you.'

She escaped to her study, closed the door and leant against it, heart pounding, her hand raised to her mouth. It wasn't OK. Never would be. He didn't want what she was offering him. A voice slid into her head. She recognized the mocking tone. Her mother's. It had been a consistent presence in her childhood for as long as she could recall, increasingly so after Charlie had left and was no longer a target for her anger and resentment. Her mother was never the kind of person to allow any opportunity to criticize or belittle pass her by. Even being dead these last twelve years hadn't stopped that voice. *Kate, as clever as you are, you can't keep a man, any man, can you? Know what you'll be when that girl of yours grows up and leaves you? You'll be me.*

Hanson let her head drop forward and silently wept.

TEN

Slowing the car to a halt outside Coultard's house, Hanson pulled down the sun visor and scrutinized her face in the small mirror. As if she didn't already know it, it told her that Monday night had been a very long one. With an impatient headshake she flipped up the visor and got out of the car. Reaching the house, she raised her hand towards the bell but before she could ring Coultard opened the door. He must have seen her arrive and from the look on his face he was less than happy to see her. 'You should have phoned to tell me you were coming. How did you know I would be here?'

'I rang your office early this morning to speak to you. They told me that you worked from home on Tuesdays.'

He stared at her, horrified. 'You shouldn't have done that,' he whispered. 'It could make all kinds of problems for me with my line manager.'

'He sounded very pleasant on the phone. This is a murder investigation, Mr Coultard and I have to talk to you. Unless you prefer to go to police headquarters?'

He abruptly turned from her and headed towards the kitchen. Closing the door, she followed. Coultard had to be in his mid-forties but his behaviour struck her as immature and dependent. She came inside the kitchen, giving him a quick evaluation. Apart from the tension on his face he looked much as he had on her last visit: the same dark grey cardigan but this time the buttoned-to-the-neck shirt was in a small, black-brown check. She didn't fully understand what he was about, which is why she was here. She wanted to know why he appeared to want to exist without drawing any official, work or social attention to himself. She glanced at his clothes again, seeing them as a form of camouflage. Yet there had been one occasion when he had made his presence felt. The evening of Della Harrington's murder. He leant against a kitchen counter, arms folded, gaze fixed on the floor as Hanson walked to the table. A couple of files were sitting on it, both closed. She sat, pulled out her notebook and gave him a direct look.

'You were outside Della Harrington's apartment building from about six-thirty on the day she died. Where were you before that, Mr Coultard?'

'I was at work. Why?'

'If that's where you were, Mr Coultard, there's no problem. That's the same place you work at now?'

Coultard stared at her. Hardly a stag at bay. More a rabbit fixed in headlights. 'I already told you that and I don't want the police going to my workplace.'

'They may not need to talk directly to your work colleagues, if that's what's concerning you, but they may want to verify your whereabouts on that day.' She gave him a steady look. 'Even ten years ago, companies were security conscious. Yours is likely to have retained records of staff comings and goings.' He stared at her. She doubted that his company would have any such records but she wanted him talking, and if making him feel under pressure was the way to do it, then so be it. So far, he hadn't uttered one useful comment. Taking her notebook from her bag, she looked up at him. 'That evening when you found Della Harrington dead, you let yourself into the building, then went up to her apartment. Tell me why you chose not to do that as soon as you arrived, or on any other evening so far as we have established?'

He shrugged, not meeting her gaze. 'I just didn't want to. I'm always prompt with any arrangements I make. Della knew that. She knew I would be there. She would usually come straight out. When she didn't, I just knew . . .' His voice died.

She looked up at him, waiting. 'What did you know, Mr Coultard?'

Still, he didn't speak. Her eyes moved to a tall wine rack to the right of him, where two wine glasses were just visible, half-filled with red wine. She glanced at her watch. Eleven-thirty a.m. If it was fresh wine, someone had started early. Make that two someones. She kept her voice relaxed. 'Is your wife in, Mr Coultard?'

'No.'

'Are you expecting her back?' The clock on the wall ticked off the seconds.

'No.'

'I need to check with you who entered Della Harrington's apartment when you were there that evening.'

He frowned, looked at the floor. 'I already told you, I went in with the maintenance man.'

She gave a slow nod. 'Yes. You did. The problem is, we've been told otherwise.' His head came up. He stared at her. 'You have been described to us as highly anxious to get into Miss Harrington's apartment that evening. Our understanding is that you were first to enter it, that you were alone when you did so and that you remained inside, still alone for at least a couple of minutes.' She waited, seeing indecision flood his face. 'You need to explain that to me, Mr Coultard. Now.'

'I . . . I was worried about her.'

'Why?'

He pulled the cardigan around himself, folded his arms. 'No particular reason.'

Hanson recorded his few words in quick, cursive strokes in her notebook, recalling Corrigan's phone call to her the previous day to tell her what he had learnt about Della Harrington's sexuality. 'There's no indication on file that you told the police at the time that you were worried about Ms Harrington.' He shrugged, said nothing. 'Why didn't you tell them?'

'It wasn't my place. It was an odd comment she made.'

'Tell me.'

He ran his tongue over his lips. 'She said something like, "You expect one thing from a man and you get something else." Della didn't like being questioned so I didn't ask for details.'

She eyed him. It was hard to imagine this timid man in the role of Della Harrington's rescuer but she had to ask. 'Did you think this man was inside her apartment that evening?'

He folded his arms tight across his chest, not looking at her. 'I . . . I just thought she might be . . . upset.'

She stared at him. 'Come on, Mr Coultard. You're not being consistent here. You need to be open about this. If you wanted to get inside the apartment to protect her . . .'

'It wasn't like that. Actually, I wondered if maybe Della had gone out. She had some of my CDs and I wanted them back. That's why I went into the apartment. To get them.'

Hanson's professional training had equipped her to maintain a relaxed facial expression and demeanour whilst listening to information of all kinds. It deserted her now. She stared at him. 'You're telling me that you went inside that apartment, saw Della's body and you stayed there, searching for your CDs, then removed them?'

'*No*. You're making it sound bad. I went straight to the shelf, found them and . . . that's when I saw her.'

The manner in which Harrington's body had been displayed was fixed inside Hanson's head. Having visited that apartment and seen how small it was, she didn't believe him. 'Don't mess with me, Mr Coultard. You could not have missed seeing Della immediately you entered that apartment.'

'I . . . I needed my CDs. They're extremely important to me.'

Hanson had heard countless descriptions from individuals of their thoughtless cruelty towards and disregard for others. And here was Coultard, socially timid, reluctant to be involved with others, a man who feared criticism yet had been able to ignore or block from his mind the sight of a woman whom he knew and apparently liked lying close by, damaged and destroyed. 'Della was someone you thought of as a friend,' she said quietly. 'You weren't affected by seeing her like that?'

His face hardened. 'You've got it all wrong. I opened up to Della. I felt safe with her. But she changed. She became distant. Told me I had to wait outside. I find that kind of rejection very difficult to cope with. I decided I wasn't interested in her any more. I asked for my CDs but she refused to give them to me. They, my CDs, my music, they're my *life*. I had to have them back. What's so hard to understand about that?' He looked down at his hands. 'I told you about wanting to cover her. That was me wanting to protect her.'

Hanson made quick notes. She doubted the chivalry he had just indicated. He had also told her during her previous visit that by covering Della he had hoped to avoid police criticism. If that were true, Steffan Coultard's principle motivation was self-interest and self-protection. Della's plight when he saw her that evening had come a long way second. By far a more likely explanation was that he'd heard Fenton, the maintenance man, express that intention when he arrived inside the apartment and had adopted it as his own to protect himself from criticism. An alternative explanation was that Steffan Coultard was not shocked by the sight of Della Harrington's dead body because he'd already seen it when he'd killed her. She closed her eyes, pinched the bridge of her nose. She wouldn't challenge him on his claim to have wished to protect Della. It would merely trigger further denials. She wanted to be away from this house. In the heavy silence between them, she slowly raised her head, her eyes on the wine glasses. One of the things she'd learned from her work was that there was a particular feel to any house in which an unknown person was present. She wouldn't challenge him on that presence. He would merely deny it and she had no power to instigate a search.

Closing her notebook, she reached into her pocket for her phone. 'Excuse me.' She looked down at its blank screen. 'Mr Coultard, I've had an urgent text and I need to leave right now but we'll be in touch. I can see myself out.' He followed her to the front door, this time watching her as she got into her car, made a U-turn and headed back the way she had come. He was soon lost to her behind the tree cover surrounding his house. With a quick right turn into a small side road, she went along it, reversed, drove back up and parked. All she had was a view of the pavement and roadside in front of his house. He might not appear at all but on the off-chance that he would, she was prepared to wait.

After ten minutes, phone in hand, starting to feel chilled, Hanson sat up. There was movement in the area of Coultard's house. Eyes fixed on the lower tree branches around it, she tracked feet in extremely high heels, moving in the direction of the road. A young woman with long blonde hair appeared at the end of the drive and stood on the pavement, waiting. Coultard now appeared. It looked as if some level of disagreement was occurring between them, the blonde woman giving expressive hand movements, Coultard possibly attempting to placate her. He disappeared in the direction of the house whilst the young woman stood at the kerb, arms folded. Hanson raised her phone, took several photographs and gave them a quick, critical look. They showed the young woman with her face turned in Hanson's direction. Hanson looked at them. They were fairly distant. She needed better. She looked up as the grey car she'd seen on

Coultard's drive reversed beyond the tree cover, came onto the road and stopped. The blonde woman got inside. The car was now heading along the road to where Hanson was parked. As it neared she raised her phone again. A large delivery lorry suddenly appeared from her right and Coultard halted close to a parked car to allow it through. 'Thank you, thank you,' she murmured, taking two more photographs. She gave them an evaluative glance. They each showed the back of Coultard's head, his female passenger sitting forward, her face turned to his and lit by the low winter sun. Slipping the phone into her pocket, she waited until Coultard was out of sight then started her car.

Watts was alone inside UCU when she came through the door. Dropping her bag and coat on the nearest chair, she walked to the Smartboard and started writing, giving a quick verbal account of her visit to Coultard. Watts watched and listened. 'He sounds like a right weirdo.'

'You haven't heard the best bit. He didn't mention that there was anyone with him in the house but he had a woman there.'

'Lucky him. Who was she?'

'I don't know but I took a couple of photographs of her. I've forwarded them to Forensics. I'm hoping they can enhance them. Here, take a look.' She held out her phone to him.

He squinted at the screen. 'Blimey, doc, you're on fire with this case. I take it that's not his wife?'

'I seriously doubt it.' The excitement she'd felt since she'd watched Coultard and the unknown woman suddenly left her. It was replaced by the weight of the previous evening's conversation between her and Charlie.

'What's up?' he asked.

'Nothing.'

'In that case, there's somebody waiting upstairs who might interest you. Come on.'

They walked into the observation room and Hanson looked through one-way glass to where Corrigan was facing a scruffy man across the table.

'Archie Fenton, the maintenance man,' said Watts. 'According to him, Della Harrington's clothes were ripped off her, as in damaged. We know that wasn't the case. Corrigan suspects Fenton's into porn, big-time, which is what probably led to his assuming that Harrington's clothing was "ripped". Fenton saw what he was expecting to see. What he's used to seeing.' Watts glanced at her. 'Given the way Harrington was displayed, given that her death was a sexual homicide, if Fenton does have a hardcore porn habit, he's moving himself very nicely into the frame of suspect. I'll get in there and we'll start the interview. After you've observed, you can tell us what you make of him.'

He left the room and within a few seconds the door to the next room opened and he appeared, took the chair next to Corrigan and activated the PACE machine. Having gone through the required preamble, he fixed his attention on the twitchy face opposite him. 'Right Mr Fenton, you've come here voluntarily. We'll keep it simple. Tell us why you described Della Harrington's clothes as having been "ripped" from her body.'

Fenton looked away from him with a frown towards the one-way glass beyond which Hanson was sitting. 'I just said it. It didn't mean nothing.'

Corrigan gazed at him. 'When we spoke to you a couple of days ago you said that you came on duty at three o'clock and remained in your office on the ground floor of the apartment building until you heard some kind of argument and went out to see what was going on.' He leant forward, causing Fenton to shrink away. 'Are you sure that's the truth, Mr Fenton?'

Fenton's eyes slid away from the two officers. 'Yes, it is. It's in my statement to the police at the time. You know it is.'

'You also said you watched TV for over three hours on a work day. Tell us what was on that was so interesting.'

'I dunno. You're asking me details from ten years back.'

Corrigan's eyes stayed on Fenton, who squirmed. 'Did you have a DVD player in that room?'

Fenton rallied, giving him a quick disparaging look. 'If you must know, I had a laptop.'

'Is that so?' said Corrigan. 'That would have been expensive kit, back then. Why the need?' Fenton opened his mouth and closed it again. 'It fits with our thinking about you, sir, that back then you were a heavy user of pornography of a violent nature. What do you say to that?'

'I wasn't.' Fenton's eyes were fixed on the table. He rallied. 'Prove it.'

Corrigan sat back and Watts took over. 'Your story is that you spent three hours in a working day watching television. On your own?'

'That's right. I might just have left my office for a few minutes. To break it up a bit. Get a breath of air, like. I had nothing else to do that day.'

'See anybody outside, did you? Somebody who might recall seeing you?' He watched Fenton's mouth form itself into a response. 'Before you say no, think about it. We need names of people who were outside Marlow Gardens Apartments that afternoon. What you don't need is us delving into your porn use, which we will do—'

'I'm not into nothing illegal!'

'. . . if you don't give us information which sounds plausible right now. What do you say, Archie?'

Fenton's tongue slid over his lips. 'I wasn't out there more than a minute or two. There were all sorts of people coming and going.'

'That's the way, Archie. You've made a start. Any you recognized?'

'I . . . I think I might have seen the bloke who handled the lettings in the area. Just in passing, like. Not to speak to. I didn't know him.'

'You mean Leonard Dobbs?'

'Yeah. That's him.'

'Hard to believe you didn't know Dobbs, seeing as you were working at Marlow Gardens. A building he managed.' Fenton's eyes drifted away. 'Who else?' Hanson watched Fenton, guessing he would go with a minimal response.

He did. 'Jim Withershaw.'

Her colleagues looked at each other, frowned. 'What's Jim Withershaw to you?' asked Watts.

'Nothing. He was the boss of the painting crew that was working on the outside of the building back then.'

'What did he have to say?'

'Nothing much.' Fenton's gaze slid away from both officers. 'He asked me if I knew anything about any pilfering around the building. I said no. I was maintenance . . .'

'So you've said.' Watts sat back, his wide face creasing into a smile. 'See, lieutenant? I told you Archie probably had something for us. Something he was doing that afternoon which gave him a break from *Naughty Nuns*, *Hot Housewives* and probably a lot worse.'

Colour swept over Fenton's face. 'I want to go. *Now*.'

Watts slow-nodded. 'You can when you've told us about the pilfering this Withershaw mentioned.'

'I didn't have a clue what he was on about, so I can't tell you nothing about it.'

Watts regarded him for several seconds, then reached out and ended the recording. He and Corrigan stood and looked down at him. 'You'd do well to remember, Archie, that we've got our eyes on you,' said Watts. 'Now, clear off.'

They returned to UCU. 'Shifty git,' said Watts. 'What he told us means another job for Jules. I'll get him to trace this Withershaw's current whereabouts. The name itself should please him because it isn't "Smith".' He looked at Hanson. 'What's your verdict on Fenton?'

'I know what you think. You think that his interest in porn could link him to Harrington's murder.'

He gazed at her. 'And you don't.'

'I didn't say that.'

'Right. Glad we got that sorted.' Corrigan raised his hand to them and headed for the door. 'Corrigan's got armed response,' he said. 'How do you fancy an outing to Moseley?'

'What for?'

'Della Harrington's other next-door neighbour is expecting us.'

The last fifteen minutes of the journey had passed in silence. Watts glanced across at Hanson. He'd known her for a few years now so he didn't need to be told that something was up with her. He'd seen her in all kinds of moods and states: enthusiastic, determined, amused to the point of helpless laughing. He'd also seen her snappy, angry and bossy. What he was seeing right now was something different. His thinking ran on, looking for a likely explanation. Corrigan? He shook his head. Like most people inside headquarters, Watts knew there was a chemistry there, although neither of them seemed able to get it together. If something had happened between the two of them, he would have picked up on it. Not from Corrigan himself. He was tight-lipped on personal stuff. Watts shook his head. There was only one way to find out what was on her mind. 'Got a problem, doc?'

'No.'

She looked out of the passenger window. Knowing a closed conversation when he heard one, Watts changed the subject. 'This Josie Clark was Della Harrington's other next-door neighbour at the time of the murder. She's the one who was off work with flu on the day it happened. At least, that's what she said.' Hanson rolled her eyes. 'Whatever she was doing, I've got high hopes of her having something to tell us.' He slid the vehicle to a halt halfway down a quiet road and they got out into eye-searing cold to walk the path to the front door where Watts pushed the bell of the small, well-maintained house. Behind his bullish face his optimism was on the slide. A decade was a long time. He'd heard it from Hanson often enough. How emotions within a situation can help fix details in memory but can also cause a lot of forgetting. What were the chances of this Clark woman remembering anything about a day or two she took off work a decade ago? Maybe she fancied a bit of work-time shopping? Seeing a shadow beyond the glass of the door he adjusted his face. It was opened by a mid-forties blonde woman who gave them a wide smile. Watts held up identification.

'Ms Josie Clark?'

'Detective Inspector Watts, come in. Isn't it cold?' They stepped into light and warmth. Watts introduced Hanson. Clark looked at her. 'A forensic psychologist? That sounds like interesting work. Come through to the kitchen and I'll make coffee. I was outside just now, pruning the jasmine, or possibly killing it off, but it's reminded me that spring must be on the way.'

They followed her into a bright kitchen overlooking the rear garden, Watts thinking that this woman was warm and welcoming like her house. He'd taken a quick look through the open door of the living room as they'd walked past. 'Scoping', Hanson called it. He'd noticed books. A lot of books. There were more here in the kitchen. Not cookbooks either. All sorts. He eyed them, thinking he should read more, but the Job involved as much as he could take. As Clark got busy making coffee, he took her ten-year-old statement from an inside pocket and passed it to Hanson, the details such as they were, already fixed inside his head. Back then, Clark was working as a librarian, which probably explained the number of books he was seeing here. Flu had kept her off work on the day Della Harrington was murdered. In the early evening, she had been awakened by loud voices inside the apartment building and footsteps on the stairs. Eventually, she'd opened her door to a police officer and provided him with this brief statement. The one now in Hanson's hand.

Coffee arrived on the table in front of them. 'I hope you like it strong. A couple of minutes before you arrived I took some pain au chocolat out of the oven. They're still warm. Would you like one?'

Watts heard Hanson's 'Please,' and said the same. He took a deep breath and sipped his coffee. This was the nearest the Job got to heaven. There was something about women who made good coffee that appealed to him. Hanson could do it when she put her mind to it. Chong always nailed it. Clark returned with the pain au chocolat and plates.

Watts looked up at her. 'I said on the phone that we're investigating the Della Harrington murder. You probably noticed it's been in the news again.'

'Yes, I saw it,' said Clark. 'I hope you get him this time.' She shook her head. 'It's dreadful what happened to Della but it must have been awful for that poor man who spent so many years in prison.'

Not picking up any implied criticism of the force, Watts let the comment go. 'We're talking to all witnesses who made statements about that day, giving them a chance to think back to it, maybe recall something they saw which they didn't think was relevant or important at the time.' Clark nodded but said nothing. He reached for her statement now lying on the table and passed it to her. 'This might refresh your memory, Ms Clark.' He and Hanson waited as she read her own years-ago words. It didn't take her long. She put it down.

'I can hardly believe it's a decade since it happened. I'll do my best.'

He nodded, glanced at Hanson who smiled on cue. 'That's all we ask, Ms Clark,' she said. 'Tell us whatever you want.'

Clark gave each of them a doubtful look. '. . . I don't know where to start.'

'You were off work that day,' prompted Hanson.

Clark put down her cup. 'Actually, I went to work but left at around midday. Like I said in my statement, I was ill. The first I knew that something had happened to Della, there was a lot of noise, voices somewhere in the building. It woke me up. I didn't feel well enough to get up and investigate. I ignored it. A while later, a policeman knocked on my door.' She pointed at the statement. 'I managed to give him that, which wasn't much. I'm sorry, but that's it.'

Watts gave Hanson a quick, sidelong look. This was her territory. She knew how memory worked plus she had a passion for detail. Right now, they needed both. He watched and listened as she got to work. 'Ms Clark, it's possible that you might recall more with a little help. Are you willing to give it a try?'

'Of course.'

'Thank you. Imagine that we've come here today because we're planning to make a televised reconstruction of the events of the day of the murder, based on what you as a witness heard and saw.' Clark nodded, looking keen but saying nothing. 'Your job is to help us with that reconstruction by telling us every single thing about that day, no matter how incidental or unimportant it might seem. Try not to monitor or second-guess what comes into your head. Just let it come. You can start anywhere you like. It doesn't matter. If you don't remember much of that day due to being unwell, you could start with the previous one.'

Clark got up, crossed the kitchen and returned with the coffee pot. She refilled their cups and her own. 'I like coffee when I'm thinking.' She sat, took several sips, her eyes fixed on the table. 'OK. I'll go with the day prior to Della's murder. I came home from my job at Aston University at around lunchtime. I can't give you an exact time but I was starting to feel really unwell. I parked my car in the residents' car park and walked to the main door.' She looked up at Hanson. 'I remember the letting agent for our building was standing there, but there was nothing remarkable about that. He was often around the building. Because of the way I was feeling, I just walked past him to the door. I had some difficulty recalling my door code. That's when he spoke to me.'

'Can you remember what he said?' asked Hanson.

'He said something about wanting to come up to my apartment to check something. I can't remember his exact words because I was starting to feel worse. I wanted to get away from him. I don't think I actually said anything, just waved him off. All I wanted to do was to get inside my apartment on my own and lie down, which is what I did.' Watts glanced at Hanson. He would have liked more precision on the times all this was happening, who else was about, but she was listening intently, her eyes on Clark and he knew better than to intervene. 'I went straight to bed and stayed there for the rest of that day and night.' Clark's frown deepened. 'I woke up early the next morning. The day of the murder. I can't tell you the actual time but I'd say it was around six. I took my duvet into the lounge and lay down on the sofa.' She shook her head. 'No, wait. I opened the curtains first. It was still dark outside. I remember I decided to watch television for a while.' Hanson's pen sped, converting every word into a series of squiggles incomprehensible to everyone but herself.

'Was the television at normal volume?' she asked.

'No. It was low. Because of my headache. I think I put it on hoping for some distraction.'

'Did you hear anything from Della Harrington's apartment?'

'Sorry, no. I just lay there, feeling sorry for myself. After a while, I remember thinking it would probably be best if I tried to go back to sleep. That's when I decided to take a sleeping pill and go back to bed. My doctor had prescribed them a couple of months before when I was finding work very hectic and having trouble switching off from it. I hadn't used them but I decided to take just one.' She shook her head. 'What a mistake. That day was the first and the last time I took anything to make me sleep. It caused me to have *such* a dream . . . the most vivid I can ever remember.'

'Tell us about it,' said Hanson quietly.

'The dream?' Clark sipped coffee, frowned. 'It was totally bizarre, but I suppose that's what dreams are, aren't they? It started with me floating on water in bright sunshine, like I was sunbathing. I felt *really* hot and I was wanting to go indoors . . . and I did . . . but it was just as hot inside. And dark. I remember feeling a bit nervous because of some strange shapes moving about. After a while I realized they were huge, black birds. They began flying around the room and I knew they were trapped. They flapped and swooped at me then crashed to the floor. And then a man came into the room and I told him about the birds. He told me not to get upset, that he was there to check on me or something, that I was a clever girl but that I should relax and leave the birds to him. Then, a woman came in. She shouted, "Get away!" and the birds just went. Disappeared.' She shook her head. 'That was it. No more sleeping tablets for me.'

'You had this dream some time during the day of the murder?' asked Hanson.

Clark gave it some thought. 'Yes. At a guess it was around lunchtime but my body clock was probably all over the place so I don't really know.'

Seeing Hanson busily writing, Watts said, 'You mentioned the letting agent just now. What can you tell us about him?'

Clark hesitated. 'I wouldn't want to cause problems for anyone by saying it, but I didn't like him much.'

'Why's that?'

'He was always hanging around the building.' Seeing Watts waiting for more, she said, 'He knocked on my door once. This was around twelve months before what happened to Della. I hadn't long moved in. He said he wanted to check the apartment for damp. I told him there wasn't any but I let him in anyway. He took a quick look around then he stood for ages in front of my window, like he was looking at the plasterwork there.' She paused. 'Only, he wasn't.'

'What did you think he was looking at?'

'I had my desk under the window. He was looking at the papers on it. I was a little shocked by that because he was a respectable businessman.'

'What kinds of papers were on your desk?' he asked.

'Letters, bank statements, whatever had come in the post that day.'

With a glance from Watts, Hanson said, 'Ms Clark, you stated that later on the day of the murder you were woken by noise and loud voices in the building. Did you recognize any of those voices?'

'Yes, I did. One belonged to Archie, the maintenance man, and another of them to a friend of Della's. I think his name was Stephen. Up to then I'd barely heard him speak but I knew it was him because I heard him going on about being a friend of Della's and that he'd come to take her to a rehearsal. His voice was loud and he was demanding a key from the woman who lived on the other side of Della. Sorry, I don't recall her name. I was really surprised to hear him speak like that. He sounded very upset.'

'Had you seen Steffan Coultard prior to that day?' asked Hanson.

Clark nodded. 'Steffan. That's him. Oh, yes. A number of times. He never spoke directly to me but there was one day I was coming up the stairs, this was a while before Della was killed and she was standing at her door. Steffan was on the landing.' She looked down at her cup. 'I wouldn't want anybody to think I was a snoopy kind of neighbour but I couldn't help overhearing. They were having, not an argument exactly because I didn't hear him say anything, but I heard Della's voice and I was struck by the way she spoke to him. She sounded very firm. Cold, actually. I didn't hear all of what she said but she was telling him to wait downstairs.'

'Did Mr Coultard respond at all?' asked Hanson.

'He turned away from her and started down the stairs. I got the impression he was upset.'

'Did he say anything to you in passing?'

'No.'

'What can you tell us about this maintenance man you mentioned?' asked Watts.

'Archie?' she smiled. 'He was OK. Approachable and helpful. When I heard his voice on the landing that evening, I felt better because I knew he would sort out whatever was going on. The next thing I heard was Della's apartment door being opened and then all hell broke loose.'

Hanson and Watts were inside his vehicle, heading away from Josie Clark's house. 'What do you think?' he asked.

'Something happened between Steffan Coultard and Della Harrington which changed their relationship.'

'Maybe he tried it on with her.'

Hanson looked doubtful. 'I don't know. I would have assumed that as he knew her fairly well, he would have been aware of her sexuality.'

'A word to the wise, doc. We don't assume nothing in this game. We follow the evidence.'

She gave him a sidelong glance. 'Slipping into the role of Watson, your idiot sidekick, benefit me with your thoughts on the dream Clark told us about.'

He glared at a small car in front of them which was intermittently speeding up then slowing down. 'Nothing much and, in case you've forgotten, that kind of thing doesn't count as evidence.'

Hanson gazed out of the window. 'I think it could be very relevant. From what Clark told us, it sounds like she was in a period of REM sleep, still aware of her own physiological state which would account for her feeling hot. She appears to have been experiencing "micro awakenings" during which she picked up other noises coming from that conscious awareness and incorporated them into the dream.' She looked back at Watts. 'It's possible that Clark's sleep was disturbed by sounds, noise of an altercation coming from Della Harrington's apartment. If so, it suggests that Harrington was killed during the early part of the one-to-six p.m. time frame. Say, around one or two p.m.'

'Doc, you know I've got a lot of time for your expertise . . .'

'Depending on your mood and what it is I'm telling you.'

'. . . but that kind of thing is no help to us. Clark told us she wasn't reliable on times that day and I doubt she would be willing to swear to what she said to us. You know what we need. Physical evidence or words accredited to an actual source.' He gave her a quick glance. 'Say I'm wrong.'

'I can't.'

They drove on in silence for a minute or two. 'Know what, doc? For the first time since we started this case I'm starting to feel a bit upbeat.'

She looked across at him. 'Nice to hear, if unexpected, given its current state. Do you think this mindset might be attributable to the effects of two, or was it three, pain au chocolat and some very nice coffee served by a very pleasant and attractive woman?'

'Smart Alec. I tell you, my being upbeat is just as well because me and Corrigan have got a meeting looming with the chief. He'll be demanding to know what progress we're making. We'll be telling him that we've got three persons of interest. One, Archie Fenton, potential sex type, definitely in the frame. Two, Steffan Coultard who is all sorts of iffy but it's number three, Leonard Dobbs the letting agent who is starting to get my interest.'

'Why, exactly?'

Watts raised his big hand, itemizing on thick fingers. 'One, it looks to me like he was hanging around the area of Marlow Gardens at the time of the murder, just like he does now . . .'

'He worked there. Still does.'

'Exactly my point. People who are around an area get to be so familiar they become fixtures. People's eyes float right over 'em. They don't notice they're around. Two, he's got an eye for the women.'

'Who says?' asked Hanson.

'I do. He was giving you the once-over at Marlow Gardens.'

Hanson's brows rose. 'Is this the good quality evidence you've been instructing me on?'

'I'm telling you, doc, he needs some serious looking at. What about the way he looks, his hair?'

'My advice is, don't go to the chief with "Exhibit One: Ornate Hair Coiffure" as a reason for your interest in Dobbs.'

Watts slid into a gap in the oncoming traffic. 'I'll drop in on Dobbs tomorrow. Shake him up a bit. He and the other two are a work in progress for me and Corrigan over the next couple of days.' He looked at her. 'What's up?'

'It's occurred to me that Archie Fenton was viewed by at least one female resident of Marlow Gardens as someone to rely on. Remember what Clark just said about him?'

'Yeah, yeah. I tell you, doc, types like him often have a sort of chameleon way with 'em. How'd you think they ingratiate themselves to get people's trust?'

'I'm clueless, but grateful. Tell me.'

'Be as sarky as you like, but it's true and you know it.'

They slowed to join a long line of halted vehicles. 'Bloody hell. What's going on here?'

Hanson sat forward, looked along the nearside of the road. 'Road works and what looks to be temporary three-way lights.'

Watts took out his phone and glanced at its screen. 'Confirmation from Della Harrington's employers. The call centre's records contain no indication that she was in any way harassed by callers to their service . . . *Yes*!' He looked up at her. 'You'll like this, doc. Forensics have identified the woman you snapped outside Coultard's house. She's a sex worker and an illegal immigrant by the name of Marija Gailitis, currently in detention at Birmingham Airport, now awaiting removal from the UK. What do you make of that, doc?'

As soon as his phone was in his pocket it rang. Hanson listened to Watts' half of the brief exchange. 'Right now, I'm going nowhere, but make it quick because I might be.' He looked at her. 'You available in the morning for a trip to the airport with Corrigan to see the woman I just mentioned?' She nodded. He spoke into the phone. 'All fixed. The doc will go with you. Me? I'm planning a little jaunt to the Jewellery Quarter for a chat with a property expert.'

ELEVEN

Gazing out at open countryside flowing past, her head back, Hanson listened to the sweet, somewhat melancholy voice coming from the CD player, '*I drove all ni-ight, to get to you* . . .' Corrigan was an Orbison fan and, in her experience, an incurable romantic. The track was one of his favourites. Through the passenger window she watched a plane rise effortlessly, then another as the airport came into view. Ahead of them she saw hotels and the Arrivals and Departures buildings.

'I associate this drive with going home,' he said.

She looked at him, reminded of something that she hadn't thought about in quite a while. This wasn't Corrigan's home. Yes, he had his lovingly renovated house close to headquarters, but brick, slate and glowing wood floors wouldn't hold him here if he decided that they weren't enough. She closed down the thought. He pointed through the windscreen to a nondescript building ahead. 'There it is. The detention centre. They're expecting us.' She looked at the low-rise construction still some distance away. If she hadn't known otherwise, she would have assumed it was a warehouse. Which it was, of sorts.

Leaving the vehicle, they approached it and were stopped by security staff who checked their identification, consulted printed lists, then waved them through a gate in the chain-link fence. They walked the few metres to the main entrance. Coming inside, Hanson was aware of the plainness, the utility of the place and the low-level noises coming from deep within it. A uniformed custody officer approached them. They showed ID once more. He nodded, hooked a finger and they followed him along corridors and through several doors, the noises around them louder now. He stopped at a grey metal door, pulled it open, stepped aside and gestured for them to enter, speaking for the first time. 'The detainee will arrive via the door at the other end of this room.' Hanson looked at the featureless space equipped with a table and four chairs. Nothing else. With another nod, the officer pushed the door closed behind them. Hanson reached for one of the chairs. It was heavy. In her experience, furniture often was in places where people were known to be under pressure.

The door on the opposite side of the narrow room swung open. A different officer held the door and gestured to someone unseen. A few seconds' wait and a woman came inside. The woman with straight blonde hair whom Hanson had photographed outside Steffan Coultard's house. The officer spoke to them from the doorway. 'I'll be back in thirty minutes, finished or not.' He pointed to a red button set into a nearby wall. 'If you're ready to leave earlier or you require other assistance, use that and I'll come.' He reached for the door and it swung closed, confirming Hanson's impression of efficiency brought to bear on human desperation. Marija Gailitis stood where she was, her face pale, watchful.

Corrigan pulled out a chair and introduced himself and Hanson. 'Please, have a seat Ms Gailitis.'

She sat, her back straight, her face composed, her hands folded in her lap. Hanson looked at the face she hadn't seen in detail until now, the eyes dark brown, their lashes black, the cheekbones high, the full lips compressed together. Given the absence of an interpreter, the indication was that Marija Gailitis had some command of English. Corrigan said, 'Ms Gailitis, we're grateful to you for agreeing to speak with us.'

Gailitis looked at him then at Hanson. 'You are welcome. I am hoping my English is good?'

They nodded. 'Can you tell us why you came to the UK, Ms Gailitis?' he asked.

'Of course. In Ukraine, there is not too much money. So, I come here. For my family and myself. Money is better.'

Getting a quick glance from Corrigan, Hanson said, 'We need to ask you about a man. His name is Steffan Coultard.' Gailitis' single response was a frown. 'What can you tell us about him?'

'I don't want to get him in trouble. He a nice man. I meet other men, not so nice.' She stared at the table. 'You understand what I say? I have to earn money. It is difficult for me here. I try to work as cleaner for agency. The boss man says I owe him money. He ask for sex to pay off debt. I know I have to get other work or I never get away from him.' Hanson felt a wave of sympathy for the young woman. Illegal she might be, she was

also a victim. 'I try to be careful, you know? I try to use this.'
She tapped her temple. 'But sometimes things go wrong for me
with men.' She smiled. The smile caused Hanson to reconsider
Gailitis' age. According to officials here, her documents such as
they were indicated her to be twenty-three. Hanson thought that
eighteen was more likely. 'I meet Steffan many months ago. On
website. He have some difficulties, you know? Sex difficulties.
He don't want it too much, you understand?' Hearing the direct,
matter-of-fact words, Hanson took a similar approach.

'What did he want you to do, Ms Gailitis?'

The slim shoulders rose then fell. 'He like me to eat lunch,
dinner with him. He make nice food. He give me wine. We have
sex, yes but not too much. He like for me to lie down. He like to
watch me.' Hanson and Corrigan exchanged a fleeting glance.

'When you say that he liked you to lie down, can you tell us
about that?' asked Hanson.

'Of course. It was not funny business. He just say to me, "Lie
down like this". They watched as she raised her arms and held
them out straight on either side. 'Then, he take photo.'

'You were fully dressed?' asked Hanson.

'What is that?'

'Did you have clothes on?'

Gailitis smiled at them. 'Clothes *on*? Of course not. Why have
clothes for bed, for photos?' The smile disappeared. 'I miss
Steffan. He is very generous man. Romantic, you know. He play
nice music when we eat.'

Hanson was thinking how best to ask the next question,
doubting that there was a best way. 'Did you ever see Mr Coultard
angry?'

'Steffan?' The wide smile came again. 'I think you do not
know him too much. Steffan never angry to me. He was generous
man who asked for not much. He was kind to me.' Her face
clouded. 'I hope I help him. He not in trouble?'

Corrigan offered her no reassuring words. 'What can you tell
us about Steffan Coultard's wife?' he asked.

'His *wife*?' Gailitis stared at him. 'Steffan have no *wife*. He
is . . . I don't have too much words for this, excuse me. He like
to be alone, like this.' She wrapped her arms tightly around
herself. 'You understand? He don't like too much talking and

going out but he need a bit of company, you know? He don't
like that too much, either. Just when he want it. He is alright,
yes? Tell him, I thank him for money and for his friendship,
yes?'

'What will you do now?' asked Hanson.

Gailitis raised her shoulders. 'I wait. For my date to go home
to Ukraine. When home, I have to think very quickly what I do.'
She looked away from them. 'I have my mother and little brother
to look after.'

They were inside the Volvo, Hanson thinking of Marija Gailitis's
concern for Steffan Coultard, one of a number of men who had
used her. Maybe there were different kinds of using.

'Why would Coultard lie about having a wife?' asked Corrigan.

'I'm not sure. Perhaps he wanted to appear to neighbours and
others to have a normal life. What do you think of what Marija
said? About Coultard wanting her to lie down with her arms
outstretched so he could take her photograph?'

'Like you, it reminded me of how Della Harrington's body
was posed.'

'What she described to us suggests that Steffan Coultard enjoys
images of women which are submissive. Watts said he thought
Harrington's killer took photographs of the scene. Something
else that got my interest is her description of Coultard's life and
his needs. I only met him twice but what she told us fits with
my impression of him.'

'Which is?'

'A man with an avoidant personality. A man who worries
excessively about how he's perceived, who suffers from extreme
social anxiety which he reduces by limiting or controlling
the social interactions he does have.'

'Does it fit with paying women for sex?'

'Very well. Making sex a financial transaction would give him
relationships on his terms, in which he would set the boundaries
without the problem of expectation or commitment.' She was
quiet for a while then, 'What do you think will happen to Marija?'

'I'm guessing she'll eventually find her way back to the UK.'

He negotiated the big interchange beyond the airport and took
a different road to the one they'd followed here. Surprised, she

looked at him. His eyes fixed on the road, he said, 'I like the work we do but right now I'm tired of sad stories. Don't know about you, Red, but I'm in need of distraction. How about a trip into Stratford-upon-Avon?'

'Stratford? Why?' She watched his mouth widen, heard him laugh. 'Only somebody who lives just miles from it would ask that.'

Watts was squinting across the street to the apartment building where Della Harrington was murdered ten years before. During the last week or two, he'd become increasingly preoccupied with time. Or, more to the point, time passing. It was part of working cold cases. They were all about time. But the Harrington case was different. It was a whole decade old, one of the worst murders he could remember in all his years on the force, yet he guessed that for many it was now just a blip in their own and the city's history. It was 'back then'. His eyes moved over the 'now': the Jewellery Quarter was being reworked or pulled down, old warehouses and factories getting a makeover, new buildings zooming upwards. At least, these were the sentiments he was getting from reading the details on painted hoardings screening the building sites around him. *'Sorry for the inconvenience but this is how we'll look soon!'* ran the words, above stylized illustrations of one of the sites bathed in sunshine and featuring sleek new buildings surrounded by trees, plus references to the multiple floors and office space that would soon become available at an eye-watering cost per square foot.

He crossed the road, walked to the hoardings and looked through a gap alongside other, curious passers-by, tracking the movements of workers in coloured hard hats swarming around and within the half-completed building in the cold and damp. It looked nothing like the illustration. All it told Watts was that these construction workers and this city were hell-bent on burying small, insignificant Marlow Gardens Apartments along with Della Harrington.

He turned away from the activity and noise, heading for a line of distant shopfronts, one of them double-width, its plate glass windows bearing the legend: 'L. Dobbs & L. Dobbs, Lettings and Sales. Serving our community since 1986'. Watts had been on its website. It told him that the business was started by Dobbs Senior. He'd also checked the original case file information.

Leonard Dobbs Junior's name had never featured in the original investigation. As soon as David Lockman's name had entered it, it looked as though force attention had fastened on him, an interloper who had brought murder to the area.

Pushing open the door of Dobbs' premises, he came inside and approached a young woman in a crisp white shirt sitting behind a desk. She smiled up at him. 'Good morning. How can I help?'

Watts flipped his identification. The smile wavered, recovered. 'I want to see Leonard Dobbs.'

She reached for the desk phone. 'I'll just check he's available.'

Watts turned to the wide windows, his attention on the corner of Harrington's apartment block just visible, then to a nearby wall and a framed photograph of Dobbs, his light brown hair almost as elaborate as Watts had seen it, shaking the hand of the Lord Mayor if the heavy chain around the man's neck was anything to go by. Seeing a date, he looked closer: 2004. He picked up the sound of the phone being replaced.

'He'll be out in a couple of minutes if . . .'

'Thanks.'

He headed for the door bearing Dobbs' name, gave it a perfunctory knock and opened it. Dobbs sprang up from behind his desk with a look Watts recognized from years on the Job. A mix of synthetic amiability and shiftiness. Dobbs found a smile from somewhere and pasted it on, extending his hand. 'Detective Inspector Watts. Back in the area again.' The smile was replaced by a sympathetic expression which never got close to his eyes. 'If it's the apartment you want to see again, I'm afraid I have to tell you, it's now occupied—'

'I want names and background information on all the residents of Marlow Gardens at the time Della Harrington was murdered.'

Dobbs sat back on his chair. 'I see. That could take some time. It's archived.' He gave a thin smile. 'That is, if it hasn't been shredded. We try to clear out the old stuff every seven or eight years.'

Watts unbuttoned his coat and sat. 'In which case, let's hope it's all in one piece, shall we?'

Dobbs hesitated then reached for the phone. 'Sienna, look out all the stored records for Marlow Gardens Apartments dating back to 2005, 2006. Yes, that's right. All of them.' He put down the phone. 'Sienna's gone to see what she can find. It might take a while. I don't want to keep you. How about I send you a note of anything . . .'

'I'll wait. As well as the info I've just asked for, I also want any contact details you've got for the painting crew that was working on Marlow Gardens at the time Harrington was killed.'

'Those details would be in the files you've requested.' He paused. '*If* we still have them.'

Watts made a show of settling himself on his chair, his face genial. 'While we wait you can tell me all you know about Della Harrington.'

Dobbs looked startled. 'Meaning?'

Watts waved his hand. 'Anything that comes to mind. I'm in no rush, so how about you start by telling me what she was like from your experience, the visitors she had back then, that sort of thing.' He sent Dobbs a sudden direct look. 'How she was with you. How you got on with her . . . that is, if you did. Stuff like that.' He watched Dobbs' mouth open, anticipating excuses and denials. He got them.

'Detective Inspector, I can assure you that running this business is a full-time undertaking. I have neither the time nor the inclination to get to know residents.'

Watts took an innocent approach. 'That's a coincidence. Your maintenance man, Archie Fenton told us much the same. I'm waiting for somebody else to come up with a similar response and I'll have the complete set.' Dobbs stared at him as Watts leant forward. 'See Nothing, Hear Nothing, Say Nothing.' He sat back, waiting. Dobbs remained silent. 'See? Nobody's saying anything.' He lowered his voice. 'What people don't realize is that during a police investigation, that way of going about things only works for so long.' He eyed Dobbs. 'It's stopping right now where Della Harrington's concerned. I'm after information and I'm the patient sort.' He let a short silence develop then brought his big hands together. Dobbs leapt at the sharp contact. '*Right.* Dobbs *and* Dobbs. Who's the other one?'

Dobbs eyed him, his earlier oiliness gone. 'My father. He died around five years ago.'

Watts knew this. It was on the website. 'So, you wouldn't

have been so busy in 2006 when Harrington was murdered. This office is a stone's throw from Marlow Gardens and the impression I've got is that you were often in and out of the place.'

Dobbs' face hardened. 'I can't think how you got that idea. This firm is responsible for managing several buildings in the area, in addition to Marlow Gardens. Ensuring that all the residents are well looked after is a full-time undertaking.' He closed his mouth.

Watts nodded. 'There you go. Resident contact. Just what I'm talking about.' Dobbs looked away from him. Watts continued, his tone chatty. 'We're in different lines of work but I'm a people person like you, which means we're not so different.'

Hearing this verbal olive branch, Dobbs went with it. 'Listening to residents' problems and sorting them out is a big part of my job at Marlow Gardens, and as I said there are other apartment buildings this firm is responsible for, which means it's a full-time undertaking which—'

'Sounds like you've got yourself quite an empire here. What did you sort out for Della Harrington?'

Dobbs straightened, started tidying files on his desk. 'I hardly knew the woman. She was pleasant enough but very reserved. I doubt we exchanged more than half a dozen words in the whole time she lived here.'

'Did she have visitors?'

Dobbs eyed him across the desk. 'I'm too busy to keep tabs on residents' comings and goings, but not that many as far as I know.' Seeing Watts' rhythmic nods, he added, 'I believe she had a sister who visited occasionally. The only other visitor I'm aware of was a man. He would show up once a week as far as I recall.'

'Ah. The boyfriend,' said Watts with a nod.

'I doubt it.'

'Why's that?'

Dobbs shrugged. 'It's only what I picked up from the police swarming over the area when it all happened. He and Harrington were both in the same choir. The newspapers at the time said she led a quiet life.'

The door swung open and the young woman Watts had seen in the outer office came inside, her arms loaded with files, the sleeves of her white shirt grimy. Dumping the files on Dobbs' desk, she turned and left without a word. 'Thank you, Sienna!' Dobbs called after her as the door closed firmly. The smile disappeared. He pawed the files, separating three of them. 'These three should contain the information you want. Give me your email address and I'll scan the relevant bits and send them to you . . .'

'I'll take them with me.' Watts pointed to one of them bearing Harrington's name. 'What's in that one?'

Dobbs hesitated then reached for it. 'Let's have a look, shall we?'

'Yeah. Lets.'

Dobbs turned pages. 'These are details of Della Harrington's initial interest in her apartment at Marlow Gardens. She first came into this office in the August, a couple of years before she was murdered. According to this, I showed her around that apartment.' His eyes still on the file he said, 'If I hadn't seen it written here, I wouldn't have remembered it. Memory's strange, isn't it?'

'Positively tricky,' murmured Watts. 'What else does your file say?'

Dobbs studied the page in front of him. 'It says she was very keen on the building and the apartment itself. She liked it because it was private and secure.' Seemingly unaware of the implications of his words in relation to what had subsequently happened to Della Harrington, he looked up at Watts. 'It was exactly what she was looking for. Back then the prices of apartments in this area were dropping, would you believe? You've seen her apartment. Sixty grand ten years ago and now she'd get three times that . . . if she was still . . .' Watts looked at him with barely concealed dislike. 'Property-wise, this city is on the move, detective inspector.'

'You don't say,' said Watts, now more than ready to leave. 'Let me know when it reaches Shanghai, I'll want to get off.'

Dobbs sent him the thinnest of smiles. 'Have you looked around this area and the rest of Birmingham city centre? Have you seen the development going on? If there was no height restriction, we'd be seeing buildings here to challenge Dubai's. Birmingham is a happening place, detective inspector.'

'Is that a fact?' said Watts, unimpressed. 'In my experience, it's been "happening" for years.' He stood, reached for the files.

Dobbs' hands closed around them. 'I've been thinking. Don't you need some sort of paperwork to take these?'

'You mean a warrant?' Dobbs nodded, looking hopeful. 'No, I don't and it's a good idea not to think too much, Mr Dobbs. It'll get you and me nowhere.'

Leaving Dobbs' premises, Watts hefted the files and walked the few hundred yards to where he'd parked. There were signs of light in this case. Coultard, Fenton and Dobbs already persons of interest and what he knew about Della Harrington's ownership of her apartment had brought a new dimension to the case, plus two massive question marks. Who bought it for her? And why? Reaching the Range Rover, he dropped the files inside, got in and drove off, smiling to himself.

His departure was marked by a man standing some metres away in deep shadow. A man who had observed Detective Inspector Bernard Watts' jaunty walk, his arms full of files, his face bearing a complacent grin. His eyes narrowed. Now why might that be? He watched the Range Rover turn and disappear from sight, then walked slowly away. Reaching Marlow Gardens, he looked up at one of the large windows on the first floor. There were lights inside, just as there had been that day. When you needed something that badly, when you had to have it and it wasn't about to be handed to you, it left you with no choices. His mouth tightened. And now the police were back. It was all starting up again. A woman passed by and he kept his hands bunched inside his overcoat pockets to stop himself driving a fist into a nearby wall. The police could do what the hell they liked, follow up their leads until there was nothing else to ask or say. They still wouldn't know him. He gave a low laugh. The woman looked back and frowned as he sauntered away, his voice low.

'I'm an *artiste* and the most cold-hearted bastard you'll ever meet.'

Corrigan held open the door and Hanson and he walked inside the busy theatre restaurant. A smiling waitress came to them and led them to a table with a view of the river. They sat. Hanson gave him an accusatory look. 'You had a reservation.'

He smiled at her. 'For one, I swear. With armed response and UCU, I don't get much time for this kind of exploration.' He looked out at the Avon visible across a stretch of grass and decorative paving. 'My mom goes nuts when I tell her about places like this.' They both reached for menus, their hands brushing.

'What do you fancy eating, Red?'

She looked down the list, feeling suddenly hungry. 'I think I'll have the steak because I won't be cooking dinner later.' She looked up to find the blue eyes on her. 'Maisie is at Kevin's until tomorrow.'

'How's Charlie doing?' he asked.

'Fine. He's gone home.'

She put down the menu and gazed out at the river. The waitress arrived, took their food order and left. Hanson felt Corrigan's attention on her. She made herself breathe then met his gaze. 'What?'

'You and Charlie got a problem?'

'He's gone back to Worcester because he's . . . There's a friend he needed to see.' Exasperated with herself, she rolled her eyes. 'He has a girlfriend.'

'Good for Charlie. How'd you feel about that?' She looked at him then away. 'I'm guessing not so good.'

'It's fine,' she said, not looking at him. She didn't need to. She knew she wasn't fooling him. Or herself. Two glasses of red wine arrived on the table. She stared at them.

Corrigan held up the menu and pointed at it. 'See? They come with the meal.' She took it from him, again their hands making brief contact. Heat rose inside her chest and onto her face. She kept her eyes on the glass, sensing him reach for his. A peripheral glance and she watched him lift it, saw his lips make contact with glass then wine. He raised his glass to her. She did the same. 'Here's to UCU,' he said.

Their food arrived. Hanson made herself relax. This was a situation which had happened between them a number of times in the past, two colleagues enjoying a short break from intense, difficult work. They ate, talking lightly, easily. The tables around them slowly emptied. She checked the time. 'I should be getting back.'

He leant his forearms on the table, gave her a direct look. 'Did I tell you that I'm real pleased we're working together again?'

'Yes, you did,' she said, tone business-like.

'Did I tell you I like—'

'Corrigan,' she warned.

'. . . hearing that deep, husky voice of yours on a daily basis?'

She grinned in spite of herself. 'Isn't that something I should be saying to you?'

He widened his eyes in mock-horror, his voice assuming an iconic falsetto. 'Gee, Minnie, what's happening to us?'

Her shoulders shook, tears of laughter came into her eyes. 'You're such a fool,' she whispered.

'Yep. I know.'

The waitress brought the bill. Hanson reached for it. He took her hand and moved it gently aside, producing his Amex card.

They walked to the restaurant doors and the waiter got their coats. Corrigan held hers as she put it on. She tugged at her hair. 'Wait. I think I'm caught up.'

'OK, Red. I got it.'

He gently unwound the deep red hair from around a button, laid it on her shoulder and gently smoothed it, his mouth close to her ear, his voice barely audible. 'I love this.'

Back at headquarters, Hanson went directly to the Post-Mortem Suite, taking a photograph with her. She showed it to Connie Chong, in-house pathologist, pointing at Della Harrington's head injury. 'How long might this woman have survived after sustaining that?'

Chong looked at it. 'I like to assist UCU whenever I can but this isn't an exact science, you know. A lot of them aren't, contrary to expectation.' She studied the treacherous-looking fissures radiating from the central area of damage to Della Harrington's skull. 'Our friend the blunt instrument by the look of it . . . I'd say if she wasn't dead immediately, the outside limit for survival would be two, three minutes at most.'

Leaving headquarters, Hanson got into her car, thinking of what Clark, Della's neighbour had told them of the dream she had had. Surely, two minutes or so was long enough for a cry, a word, a few faltering steps away from someone Della had allowed inside her apartment as a friend? She came onto her drive and got out of her car. She wasn't used to a full lunch or alcohol in the middle of the day. She headed into the house, dropped her briefcase and bag on the hall floor and went to the sitting room where she sat in a corner of the sofa, pulling the travel rug over herself. She listened to the silence, thinking of Corrigan until it was broken by the jingle of a tiny bell. Mugger sidled through the door, ran to her and jumped onto her lap. She stroked his warm fur. She and Corrigan had known each other for, what, four years? Maybe a little more. Long enough for them both to know that whatever there was between them wasn't going to progress. He knew how she chose to live her life because she had told him. Her way of dealing with her lack of trust in men was to have short-term sexual relationships with those she knew who appealed to her and accepted her 'No Commitment' terms. It was a pragmatic arrangement that suited her and them. Needs were met. Nobody had expectations which weren't. Nobody got hurt. Kevin's response to such pragmatism was typical. He used it as a criticism to hurl at her when it suited him, ignoring his own history of serial conquests throughout the time they were married. She left the sofa for the kitchen, returning with a glass of wine. *Kevin Osborne is a hypocrite with the self-awareness of a house brick. The way I choose to live my life is honest. No lies. Maisie isn't aware of it. Nobody ends up . . . disappointed.* She knew that Corrigan had been disappointed when they'd talked about it. His was a Catholic upbringing and he wanted – needed – commitment. A relationship between them would never work. They wanted different things.

Marija Gailitis was back inside her head. A woman who needed money, had sex to get it, yet also saw something like romance in the transaction she had had with Steffan Coultard. She sipped wine. Watts had said it. This case was all about needs. She eased Mugger aside, threw away the rug and got up from the sofa. Seeing his reproachful look, she said, 'Think about it. Charlie Hanson. Kevin Osborne. They both left when it suited them. I'm in charge of my life now. That's how it's going to stay.' She headed for the kitchen again. 'I'll probably end up with you as my only confidant so you'd better improve your language skills.'

TWELVE

I n mid-morning cold, Watts watched Corrigan's black Volvo slide to a halt at the kerbside in response to his call twenty minutes before. He walked to it, spoke through the open window, breath billowing. 'Jules texted me last night. He'd found details for Jim Withershaw, the boss of the paint crew that was working on Marlow Gardens at the time of the murder. Deceased now, but Jules gave me details of one of the crew back then.' He jerked a thumb towards the row of houses behind him. 'Wayne Chatterton. He's in his late twenties now. He's got form for theft, being a general pain in the arse and he's at home.'

They approached the house, the most rundown in the middle of a bleak terrace. As much as Watts disapproved of what he'd recently seen of Birmingham's future, he wasn't that thrilled with its old face. He'd phoned the local Job ten minutes earlier and learned that Chatterton was wearing a tag, the result of antisocial behaviour targeted at the neighbours. He'd also been told that Chatterton was seemingly content to remain inside this godforsaken looking dump for most of the twenty-four. A crumbling tarmac path led them to a scratched and dented front door. Watts pounded it. Somewhere beyond, a loud television or games console was in operation. He hit the door again, harder this time. The volume of the TV-game console lessened, followed by a querulous female voice. 'Wayne? *Wayne.*'

After a brief lull the door was opened by a heavily-built, barefoot male dressed in tracksuit bottoms, a pyjama jacket, open at the front. The vest beneath it didn't invite close scrutiny. He merely looked at them then turned and went through a door off the hall. They followed him into a small, smoke-filled room where Chatterton sat and lit a cigarette. Both officers tested the air. The merest whiff of weed and Chatterton would be on his way to headquarters. Nothing. The female voice came again. Corrigan nodded at Watts and headed for a door leading off the room.

Chatterton half-rose, his face belligerent. 'Hey, *you*. Who do you think *you* are! You can't just force your way in here, then walk around as though you own the f—'

'You opened your door to us. That was an invitation.' Showing his identification, he said, 'Detective Inspector Watts. That was Lieutenant Corrigan who just went in there, and actually, Wayne, we'll do whatever it takes to get what we're after.'

The female voice was still evident but subdued now. Chatterton's eyes narrowed as he picked up Corrigan's words. His lips curled. 'Bloody foreigner. You should be giving jobs to people that was born here.' He dragged on his cigarette. 'And you're wasting your time trying to pin anything on me.' He pulled at one pyjama leg, turning his bare foot this way and that, displaying the ankle tag. 'You can tell the neighbours or whoever else phoned you to get stuffed. It wasn't me. I don't do nothing. I don't go nowhere.'

Watts' gaze drifted around the hazy room, over the sagging sofa, cup-ringed coffee table and up-to-the-minute, wall-mounted television, bigger than Watts' own. 'Sounds like a quiet life. No commuting to the office for gainful employment? No business lunches? No Bolly on the old expense account?' He caught Chatterton's smirk. It told him that Chatterton was not a total idiot. Just lacking whatever it took to shift himself from this house, his life, to something better. Chatterton preferred to make a nuisance of himself and live off his mother. And his father. If he had one. Watts lifted the games console off one of the armchairs, shoved it along the carpet with his foot and sat. Corrigan emerged from the other room with a quick headshake. It told Watts that the mother had been no help. He regarded Chatterton for several seconds.

'Cast your mind back ten years, Wayne. That should give you a hint as to why we're here.' Chatterton took another long drag at his cigarette then crushed it into an already two-thirds full saucer, assuming a puzzled air. 'Don't know what you're on about.'

'Try Marlow Gardens Apartments, Jewellery Quarter. Della Harrington.'

Chatterton was looking bored. 'Who?'

Watts planted his big hands on the arms of the chair, pushed himself upright. 'OK, Corrigan. We're finished here. Chatterton, you're coming with us to headquarters.'

He looked up at them, his broad face aggrieved. 'Hang on! You never give me a chance to think. I've just remembered that place, but I don't know anything about the woman you mentioned.'

'Let's see, shall we?' said Watts, still standing. 'Start by telling us everything you remember about Marlow Gardens, and I mean everything.'

Chatterton lounged against the sofa, adjusting his vest and pyjama jacket. 'All I remember is that the painting lark I was on back then was a doddle. It paid well for an eighteen-year-old kid like me with no experience.'

'And an aversion to regular work,' added Watts. He watched a wide grin appear on Chatterton's face. 'You know, Wayne, when people say "exterior painting" to me, I think "windows". Then I think "*open* windows". Tell us about whatever little side-line you had going at the time you were working at Marlow Gardens.'

Chatterton looked scornful. 'I didn't have one, although I've got a motto: if people are stupid enough to leave their windows open and stuff in full view, they're asking to have it nicked. It serves 'em bloody well right.'

'What do you think, lieutenant? Does that sound like an admission to you?'

'Could be,' said Corrigan, his eyes fixed on Chatterton. Barely ten minutes in and Watts was wanting to give Chatterton's round face a smack and regretting that he couldn't. 'I've got a motto, Wayne: I hate being buggered about when I'm after facts. It gets me right narky. Get dressed.' He reached into his pocket, brought out his keys and glanced at Corrigan who turned to the door.

Chatterton got the point. 'Just simmer down, will you? I'm ADHD. I don't respond well to pressure.' He lit another cigarette, blew out smoke. The dull ache inside Watts' head was threatening to bloom into a leaden thud. Corrigan was still at the door, eyes fixed on Chatterton, who said, 'That painting job was alright and so was Jim, the gaffer but, speaking *hypothetically*, nobody passes up chances, do they?'

'We're all ears, Wayne. We're investigating a murder which happened while you were working in that building with your "open windows" motto and your sticky fingers.'

'Look at my form,' said Chatterton. 'If you find a single thing on it which says "sex", I'll fix you up a date with my old lady.'

'You're telling us that sex featured in that murder,' said Corrigan.

Chatterton smirked, looked away. 'Everybody knew. The plod was all over that place, nattering to each other, trying to get their photos in the papers. For anybody with half an ear it was obvious what had happened to that woman.' Chatterton sent Watts a crafty look. 'There was somebody at Marlow Gardens who come to me with a proposition not long after we started work there. He said he'd give me a list of which apartment windows would be unlocked and when so I could help myself to whatever was there, plus what he was after.'

'Which was?'

'He wanted women's stuff.' Seeing them exchange looks, Chatterton rolled his eyes. 'You know: underwear. Fancy stuff. He wanted me to go through laundry baskets for it, the dirty bastard. I told him to get stuffed.'

'Name!' barked Watts.

Chatterton blew more smoke. 'I'm no grass but it was the maintenance man who worked there. See? I don't mind helping the law when it suits me. I left that Marlow Gardens job barely a week after that woman got done in. Something about the place put me right off.'

Watts eyes narrowed. 'Like what?'

Chatterton shrugged. 'Dunno. Our old lady said the murder upset me. Made my ADHD worse. She was the one who said to pack the job in.' He sent Watts an appraising look. 'That murder is history, but there was a scam going on in the apartment building next to Marlow Gardens.'

Watts frowned. 'What sort of scam?'

'I heard that one or two of the younger women living there were a bit skint because of the recession and had problems paying their rents.' He winked. 'But it got sorted.'

Watts and Corrigan exchanged looks, 'Who did the sorting?' asked Watts.

Chatterton peered inside his cigarette pack. 'Couldn't say.'

'The maintenance man?'

Chatterton hooted with laughter then coughed himself red-faced. Gasping, he dragged his sleeve across his eyes. 'Get real. He's the one that told me about it. He didn't have the nous or the funds for that kind of caper. No. His interest stopped at dirty underwear. I was only eighteen but I was no fool. Stuff goes missing from apartments like that and the first thing the police ask is "Who had access?", and there's me painting windows, a lot of 'em open.' He looked scornful. 'Leave it out.'

'Who was running the rent scam?' Getting no response Watts shouted, '*Name!*'

'Simmer down, you'll get my old lady in here. I don't know. The maintenance man never said.'

Outside the house Watts turned to Corrigan. 'I'll see you back at headquarters. Make a start on the progress report for the chief. We're seeing him on Monday and he'll be expecting Persons of Interest and reasons why. I don't know about you, Corrigan, but one day I feel we're making progress and the next it's like we're knitting smoke.' He gazed at houses either side of Chatterton's, saw a curtain twitch. 'Any road up, we've got names to give the chief, one of them Fenton who we know is into heavy porn and God knows what else.' He looked at Corrigan. 'Got any idea as to who might have been helping young women with their rents back then?'

'Sure have,' said Corrigan.

'And me.'

The young woman looked up as Watts pushed open the door and walked inside. He was searching his head for her name and not finding it. She watched as he approached her desk. 'Mr Dobbs isn't here.'

'It's not Dobbs I've come to see. It's you.' She stared up at him, biting her lip.

'I want to ask you a couple of questions about this place.'

'What sort of questions? Not that it matters.' She sat back. 'I'm working my notice.'

'Oh? How did that come about?' he asked, wondering if Dobbs had sacked her. Looking into her face he guessed that she was probably no more than early twenties. Way too young to have any direct knowledge of the Harrington murder. He was still glad he'd come. When he was here before she'd been on the ball, knew how this place operated.

'It was my decision. I don't like it here.'

Watts pulled a chair closer to her desk. 'I want to know about this lettings business. I want to know about young women who rented apartments at Marlow Gardens, plus the building next-door to it ten-plus years back.'

A deep flush climbed her neck and spread over her face. 'It sounds like you already know.'

'I'll know more if you talk to me about it.'

She looked away from him to the window. He waited, seeing indecision and self-protection battle it out. She looked back at him. 'Leonard Dobbs is an absolute pig. I've been here nearly two years but I realized it from the first week.'

He waited, seeing more struggle going on behind the smooth face. Finally, he asked, 'What exactly was it that you realized about him?'

'That I had to watch him. Most of the time, I was on my own here with him.' Her face flared again. 'I'd be in the filing room or the one where the coffee and the photocopier are kept and he'd follow me in there. Come up behind me and stand really close with an excuse that he had something to say about work or whatever.' Watts nodded, wanting more but conscious he was now winging it and worried about stepping in too soon. He wished Hanson or one of the female PCs trained in talking to young females was here. She continued, her voice so quiet he had to strain to hear what she was saying. 'The second week I was here he touched me. Put his hands on my waist. Slid his hands downwards.'

Watts wanted to know how she'd responded but decided against asking. It might sound like criticism if she hadn't done anything. He went with: 'What happened?' Several possibilities arrived in his head, none of them good.

'I told him to take his hands off me and that if he came anywhere near me again, I'd report him to the police.'

'What did he say?' asked Watts.

'Nothing much. He laughed, sneered at me, said the police had better things to do with their time. But it worked. He never put his hands on me again. I'm sure he'd have loved to get rid of me but he was nervous what I might do or say, if he did.' She stared across at Watts. 'You're wondering why I stayed here, aren't you?'

'I'm sure you had your reasons.'

'Yes. I had. This job pays well. I have to pay my mom for my keep. I have to pay my fares. As long as he stayed away from me it was alright, although that didn't mean I changed my view of him. At best, I tolerated him. Ever since this murder case was reopened, he's been really edgy. Snapping at me. I decided I'd had enough. I hoped he wouldn't insist I work out my notice. He didn't. He's glad to be rid of me, particularly with the police around.' She waited. 'You said you had some questions?'

'I have, yes.' Wayne Chatterton's words were loud and clear inside his head. 'It's about young female tenants who lived at Marlow Gardens and the apartment block next to it ten years back. The ones who got into financial difficulties and were given . . . let's call it assistance to sort them. You might not know anything about that . . .'

'Oh, I *do*,' she whispered. 'I'll tell you why. It's still happening. I've got no real proof as to how he goes about it but he finds out that they're struggling and he doesn't waste any time. If they're single and under twenty-five, he's straight in there . . . sorting the situation out to his own advantage. If you get what I mean.'

'Sorry to ask, but can you be specific?'

She raised her head, face colouring again. 'I'm pretty sure he makes them have sex with him.'

'How do you know this?'

'I got friendly with one of the girls about twelve months ago. She was my age. Dobbs was fuming when he found out we were friends. He went on about it being a "conflict of interest" and "unethical".' Her lips curled. '*Him,* going on to me about ethics. Anyway, that friend lost her job a few months after she moved in to Marlow Gardens. She told me she was really worried about finding another job and how she was going to afford her apartment in the meantime. Part of my job spec here is to keep the accounts up to date. After a few weeks of there being no rent payments from her, I noticed that her rent was suddenly up to date and being paid regularly in cash, although I knew she hadn't found another job.'

'Did you ask her about it?'

'How could I? For all I knew, her family might have stepped

in and lent her the money.' She shook her head. 'That's not what had happened. She'd already told me they didn't have much. Then, after a week or two, I noticed that she'd gone really cool towards me. She didn't drop into the office any more or ring to suggest a coffee.' She rubbed her arms. 'That's when I put two and two together and realized that Dobbs was behind it all. He put pressure on her and it led to her refusing to even come near me or this place, let alone tell me anything. Like I said, he's a pig.' She gave Watts a direct look. 'Once I found out about her, I went through the accounts. I found others. Other women who had had rent problems which were suddenly sorted out.' She studied Watts. 'They might have agreed to what Dobbs was suggesting but they were on the verge of losing their apartments, their homes and had no money coming in. I don't care what the law says about that kind of situation. To me, that's no different to rape. He was forcing them. Where's the difference between that and some stranger attacking them? Because he owns this place he thinks he can do whatever he wants. He's right. He *can*. They don't have a choice. Or a chance. I detest him.'

'When are you expecting him back?'

'I'm not. At least not today. He's in Manchester, looking after his "business interests". Or, so he said. I think he's got a woman up there. More than one, for all I know.' She shrugged. 'I'm finished here as of five o'clock this afternoon. He's got a temp coming in in the morning. I'm just glad I'll never have to hear his smarmy voice or look at his stupid hair again.'

'When did he say he'd be back?'

'I booked him on the early morning train, arriving at New Street at around ten tomorrow morning.'

'Have you got any details of the women you mentioned? Names, dates?'

She gave Watts a direct look. 'Give me ten minutes and I'll print them out for you.'

He watched her go, his mind taken up with Della Harrington. She didn't fit the profile for a young, vulnerable tenant this young woman had described. Harrington was thirty. More to the point, she wasn't a tenant. She owned her apartment. Dobbs would have had no hold over her. Watts frowned, turning over the possibilities as they arrived inside his head. Was it possible that

Dobbs was behind the purchase of Harrington's apartment? But why would he do that? Harrington wasn't into men, regardless of how trustworthy or otherwise they might be. Josie Clark had described Dobbs coming into her apartment, looking at papers on her desk. Another single woman. Like Harrington, a bit older than his apparent preference. Perhaps Dobbs liked to keep in practice? He ran his hand over his thumping head knowing that dinner tonight would be a large coffee, two painkillers, and a close read of whatever this young woman returned with. He searched his memory for her name. Hanson put in a sudden appearance inside his head. She didn't approve of 'young woman' or 'she' and even less, 'love'. 'Use their *names*', she'd said countless times. Now he remembered it.

'Here you are,' she said, coming from the back of the premises and handing him a slim file.

He glanced inside it then up at her. 'Thanks very much for this, Sienna. We appreciate it.'

THIRTEEN

The announcer's voice echoed across New Street Station's cavernous concourse, announcing the arrival of the Friday morning Manchester train. They moved at speed, Corrigan pointing up at the arrivals board. 'Platform change! It's this way.'

Arriving at the passenger exit they waited, scanning the faces of the crowd surging towards it. Watts caught a glimpse of a camel overcoat and blow-dried hair. 'He's here.' Watts showed identification to the barrier staff and waited as Dobbs came further into view, his face relaxed. Looking sleek, pleased with himself, he arrived at the barrier and held out his ticket to staff without so much as a glance, his eyes drifting over people on the other side. Tension flooded his face as Watts stepped forward.

'Mr Dobbs, come through the barrier to us, please.'

He came slowly, his colour draining. 'I . . . I want my lawyer. *Now.*'

Corrigan eyed him, his voice low. 'You're gonna need one.'

Dobbs stared at the young constable standing to one side of the door of the interview room then sent Watts and Corrigan furious looks across the table, his mouth firmly closed. This was how Dobbs had been since he'd recovered from the shock of being picked up. All the signs were that he wasn't about to give them anything.

He finally spoke. 'This is an *outrage*. My lawyer is on her way. Until she arrives I'm not answering any questions.'

'Suit yourself,' said Watts. 'You're under arrest and I've given you your rights. You can wait here until she does.'

They left the room, Dobbs' eyes following them. They came into UCU to find Hanson poring over papers and Julian on his laptop. Watts sat heavily. 'We've arrested Dobbs.'

'I heard,' she said. 'For what?'

'Suspicion of historical and current sexual exploitation of female tenants at Marlow Gardens and the building next door.

Sienna, the young woman who worked in his office, is right. He's a pig. We've left him waiting for his brief. I'm hoping we can wring the details out of him when he's ready to talk.'

Hanson's eyes were fixed on his face. 'Hoping?'

'Like I said, he's a pig. My guess is he'll deny everything.'

'You think he's a suspect for Della Harrington?' asked Julian.

Watts frowned. 'On the ball, Captain Obvious. Move these books. Me and Corrigan need the table so we can start to sort out what we tell the chief on Monday about the progress we've made on her case.' As Julian gathered textbooks together, Watts looked across at Hanson. 'It's coming together. It was always about sex but we didn't realize the half of it. That building, the area was a playground for that sleazy bastard Dobbs to exploit young women with money worries who were unlucky enough to rent apartments he managed. I'm banking on him not knowing what Sienna his PA has told us. She's left her job now and she won't be having further contact with him so he can't pressure her. Leonard Dobbs is a predator. You tell me what sexual predators do.' Without waiting for a response, he said, 'They zero in on vulnerable women but also other males who are like-minded.' He saw her frown, guessed that she was full of questions as always. 'Coultard uses sex workers. We don't know what else he might be into. Like Dobbs, he hasn't got a clue that we know what he's been up to. And then there's Fenton and his porn habit and whatever else turns him on, which we'll be asking him about.' He shook his head. 'I know what you're thinking. That we can't trust Chatterton. You're right but what we've now got is a common thread running through this investigation. Three sexually deviant males, each of them with their eyes on females within a stone's throw of Della Harrington's apartment at the time she was murdered. Too much of a thread to ignore.' He tapped Corrigan's draft report to the chief lying on the table in front of him. 'It's all in this and in an hour or so we should have more.' He looked at her. 'OK. Let's have it. What's on your mind?'

'Coultard is a loner. I find it difficult to imagine him in league with anybody, particularly somebody like Leonard Dobbs.'

'Are you saying it's not possible?'

'Of course not,' said Hanson. 'And where, how, does Fenton

fit into it? Where's the evidence of him being directly sexually abusive towards a woman?'

'Think of all your theory, doc. Think of all the deviants you've worked with and you tell me that blokes like Fenton never progress to hands-on assault.'

'You know I can't say that.'

'Right. And what else do we have on Fenton? I don't need to spell it out for you. He had a passkey to those apartments. He could have gone into Harrington's apartment, wanting a look through her underwear, say, and she came back unexpectedly and found him. What might he have done in a situation like that? I see endless permutations involving him and those other two bastards.' He looked at her. 'Why the frown?'

'Clark and Tyler, her neighbours, weren't in any way negative or critical of Fenton. The impression I got was that they regarded him as trustworthy to a degree, particularly when Coultard was acting out, demanding the key to Harrington's apartment.'

'Yes, and I'll tell you why. Clark and Tyler had a couple of protective factors. Both of them were older, more sophisticated. Forster was sharing her apartment with her boyfriend at the time. Fenton wouldn't have been sniffing around them and neither would Dobbs. He prefers 'em young and vulnerable.'

'Exactly. We're back to why Dobbs, or any of your "permutations" would be interested in Della Harrington? She was thirty. She wasn't short of money.'

'That's what we're going to have to find out. With or without Dobbs' help.' Watts was now on a roll. 'Three sex types inside or around Marlow Gardens at the time Harrington was killed. We know what was done to her. That kind of posing tells me a couple of things about who killed her. It was a porn-inspired sex homicide, committed by somebody driven to make real what he habitually watched . . . and maybe take pictures of it before he left.'

She stared at him. 'You mean *snuff* porn?' She looked at Corrigan. 'You think the same?'

'We're considering all the possibilities the evidence is suggesting right now. Fenton is a user of porn. Why not a producer, too?'

'There's something else,' said Watts. 'There had to be a man in Harrington's life. A well-hidden man.' He saw Hanson's mouth open. 'I know what you're going to say, doc. That she was gay, but put that to one side and think about it.'

She closed her eyes, opened them. 'Watts, you're the DI responsible for the management of this case and I am thinking about it. I'm even willing to consider the Loch Ness Monster as a suspect on your say-so.' She looked at them, hands raised. 'Done it. It wasn't Nessie.'

'Very droll.'

'We need more facts about these three men, yes, I *know* they were in and out of that building, but so were a lot of other people and we don't know anything about them either.'

'And we're not likely to,' snapped Watts. 'We're ten years down the line, there's no time or money to chase a lot of passers-by and callers-in. On Monday we tell the chief about Fenton, Dobbs and Coultard.' He stopped. 'That's another thing: I want to know where Coultard's wife is. She might have a lot to say about him.'

'According to Marija Gailitis, he didn't have one.'

'If she exists, we have to talk to her. Look, I'm not saying that those three were directly involved in killing Harrington, although I'm ruling nothing out. What I am saying is, we need to consider that maybe one of them killed Harrington and the other two had minor roles in it. It's obvious there was nothing about Fenton that would have appealed to Della Harrington, enough for her to give him ideas, but you've said it yourself often enough, doc. "Don't judge a sex offender's risk before you know *all* that he does." We don't know about that because we don't know Fenton. All I'm saying is he could well have taken photographs of that death scene because as far as I'm concerned, what we do know about him is screaming, "Deviant".'

Hanson was silent because right now she couldn't say he was wrong. 'I suppose it's possible he could have been drawn into murder by somebody with a forceful personality,' she said.

'There's an idea,' said Corrigan. 'Once we promote all three to suspect, we'll need an evaluation of their personalities.'

'We'll delve into Fenton and his interests once we have him in,' said Watts. 'I can't see any woman wanting to get up close and personal with him, but ten years back it looks like he had more going for him.' He pulled a writing pad towards him, wrote quickly then looked at Corrigan. 'The key word in this case since we first saw Harrington's crime scene photos has always been "sex". That's not changed.' He jabbed each name with his pen. 'Coultard, Fenton, Dobbs. All different. All of them dodgy. All hanging around that apartment building, *plus,* Fenton and Dobbs had ready access to the insides of the apartments. There's a possible duo for a start. What do you think, Corrigan?'

'All possible at this stage.'

Watts eyed the wall clock, then Hanson. 'Cheer up, doc.'

'Do you have any idea how annoying that phrase is?'

'Yes.' He grinned. The phone rang. He grabbed it. Without a word, he ended the call. 'Dobbs' brief has just arrived.'

They came into the interview room where Dobbs was talking in a low whisper to a woman, his eyes fixed on the constable standing to one side of the door. Both Dobbs and his lawyer straightened. Watts and Corrigan took seats opposite them. Watts' hand went to the PACE machine. 'Glad you've arrived,' he said to the lawyer. 'Now we can crack on. I arrested your client, Leonard Dobbs at New Street Station this morning, based on information received . . .'

'I haven't seen that information,' she said, coolly.

'. . . which supports what we know of your client's sexually exploitative behaviour in and around Marlow Gardens Apartments.'

'I want that information, please,' she said, adding, 'I also want to know how you came by it.'

Dobbs pointed at Watts. 'I know how he got hold of whatever he thinks he's got.' He looked at her, his facial expression triumphant. 'Sienna Barton, my ex-PA.' He grinned across the table at both officers. 'I'll tell you about *her* . . .'

His lawyer intervened. 'Mr Dobbs, my advice is to say nothing until Detective Inspector Watts and Lieutenant Corrigan have divulged what they believe is information against you.'

He ignored her, his eyes fixed on Watts. 'I'm not waiting around, listening to a lot of rubbish. I don't know what Sienna Barton's told you, but you need to know about her. She's a grasping, poisonous little—'

'Mr Dobbs, *please.*'

He shook off his lawyer's hand. 'Did she tell you we were "involved", from just a couple of weeks of her coming to work for me?' Watts and Corrigan stared at him. He grinned. 'She didn't, did she? Her problem is, she thought it was going somewhere. I told her it wasn't. That it was just sex. She went barmy. Threatened to tell my wife.'

'And?' asked Watts.

'Mr Dobbs, please, *stop* . . .'

'I told her to do whatever she liked.'

Dobbs sat back, looking straight into their eyes, still smiling. 'My wife knows how hard I work. She's a very accommodating woman. Sienna thought better of it. She wouldn't have been able to prove anything and my wife would have dismissed anything she said. Sienna Barton was on the make.' He paused, giving Watts and Corrigan canny looks. 'Whatever she told you or gave you, it's all false. Just ask yourselves, who did all of the word processing in that office? Who was in a position to falsify or change things?'

'We've got information of financial transactions between you and young, female tenants in the area close to your offices,' said Watts.

'And I'm telling you, it's all rubbish. False information fabricated by a woman in my employment to get at me. Come on! A woman scorned and all that?'

His lawyer intervened, her eyes on Watts. 'If you obtained this information from the young woman identified by my client, you need proof that it's reliable. Do you have that?'

'We'll verify it,' said Corrigan. 'We'll obtain proof that Mr Dobbs used his professional situation to obtain sexual activity . . .'

'You'd better listen to my lawyer when she's telling you something about the law here,' Dobbs hissed. He and Corrigan locked eyes. 'Hang on,' whispered Dobbs. 'You two are investigating that murder in Marlow Gardens years ago.' He turned to his lawyer. '*Do* something. They're not interested in anything Sienna Barton told them. They're out to pin that old murder on *me*.'

His lawyer gave Watts an evaluative look. 'I'm asking you again. Are you able to verify the information you've acquired within the next twenty-four hours?'

Strands of Dobbs' hair were now hanging limp on his forehead. He pushed them away. 'Never mind that crap. I want out of here now.'

She looked at her watch. 'Actually, make that nineteen hours you have left if you insist on holding my client.' Watts and Corrigan said nothing.

She stood, nodded to Dobbs who also stood, smirking. 'I think we're finished here,' she said.

They came into UCU, Watts' face thunderous. He dropped his file on the table and looked at Corrigan. 'The names we got from Sienna Barton. Give 'em to Jules. As soon as he's got their whereabouts we'll follow 'em up.'

'What happened?' asked Hanson.

She listened to Watts' terse account of the scene which had just played itself out in the interview room. 'The main thing for us is that Dobbs has been arrested. Once we get the information from Jules, we'll talk to the women then get Dobbs in again. We know he's pressured women for sex so he's well on his way to suspect for the Harrington killing. I want to move him to prime suspect.'

Hanson listened as he and Corrigan began to put together the case they were taking to the chief. It sounded convincing and yet . . . Pen in hand, she stared unseeing at the notes in front of her, realising that her initial dissatisfaction with the Harrington crime scene was back. She looked up at her colleagues. If she had any doubts, no matter how vague or inexplicable they were, she had to say before they saw the chief. She had looked through the list of facts pertaining to that crime scene which she'd put together whilst they were upstairs talking to Dobbs. The case was now moving at speed and she couldn't see Watts being willing to wait whilst she explored her thinking on it.

Watts stood. 'OK. What we're going with is Della Harrington, victim of sexual homicide and three names: Steffan Coultard, Archie Fenton and Leonard Dobbs, each of them with strong connections to Marlow Gardens at the time of the murder. Dobbs still does, plus he's used his position in respect of that building and one next door to pressure females for sex. Anything you want to add, doc?'

She had to say something.

'Is it?'

'Is it what?'

'Is it a sexual homicide?'

He stared at her. Corrigan did the same. 'What do you mean?' Watts asked. 'You're not making a lot of sense here. This case is what it is. What it's always been. You said it yourself when you looked at the pictures of Harrington, saw the posing of the body. What's your problem?'

'I don't know. I'm just not satisfied with what I've seen.'

He gave her a steady look. 'You want us to go to the chief, lay out the case then tell him you're not "satisfied". You know the names we've got and why. Come on. Never mind the i-dotting and the t-crossing, what do you *think*?'

'I . . . I agree with you on the three persons of interest. I've heard what you have on Fenton. I met Dobbs at Marlow Gardens very briefly, remember? I saw the way he looked at me. It fits with what Sienna the young woman who worked in his office said about him. I've talked with Coultard twice. I know how emotionally avoidant and isolated he is, plus we know he was meeting his sexual needs with a sex worker, possibly other women like her.'

'So? Where's your problem with that?' said Watts.

'I don't think it's . . .'

The phone rang. Watts reached for it, adding quick notes to the case he and Corrigan were taking to the chief. 'Speaking. Yeah . . . yeah.' He stopped writing, straightened. 'You what?' Hanson and Corrigan looked at him, then at each other. He put down the phone.

'What is it?' asked Hanson.

'There's been an incident at David Lockman's house.'

'What kind of incident?' she asked.

'Damage to a window. Somebody put something through it. Lockman's spent all of yesterday in hospital.'

'He's been *attacked*?' she said, horrified.

'No. Seems he took an overdose. He's at home now.'

She watched as they stood and gathered papers together.

'Don't know about you, doc, but it's time to give it up for today. Me and Corrigan will follow up these young women over the weekend. If you have any ideas about the case, let us know. Monday, we take what we've got to the chief.'

'What about David Lockman?'

'What about him?'

'Aren't you going to see him? Ask him what happened?'

Watts shrugged. 'He's not our concern. Local police have picked it up. That was them on the phone. I feel as sorry for the bloke as you do, but he's not part of what we're doing here. We've got enough to do and we need to give him a wide berth, given that he's lawyered up for his compensation fight.'

She watched them head for the door and out. Watts was tired. He was also irritated with her. She understood why. The Harrington crime scene photographs ticked every sexual homicide box: the indications of the killer's planning, the control he took when he entered her apartment, the display of the body, followed by what appeared to be a quick search for valuables which he took with him before slipping away from the building. The fact that he left no DNA in the form of semen was no argument against it being sexual homicide. Hanson had talked with enough offenders whose hatred or fear of women was such that they were unable to sexually engage with a victim either prior to or after death, or could only do so indirectly, collecting and taking any semen away with them. She paused, thinking of Fenton. He was a pornography aficionado who probably had a lot of experience of that kind of indirect sexual satisfaction. And then there was Coultard, uncomfortable with women, unless he made it a monetary transaction. Another thought occurred. Had Della Harrington's killer managed to slip away from that apartment so efficiently because he was a regular presence around and inside that building? Because he didn't have far to go to be out of sight inside his office? All of that applied to Dobbs and to Fenton. She saw why all three had to be at the very least persons of interest in this investigation. She closed her eyes, suddenly weary. She was criticising a strong case her colleagues had constructed by querying the basic premise underlying it, yet she wasn't able to vocalize her dissatisfaction. Little wonder Watts was annoyed.

She got up, went to what was loosely termed the refreshment centre, poured herself a glass of cold water and drank it. Back at the table she looked down at the thick bundle of crime scene photographs. She reached for them, laid them one by one on the table and sighed. 'OK. What do I see?' She let her eyes drift over them. The killer's behaviour with the body would have been time-consuming. Someone could have called at that apartment at any time, which suggested he felt at ease there. She frowned. Had he been inside it before? She pushed back her hair, feeling tired yet unable to give up until she understood. All of what had happened to Della Harrington was planned. Her killer had brought with him his rich fantasy life to that small apartment. And yet, he'd omitted to bring one key element to that scene: the knife. He'd relied on finding a suitable blade at the scene with which he would inflict the tiny, bloodless cuts to Harrington's arms. He'd been sufficiently in control to leave her where she had fallen in order to locate it. She ran her finger along the small line above her nose. *Where the hell am I going with this?*

'Kate?'

Startled, she looked up. Julian had come into UCU. 'Sorry. Didn't mean to make you jump.'

She sat back, pointing at the data in front of her. 'I'm trying to square a circle and inevitably failing.' She looked at him. She'd been his lecturer for three years, and his PhD supervisor for two. He had a mind for the theoretical. 'You've seen the crime scene photographs, Julian.'

'I had a quick look at them.'

'What did they say to you?'

'Sadistic sexual homicide. Basic 101, Crim. Psych.'

Hanson's eyes moved over her notes, the open textbooks. What he had just said echoed Watts' and Corrigan's thinking and her own, if she ignored whatever was troubling her. 'You're right. We know Della Harrington's killer was organized. He arrived with a plan. He murdered her by following that plan. Nothing went wrong for him in that apartment . . .' She paused, looked up at him. 'We know something else about sexual attackers.'

'Their predisposition to repeat their behaviour?' He came to the table, looked at the photographs. 'If he was so sure of himself, it could be because he'd done it before.'

'Which means he could be in the system.'

'Shall I do a date search?' he asked.

'Please. Look for any solved or unsolved sexual homicide

cases over the last two decades which echo the main features of the Della Harrington murder.'

Julian went to the desktop and logged on. 'Why didn't the original investigation team do this?' he asked.

'Because they set their sights on David Lockman much too soon.'

The click of computer keys increased Hanson's tension. Restless, she got up, went to the window. They had a sexually deviant killer whose actions showed him to be supremely confident inside Harrington's small apartment. He had taken command of that situation quickly but once she was dead he also took his time. He knew exactly what he wanted to do. All possible signs that Harrington's murder was not his debut.

'Kate?'

She turned, came quickly across the room to where Julian was sitting, her eyes fixed on the screen. 'You've found something.'

'No.'

'Nothing?'

He scrolled slowly down the screen. 'Have a look. There's nothing which fits with the Harrington case.' She raked her hair from her face, absorbed data, watched it move upwards. After a few minutes she straightened. As he'd said, there was nothing.

She returned to her notes, stared down at them. 'A decade has gone by since he killed Della Harrington. What do you think the chances are that she is his only victim?'

'It goes against the theory,' he said. 'Maybe he was, and is, very mobile. In which case, he could have committed similar murders outside the UK. Want me to take a look?' Hanson gathered together notes and photographs. She had to get away from this room, this case. The topmost photograph caught her attention. The one showing the tiny lines of bloodless cuts to Harrington's arms. 'Do you want a Europe-wide search?' he asked, turning on his chair to look at her. She was staring, transfixed at the photograph. 'Kate?'

'How could I have been so *slow*?' she whispered. 'Julian, define sexual sadism for me.'

'A sexual perversion which requires the infliction of pain and/ or humiliation to another which puts that person in fear . . .'

She stared at him. 'Exactly. Della Harrington's post-mortem

photograph indicate a massive blow to her head. Chong's estimate of her survival time following it was a couple of minutes, max. Every single thing he did to her came after that blow. The stripping, the posing of her body, these two lines of small cuts to her arms . . . they were all post-mortem. None of those things he did to her would have caused her fear, pain, humiliation or anything else. She was beyond response. Dead. There *was* no sadistic payoff.' Her hands were shaking as she pushed the photographs into their envelope. 'I can't believe I didn't get it, and on Monday Watts and Corrigan are making their case to the chief, a case they don't doubt is a sexual homicide.'

'Jeez. Warn me when you decide to tell them. Watts is going to go ape sh—'

'I should have told them when I first had doubts. They're offering Steffan Coultard, Archie Fenton and Leonard Dobbs as suspects in Harrington's murder because all three of them are known to have exploitative sexual interests of some kind. If the Harrington case isn't a sexual homicide, they don't fit.'

'They may not fit for sadism, Kate, but can you be one hundred percent sure that none of those three was involved in her murder?'

'No. I can't.' She closed her eyes, let her head fall back. 'God, what a *mess*. One or other of them could have done it. If so, we have to look for an underlying motivation.' She frowned. 'Which means we're back to the start of the investigation with nothing.'

'Except for Coultard, Fenton and Dobbs,' said Julian. 'You still have them to explore further. Watts and Corrigan have to go to the chief with their names.'

Julian went out, leaving Hanson staring straight ahead at nothing. The Harrington case was turned on its head if it wasn't sexual. What other motivation could be hidden within it? Did he want to silence her? If so, about what? What could Della Harrington have possibly known that was sufficient to get her killed? Leonard Dobbs slid into her head. Might Della have found out what he was doing at Marlow Gardens and the apartment building next door? There was the other possibility mentioned by Watts: that Della had had a secret man in her life. If so, was he responsible for her murder? And what were the chances of their identifying him after a decade? It would take massive resources which they didn't have. Next time she saw her colleagues, she had to talk to them about what she was thinking. She stared ahead, thinking of Harrington's killer. *What have you told me about yourself, so far? That you're cool under pressure. How about, ruthless? Forget, 'cool'. Make that cold.* She shook her head. Julian was right. Watts wouldn't take any of this well.

She gathered up papers and pushed them inside her briefcase, feeling spent. She should have been home fifteen minutes ago. She was taking Maisie and Chelsey bowling.

FOURTEEN

Hanson came into an empty UCU on Monday morning to the sound of the phone ringing. Dropping her belongings on the table she reached for it. 'Unsolved Crime Unit, Police Headquarters, Rose Road.' The voice in her ear was faint.

'Hello. May I speak to Detective Inspector Bernard Watts, please?'

She absently registered the grammatically correct phrasing, the pleasant, somewhat diffident tone. 'I'm sorry, DI Watts isn't available right now but I can take a message for you.' She reached for a pen.

'Would you tell him that David Lockman called? My contact number is . . .'

She froze, her one thought that she had to end the call. 'Mr Lockman, he's very unlikely to return your call.'

'I understand, but I'd very much appreciate you letting DI Watts know that all I want from him is a general indication of how his new investigation is progressing.'

She wouldn't give this man anything but he deserved honesty. 'I'm sorry, Mr Lockman, but he's unable to do that. All I can say is that the Unsolved Crime Unit is committing all of its time to the case.'

'Who am I speaking to?'

'My name is Kate Hanson. As I said—'

'Ms Hanson, you mentioned time. I doubt you can tell me very much about that. I've become an expert on it over the last ten years. What I also know is that I'll never have a life or any real freedom until Della Harrington's killer is identified.'

She took this to be an oblique reference to what they had been told had happened to him the previous week. She understood. Without someone identified by UCU as responsible for Della Harrington's death, his future would continue to be blighted, no matter what the appeal court had ruled.

'I'm truly sorry, Mr Lockman.'

'I'm sure you are but it doesn't help me. Something happened at my home last week. Someone took the top off a stone sundial in my front garden and used it to smash my window.'

'We heard you were in hospital . . .'

'I'm home now. I'm fine,' he said, tone clipped. 'Except for acute embarrassment at losing track of how many Valium I'd taken, plus guilt for causing unnecessary work for people who've got better things to do.'

'I will let DI Watts know that you called and what you've said.'

'Thank you.'

Replacing the phone, she added words to the message pad. The door swung open and her colleagues came inside. She gave them a quick evaluation. 'You don't look chewed out so I'm guessing the meeting with the chief went well?'

Watts blew air through his lips and sat as Corrigan switched on the kettle. 'As well as it could. He's accepted Coultard, Fenton and Dobbs as persons of interest, with Coultard and Dobbs under consideration as potential suspects. He wants us to push one of them up to prime suspect.'

She looked at him. The case was moving on and it was all wrong. 'We need to talk about . . .'

Watts stretched his arms, let them drop. 'I feel like I've done nothing else but talk for the last couple of hours, doc. And there's going to be more verbal fencing because we need all three in here for interview. We'll start with Dobbs because we've now got evidence on him. Me and Corrigan were in here at the weekend. We made contact with three of the women Dobbs took sexual advantage of. One of them was willing to talk to us. She confirmed what Sienna Barton told us. She's now made an official complaint against him. He doesn't know about that. I want him in again, ASAP.' He looked across the table at her. 'I want you observing that interview and any others we fix up involving Coultard and Fenton. We want your eyes, your ears and everything you know about sex types.'

Watts lifted the phone and spoke briefly to Dobbs. From what she could gauge from his face she guessed that Dobbs wasn't pleased at what he was hearing. Replacing the phone, he looked at her as she reached for her bag and keys. 'Hang on, doc. He'll be here in an hour with his brief. Where are you going?'

She wouldn't tell him that since Charlie had left she'd heard nothing from him. That she felt adrift and alone. 'I have to call in at my house but I'll be back in time for the interview.' She handed him the message slip. 'I took a call for you earlier. From David Lockman.' She watched him read it then let it drop on the table.

'He'll have a long wait.'

Hanson returned to headquarters. Charlie wasn't at her house and he hadn't called. She wouldn't ring him. The situation had to be left with him. Whether he came to live with her or he didn't was his choice. Nothing had changed. She'd been alone for the last ten-plus years. She could do more of it.

She entered the observation room, watching her colleagues face Leonard Dobbs and his lawyer. Watts' eyes went from the lawyer to Dobbs and stayed there. 'We'll get straight to it, Mr Dobbs. We have confirmation from a female complainant that you exerted pressure on her for sexual activity in exchange for financial help with her rent. What do you say?'

Dobbs glanced at his lawyer. 'I say it's rubbish. I won't even dignify it with a response.'

'I need details of what you have in respect of my client, detective inspector,' Dobbs' lawyer said.

'I'll give you details. There's three women your client placed under sexual pressure in 2007. Dates and names might refresh his memory.' He read the details in front of him. 'In May, 2007, Anna Squires, age nineteen. In August, Kitty Garvey, eighteen. In October, Lisa Johnson, also eighteen. Miss Johnson has made a statement—'

'I've just told you, it's rubbish,' snapped Dobbs, his colour rising.

'There's more.'

'So, what? It's all lies.'

'Now that we've got an official complaint against you, we're continuing our investigation into your exploitative activities involving the other named women.'

Dobbs shook his head. 'This is ridiculous. I don't know what you've been told but I'm telling you now, she, they are all liars.' His eyes narrowed. He pointed at Watts' face. 'Hang on. That last name. Johnson. I remember her.' He sent his lawyer a smug glance. She remained straight-faced, not looking at him. 'I'll tell you about Lisa-bloody-Johnson. I had to throw her out. She was bringing men back to her apartment. I don't mean the occasional boyfriend. I'm talking about a constant stream of different men. There's your reason for her complaint. You show up at her door, she goes into a panic in case it all comes out what she was back then and she decides to throw dirt at me to deflect attention from herself.'

'You think any of what you just said makes a difference to what we're talking about here?' asked Corrigan.

Dobbs stared at him. 'I don't know how stuff like this goes down where you're from, but character counts for something here. Check her out. You'll find she's a little slag *and* a liar.'

Watts regarded him with barely concealed loathing. 'We have her written statement that you went to her apartment, that you offered a way for her to pay her rent, which involved having sex with you.'

Dobbs folded his arms, looking self-assured. 'I offered to help her by covering the rent she hadn't paid, plus a couple of months to give her a chance to sort out her situation. I made it clear it was a loan. I had a daughter of around the same age back then.' He placed his open hand against his chest. '*I* would hope that anybody, any man who's able to help any young woman in a situation like that would do what I did.' His eyes went to his lawyer who was busily writing, then back to the two officers. 'She was pleased to accept my offer. She grabbed it with both hands. You tell me, where's the problem?'

'Do you admit to having sexual activity with Lisa Johnson?'

Dobbs gave Watts a crafty glance before replying. 'She came on to me. It was consensual. Nothing to do with any money.'

'Taken by your charm and looks, was she?' Watts got a look from Dobbs' lawyer. 'Tell us about Anna Squires and Kitty Garvey.'

'What about them?'

'Do you admit to having sexual activity with either of those women?'

Dobbs looked to his lawyer. Watching the situation unfold, Hanson had guessed that this woman was deeply uncomfortable with the situation, but as a professional she wouldn't show it. She watched as the lawyer whispered briefly in Dobbs' ear. He folded his arms, looked up to the ceiling.

'No comment.'

To every question which followed, Dobbs' response was the same. Hanson watched as he was charged with a total of six sexual offences. She looked at her colleagues' faces, knowing that they were thinking about what had happened to Della Harrington and about Dobbs' possible involvement in it.

'We'll be in touch, Mr Dobbs,' said Watts.

Hanson was sitting at the big worktable, hands supporting her face as Watts and Corrigan returned to UCU. Watts continued on to the Smartboard, activated it and pulled screens of information onto it, one after another. After a minute of heavy silence, his back still to the room, he said, 'You don't believe Dobbs killed Harrington, do you, doc?'

'I don't know. Having watched him in interview I see that he's a very unpleasant individual.'

'Would you be happier if it was Steffan Coultard we were interested in?'

'No. I've been to his house, spoken to him twice. I know his personality type. His internal world is filled with feelings of ineptitude, inferiority and fear of embarrassment. I struggle with the idea of his attacking a tall, statuesque woman like Della Harrington.'

There was a short silence before Watts responded. 'I hear what you're saying but tell me something. Was it a surprise when you discovered his involvement with Marija Gailitis, a sex worker?'

'Yes . . . yes, it was.' He turned to her, his thick brows raised. She shook her head. 'If you're thinking that that challenges my perception of him, it doesn't. Marija got the money she needed and he got sex without expectation or complication.'

Watts slow-nodded. 'Right. Sounds to me like he's not that different to Leonard Dobbs.'

She ran her hand over her forehead. *God, is there no end to the complications in this case?* She wouldn't challenge the three persons of interest her colleagues now had, but she had her views and he needed to hear them. 'Coultard set a financial agenda between himself and Marija. He would have known she needed money and she gave him the social and sexual experiences he doesn't have the confidence to establish. He doesn't have Dobbs' misogyny. Corrigan will tell you that Marija spoke with some warmth about Coultard.'

'That's true,' said Corrigan.

'I'm guessing that she understood him, was sympathetic towards him. Dobbs' way of connecting with women involves coercion. I doubt you'll find a female who knows him who expresses sympathy for him.' A different thought occurred to her. 'The original investigation had documents which indicated that Coultard was married. I've seen no indication that they followed it up. He told me he was married. Marija told us that he isn't . . .'

'Which makes him a liar as well as a shifty type who buys sex,' said Watts.

'I know where you're going with this. I've already explained my doubts about Della Harrington's murder being about sex. Of those three men, Coultard looks to me to be the least likely suspect, but it's your decision, yours and Corrigan's as to how you proceed. Coultard doesn't yet know we've identified Marija?'

Watts shook his head. 'No. He's due here in an hour and would you believe it, he's waived his rights to representation. I'll be asking him some questions about 'er indoors.' She got up and went to fetch her coat. 'If that's a reference to a possible wife, I'd say it's best left unsaid.'

'Where you off to?' Watts asked. 'I want you observing the interview with Coultard. I want you to tell us what else you make of him.'

'I'm due at the university in fifteen minutes. I'm there for the rest of the day.'

'*Great*. Just when we need you.'

She swung her bag onto her shoulder, aware that over the last few days she'd not been pleasing anybody. She walked to the door. Pleasing people wasn't what she was here for. 'I'll look over the recording of the interview later and let you know what I think.'

*   *   *

They came into the interview room. Coultard tensed, his eyes darting from Watts to Corrigan.

'Thanks for coming in, Mr Coultard.' Watts prodded the PACE machine as they sat. He eyed Coultard. 'Can you confirm that you're happy to continue with this interview without representation?'

'Yes. I'm assuming this is about Della. I just want to get this over and go home.'

Watts produced the photograph of Marija Gailitis taken by Hanson and slid it across the table. 'Tell us who this is.'

Coultard looked at it, his eyes widening. 'She . . . she cleans for me. Us. My wife employs her . . .'

Corrigan pointed to it. 'Sir, we already know her identity: Marija Gailitis. She's a Ukrainian national, a sex worker and an illegal.' Coultard turned his face away from them. 'Come on, Mr Coultard. We know about her so you might as well give it up.'

Coultard let his shoulders slump. 'If you know, what is there left to say?'

'Quite a lot,' said Corrigan. 'Tell us where your wife is.'

They both watched as shock and what looked like panic crossed Coultard's face. He slid his tongue over his parched-looking lips. '. . . She left.'

Watts nodded, his eyes never moving from Coultard's face. 'When did she leave?'

Coultard looked down at his hands. 'About two years ago,' he whispered.

Watts glanced at Corrigan and made a show of opening his notebook. 'Right. Let's have some details about her, shall we?'

Sweat appeared on Coultard's upper lip. 'I can't . . . I don't want to get into that. I don't want to talk about her.'

Watts and Corrigan exchanged glances. 'OK, sir,' said Corrigan. 'Let's talk about Della Harrington.' Coultard's panic stayed put. 'We know you both belonged to the same opera group, that you offered her lifts to rehearsals.' Coultard stared down at the table. 'Tell us when and why she gave you the code to the main door of her apartment block.'

'I . . . I don't recall.'

'Sir, we know that in the past you would arrive and go up to her apartment. At some point that arrangement changed.

She began to insist that you wait outside the building on your arrival. You need to tell us, why the change?'

Sweat now slicked Coultard's face. He looked from one officer to the other. 'I . . . it was a misunderstanding. One evening, months before she was killed, I arrived at the apartment early. I was feeling confused. I went into the wine bar across the road, had a couple of glasses of wine. I don't drink as a rule.' They glanced at his pudgy waistline.

'And?' asked Watts. 'What were you feeling confused about?'

Coultard looked away. 'I wanted to know where I stood with Della but I don't like those sorts of conversations. Never have. I came back. Went upstairs to the apartment. Della let me in. There was somebody else already there. I hadn't expected that. It threw me.' The tension inside the room climbed.

Watts glared at him. 'You're smart enough to know that any friend or associate of Della Harrington's back then would be of interest to her murder inquiry, yet you never mentioned this to officers at the time. Nor to Professor Hanson when she came to see you.'

Coultard's eyes slid away from them. 'I didn't think it was relevant. This was months before her murder . . .'

'*We* decide what's "relevant" here.' Watts got his irritation under control. 'According to you, "months" before the murder you're inside the apartment and you find somebody already there. Who was it?'

'It was a woman.'

Watts gave him a weary look. 'And?'

'I thought she was a work colleague of Della's.' They eyed him, waiting out another pause. 'I can't tell you who she was. Della introduced her and then the woman left. I saw her for barely a minute. I didn't take much notice. Like I said, I had other things on my mind.'

'You said Della introduced you,' said Watts. 'She would have said this woman's name.'

Coultard shrugged. 'It was something unusual. I can't remember what it was.' Feeling Watts' intent gaze on him, he looked up and then away. 'It might have been Rhonda, or something. I wasn't listening.'

'What happened then?'

'Like I said, she left.'

Watts gave him a steady look. 'Mr Coultard, we're getting nowhere fast here. Tell us what these "things" were that you had on your mind.'

Coultard looked fazed. 'What?'

Watts' thick finger jabbed the air between them. 'You've just told us you took no notice of this visitor because you had things on your mind.'

Coultard rocked slightly on his chair, avoiding their eyes. 'It was nothing. Just . . . something I had to sort out with Della.' His voice was now almost inaudible. 'I was getting mixed messages from her.'

'Keep your voice up, Mr Coultard,' advised Corrigan. 'Tell us about the mixed messages.'

Coultard fingered away the perspiration on his top lip. 'I . . . we were friends. Or that's what I thought but it was unclear if Della had considered we might be . . . more. I decided to tell Della that I liked her.' He avoided their eyes. 'I find that kind of thing very difficult. Very challenging. I don't like to raise issues. I'd rather leave that to the other person. Or, just leave it.'

'We hear what you're telling us,' said Corrigan. 'Those kinds of overtures can be difficult. How did she respond?'

'She didn't.'

Watts folded his arms, his face set. 'Come on, Mr Coultard. You've decided to tell Della Harrington that you're attracted to her. How did she respond to that? What did she say?'

Another faint flush crept over Coultard's face. He bowed his head. 'She laughed. She said she wasn't interested. I couldn't understand it. We seemed to get on well. We sang together. I'd lent her some of my CDs . . .'

'What did *you* say or do?'

'I didn't say or do anything. I prefer to avoid confrontation.'

'You were angry with her.'

'No, I wasn't. I avoid expressing feelings. I find anger particularly difficult to cope with. I just wanted to get out of that apartment. I realized it was all a terrible mistake.'

'Where did you go?'

Coultard gave Watts a fleeting glance. 'I didn't go anywhere.

I just went down to my car and waited for her so we could go to rehearsal.'

'Given what you've told us,' said Watts, 'that must have been an uncomfortable few minutes' journey.'

Coultard frowned. 'No. It wasn't. I'm not the kind of person to . . . pursue things in that kind of situation. I was glad to let it drop. After that, she insisted I wait outside each time I called. That suited me. I wasn't going to make a thing of it after the way she'd responded to me.'

Corrigan regarded him. 'Do you think some people, some men might have found the outcome of that conversation with Della Harrington upsetting, particularly given your feelings for her?' Coultard didn't respond. Corrigan pushed on. 'A feeling of anger on your part might be regarded as understandable.'

'I wasn't angry. I just told you, I don't allow myself to get angry.'

'OK,' said Watts with another weary look for Corrigan. 'Fast forward to the evening you found Ms Harrington dead . . .'

'That wasn't just me. The maintenance man was there as well.'

The two officers exchanged quick looks. Watts leant towards Coultard. 'In your original statement you said you and Fenton went into that apartment together but that isn't strictly true, is it?' Coultard said nothing, his eyes flicking from him to Corrigan and back. 'There's something else about that evening we want to ask you about. You made quite a scene inside the building just prior to the finding of Harrington's body. In fact, you had a stand-up row with Harrington's next-door neighbour.' He eyed Coultard, waiting. 'For somebody who says he doesn't like confrontation, who avoids getting angry, that's very interesting to us.'

'That woman, the neighbour, was being very difficult towards me,' he whispered.

'We're guided by what other witnesses have told us, sir,' said Corrigan. 'According to them it was you who created the distur-bance. You actually put another witness in fear with your shouting.' Coultard squirmed on his chair. Corrigan kept his eyes fixed on him. 'Did you have a reason for creating that disturbance? Was it a way of marking your presence at Della Harrington's door at that particular time?'

'What? I don't understand what you're saying,' whispered Coultard. 'Why would I do that?'

'Maybe you thought it was a real handy way of fixing witness attention on you and the time you arrived, sir. Particularly if you had already been inside that building earlier in the day.'

Coultard's eyes widened. 'You think I killed Della.'

'If you did, it's time to tell us.'

'I didn't,' he whispered. 'It wasn't like that.'

'Tell us what it was like,' said Watts.

'Della phoned me on the afternoon of the day she died. She said she was expecting a visitor and she might be a bit late getting ready. She didn't sound very happy. I asked her if she was alright. She said yes and that I should wait in the car park for her as usual.'

'Why didn't you mention this before?' snapped Watts. 'We know you told Professor Hanson you were anxious to get inside that apartment to collect some CDs.'

'I *was*.'

'You didn't tell her about getting this call from Della Harrington.'

'I . . . I didn't want to get any more involved in this than I already was.'

'You're involved now, take my word for it,' said Watts, pointing at his own neck. 'Right up to here.' Coultard looked away from him. 'What did you make of what Harrington said to you during that call?'

Coultard shrugged. 'I thought she didn't want me seeing this person, this visitor, whoever it was.'

'Carry on.'

'I arrived, parked and waited. She usually sent me a text that she was on her way down. She didn't.' He looked from Watts to Corrigan. 'I didn't want to go into the building because she'd told me not to, but time was getting on. We had an important rehearsal. I thought about the phone call and I started wondering if she was alright. I decided to go up to her apartment.'

Watts looked at him, unwavering. 'I've got an iffy feeling about that, Mr Coultard. You've told us you avoid anger and confrontation. Now, you're telling us you went up to that apartment, knowing there might be somebody inside it who, according to you, Della Harrington wasn't happy about.' He waited. 'Come on. Let's have it.'

'All I could think about was getting to the apartment. I was wondering if she'd gone out for some reason . . . If she had, I could get my CDs. I already told Professor Hanson how important my CDs are to me. When I reached the first floor and requested Della's key, the neighbour was very challenging towards me.' He looked down at his hands. 'It upset me. Caused me to feel a bit angry. The situation got the better of me. I got the key, went inside the apartment, got my CDs . . . and then, when I saw her . . .' He put his hand over his eyes. 'Please. I have to get out of here. I'm feeling unwell.'

Watts glanced at Corrigan, then looked at Coultard. 'Before you do, you need to hear this so I'll make it as plain as I can. We're not satisfied with your account of what happened at Marlow Gardens on the evening Della Harrington was killed. It sounds to us like you knew something had happened in that apartment. There's something else we're not satisfied with: your lack of an explanation as to the current whereabouts of your wife. We'll be following up both matters and we'll be contacting you again to do that. Do you understand?'

'Yes. Can I go? There's things I have to do.'

After cautioning Coultard for withholding information from the original investigation they let him leave and took the information they had obtained directly to the chief.

'Sounds like a rum sort,' he said. 'What do you think of him for the Harrington murder?'

'He's a real possibility. We think it's possible that in the months after she rejected him, he dwelt on it and killed her,' said Watts.

'What about the whereabouts of this wife of his who may have left but might not exist at all?'

'We've searched marriage records. There isn't one for Coultard but it might have been a common law arrangement. Based on what we know about him and his sexual arrangement with the Ukrainian woman, we're increasingly suspicious where he's concerned.'

The chief slow-nodded. 'Start the process of applying for a search of his property and gardens. Has Professor Hanson met him?'

'Yes. She says his personality makes him socially and emotionally avoidant.'

'Give him a chance to think over his visit here, then get over to his house later today. If this wife does exist, he has to tell us where she is, but bear in mind what Hanson said about him and be subtle. We don't want accusations of heavy-handedness, even if he has done his wife in as well as the Harrington woman.'

'We'll give him a chance to calm down. He was happy enough to speak to us earlier without a lawyer,' said Watts.

'That could well change,' said the chief. 'Especially when he's had a chance to think about what's happening to him. When you're at his house, give it a low-key once-over for anything related to a wife. See how he deals with inquiries about her. If you find your suspicions growing, bring him back here. If you're still unsure whether there was or is a wife, prepare a MISPER report. Take the opportunity to ask him some more questions about Della Harrington. Keep me posted so I can sanction a house and garden search, once you decide it's necessary.'

On Hanson's arrival in UCU in the late afternoon, Corrigan briefly related their interview with Coultard as Watts slid the DVD recording of it into the player. She sat close to the screen, watching and listening. The only sounds inside the room for the next several minutes were her colleagues' voices and that of Steffan Coultard. After several minutes the interview scene was replaced by a blank screen. Watts got up and removed the DVD. 'My verdict on Coultard is that he's a liar and probably worse. We think that at the very least, he knew something had happened in that apartment. Explain that, doc. How would he know, unless he was inside it?'

'I know what you're saying,' she said. 'But what I just heard and saw confirms his social avoidance, his anxiety about attracting the censure of others. If it's true that Della told him she was expecting a difficult visit from someone, I think it's possible that whilst he anticipated Della being upset, she was no longer a priority for him because she had already rejected his overtures. His focus had switched. He wanted his CDs. I'm not saying your suspicions about him are unfounded. I'm outlining the type of personality you're dealing with so you have the best chance of understanding him and the choices he makes, but you might still be right about him. He did lie.'

Watts was looking frustrated. 'All this denying that he was angry, that he doesn't "allow" himself to get angry: I tell you, I don't trust a word he says. You've told us he has a problem with women. I think you're right about that, doc. We've got witnesses who described him rowing with Forster, the next-door neighbour. *She* told us she was reluctant to open her door to him, and the next thing he does is go into that apartment where Harrington is spread-eagled on the floor and he's looking for his bloody CDs. Or so he says. My question to you is, is it possible that when Coultard is under pressure, sex-wise or any other-wise, he's capable of losing it and doing what was done to Harrington?'

The silence in the big room was profound. She looked up, seeing Corrigan's eyes on her, Watts waiting for her response. 'I can't rule it out. I've met him just twice and the information we have on his life is still limited.' There was a short silence. 'What's your plan now?' she asked.

Corrigan told her what the chief had said. 'We're going to Coultard's place to talk to him. We're hoping he'll be more relaxed there. Any advice?'

'Yes. Avoid any reference to plans for a search of his property. He would regard it as further criticism of himself which could make him increasingly stressed and limit what he's prepared to tell you.'

Watts thrust his hands in his pockets, clearly irritable. 'If you were telling us that Coultard is a self-centred bastard, I'd be the first to agree. My view of him is that he sees himself as Number One. Nobody else matters.'

FIFTEEN

They arrived at Coultard's tree-screened house, the sun well on its way to setting. Watts pressed the doorbell and they listened to its echo in the house beyond. He kept his voice low, talking from the corner of his mouth. 'You can lead this, Corrigan, because he makes me narky. All this pussy-footing about like the chief and the doc have suggested is more your way of operating than mine. Meanwhile, I'll be looking around for any signs of his Mrs and hoping I find some.' He eyed the extensive front garden. 'I don't fancy having this lot dug up, nor what's probably out the back.' A shadow appeared against the glass. The door swung slowly open. Steffan Coultard stood in the doorway, his face expressionless.

'Mr Coultard, is it OK if we come inside and speak with you?' asked Corrigan.

Coultard nodded, stepped back and they went into the house. Without a word, Coultard closed the door then led them into the kitchen. Watts' eyes roamed over it as Corrigan spoke. 'Sir, you've talked to us about Della Harrington. If there's anything else you've thought about since we saw you earlier and that you'd like to add, we'd be real pleased to hear it.'

Coultard stood, his arms hanging at his sides. He finally spoke, his voice muted. 'I can't think of anything.'

'Your wife didn't know Della Harrington?' Coultard shook his head. 'It would be a real help to us if we could speak to your wife. When was the last time you saw her?'

'About three weeks ago.'

'Where was that?' asked Corrigan.

'Here.'

'Why did she come here?' Coultard didn't respond. 'Do you know where she is right now, sir?'

'No.'

'Do you have any concerns about her?'

'I don't know what you mean.'

'Was there any disagreement between you the last time you were together?'

Coultard shook his head. 'No. She was here and then she left. I don't see the relevance of your questions.'

Corrigan gave him a direct look. 'It's relevant because right now, we don't know if something has happened to your wife.' Corrigan looked around the kitchen and finally at several open files and an envelope on the table. 'Been working from home, sir?'

Coultard's eyes followed Corrigan's. 'A little.'

'We've reviewed our interview with you this morning. How do you feel about officially reporting your wife as missing?'

Coultard gave this some thought. 'Is it a rule?'

'It's standard procedure, sir.'

'In that case, I'll do it now to you.'

'Best to do it at headquarters.'

'I'm rather busy today,' said Coultard, his gaze fixed on the table.

'You need to do this for your wife, sir. It shouldn't take long and we'll arrange for someone to bring you home again.'

Coultard stared up at Corrigan for several seconds, then pointed towards the kitchen window. 'See? The sun is setting just beyond the garden. Isn't it lovely?' Corrigan allowed the silence to run on. 'I'll get my coat, shall I?'

'You do that, sir.'

They watched as he left the kitchen. Watts waited a few seconds then moved to where Corrigan was standing. 'I know what the doc thinks of him, but right now his attitude has got the hairs on the back of my neck standing up.'

'Know what you mean,' said Corrigan. 'This place sure is cold. Let's hope a change of scene gets him talking.'

'As far as I'm concerned,' whispered Watts, 'once we get him to headquarters he won't be going anywhere until we have some answers that make sense.'

Corrigan looked around the chill kitchen with its bland cabinets and its silent gadgets, his attention settling on the rear garden, now shrouded in darkness. 'Living in this place would be enough to sap anybody's emotions.'

'I couldn't live in a house this cold,' said Watts. He walked towards the window and looked out at the garden. 'Once we're at headquarters, we'll get him to do the MISPER on his wife, see what he comes up with by way of a description and other details, then start the ball rolling with more questions about Harrington. We'll keep it low-key. By the time we've done all of that, we should have the paperwork to search this place from top to bottom and outside.' Watts dug for his phone. 'I'll give the chief a heads up that we're bringing him in.' He spoke into the phone, listened, pointing upwards. 'What's taking him so long?'

A muffled thump sounded from the upper floor. 'I'll go see.' Corrigan left the kitchen and followed the hall, his long legs taking seconds to cover the brown-carpeted stairs to the upper-floor landing. 'Mr Coultard?' Straight ahead was a half-open door. He went to it, pushing it fully open, stopped by the first vibrant splashes of colour in this whole drab house: bright poppies on a cream window blind, their fat, red petals sliding from it to the floor and falling onto brown leather slippers protruding from beyond the bed.

'Sweet Jesus *Christ.*' Corrigan went to him, knelt, pressing his hand against the gaping wound in Coultard's neck, turned to the open door, his fingers, his hand awash as he looked up at Watts' shocked face.

'Get an ambulance here. *Now!*'

Inside her warm kitchen, Hanson sliced plump tomatoes, watching the point of her knife pierce the bright red skin, exposing flesh and seeds. She felt more relaxed than she had during the last couple of days. The first opportunity she got, she would tell her colleagues that she was now sure that Della Harrington had not been the victim of a sexual homicide. She thought of Charlie. She'd accepted that he had a woman friend. She was happy for him. She didn't want him alone and lonely at this stage of his life. She sliced more tomatoes then glanced at the neat, round pizza base which Maisie had produced following a lot of energetic prodding and pressing, plus some over-enthusiastic lifting and tossing which had resulted in her fingers going straight through it. 'It looks great now you've worked it again,' observed Hanson. 'Are you ready to top it, while I get the salad together?'

'Yeah.' Maisie rummaged inside the fridge. 'Topping's the best part of making pizza.' She came across the kitchen carrying numerous items including a pack of mozzarella balls and a bowl of tomato sauce. She set them all down and spread the vibrant red sauce thickly over the dough. 'Now for it.' She pointed to a dish. 'See? Chopped olives, mushrooms, bits of basil. I'm also including two anchovies.'

'Only two? We both like them.'

'Yeah, but they go a long way, if you know what I mean.'

Hanson smiled. 'I do. Strong flavour.' A small movement from the corner of the kitchen caught her attention. She watched Mugger emerge from his basket with his nonchalant stretch-and-sniff routine. He padded towards them, head up for possible windfalls. She chopped small red peppers as Maisie carefully arranged the various ingredients on top of the tomato sauce. 'This is why I like pizza, Mom. These things are all so different in looks and taste but they all kind of fit together, don't they?' . . . *All different . . . all fit together.* The words echoed inside Hanson's head as she went across the kitchen to wash her hands. She gazed out of the window at darkness. Maisie's words were an apt description for the features she had anticipated seeing during her first examination of the Harrington crime scene photographs. She had found them. Yet they were all wrong. They didn't fit together at all. Watts was aware of her dissatisfaction. Hearing the detail wouldn't make him any happier but he had to know about them.

'Come *on*, Mom. Get it in the oven. I'm *starving.*'

Hanson carried the pizza across the kitchen on its wooden board, slid it inside the oven and set the timer for ten minutes. Maisie held up a hand and Hanson did the same, their palms making contact. '*That* is your best to date,' said Hanson. Her phone rang. Anticipating a call from Watts, she reached for it, saw Corrigan's name.

'Hi . . . Where are . . .?' Her eyes widened. Conscious of Maisie's proximity she moved away, reducing her voice to a whisper. '*What*?'

Almost four hours later her two colleagues arrived at her house. They looked worn. She brought out two small glasses and passed Corrigan the whisky. He poured a measure in each. Raising the bottle, he gave her a questioning look. She shook her head. They sat together at the kitchen table in silence. 'What happened?'

'Coultard cut his throat,' said Watts. 'Paramedics took him to a hospital local to his house. We followed. It doesn't look good.'

'Any idea what prompted him to do it?' She watched Watts reach for his coat and take a folded sheet of paper from an inside pocket. 'Looks like he planned it.' She took it from him and saw it was a photocopy, half-a-dozen words on it. She looked up at him. He shrugged. 'We read it over the phone to the chief. Coultard's a person of interest but from what you've said about him and how he lives, we're agreed he could be vulnerable to persuasion for self-harming. The original's being processed in case there's anything on it which suggests somebody might have encouraged him to do it.'

'Do you think it likely?' she asked. They looked uncertain. She looked down at the brief, handwritten words, neat and unobtrusive in style, like Coultard himself.

I don't have a life. I don't trust. Tell Marija.

The last two words were crossed through. Hanson passed it back to Watts. 'He doesn't deny killing Harrington,' he said. 'As far as he knew, that was his last communication but there's no reference to her at all, nor his wife.'

Hanson looked down at Marija's name, the firm straight line through it. 'What did the chief say?'

'Not a lot,' said Watts. 'For him, this is about protecting the force. Me and Corrigan have to submit a report each, setting out what happened at Coultard's house.'

'Is Coultard's property being searched?'

Corrigan raised his glass and drained it, looking exhausted. 'Being done right now.'

Hanson looked from his face to his hand, saw the red stain along the edge of his shirt cuff. He caught her glance, looked at it, put down the glass. 'Guess I'll head home.' He stood.

She did the same, not wanting him to go. *Stay here. Stay with me.* 'Nothing yet on Coultard's wife?' she asked, wanting to hold him as he pulled on his overcoat and turned to her.

He shook his head. 'I've got real serious doubts he was ever married.'

'Tell the doc what else you're thinking,' said Watts.

'I've thought about what you said. About the Harrington murder. I've gone through every one of the scene pics, kicked the tyres of the whole case. I doubt it was a sexual homicide.' Hanson looked at Watts, guessing that he was still holding onto the possibility in the absence of anything else.

Watts got to his feet, avoiding her gaze. 'We've still got Dobbs and Fenton. Given what we know about Dobbs' sexual shenanigans, there's still a lot of mileage in him as a suspect for Harrington. We're pressing on with our investigation of the two of them.'

She went with them to the door, watched as they walked to their vehicles. In the steadily falling rain, she saw Watts raise his big hand and place it on Corrigan's shoulder.

SIXTEEN

Chong was cold, damp and busy, although none of these states would have been immediately obvious to a casual observer. She was sitting inside the open tailgate of the forensic van she had driven here at four forty-five that morning, transporting herself and five forensic colleagues to this godforsaken-looking area. She chided herself. It was probably picturesque in good weather. It wasn't looking its best, given the hour and the weather. Come to that, neither was she. She stared through relentless rain, sipped steaming coffee, her eyes moving over farmland on the edge of Birmingham's southern boundary. She glanced at the brightly lit forensic tent some metres away. It had taken her white-clad colleagues less than thirty seconds to erect it, the rear of it hard against the field's fencing. No matter how cramped the space was inside, she would soon be glad of its shelter. She watched the shadows of her colleagues' synchronized movements move across it and sipped more coffee. Six ten a.m. now and from what she was seeing her job inside that tent was about to start. She straightened as the tent flap was pulled aside, one of her colleagues emerging to beckon her. Throwing coffee onto sodden grass, Chong pressed the plastic cup onto the top of the thermos, pulled the hood of her forensic suit over her head and grabbed her metal case.

Reaching the mouth of the tent she nodded to the local, uniformed officer waiting at its entrance, his clipboard covered by protective plastic. 'Connie Chong, pathologist. Headquarters, Rose Road, Harborne.' He recorded the details, pulled aside the tent flap and she went inside. Within the limited space one of her forensic colleagues was photographing an area of disturbed ground, three others were fingertip-searching the grass and sodden earth surrounding it for potential evidence. The senior forensic worker stepped carefully towards her.

'You and I have upset the gods to be pulled out here on a morning like this.'

He grinned, his plump face pink and shiny within his hood. 'Let's hope whatever we did was worth it.'

'I can't think of anything,' said Chong, 'but I'm hoping you have more of a social life than me.'

He rolled his eyes in an 'as if' response. All she knew about him was that he was unmarried and lived with his pernickety mother.

'Who phoned it in?' she asked, following him to a small, clear plastic window to one side of the tent where he pointed to a stolid-looking male in a waterproof hat, jacket and rubber boots standing some distance away. 'He farms the land here.'

'What was he doing out here in the middle of the night?'

'According to him, a neighbouring farmer rang him to say there was a problem with his fence.' She followed where he was pointing to the unzipped rear wall of the tent and broken fence posts. 'Apparently, there's been some animal rustling and farm equipment thefts around here in the last year. He came down to fix it as soon as he got the call and started by cutting back the thick hedge.' Another finger-point to a dark mound close to the area of fence. 'He found that.'

'I want to see it.'

They walked the short distance and stood looking down at dark earth surrounded by wet grass. In the middle of the earth was a darker mass of earth-stained, woven material, holed in places, scraps of what looked to be black plastic protruding from it and now fluttering in the draught, the whole of it bound by soiled rope.

Chong went onto her knees, opened her case and took out her camera, picking up a familiar aroma. Firing off several shots, she moved on to what she had identified as hessian sacking. On her heels, she lowered her face towards it, seeing the unmistakeable signs of animal predation. Pulling carefully at a large piece of black plastic, the aroma changed to a thick odour like no other, filling her nasal passages, immediately identifiable to any pathologist in a nanosecond. She looked up at the forensic officer.

'Could be worse?'

He grimaced. 'Enough for me.' He watched as she ran a gloved hand over the bulky shape.

'Human?' he asked.

'Yes. Whoever's inside looks to be neatly folded and packaged.'

'Or disarticulated into convenient pieces 'n' parts,' he said, tone still cheerful.

She got to her feet and looked down at the moist earth surrounding the dark bulk. 'I won't do anything here, beyond recording the scene—' she pointed to it – 'after which I want it removed and taken to the van for transfer to headquarters' PM Suite.' She looked up at him. 'You and the team can carry on here, work the immediate area for anything which might have been left behind by the killer. *Or*, they stay and you come back and give me a hand in the PM Suite. Igor, my pathology assistant, isn't due in until around ten.'

'Call that a choice?' She had worked with this officer in the past, knew him to be methodical as well as invariably upbeat. 'I'm with you and it,' he said, 'rather than hang around here.' He straightened, beckoned to two colleagues and pointed at the mounded shape. 'We'll be moving it in around fifteen minutes. It looks heavy. Hope you polished off all your porridge this morning.'

Four hours later, Chong was inside headquarters' Post-Mortem Suite, the bulky shape crouched on one of the steel examination tables. Gowned, masked and gloved, she approached it, speaking over one shoulder to Igor, her pathology assistant. 'I've recorded where I'm at so far. It's getting tricky now, so I need to focus while you note down my prelims.' He followed her to the table and stood, pen and clipboard in hand as she talked, pointing to rope bindings now coiled inside a metal dish, mired hessian already cut and lifted away from the remains within it. Now she did the same to the heavy-duty black plastic. After several more minutes of careful work it lay, cut and lifted away. What was inside was now fully visible.

'Crank up the extract system to max please, Igor.'

He left the table and she looked down at the remains. Her hunch had been correct. The body had been folded into position soon after death. Igor returned and stood, pen poised as Chong began. 'Examination of remains found at Badham Farm on the southern border of Birmingham at six ten a.m., on . . . insert today's date. Victim buried with lower limbs folded at the knee, upper body resting on thighs, arms positioned close to sides and pointing back towards feet.' She paused to allow for Igor's note-taking. 'Position of remains held in place by an initial layer of heavy-duty black plastic then a layer of hessian. No distinguishing features to either of those materials. All secured by rope bindings, nothing unusual noted.'

She walked around the examination table, reached for a ceiling-mounted lamp and pulled it closer to the table. 'Remains mostly skeletonized. A single individual. Gender, age, race, nature of injuries and cause of death undetermined at this time.' She lowered her head to the table, gazed at the folded legs, the upper body resting on them, then up at Igor. 'Once I've had a chance to straighten it out and examine the pelvic area I'll know for certain, but for now, add likely female.' Taking a disposable measuring tape from its wrapper she opened it and measured the lower legs from knee to heel. 'Another guestimate is tall. Height estimate in the region of 175 centimetres or five nine.' She straightened, glancing at her assistant still writing. 'OK?'

He made a small stab of pen on paper. 'Got it.'

'Almost finished for now.'

She lowered her face to the examination table again, eyes moving along thigh and shin bones. She reached for a tray laid with various implements. 'Now taking samples for DNA identi-fication.' Placing the samples into clear, Perspex tubes, she added details to their labels, plus her own signature. Moving along the remains, she focused on the area of the head, what remained of the face pressed tight against the knees. 'A quantity of long hairs visible, colour and exact length not yet established.' She reached for long tweezers and applied them to the hair. Individual hairs came away easily. She pushed them carefully inside a clear plastic tube, snapped on its lid and wrote on the label. 'Hair sample taken, also for DNA purposes.'

She stood away from the table and tugged at her coveralls, waylaid now by her early-morning start. 'I'm in urgent need of caffeine,' she murmured. 'OK, Igor. I'll take a couple of shots of it, then you can move it into the refrigerated store. I'll send off the samples for DNA analysis and I'm done.'

'Long hair,' said Igor. 'Looks to be female.'

'I'm guessing that you bump into DI Watts in that simple world you both live in. Hand me the camera, please.' She took several shots and checked each one. 'This is a homicide dating back a decade or so. I'm hoping for the cavalry in the form of a DNA match.'

'And if the cavalry doesn't come?'

'After I've done a full post, it will go into the long-term cold store where it can wait some more.'

Inside UCU the mood was sombre when Hanson arrived. She glanced at Corrigan sitting low on his chair, his face preoccupied. She turned to Watts standing at the window, rain streaming down it. He spoke, his tone flat. 'Accident and Emergency phoned. Coultard is still with us. If he survives, we'll go and see him. Try to get the reason out of him as to why he tried to kill himself. Guilt because he killed Harrington would suit me. If you can think of a lead we haven't followed up in respect of Fenton or Dobbs, or a witness we haven't spoken to, tell me now.'

'You're still investigating Harrington as a sexual homicide?'

He shook his head. 'Right now, all I'm doing is looking at those two for an answer. Make that three if Coultard survives. I know you're all about the "why" of a case, but for us it's getting whatever we can from the POIs and comparing it to hard evidence.' He left the window and came to the table. 'Have a look at this, if you haven't seen it already.'

She took the newspaper from him, read the big, black headline: 'Birmingham's Unsolved Crime Unit Failing Della Harrington?' She folded it and dropped it onto the table. 'What about a visit to Esther Collins?'

He looked at her. 'Are you serious? After her performance at Lockman's trial? She helped send him to prison.'

Corrigan looked up at her. 'The appeal court judges were real critical of her.'

Watts was clearly exasperated. 'Come on, doc. She was a liability back then. Now, she's ten years older.'

'What about her wider potential as a witness?' she asked. 'Collins was inside her apartment that day, and probably on many others, judging by the case information which indicates her sitting at her window for long stretches of time . . .'

'Yeah, busy identifying Lockman who had nothing to do with anything and getting him a life sentence.'

'She might have seen something.'

Watts' eyes rolled. Corrigan was looking doubtful. 'She was unreliable ten years ago, Red. I can't see her recall having improved since then.'

Hanson understood their doubts. She had similar ones. She'd read and reread the transcripts from Lockman's trial and that relating to the Court of Appeal's decision. Both sources questioned Esther Collins' ability to provide reliable information, the second particularly damning.

Hanson looked up to find Watts' eyes on her. 'Doc, if you're thinking that whatever she might have to say is better than nothing, I'm telling you now, it won't be. If we assume that anything she's got to say is reliable, you know what will happen? We'll spend hours following it up and like as not ending up where we are now: next door to nowhere.' He pointed at the newspaper. 'They'll love it and the chief won't sanction any follow-up costs anyway. Forget it.'

She stood. 'OK. I'll be at the university if you need me.'

She left UCU and had reached headquarters' main entrance beyond which the rain was now pounding. She ran to her car which was in the far corner of the car park, hurled her briefcase and bag into the boot, ran to the driver's door, got inside and slammed the door. Panting, chilled, she reached for Maisie's school scarf, dried her face with it and looked at herself in the driving mirror. Her hair had transformed itself into a mass of russet springs. *What a bloody mess. Me. Case. Everything.* She reversed out of the parking space and headed for the exit, noting several vehicles with steamed-up windows parked close to it. Press taking shelter. Wipers speeding across her windscreen, she drove across Harborne in the direction of the university and a stack of student papers awaiting grading. Ignoring the turn that would take her in its direction, she continued on. There was something she had to do, something which felt like unfinished business and she didn't have far to go.

Igor followed the stairs down to the Post-Mortem Suite, whistling as he went. Chong had ordered a full instrument sterilisation whilst business was quiet. Nearing the suite, he stopped whistling. The phone was ringing. He sprinted the short distance along the corridor and through the door. He hadn't switched the phone to 'Message' and Chong was a stickler for rules. Twenty-four-hour phone availability was one of them. He grabbed the phone. 'PM Suite, headquarters.' He listened to a voice he recognized as coming from the lab which conducted sample tests. He wrote down the result, pausing at the name he'd just been given. 'Spell that, please.' He added it to the message pad, murmured quick thanks and ended the call. Adding day, date and time to the message he dropped the pen and headed for the sterilising equipment with a cheerful whistle.

Twenty minutes after arriving at Esther Collins' retirement home, Hanson was feeling damp and chilled, despite the warmth of the neat sitting room, and very discouraged. Yes, Collins did remember the day Della Harrington died. She had also described at some length the criticism of her evidence during the original trial and more recently in the appeal court. She had a lot to say about the legal process. 'I wanted to assist the police because I believed I had information which would help them. I was spending a lot of time at my window in those days because I'd had an operation and my doctor advised me not to put weight on my leg.' She leant towards Hanson. 'That murder was shocking but there was something even more shocking.' She paused for effect, her eyes fixed on Hanson. 'Giving evidence in court. It was *the* most horrible experience I ever had. I was harangued by the barristers, the judge kept giving me impatient looks and then, to cap it all, when that man went back to court recently it was in the papers again and I was blamed *again*. I was relatively young at the time but they were all out to portray me as gaga. There's too much of that attitude to the elderly these days.' She stopped, hands clasped together, chest rising and falling, still outraged. Hanson did a quick computation of Collins's age at the time of the murder. Seventy? At eighty or so now, she was bright, aware and there was nothing 'gaga' about her that Hanson had so far discerned. The small eyes behind the glasses fastened on Hanson. 'Do you always wear your hair like that, dear?'

Hanson reflected that even when Watts was in a low mood he

could still make good sense. She'd asked Collins what she recalled seeing from her window on the day of the murder but Collins had been dismissive, her focus returning to her courtroom experience. Hanson knew she was getting nowhere. Time she left. Looking up, seeing Collins's bright-eyed face, she decided to give it one more shot. 'You said you saw Mr Fenton and Mr Dobbs and also a youth in paint overalls on the day of the murder.'

Collins nodded. 'Yes. Every time I saw them, either alone or together, do you know what I thought? Up to no good. *That's* what I thought about all three of them.'

Hanson smiled. Collins was clearly on the ball when it came to summing up people. 'You didn't see anyone else?'

'No. Only Della Harrington.'

About to close her notebook, Hanson stopped, looked up. 'When was this?'

'On the day we're talking about. The morning of the day she was killed.'

Inside her head Hanson was in overdrive, interrogating the file information which related to that day. 'Do you recall what time you saw Della, Mrs Collins?'

'*Ha.* I'm not falling for that again. That's what they criticized me for at court. That I kept changing the time that I saw that awful man.'

Sidestepping the reference to David Lockman, Hanson asked, 'What was Della doing?'

Collins looked impatient. 'What do you mean, what was she doing? She was just *there*, when I looked out.'

Hanson had now located the file reference for Della on that day. 'She was jogging.'

'No, she wasn't. I watched her leave Marlow Gardens' main entrance, just below my window. I thought how well-dressed she was. I even remember what she was wearing. She generally wore rather plain things to my way of thinking, or those exercise clothes which don't flatter the fuller figure.' She shook her head. 'No. The morning I'm talking about, she had on smart brown trousers and a tweed jacket. I thought she looked very nice.' Collins twinkled at Hanson. 'I was a bit of a clothes horse in my time, you know.'

'Did you see her return to Marlow Gardens?'

'No. I didn't see her again, but I can tell you where she was going.' Collins eyed Hanson, looking pleased. 'The post office.'

Pen poised, besieged by doubts, Hanson asked, 'How could you know that, Mrs Collins?'

'Because she was carrying a *parcel*.' She gave Hanson a triumphant look. 'I'm quite sure.' She raised both hands. 'It was about so big, wrapped in brown paper.' Hanson noted down the details, including Collins' estimate that it was similar in size to a mail-order catalogue. The only known sightings of Della Harrington on the day she was murdered were of her in grey top and sweatpants, jogging in the area in the late morning of the day she was killed. The same grey top and sweatpants found on and around her body at about seven p.m. that evening. There had been no other sighting.

Masking her doubts but wanting to follow the issue to its bitter end, she said, 'Mrs Collins, I really need you to try and identify the time you saw Della.'

'. . . I'd say it was about eleven-ish or maybe twelve-ish that morning.'

Hanson reached up and rubbed her temple which had begun to throb. 'You didn't report that to the police at the time?'

'Why would I? She was still alive when I saw her. How would that be relevant?'

Hanson took some deep breaths. 'You're sure that when you saw Della on her way to the post office it was on the morning of the day she died?'

'I am, and for one simple reason: it was my seventieth birthday.' She looked from Hanson to a photograph in a silver frame on a small table next to her chair. 'About half an hour after I saw Della, my nephew Raymond arrived to take me out to lunch. Such a sweet boy.' Hanson gazed at the photograph of a middle-aged, somewhat overweight male with thick-framed glasses.

'Mrs Collins, can I ask the date of your birthday?'

'8th November,' she replied promptly.

Hanson absorbed this, realising that she couldn't leave the issue there. 'Does your nephew live locally?'

'Oh, no. He has a very important job in Edinburgh.' She gave Hanson a speculative look. 'Shall I ring him to confirm what I've told you?' Not waiting for a response, she produced a mobile phone, tapped it and waited. Hanson saw delight arrive on her face as her call was picked up. 'Raymond, dear, this is Aunt Esther.' Hanson heard a deep voice, watched Collins move the phone away from her ear. 'He has his own department where he works, you know.' Putting the phone to her ear again, she said, 'Raymond, do you remember that ghastly murder at Marlow Gardens when I lived there? Good. I've got someone here from the police asking me questions about that day and she wants to know where I was.' She laughed into the phone. 'Apparently, I need an *alibi*. Can you have a quick word with her?' She nodded several times, handing the phone to Hanson who introduced herself to Collins' nephew.

'I'm asking your aunt about the day of the murder. She tells me that you took her to lunch for her birthday. Can you confirm the date, please?' It was Hanson's turn to nod. 'Thank you.'

She handed back the phone to Collins who spoke into it. 'Aunt Esther here again, Raymond.' Hanson watched her face light up. 'You are? How splendid. I'll see you then. Bye-bye.' Ending the call, Collins smiled. 'He's coming down to Birmingham next week and he's taking me out to dinner and the theatre.' She smiled at Hanson. 'Did he give me an alibi?'

'Yes, Mrs Collins. What he told me was fine.'

Hanson trudged through still-heavy rain to her car, got inside and sat, tracking individual raindrops as they slid down the windscreen. Della Harrington had died on Thursday the ninth of November. Collins had been right about her birthday: the eighth of November. Her nephew had confirmed it and also that he had taken his aunt out for lunch that day. The day prior to Della Harrington's murder. Which explained why not a single person had come forward with a sighting of Harrington dressed as Collins had described. Hanson closed her eyes. Aware of the criticism of Collins' reliability and Watts' expressed doubts about her value as a witness, she had still come here and now she was cold, wet, had a headache and had wasted most of what was left of the afternoon.

She started the engine and headed for the nearby Hagley Road, her leaving tracked by a man who turned and began walking away, a speculative look on his face. According to what he'd read in the newspapers, the police unit she was working with was struggling. He frowned. He'd watched her going to and from headquarters and also the university where she worked. He knew where she lived. He'd followed her here. If you watched people in different contexts it helped to build up a picture of them and how they operated. What he now knew about her didn't please him. She was pushy and driven. The kind who wouldn't let anything rest. He reached his car in the gathering afternoon darkness.

She had all the makings of a bloody nuisance. The question was, how did he stop her?

Inside her room at the university, Hanson was on the phone to Watts. She'd told him about her visit to Esther Collins and the information Collins had provided. 'Like you said, we can't trust her on facts.' She waited. 'This is where you say, "I told you so".'

'No, doc, you're alright. I know how much you like t-crossing and i-dotting. Don't know about you but I'm beat and Corrigan here looks about the same. Give it a rest and we'll see you tomorrow.'

Call ended, she looked at the pile of student papers, her mind still on the case. Elbows on the desk, she tried pushing her fingers through her damp, matted curls. How could she make any kind of progress in understanding this case, if she didn't have a clue where to start or what to look for? She was sure of only one thing: the motive behind Della Harrington's murder was not sexual. Hands clasped to her mouth, she stared ahead. "Give it a rest", Watts had said. She shrugged her way into her coat, pushed the student papers into her briefcase and headed for the door and home.

After several hours of uninterrupted work inside her silent house, Hanson placed the last graded student paper onto the pile with an air of finality. Tired, she left her study and headed for the kitchen, the sound of Mugger's bell telling her that she was being followed. She looked down at him and smiled. He gave her a yellow-eyed look and a plaintiff miaow. 'OK, smooth-talker. One very small snack before bedtime.'

She fetched the packet from the cupboard under the sink, shook a few biscuits from it into his plastic bowl. Placing it on the floor she watched him eat, realising that she had eaten nothing since she'd arrived home. Maisie was spending the night at Kevin's place. On such evenings Hanson's domestic routine tended to slide. She fetched bread, cut two slices, eyed an avocado, shook her head. Too late. Pushing the bread into the toaster she stared at it, an idea she'd had earlier insinuating itself inside her head again. She closed her eyes against it. *No.* No way. She daren't. It went against everything she believed in, principle among them loyalty. The idea persisted. Undeterred by the hour, she busied herself with coffee-making. Toast shot into the air. She grabbed it, applied butter and honey and carried it with the coffee to her study. The idea remained, steadfast. Esther Collins wasn't the only presence at Marlow Gardens on the day Harrington died who also had witness potential. Merely giving the idea consideration made her feel edgy. She shook her head. No. She couldn't do it. Her heart sped. It might achieve something. But if it did, she would have to declare how, which would put West Midlands Police in a bad situation. She bit her lip, heart rate climbing. She also risked alienating two people who were hugely important to her. It had the potential for sending shockwaves through other parts of her professional life. She looked at her watch: nine forty. Too late to ring? Heart now racing, she located her phone. Flicking the pages of her notebook, she made a quick deal with herself. If she hadn't made a note of the number it would be a sign that this was a *really* bad idea and she would forget . . .

She stared down at the number. She knew the chief's attitude to her. Yes, he valued the expertise she brought to UCU's cases but he also regarded her as a transgressor of rules. She frowned. He would, of course. His whole professional life was bound by them. Hers was entirely different, based on scientific method, plus a willingness to think creatively to solve problems. She took a deep breath. Time to get creative. If there was the slightest chance of moving Della Harrington's case forward, she had to take it. She tapped the number into her phone and waited. Her call was picked up. She got a terse, 'Hello?'

'Mr Lockman, this is Kate Hanson.'

When he finally spoke, his voice was cool, distant. 'Ms Hanson, I've made my lawyers aware that I rang police headquarters, that I spoke to you.' She closed her eyes. *Damn it!* If she'd given this idea more thought, she might have anticipated that he would. 'Obviously, they weren't happy about it. They are very clear that any further conversation I have with you because of your involvement with West Midlands Police could jeopardize my compensation claim.' There was a brief silence. 'This isn't about money. It's very important to me that the claim succeeds. It would be an acknowledgement by West Midlands Police that it as good as ruined my life. I hope you'll understand when I say that I have to end this call . . .'

'*Wait*, Mr Lockman.' She felt her face heat up. 'I'm also taking a risk here but I must talk to you. You were in the vicinity of Della Harrington's apartment on the day she was murdered. That means you could be a valuable witness during the time you were there.' She waited. 'Please, Mr Lockman. Like you, Della has waited a long time for justice. I understand your reluctance. Is it possible for us to agree a meeting, just between the two of us? Somewhere neutral?'

SEVENTEEN

Early the following morning, Hanson came inside The Button Factory, a contemporary bar-restaurant in the Jewellery Quarter which David Lockman had reluctantly suggested as a meeting place. His choice had surprised her until she'd arrived and realized that it was not in the vicinity of Marlow Gardens. She looked around. The bar was very quiet at this hour of the morning. She was the only customer apart from two men at a far table. Choosing a table in a distant corner with a view of the door, she went to it. The tension which had started up immediately after her phone call to Lockman had kept her from sleep. She'd managed to keep it at bay whilst driving here. Now it was back, filling her head and chest. She pushed thoughts of her UCU colleagues and headquarters from her mind, told herself to relax. UCU needed help with this case. David Lockman had been in the area that evening. He might know something without being aware of it.

A sudden movement at the main door stopped her thoughts. She straightened, clasping her hands tight. He was here. She watched him glance around. He'd lost the gaunt, hollowed-out look she had seen on the television at the time of his release. He still looked pale and thin. Of course, he did. He'd been in hospital. Should she mention that? He was walking towards her now, unsmiling. Reaching the corner where she was sitting, he held out his hand. She took it in hers. 'I've been doing my homework and I owe you an apology, *Professor* Hanson.'

Never one to demand the use of her title, Hanson shook her head. 'Not a problem, Mr Lockman.'

'May I get you a drink?' he asked.

'Coffee would be fine, thank you. Black. No sugar.'

He turned and walked to the bar. She watched him go, saw the loose fit of his overcoat on his shoulders, watched his brief, verbal exchange with the waiter. She frowned. Was it her imagination or had the waiter just given him a double take? She imagined the stress Lockman must be under, second-guessing on a daily basis the responses of others towards him. Little wonder he looked tired.

He came back to the table, took a seat opposite her. 'He'll bring our coffee in a minute.' He looked around the almost empty bar then out of the windows. 'I come here occasionally. I mean to the Jewellery Quarter.' He gave her a direct look. 'I come because I need to be here. I'm not sure what it is I'm trying to prove. Maybe that I have the right? I don't think it matters why I come. I just do. Being here feels like progress of a sort.' He looked at her and she noticed more tiredness around and within the brown eyes. 'Tell me again why you want to see me.'

'Like I said on the phone, you were in the area of Marlow Gardens on the day Della Harrington was murdered. That makes you a potential witness on that day, Mr Lockman.'

He gave her a direct look. 'You'll have seen the police files so you'll already know everything I told the police. You probably have a fuller picture of what happened that day than I had. Or have.'

'I've gone through them, yes, but it's just words on paper, compared to talking to someone who was actually there.' She leant forward to emphasize her words. 'People don't always realize the relevance of what they see. I thought if we talked about it, it might remind you of something long forgotten.' She sat back. 'I don't have any idea what that something might be, of course.' They were silent as the waiter arrived with their coffee, placed it on the table between them and went away.

Lockman stirred his and spoke without looking at her, his voice barely more than a whisper. 'As I drove here, I was thinking about what happened that day. Not that it's out of my mind much. The whole thing, the case the police built against me, it felt like a ten-ton truck when it arrived. The speed, the way everything I said was used against me. I felt powerless to stop it. I was powerless. I had nothing to do with that woman's death but it felt like I was stuck behind a glass wall whenever I tried to argue against what they were saying.' He looked away.

'You had the same lawyers then that you have now?' She immediately regretted mentioning them. She didn't want him cautious, censoring his words or worse, having second thoughts about being here.

'Yes. I told them everything I knew, anything I could think of to help them fight my case. Which they did as best they could. I soon realized that they felt much as I did. They'd go into discussions with prosecution lawyers feeling confident and come out bemused.' He shook his head. The shadows beneath his eyes seemed to have deepened in the short time since he'd arrived. 'I appreciate your optimism, Professor Hanson, and I understand what you're saying, that if I think about that day I might recall something that could clear my name but—' he shook his head – 'it's not going to happen. There isn't anything.'

Despite his words, she felt marginally upbeat. He was willing to talk to her. Now, she had to move to the specifics of the case against him. One in particular was of paramount importance.

'Tell me why you came to Marlow Gardens that day.'

He gazed at her. 'I'm assuming you know about the phone call made to my home?'

'I've read about it. What I'd like is for you to talk me through that.'

He regarded her in silence for several seconds and sighed, his voice delivering the information in a flat tone. 'I got home and found a message had been left on my answering machine asking me to go to the Jewellery Quarter, to a specific apartment in Marlow Gardens.' He looked at her. 'Have you any idea the number of times the police asked me about it? No matter how many times I told them, they rejected what I said. I couldn't tell them any more because I didn't know any more. They still didn't let up. They became increasingly dissatisfied and suspicious of me.' He moved his hand in a circular gesture. 'That's how it was, round and round and there was nothing I could say except to keep repeating what I knew had happened.' He shook his head. 'I'm sorry, but I just don't see how my talking to you about that call helps my current situation.'

She understood. It was what she had anticipated. He wasn't the first released prisoner she had talked to in the course of her forensic work, but having taken the risk of meeting him, she had to encourage his thinking, get him on side.

'Did your legal team ever indicate that it had any kind of problem with that message?'

He considered the question. 'One or two of them thought it was odd. They did everything possible to follow it up. They got nowhere. When I heard myself describe it, I understood their thinking.' He looked directly at Hanson. 'My biggest regret is that I deleted it. That was something else the police used against me. They were determined that I was guilty.' He gazed at her. 'I was never inside that apartment, I didn't arrive in that area until just before six, yet I'm supposed to have killed a woman whose body was found barely an hour later. The effect on my wife and kids, my mother . . .' He stopped, got control of his voice. 'That's all history now. Something I have to live with.'

'Did any of your lawyers express a specific view about the message to your house phone?'

'They did ask me if I thought it was some kind of . . . well, joke, I suppose. A joke that went wrong.' He ran a hand over his hair. She noted that unlike photographs taken at the time of his arrest, it was now shot with grey. 'What would have been the point of that? It would have had to be someone who knew me well, which makes me feel very uncomfortable. If it was a joke, surely that person would have come forward and said so, as soon as they saw what was happening to me?' His words triggered Hanson's recall of a high-profile serial murder case in Yorkshire many years before. During that long investigation an unknown person had sent several cassette recordings of his own voice, mocking investigating officers for their lack of progress. Those recordings diverted police attention from the real killer, prolonged the investigation and ultimately increased the victim toll. That person had never come forward but he was eventually identified and arrested. She didn't share David Lockman's optimism about human nature in such a context, but she was glad to know he still had some.

'If someone had left that message as a joke, it might have been very difficult for him or her to admit responsibility once you were arrested.'

'Her. It sounded like a woman's voice. I suppose so, but don't look to me to sympathize. If it was some kind of joke, she should have done the right thing and come forward. And, in case I'm correctly anticipating your next question, no, I still can't think of anybody who might have done it.'

'You're absolutely sure it was a female voice?'

'Yes.' He studied Hanson. 'If you're thinking that there was a disgruntled woman in my life back then you are way off track. I was happily married. Had two great kids. There was nobody.' He straightened, pushed back his shoulders. 'The way I deal with all of this is I try not to think about any of it too much. I've started writing again, which is good because it fills my head. Before all of this happened, writing and my family were my life. I did nothing else, beyond publicising my books. All the people I knew back then were in the book world . . .' He stopped, looked down at the table, reached for his coffee, his hand shaking. 'Sorry. All that has nothing to do with what you're here for.' A silence grew between them. He looked up at her. 'You're a forensic psychologist. Criminal acts are what your job is all about?' She nodded. He smiled for the first time. 'Before all of this happened to me, I read a fair bit of crime fiction. I enjoyed them. They were light and distracting. An easy read compared to the literary stuff I was producing.' He looked away. 'I don't read it any more. Not now I know the grim reality of crime.'

'I understand what you're saying.'

She was ready now to ask for what she wanted from him. She had to get it right. There wouldn't be another opportunity because she doubted he would agree to meet with her again. For her part she wanted this to be their only meeting. She felt uncomfortable keeping secrets from her colleagues. 'Mr Lockman, I need you to talk me through that whole day, all that you remember of it. It's possible you might recall something, something so small or inconsequential that you didn't see its relevance at the time.'

He looked at her and she could see he was unconvinced. 'If there was something like that, surely I would have realized? I spent every waking hour while I was on remand thinking about it, talking to my lawyers, being interviewed for hours. It dominated my life, my thoughts for months. And if it was as small and inconsequential as you say, what are the chances I'll remember it now?'

She recognized that what he was saying was valid. She still had to get him thinking. 'How about I go through with you my understanding of the series of events which led to you being in the vicinity of Marlow Gardens and those which occurred whilst you were there. Hearing me say those things might remind you of something. Something I don't know.'

He nodded, waiting.

'Presumably, the phone message arrived whilst you were out.'

'Yes. I came home just before two o'clock that afternoon, heard it bleeping and made a note of the details.'

'And you went to the address given.'

'Not straight away. The message didn't specify a time for me to be there and I'd arranged to call in on an amateur theatre group in my area.'

'Tell me about that,' she said.

'I'd agreed to help the actors deliver dialogue. Some find it tricky and they asked me to advise them. I was pleased to help because I liked to support local theatre. I was there a while.' His face darkened. 'That was something else the police used against me. They said that my presence there didn't provide an uninterrupted account of my movements that afternoon. Of course, it didn't! I was working with individual actors in a large community centre with other things going on . . .' He looked down at the table. 'Sorry. Even now, I can get a bit irritated by how things went. I left the centre at around five fifteen, five thirty and drove to the Jewellery Quarter.'

'Let's consider the undisputed facts,' said Hanson. 'First, that whole chain of events leading to your arrest was set in motion by the message which was left on your home phone. Second, you came to the area at the suggestion of whoever left it. Third, you went to the main entrance of the apartment building. Fourth, you couldn't find the specific apartment and, fifth, you asked passers-by for help in finding a similar apartment building but none was able to assist you.'

'That's an accurate summation.' He nodded.

Hanson felt something nudging inside her head. Unable to get hold of it she said, 'Think about those specific occurrences. Is there anything about any one of them which at the time made you think, *that* was odd, or gave you pause for thought?'

'Not that I remember. As I said earlier, the police went on about the phone message itself being odd and I could see where they were coming from, but it didn't seem odd to me at the time. I just did what it said.'

'You're totally convinced it was a woman's voice?'

'Yes.' He looked at her, frowned. 'At least, that's what I thought.'

She leant closer, her eyes on his. 'That voice is key to what happened to you, Mr Lockman. It was the sole reason you were in that area that day. Was there anything about it, any quality, maybe a choice of words, a turn of phrase which stuck in your mind?'

He shook his head. She now noticed the deep lines etched on his forehead, deeper ones from his nose to his mouth. 'No. Not that I recall. The voice sounded young but that was only an impression. There was nothing else that caught my interest. My attention was on the actual words I was hearing.'

'What did the caller say to you?'

'She said she was a photographer, that my agent had asked her to call me and set up a meeting so that she could take a cover photograph of me and show me some of her ideas for the cover itself.'

'You understood her to be referring to the book which later became a best seller in the months prior to your arrest?'

'That's the one.'

Hanson didn't pick up any pleasure or pride in the three words and didn't see any in his face. 'Can you recall receiving any unusual calls prior to that one?'

He frowned, shook his head. 'No. I remember getting one or two hang-ups, which I suppose might be classed as nuisance calls but that's about it.'

'Tell me about them.'

He shrugged. 'There's nothing to tell. The phone rang, I picked it up, got nothing but silence so I hung up.'

'You said there were one or two?' She watched as he thought about it.

'Possibly three or four over the course of about ten days.'

'Can you recall when that was in relation to the Harrington murder?'

'I'd say about two, three weeks before, but that's only a guess.'

She made a note. Without looking at him she asked, 'Would you describe the publishing world as competitive, Mr Lockman?'

'I suppose so. A little. Why?'

'Is it likely you had enemies?'

She looked up. He was staring at her, incredulous. *'Enemies?'* He laughed for the first time since he'd arrived. 'Of course, not.

I had no enemies. Writers lead quiet lives but on the limited occasions when we get together, we have a great time. We talk for hours about everything to do with our experience of writing.' He stopped. 'That's one of the aspects of being a writer that I need to get back. If I can.'

She watched him raise his coffee cup, saw the slight tremor in his hand. There was a question in her mind which was clamouring to be asked. 'Mr Lockman, I don't want to cause you any upset, but are you able to talk about your wife?'

He looked away from her. 'Professor Hanson, I've had ten years to think about what's happened to my life and from all possible perspectives.' He looked at her. 'You're considering the possibility of a problem between us which somehow led to my being arrested.' He looked back to her. 'You're thinking my wife might have been involved with someone else?'

'I'm sorry to have to ask.'

'No need to apologize. Ally and I met when we were nineteen.' His voice dropped. 'There was never anyone else for either of us. She stuck by me throughout the investigation, the trial. It was horrendous for both of us. It had to have impacted on the children, even though they were young. When I was sent to prison she experienced . . . unpleasantness, because of what had been written about me in the media. We both knew the situation couldn't continue. I was worrying about her and the children, she was worrying about how I was coping. The pressure on both of us was intolerable. Following my being sentenced my lawyers suggested that Ally should be helped to relocate to a new area.' He gazed down at the table, running his fingers over it. 'I was going to be in prison for years. I couldn't put her or the children through that. I agreed. Ally and the children live in north Wales now. It's a beautiful area. Or so I'm told. The children are happy and so is she from what my lawyers tell me.' He looked up at Hanson. 'We're divorced. Ally married again. I still provide financially for the children, because I can afford it and I want to. They're mine and they're welcome to every penny. I'm glad now that we decided to part. It wouldn't have been good for Ally or the children to experience the stigma of what people believe I've done.' He gazed out of the window. 'And, it's still there, as I'm trying to adjust to life outside prison, which tells me that it was best that I let my family go. They didn't deserve to be a part of that.'

Hanson felt she now had a real sense of what he had endured from justice gone wrong. 'I'm sorry to have to ask these questions, Mr Lockman.'

He sat back from the table, his face drained. Hanson wondered if she dared ask him what was now on her mind. There was only one way to find out. 'The coffee cup and the bookmark. What do you think of those as evidence against you?'

'What do I *think* of them?' He shook his head. 'Nothing. Except that I used to go to that particular chain of coffee shops occasionally. That cup must have been one I'd used and left there, or somewhere. I can't give you an explanation as to why anyone would take it and keep it. I mean, why would anybody bother to do that? As for the bookmark, a lot of authors use small items like that as a thank-you to fans of their book. The police told me that the cup and the bookmark were inside the murdered woman's apartment. I didn't believe them. It sounded crazy to me. They showed me her photograph. Their theory was that I had met her at some time because there was something written on the bookmark. It was my handwriting but I didn't remember her among all the hundreds of people I'd seen at bookshop events and festivals.' He gave her an evaluative look. 'I'll tell you something now, Professor Hanson. If I heard of someone else being in my situation, with the same case against him, I'd be thinking, "Guilty as hell"!' He shook his head. 'And if my lawyers knew I was saying that, especially to you, they'd be furious. They'd be furious I'm here at all.'

'You still have no thoughts on how the cup and the bookmark came to be in Della Harrington's apartment?'

'No. I said to the police at the time, if I were guilty and I saw them inside that apartment, wouldn't I have taken them away with me? They wouldn't listen. They weren't interested.'

Knowing where those small items were found, Hanson could guess the police thinking at the time: Lockman as prime suspect wouldn't have known their whereabouts, inside a wardrobe, one of them inside a handbag. She studied his face, seeing exhaustion in every line. She couldn't subject him to much more. 'Mr Lockman, I know this is difficult so it's best if we finish now, but could I ask you to think about the questions I raised earlier about the phone call, about anyone you might have seen that day, anyone who might possibly have had a grudge against you?'

He nodded and stood. 'If I think of anything, I'll ring you.'

She took the small drip mat from her saucer, quickly wrote her name and phone number on it and held it out to him.

He took it. 'Goodbye, Professor Hanson. I don't think our meeting has achieved anything but I want you to know that I appreciate your interest.'

She watched him go, thinking that that was that. She was not hopeful of his recalling anything useful. Having seen the impact of this meeting on him, she wouldn't put him through it again. He'd suffered enough.

Her phone rang. Seeing the caller's name, she felt a quick rush of guilt. 'Hi,' she said, keeping her voice light.

'It's me, doc,' said Watts with his usual greeting, regardless of whether he was calling via landline or mobile. 'What are you up to?'

'Why?' she countered, tension rocketing.

'Get yourself to headquarters, soon as. There's been a big development in our case.'

EIGHTEEN

She came into UCU to find Julian alone. 'Where are they?'
'Post-Mortem Suite.'
Her head full of questions there was no time to ask,
she dropped her coat and bag, headed out of the door and down
one flight of stairs to the basement. Igor let her in. She took
white coveralls and latex gloves from him, shrugged them on,
her eyes fixed on her two colleagues standing at the steel examination table. Chong was facing them across something dark and
oddly supine. Odd, even for this environment. The odour now
drifting slowly towards her was familiar, not the worst she'd
encountered down here but not far off. Reaching the table, she
looked down at the remains.

'Who?' she asked.

'According to the two musketeers here, you've had mention of
a friend of your murder victim, Della Harrington,' said Chong.

Hanson's head shot up, her eyes widening. 'Yes. A woman
called Rommy.'

Chong grinned at her. 'I do like quick recall. It denotes keenness.' She nodded at what was lying on the table. 'Time for a
formal introduction. This is, or rather, was Romily Petersen.'
Hanson opened her mouth. Chong raised a hand. 'Wait. I have
more. Romily Petersen was a single woman, a successful photo-
graphic model. She worked for all of the glossy magazines:
Vogue, *Harpers*, you name it.' She reached for a buff envelope,
drew out several photographs. 'Take a look at her.' They did.

'Blimey,' said Watts. Corrigan gave a low whistle. The woman
was stunning.

Chong continued. 'Around twelve or thirteen years ago, at age
thirty, Petersen decided on a change of career direction. She left
the UK in 2004 for a job in Paris, working for the major couture
houses to stage their collections, apparently very successfully. A
year later she was reported missing to the French police. I've
talked to them. They were very helpful. They have a similar

set-up to UCU, which sounded like *Affaire Non Resolve.*' She looked at Hanson. 'Your French is probably better than mine so I'll leave that with you.'

'They sent you these photographs?' said Hanson.

'No. The French police gave me the contact details of an extremely pleasant and attractive-sounding Monsieur Phillipe Mannion.' Watts' eyebrows lowered. 'He supplied them and he's happy to talk to UCU, answer any questions.'

Hanson picked up Petersen's photographs, her eyes moving over smooth blonde hair, the wide mouth, flawless looking skin, a reed-slim body beneath the couture clothes. Switching her attention to the remains in front of them, they were all the more shocking. They were lying face up and mostly skeletonized with dark patches of what looked to be flesh still adhering in places to the upper legs and abdomen. The legs were partially flexed, as was the upper body, giving it the appearance of being frozen in mid ab-crunch, the arms close to the sides. Hanson's eyes drifted over the surface of the remains, seeing other darkly fleshed areas. Some appeared desiccated. She looked up at Chong, Watts and Corrigan doing the same. 'What happened to her?'

'Whoever killed her did so with that ubiquitous weapon the blunt instrument to her head. Come and see.' They followed her. Chong gently moved the hair, pointing to the skull. 'See that?' They looked at the hole to one side of it. Hanson wanted to know if the injury had led to immediate death but knowing Chong's dislike of interruptions, she didn't ask. Chong pointed, tone matter-of-fact. 'That blow rendered her unconscious, probably dying. There are indications of damage to the frontal aspect of the neck, suggesting that her killer strangled her to ensure that she was dead. After death, her body was arranged.' Their heads rose. She gave them a discouraging glance. 'No conclusion-leaping down here, please. I'm not talking posing. I've found no biological evidence of sexual activity anywhere on the remains. In my opinion the arrangement of the body was one of convenience for ease of transportation. Her legs were folded, her upper body pushed down onto her thighs with her arms at her sides and pulled backwards.' She saw uncertainty on their faces. 'Imagine a cooling down pose in yoga.' Watts still looked adrift. 'She was bound in that position, wrapped in plastic and hessian, transported then shallow-buried close to the edge of a field on the southern outskirts of Birmingham. The variations in tone, the presence of these patches of darkened flesh, whilst much of the rest is skeletonized attests to what was done to her.'

Her gloved hand swept over the remains. 'Romily Petersen. Five-eight for those of us who prefer old money measurements, or 172.72 centimetres, according to details the French police circulated following her disappearance. This is definitely her. DNA says so. Any questions?'

'Yep,' said Corrigan. 'Where exactly was she found?'

Chong consulted her notes. 'Badham Farm. It's a couple of miles outside the village of Alcester. Very handy to the motorway network. At the time she disappeared, Petersen still had a house just south of Birmingham, although she'd been living in Paris for several months. Take a look at the mouth.' Chong invited, training a small light source onto the face. Hanson did so. What she saw made her wince. 'I know,' said Chong. 'In life, Petersen had no need of orthodontics. Those fashion shots you've looked at show teeth as close to natural perfection I've seen.'

'Why would anybody destroy her teeth?' asked Corrigan. 'Those kinds of injuries suggest a killer who wanted to make identification difficult. But that sort of damage is pointless since we got DNA technology.'

'Well said.' She looked at Hanson. 'As to why, I leave that kind of theorising to you.'

'Perhaps her killer did it to symbolically silence her,' suggested Hanson. 'Or, maybe he was angry at something she said to him and that anger found full expression with a blow to her mouth.' She looked at it again. 'Or, maybe his aim was poor.'

Chong gathered the fashion shots together. 'Sad, isn't it? Like your victim, it wasn't her time.'

Hanson was thinking of a single unidentified fingerprint found on the inside of Della Harrington's bedroom door and a narrow cream-coloured belt with a faint blue stripe. 'How did you match her DNA?'

'She had an older brother at the time she disappeared. He'd complied with a request for DNA samples which were stored on UK and French databases in the event that she was deceased and her remains found.'

Hanson looked up. 'She "had" a brother?'

'He died in 2010 from a stroke.'

'What happened to her house?' asked Watts.

'There was a cousin in New Zealand, distant in all senses. Petersen's sole surviving relative. He inherited it, came here, sold it and promptly returned to New Zealand.'

Watts was looking increasingly restive. 'One of these days we'll get a straightforward case.'

'Wouldn't bet on it,' murmured Chong as she drew a sheet over the remains.

'What happened to her belongings, the stuff she left behind in Paris?' he asked.

'Monsieur Mannion surrendered them to the French police. They're on their way here.'

Hanson looked up at Chong. 'There was an unidentified fingerprint found inside Della Harrington's bedroom.'

'An index finger.' She pointed to the hands. 'You can see the poor state they're in, but I've matched one of her prints to it.'

'That's brilliant,' said Hanson. 'How'd you manage it?'

Chong lifted her gloved hand and wriggled her fingers.

Watts stared at her. 'You *didn't*.'

'I removed the skin from both of her index fingers, did the best I could to ease them out to something approaching their original size then placed them on my own fingertips.' She glanced at Watts whose gills would have been green if he'd had any. 'I wore *gloves*.'

'Even so,' he muttered.

Chong stared at him. 'Listen, I've "gloved" the skin of a complete hand in my time, slipping it onto mine to raise finger and palm prints. Even if I say so myself, I got remarkable results. I don't see your problem.'

'When did she die?' asked Hanson.

'Given what we know from official records of her travel movements between France and here, she was killed some time after mid-January, 2006.'

Back in UCU they discussed this latest development. Hanson glanced at Watts' heavy face. 'This is a real breakthrough,' she said. 'Romily Petersen and Della Harrington were friends, probably intimate friends. Connected in life and now connected in death. What we have to establish is why.'

'The French guy, Mannion, might be able to tell us,' said Corrigan. 'Both Harrington and Petersen would have been at statistically low risks of violence due to age, employment and lifestyle, so it looks like they were murdered by the same person.'

'Not necessarily,' said Watts. 'The two murders are different. We've got Harrington dead inside her apartment, trussed up in a way that still shouts sexual homicide to me and now we've got this Petersen woman trussed up, but in her case for convenience, according to Chong.'

'Trussed,' repeated Hanson, chin resting on one hand. 'Well-spotted.'

'Just a figure of speech. OK, they knew each other but why the differences in the way they were killed . . .?' He clicked his fingers. 'How about this? They're both part of a sex-homicide series. Petersen was the first victim. He knocked her out but lost his nerve. Instead of carrying on like he did with Harrington, he got rid of her as quick as he could. Harrington was his next effort. This time, he felt more at home, so to speak. He did exactly what he wanted to her. You've said it yourself, doc. Sex types learn as they go along.'

'So, where are the others? It's been ten years since Harrington was killed.'

'Maybe he's taking a long sabbatical,' said Corrigan.

Watts slid papers out of an envelope. 'These are this Mannion's contact details.' He pushed them towards Hanson. 'How about you have a chat with him?'

She reached for them. 'I'll ask him what he recalls of Petersen's disappearance. Any other ideas you want to raise with him?'

'Go with that and see what you get from him.'

She dialled the number, switching the phone to loudspeaker. Her call was picked up. She got a deep male voice. 'Monsieur Phillipe Mannion?' Getting an affirmative, she continued in halting French, introducing herself and her involvement with West Midlands Police. 'I apologize for calling you at this time, but we're anxious for any assistance you might give us in relation to Romily Petersen and her disappearance.'

'Ah,' said Mannion, continuing in near-perfect English. 'I have not long been informed that she has been found, which is very distressing for me.'

'I'm sorry. Are you able to clarify the nature of your relationship with her?'

'We were lovers some years ago, then friends. Romily had experienced some stress about her sexuality and had finally come to terms with who she was. She had met someone.'

Hanson and her colleagues exchanged looks. 'Do you happen to know anything about that person?'

'She had a woman friend in England.'

Hanson's hand tightened on the phone, eyes fixed on those of her colleagues. 'Do you know that woman's name?'

'I am sorry, but no.'

'Do you know why she left Paris to come to England?'

'She had visited England several months before to visit her friend. I assumed that is why she left again.' She listened as he described giving Petersen's belongings to the police. 'They requested them and I could not keep them here in my apartment. It was too distressing. Plus, I'm married now, so it was a little problematic. If you have any further questions, you are welcome to contact me again.'

Hanson thanked him. 'We may do that, Monsieur Mannion, once we receive Ms Petersen's belongings from the police.' She put down the phone and looked at her colleagues. 'Romily Petersen came here to see Della Harrington.'

'I'll go with that,' said Watts. 'Better than having thousands of possibilities to choose from which gets us nowhere.'

'It's logical that she was making that return visit to see Della Harrington,' said Corrigan. 'Maybe she and Della were progressing their relationship.'

Watts frowned. 'There's no indication that Harrington was "out" so it's unlikely that trawling gay websites and clubs will get us anywhere. I'm telling you, I can do without this Arthur-'n'-Martha complication.'

'Moving swiftly on,' said Hanson, 'according to information from the French police, Petersen intended to be gone for only three days. After five days and she hadn't returned to Paris, Mannion reported her missing. The police went to see him, asked a few questions but as there was proof that she had left France for England of her own volition and had not returned, they didn't pursue it further. Once it became clear to the French police that she was missing, Monsieur Mannion sent her belongings to them. I don't know about you two, but I'm looking forward to getting them.' She reached for the Harrington crime scene photographs and started going through them.

'I don't see what you've got to look so chipper about,' said Watts.

'I can see a connection.'

'To who?'

'It isn't a "who",' she said. 'It's a "what".'

Corrigan left the table for the bank of filing cabinets. Pulling out a lower drawer, he took out the box of forensic evidence in the Harrington case and brought it to the table. Removing the lid, he reached inside and brought out the narrow belt which had featured in one or two of the Harrington crime scene photographs. He held it up. 'This is physical evidence of a connection between these two women. Harrington was murdered inside her apartment. The same apartment where Romily Petersen's fingerprint was found in the bedroom. We don't know when that print was left but what we do know is that this belt was lying close to Harrington's body.'

Watts left the table to trudge to the window where he stood for a minute or so, his back turned towards them. She looked at Corrigan. He shook his head, looking as nonplussed as she felt. Watts came back to the table. 'The more I know, the less I understand. Let's stick to what we do know about Harrington. I've believed all along that it was a sex homicide. I'm thinking about our persons of interest: as far as we know, Coultard, Fenton and Dobbs are heterosexual. All three are into exploiting and degrading women. What if Harrington and Petersen were the victims of hate crime? Killed by somebody who knew they were gay and wanted to punish, destroy them?'

NINETEEN

Hanson threw down one of her cards with an air of triumph. Maisie gave it a sober look. 'Mom, it's time we faced it. You'll never be much of a poker player.' Hanson gazed at the card then at her daughter. 'I thought it was a good move.'

'It might have been if I hadn't guessed what you were up to all through that game. It shows on your face. Plus, you don't take risks and you don't pay attention.'

That last criticism was one Hanson knew to be true. Her mind was elsewhere, filled with the latest events at headquarters. She watched as Maisie returned the cards to their box. 'I recall you telling me that a positive attitude is essential for a poker player so that's what I was being. Positive.'

'Hate to break it to you, Mom, but it wasn't working. I can't get a decent game since Grandpa went home. I wish he was here. When's he coming back?'

Hanson got busy folding newspapers and straightening magazines. 'I'm not sure. How about another game? I'll be sphinx-like this time.'

'Yeah, right.' Maisie got off the sofa. 'I think I'll go and finish my Eng. Lit. assignment.' She jabbed two fingers at her open mouth. Maisie's academic prowess was strictly mathematical. She regarded all other subjects as a chore and a device to keep her from it. They came out of the sitting room together, Maisie heading upstairs and Hanson to her study.

The desk lamp was already on. In the small pool of light, she saw the several books she'd taken down from one of her shelves after her meeting with David Lockman. She ran a hand over them. A single theme linked them: miscarriage of justice. She ran her finger along their spines. If they were going to be of any help, she had to reread them.

The doorbell sounded. She left the study and went to open the door. Corrigan was standing there. 'If this is a bad time, just say.'

'No. Come in.'

He followed her into the sitting room. Maisie was there, textbooks on either side of her, her iPad on her lap, her eyes on the television screen. 'I thought you were upstairs, working,' said Hanson.

'I had to come down here and do it or be driven mad by the stupid woman in this book wittering on about the men she knows, and their houses and the money they've got and which one is the best marriage deal.' She groaned. 'If I'd been alive back in the olden days and people expected me to mess around like that, I'd have drunk drain cleaner. That's if they had any. Which they probably didn't. Hi, Joe.'

'Hey, Catswhiskers.' He grinned. 'How's the math?'

'Brilliant, actually. In October, I'll be spending half my school time at uni, and—'

'That hasn't been decided yet,' said Hanson.

'That's what Daddy says I'll be doing.'

Hanson kept her face bland, doing a silent count to twenty. 'Your father and I are in agreement. It needs thinking about. It's not easy for you, mixing with students who are so much older.' Her mind spun back a little over a year to an incident inside the School of Psychology computer lab when one of those students, male and nineteen at the time, tried to take Maisie's coursework from her. Maisie had stopped him. With a kick.

She gave her mother an exasperated look. 'I know what you're on about and that's total history. I was just a kid, then. You *always* rake stuff up, Mom.' She switched her gaze to Corrigan. 'I bet you didn't do that with your daughter when she was my age, did you, Joe?' Her phone shrilled. She grabbed it, leapt from the sofa. 'That's Chel. See you.'

Hanson watched her rush for the stairs then looked at him. 'Come on. I'll make coffee whilst regaining my sanity.'

They went into the kitchen where Hanson assembled cups, giving him a quick glance. He was looking thoughtful. She guessed he was thinking about Coultard's attempted suicide. She brought the coffee to the table, breaking the silence. 'Here you go.'

'Thanks.'

She watched his lips as he drank. 'Things seem to be on the move with the Harrington case,' she said.

'Sure looks that way.'

'Something on your mind?'

'Yep.' He looked at her. 'I've told you about my mom.'

Hanson smiled. 'You have.'

'She gives good advice. She reckons I let situations slide.' He gave Hanson a direct look. 'She's right. I'm done with kicking this can down the road. It's time I went with what I want. You're coming to my place for dinner, Saturday. Before that happens, I need to be straight about what I'm thinking – make that "hoping".'

Hanson looked at him, getting the same feeling she'd had as a small child the first time she'd walked on ice, felt it move beneath her feet. 'Corrigan, if I'm getting the drift of what you're saying, it seems to me there's something we still need to get straight between us.'

'If you're about to tell me you've got no use for commitment, I already know. I'm not looking to change you.'

'I'm not sure about that. You want to move things on between us.'

'That's true,' he said.

She shook her head. 'It's not going to happen the way you want. I'm not about to change the way I live my life.' She looked away from him. This had to be sorted. Now. He had to understand and accept why she did what she did when it came to relationships. 'The relationship between Charlie and my mother was toxic on her side. I'm only surprised he stayed as long as he did. When he left she decided that whatever toxicity she had left over, she would use on me. I didn't see him from when I was fifteen until I was twenty-something, and then hardly at all for years after that. I don't need to tell you about Kevin. I heard Maisie describing him to a friend recently. She called him a "womaniser". It was a bad moment for me because she's not yet fourteen. I'm telling you this so you know that the way I live my life and the men I allow into it, it has to be on my terms. Maisie isn't aware of that. It works for me. It's not about to change. You know most of this. We've had this kind of discussion before.'

'Would it help any if I said I accept your terms?'

'I'm not convinced you do.'

He came and stood close to her. She felt his heat. 'Let's slow the tempo. About this dinner I'm making for us. You easy with steak-au-poivre?'

She looked up at him. 'Very easy.'

TWENTY

'Want anything, Kate?'

Hanson looked up at her personal assistant standing at the door. 'No thanks, Crystal. I'm going to headquarters in ten minutes if you need to contact me.'

The door closed and Hanson turned her attention back to the slim book in front of her on the desk. It was one of several she had skimmed through late the previous evening to refresh her memory. One she hadn't read for some years. A true account of events which occurred in Liverpool in the 1930s and which had led to a woman being brutally murdered in her home and her insurance agent husband facing the gallows. Reaching for a pen, she began listing the main events. On the evening prior to the murder, a message was left for him at his chess club. The unknown caller was offering new business, gave details of his address and suggested that they meet there. The following dark, wintry evening the husband set out to visit his caller but on arrival at the designated area, he had been unable to locate the address. He had asked for directions from several passers-by, one of them a police officer. Still unable to locate it, he had abandoned his efforts and returned home. Experiencing difficulties opening his own front door, he went to his next-door neighbour's house with a request that the neighbour accompany him to the back door. This time the husband managed to get inside where he and the neighbour found his wife beaten to death.

Looking down the list she'd made, Hanson felt a small frisson of excitement. She cautioned herself. There were differences between it and the Harrington murder but one aspect was now chiming with a vague idea she'd had when she'd met David Lockman. An idea too elusive to express at the time. Now she could see it, as plain as the printed pages of the slender book in front of her. She reached for her phone. If she was going to ring him, suggest another meeting, she had to do it here. Now. She tapped his number and waited. Her call was picked up.

'Mr Lockman, this is Kate Hanson.'

'Professor Hanson.' His voice didn't sound encouraging. She took a breath. She had to get him on side. 'Mr Lockman. I need to talk to you again.' She got several seconds of silence before he responded.

'I'm sorry but I can't do it.' She gripped the phone, tension climbing. Had he told his lawyers about their meeting? 'I found it very upsetting to talk about the case,' he said, 'but more to the point, my lawyers have worked tirelessly on my behalf, still are, and I don't like keeping things from them.' Hanson now felt a surge of guilt. It was exactly what she was doing to her colleagues.

'Please, Mr Lockman. I have an idea which I need to put to you and see what you think. It's really important, or I wouldn't be contacting you again. I can't make any promises, but it could open up our inquiry into Della Harrington's murder.' He wouldn't know about the recent breakthrough in the case. The finding of Romily Petersen's remains had so far been kept from the press and in any event, it was irrelevant to Lockman's conviction and his life sentence. She heard him exhale.

When he spoke, he sounded weary. 'You have specific work commitments so you suggest a day and time.'

'This afternoon at three o'clock?' She waited, gripping the phone.

'Will it take long?' he asked.

'I don't think so. Shall we say the same place?'

With a perfunctory 'Yes', he was gone.

She found UCU empty when she arrived and went upstairs to the main squad room where Julian was surrounded by printouts, deep into data searches. As soon as he saw her he said, 'The chief's gone ballistic about the Romily Petersen angle. He thinks it'll slow UCU's investigation down.'

Stressed because of the arrangement she'd made with David Lockman, Hanson snapped, 'What does he propose we do? Re-bury her and pretend we never saw or heard of her?' She saw several officers grin, heard a couple of laughs. She told herself to relax. 'Where are Watts and Corrigan?'

'Corrigan's gone to see Dobbs to find out what he knows of

Harrington's associates and Watts has got the chief to agree some feet on the street to help him find Fenton.'

'Why the sudden urgency to find Fenton?'

'Watts suspects he's a substance user. He asked me to search against Fenton's name.' He reached for one of the printouts. 'I got a hit. Listen to this. On Sunday, 10th August, 2003 his car was stopped on the A42 heading out of Birmingham towards Solihull. Fenton was driving. The cops breathalysed him. He was over the limit.'

'One hit for alcohol over ten years ago doesn't say "substance user" to me. How's that relevant to us?'

'That's not the whole story. He wasn't alone. There was a young woman with him.' She watched him reach for more data. He passed it to her. A young, slightly worn face gazing up at Hanson from the printed photograph.

'Who is she?'

'Her name is Dawn Wilson. She was seventeen at the time that was taken, eighteen when she was found in Fenton's car. Here's her sheet.'

Hanson took it, her eyes moving quickly down the listed details of a difficult young life dating from when Wilson was barely fourteen, which included truancy, drug use and latterly prostitution. She handed back the details, images of child-woman Maisie tsunami-ing into her head. 'What was Fenton's explanation for her being in his car?'

'He told officers that she was a neighbour's daughter. That turned out to be true. The 10th August was a hot day. He said he'd offered to take Dawn for a drive. To get some air.'

'Oh, yes?'

'It gets worse. Around the end of August, Dawn Wilson's mother reported her missing. Dawn lived at home but she didn't have much of a daily routine and had a tendency to disappear for days, so the mother wasn't able to confirm the exact date that she went missing.'

'I'm not seeing a happy ending to this,' said Hanson.

'There isn't one. Dawn Wilson hasn't been seen since.'

Hanson sat on the edge of a nearby table, the possibilities of what happened to the young woman filling her head, none of them good. 'You've told Watts about this?'

'Yes.'

'And he thinks that whatever happened to her, Fenton was involved?'

Julian nodded. 'He's out there checking all of Fenton's associates and "haunts" both now and back then. So far, he's not tracked him down.' He watched Hanson head for the door. 'Where shall I say you are, if Watts or Corrigan phone in?'

She stopped, her back still towards him. 'Just say, I'm following up an idea which might come to nothing.'

Hanson was inside The Button Factory. This time, David Lockman had arrived before her. She wasn't taking that as a sign of his keenness. More an indication that he wanted their conversation done with so he could leave. She waited as he brought coffee to the table, placed one of them in front of her then sat opposite.

'I'm sorry if I sounded brusque on the phone but I found our previous discussion difficult. I couldn't get it out of my head.' He looked up at her. 'It brought it all back.' He sighed, ran both hands through his hair. 'Not that it ever goes away.' He looked more tired than when she'd seen him before. 'And as I said on the phone, I don't like having secrets from my lawyers.'

'I'm sorry that our discussion upset you, Mr Lockman, but I had to contact you again. I want to explore an idea with you. It's only a possibility but I need you to consider it, if you will.' He merely nodded. 'Last time we met, we talked about the phone call which brought you to this area. I've thought about that message. It contained several expectations of you. It brought you to this area and that apartment block on that particular day.' He nodded absently, still saying nothing. 'It seems to me that that phone call encapsulates the whole of the case which was later brought against you. That message was very skilful. It was specific and it was aimed at you. It got *you* to that area. It got *you* to Marlow Gardens Apartments, the scene of Della Harrington's murder. The focus, the intent, was all on *you*, Mr Lockman.' She sat forward. 'You and I need to think about that phone message, who might have left it and why. Why was it so important to that person to get you to that location on that particular evening?'

His head came up. He stared at her. 'Are you saying that you think I was *framed*? It did occur to me that the police were somehow involved . . .'

'No, Mr Lockman, I need you to tell me more about that message. We have a description of it in one of your statements but that was over ten years ago. If you could talk me through it here, you may recall more.' She waited as he considered what she had said.

'Like I told you last time, it was a woman's voice. Young, I think. She said she was a photographer. She asked me to come to her studio.'

'Did that sound at all strange to you, that she was giving an address which was residential, rather than office premises?'

'No, because I didn't know the area. I'd never heard of Marlow Gardens. I remember feeling pleased to have the opportunity to be directly involved in putting together a book cover. It hadn't happened before.' He stopped. 'I suppose that was one thing that was odd about it. Anyway, I wrote down the address she'd left and that was it. I deleted the message, never realising the problems it would cause me. Why would I? When I got there and saw the apartment building, it wasn't quite what I'd expected. Some of the lights were on inside and I could see that the apartments themselves were pretty small.' He shrugged. 'I just thought, how much space does it take to put together a cover using a computer programme? Like I told you, she'd also mentioned taking a cover photo but that wouldn't have required significant space.'

Hanson sipped coffee. He hadn't recalled anything which fitted with her thinking: that somebody had wanted him in that area so that he would be blamed for the Harrington murder. She wasn't done with the idea but now she needed to raise something else with him. Something he might find challenging. 'Did the police divulge the full nature of Della Harrington's murder to you?' She watched dull colour sweep on his face, saw his mouth set in a line. Obviously, they had.

'I got the full details once I was in prison. As a prisoner claiming wrongful conviction I was provided with all of that information, including photographs.' He paused. When he continued, she picked up a tremor in his voice. 'I saw what was done to her. To me it was obvious that some kind of sex attacker had killed her. Probably somebody already on police files. My lawyers pursued it but it did no good. They didn't find any known sex offenders or offences which fitted Della Harrington's murder.' He shook his head. 'And by then, as far as the police and then the system was concerned, they already had me and that was the end of it. To have people believe you're the kind of person who could do something like that, to have people look at you and believe you're capable of . . . I was the target of a lot of animosity whilst I was in prison.'

She glanced at the scar she had noticed on his neck. She'd assumed it was prison-related. 'I'm sorry,' she said.

He looked directly at her. 'Professor Hanson, I'm grateful for your interest, your hard work but I've had enough. Talking about it merely reminds me that yes, I'm free now, but my life isn't that great. Ally and I didn't have a chance to get to know our neighbours. They're nice people but I know they're wary of me. I understand.' He looked towards the window. 'The only person who comes to the house is a local woman to clean once a week. She lets herself in, gives the place a thorough going over and four hours later she takes the money I've left for her and she leaves. I make sure I'm not there. I don't want her to feel uncomfortable, although she didn't seem bothered at all when she came in response to my ad. The only one who did, by the way.' He shook his head. 'I can't talk about this anymore. I have to get on with my life as it is now.' He moved as if to stand.

'*Please*, Mr Lockman. Just bear with me for a few more minutes. You would have seen the names of all of the people involved in the original investigation.' She reached into her bag. 'I've brought a list of them. Take a look.' She pushed it across the table towards him. 'See? That's a comprehensive list of all police personnel, witnesses, residents of Marlow Gardens, everyone who was mentioned in any way by name during the investigation. I need you to look at it. Many of the names are peripheral to the case but I want you to consider every one of them, if you will.'

He looked at it, then up at her. 'What would I be looking for, exactly?'

'Any names which catch your attention, makes you pause or means anything, *anything* at all to you. Even if you can't think why.'

He looked down at the names. Hanson sipped coffee, watched as he moved slowly, steadily down the listed names on the first sheet without a pause. He turned the page and continued on. Halfway down he stopped, looked up. 'I'm sorry but I'm not getting anywhere. I'm still not entirely sure what it is I'm looking for. So far, all I can say is that I recognize officers names, obviously, but the rest I didn't know ten years ago and I still don't.'

'What you're looking for is any name which gets your attention. It doesn't matter why. Take your time.' She stood, reached for her bag. 'When you've finished, go through them a second time. I'll be back.'

Hanson headed for the Ladies room. Inside she took her phone from her bag, tapped a number. Her call was picked up. Watts' voice came into her ear. 'Hi, I was in earlier and Julian told me about the new information relating to Fenton. How's it going?'

'It isn't. We've been out looking for him. He's nowhere and I'm knackered and starving.' She pictured him, mug in hand, perhaps an iced bun topped with a glacé cherry clamped in the other. She smiled. It was oddly comforting. 'What you up to, doc?'

She lost the smile. 'I'm not up to anything,' she snapped.

'Simmer down. It's just an expression.'

'You're full of "expressions" and most of them are really irritating. I'll see you later.' She jabbed her finger at her phone, dropped it into her bag and shook her head. *Don't lay your guilt on him. It's all yours.*

Heading back to Lockman she could see his head still bent over the list, his brows drawn together. It didn't look hopeful. She sat opposite him. 'How's it going?'

'There's nothing here that means anything to me.'

She put out her hand for the list. 'It was a long shot but I thought it was worth—'

'Wait,' he said. She looked to where he was pointing. 'Karen Forster.'

'What about her?'

'The name itself means nothing but it stopped me for some reason.' He sat back, shook his head. 'Sorry, that's it. My recall for anything around that time is completely shot. Which doesn't help, does it?'

'Don't apologize, Mr Lockman. You were under considerable

stress back then.' She took the sheet, folded it and put it inside her bag.

He looked away from her to the window. 'This meeting wasn't a lot of use to you, was it?'

'I need to think about it.' She stood.

He did the same, extending his hand which she took in hers. 'Professor Hanson, I apologize for my negativity. I doubt we'll meet again, but I want to thank you for your interest in my case. I suppose that should be Della Harrington's case. If anything comes of today, would you let me know?'

'Of course. Good luck.'

She watched him leave, waited a few minutes, then left The Button Factory and headed for her car, unaware of her progress being tracked. She'd reached her parking spot when her phone pinged. Reaching into her pocket for it, she gazed at its screen. A text from Corrigan. Could they bring forward the date they'd agreed to this evening? Smiling, she replied, then texted Erin, one of her third-year students who had stayed with Maisie in the past when Hanson had to go out. Despite knowing and liking Erin, Maisie would be furious at this indication that she needed a sitter. Dropping the phone into her pocket, she left the parking area and drove away, eyes tracking her.

'You *really* are a bloody nuisance, aren't you?' he said quietly as he watched her go. 'Do you know what happens to bloody nuisances? They find themselves in deep, *deep* trouble.'

Corrigan opened his front door at her first ring. He was in black jeans and a blue Oxford shirt. He reached out his hand to her. She took it and he drew her inside the house. The whole place smelled delicious. She realized she hadn't eaten for hours. Her hand still in his, they walked into the large sitting room. There was a fire in the hearth, wine glasses waiting on the low table. She watched him go to a wooden chest, lift a bottle of red wine, his dark brows rising as he looked at her.

She nodded. 'Half a glass, please.'

'Cutting back, Red?'

She smiled, took the glass. It was a joke between them. He knew she had no head for alcohol and rarely drank. She wanted to tell him that for this evening she had a reason for wanting to keep a clear head. She wanted to savour all of it. It had been a long time coming. Instead she raised her glass. He did the same.

'To us, Red.' He held up his glass. 'See?' He pointed to where the light from the fire heightened its colour. 'Just like your hair.'

She put down her glass, took his and put it next to hers. 'Corrigan, this meal you've made for us—.'

'Ah. I decided against the steak.'

'You haven't replaced it with anything temperamental? Such as a soufflé?'

He gazed down at her. 'Nope. A casserole. Estimated cooking time around three weeks.' He folded his arms around her.

She looked up at him. 'I'm hungry, Corrigan.' She sat on the sofa, took both his hands and pulled him down, his weight against her sublime. 'Where was I?' she whispered, running her hands over him.

'Talking about hunger,' he whispered. 'Should I say I'm real pleased you're here.'

'. . . No need.'

They grinned at each other. He lowered his head to hers. His phone rang. He ignored it. It kept ringing. 'Hot *damn*,' he said against her neck. She watched as he stood and reached for his phone, his shirt pulled from his jeans, hair ruffled.

She heard Watts' unmistakable voice. 'The chief wants to see us. Bring Hanson with you.'

She started buttoning her shirt.

TWENTY-ONE

Watts got to his feet as Hanson and Corrigan came into UCU. 'He's waiting for us and he's mega-pissed off about something.'

'Any ideas?' asked Corrigan.

'No, but he's about to tell us and I don't think we're going to like it.'

In the early-evening, relative quiet of headquarters, they left UCU and took the stairs to the chief's office. Watts knocked, got a perfunctory, 'Come in.'

The chief's massive girth was crammed into the chair behind his desk. He didn't look at them as they came inside. Instead, he kept his eyes on a letter in front of him. Without inviting them to take seats, he signed it, put it to one side and reached for another. They stood, exchanging brief glances. Finally, he stopped what he was doing and looked up at them. His eyes moved to Watts. 'Had a busy day, detective inspector?'

'I've spent the best part of five hours looking for Archie Fenton, trying to follow up what we've found out about his association with Dawn Wilson, the teenager who's been missing this last eight years. I didn't find him. The girl might have no connection to the Harrington case, but I'm not about to drop it as a line of inquiry. It could strengthen the case against Fenton as a suspect for Harrington. I'll give it another go tomorrow. If I don't find him I could be asking for more officers.' The chief nodded. His eyes moved to Corrigan. 'How about you, lieutenant? What have you been doing?'

Hanson felt a first twinge of unease. Watts. Corrigan. Her turn was coming.

'I went to see Leonard Dobbs, our other potential suspect,' Corrigan said, 'to find out what he knows about Della Harrington's private life and if he was at all aware of Romily Petersen. As anticipated, he denied all knowledge of Petersen and couldn't or wouldn't volunteer anything about Harrington. We know he's a sexual predator. We couldn't arrest him the other day, but we're not about to drop him as a potential suspect for Harrington's murder. I'll see him again and when I do, I'll up the ante for both women. See how he responds.'

The chief nodded again, turned his head and the full force of his gaze to Hanson. 'Your turn, professor. Tell us what you've been doing.'

Hanson's heart squeezed. Her two colleagues had no idea where this meeting was going but she had. She met his gaze, knowing that her situation was spinning beyond her control. She kept her response vague. 'I had work to do. At the university. Things connected to the Harrington murder.' The chief's eyes locked onto hers. She didn't allow her own to waver. Panic bloomed inside her chest. The chief wasn't fooled by the limited explanation she'd just given. He knew. She couldn't look at her colleagues. Didn't dare.

In the charged atmosphere, the chief pulled open a drawer, took out a thick, shiny A4 and laid it in front of him on the desk, face down. 'I want all three of you to take a look at something.' He slowly turned it over. Hanson froze. She picked up Watts' low gasp, felt Corrigan tense beside her. She stared down at the photograph of herself and David Lockman, his gaze fixed on something on the table between them, she pointing at it, her face animated. She recognized the scene and the exact moment it had been taken during her second meeting with him. She felt the chief's eyes on her. She glanced at Watts who was staring at the photograph. Corrigan appeared to be having trouble processing what he was seeing.

'Well?' said the chief, his eyes fixed on her face. 'What do you say?'

She stared at the photograph. No words came. The chief was experiencing no such problem. His came in a torrent. 'You know my position on the Unsolved Crime Unit talking to David Lockman. It was in a memo in bold type that it wasn't to happen. A clear, unambiguous *order*.'

Inside her head the silence was deafening as he continued to stare at the photograph, she smiling at Lockman, weak sunlight on their faces. 'This doesn't look to me like the first time you'd met him.' She said nothing, couldn't look at her colleagues. She could imagine what they were thinking.

The chief got up from his chair, walked ponderously across the room, then back again, his face ashen, beyond angry. He raised his arm, pointed at her. '*You* went against an explicit order. You went and met *him*. His lawyers know about it. They've got the same photograph from a member of the *press*.' He glared at her. 'I've managed to get hold of the photographer. He was acting on a tipoff. He's agreed not to do anything else with it for now. I've been onto Lockman's lawyers. To say they're angry doesn't begin to describe it. They've spoken to the chief constable. They're accusing *you*—' he jabbed his finger at her – 'of interfering in Lockman's compensation case.'

Hanson met the chief's gaze, aware of restlessness from Corrigan. 'I had good reason to do what I did.'

'You think that makes all of this OK?' the chief roared. 'I don't *care* about your "reason".'

Hanson's own anger spiked. She got her voice under control. 'You should. Because David Lockman was in the area on the day Della Harrington was murdered. It's time we reconsidered his role as convicted killer and instead looked at him as a potential witness. I thought that if I spoke to him, he might remember . . .'

'That what you *thought,* is it? Care to tell us how successful it was?'

'It wasn't, in terms of—'

'You went against my explicit order and it got you nowhere.' He jabbed at his wide chest. 'But it's caused *me*, this force, a load of legal problems.'

The tensions and frustrations of the day, not least of which was the unfinished business between herself and Corrigan, melded into a tight knot of fury inside Hanson. 'I'm not an officer here. What I do is bring my professional skills and theoretical knowledge to assist this force.' She and the huge officer were now locked in a face-off. What she'd said had done nothing to improve her situation. There was nothing she could say that would.

The chief glared down at her. 'I'll be speaking to the vice chancellor first thing in the morning. Meanwhile . . .'

She seized her headquarters ID attached to its blue lanyard, emblazoned with 'West Midlands Police', dragged it over her head, went to his desk, dropped it and turned.

'Now it's time for you to listen to me.' Another wave of colour swept over his heavy face. She was aware of her two colleagues moving closer. 'The Della Harrington murder is a very complex case. When I arranged to meet David Lockman, I believed I had a way of getting an insight into that complexity. I met him twice.' On hearing it confirmed, the chief's face turned vermillion. 'On the day Della Harrington was killed, I believe that an unknown individual had a strong interest in ensuring that David Lockman was in that area. If you reject that as a possibility, there's no place here for me.'

'You're right,' he shouted. 'There isn't. We'll get somebody else. Somebody who has all the expertise, the theory, but knows that rules are rules.'

'You do that,' she whispered.

She walked away from him to the door, stopped and walked back, seeing her colleagues' shocked faces. She stared up at the chief. 'But before you do, I'm telling you that theory isn't enough. I work here because there's something else just as important. This place is part of the justice system. The Unsolved Crime Unit is about justice denied. Think about that whilst you're searching for this "somebody" who can supply you with this theory you seem to think is all that matters.' She turned away, then back to him, her hair flying around her face. 'I can't work out where the hell you *live*. Don't you see the news? Don't you *see* the injustice done to women, children, men too? There's not a place we can point to on this planet that's free of it and we can't do a damn thing about it.' She pointed to him. 'Yet *you* are lucky because this force can get some justice . . . for Della Harrington, for Romily Petersen and all the cold cases which follow. Yet you won't open your mind and listen.' She stopped. The silence in the room was deafening. 'There's something else you need to know. You won't find anybody better. I'll tell you why. I've got the theory but I also care about the justice.'

She turned, walked to the door and out without a backwards glance.

Coming onto her drive she saw Charlie's car parked there. She stopped, cut the engine and sat, exhausted, still shaking. Fetching her briefcase from the boot, she walked slowly towards the house.

Opening the door, she saw Charlie smiling at her from the kitchen doorway. 'Hello, Kate.' The smile faded.

She went to him, rested her face against his chest, felt his arms around her. 'Is Maisie in?'

'She's at Chelsey's house. I hope I did the right thing. I said it was OK for her to go. By the way, a student of yours called here. Erin?' It was the final straw. Hanson's shoulders shook as the tears came. 'Kate? What's wrong? What's happened?'

She looked up, saw the concern on Charlie's face. 'It's been a hard day. Give me a few minutes and I'll get dinner together. You are staying?'

'If that's OK.' His arm around her, he walked her into the kitchen, where he pulled out a chair. 'Sit down. I'll organize dinner, but first I think some wine might help. I've found a nice Bordeaux already opened, if that's alright?' He held up the bottle.

She nodded. He brought two glasses to the table and she watched as he poured wine into them. She leant against the back of her chair, stared at the half-filled glass Charlie had placed in front of her. *Why not?* She reached for it as he sat opposite.

'Tell me what's happened.'

She shook her head. 'Just frustration on all kinds of levels I won't go into.' They sipped wine. Charlie was still waiting. She took another sip. He'd know about it sooner or later. She might as well get it over with. 'Something's happened at headquarters and . . . I think I've just committed professional suicide.'

'Surely, it can't be that bad?'

She couldn't bear the sympathy and concern on his face. She looked away, stared into her glass, moved it gently, causing the wine to swirl. Like your hair, Corrigan had said. She closed her eyes. On all levels she could think of, professional and personal, her life was now a mess. 'My work with the Unsolved Crime Unit is finished, Charlie. It doesn't matter why, but I think it's going to have big repercussions for me because . . .' She steadied her voice. 'Watts and Corrigan mean a lot to me. We were doing good work and . . .' She drank more wine, forcing it around the lump inside her throat. 'That work contributed to my promotion to professor. You know how academe works. What I did with UCU was highly visible. High visibility attracts students.'

He took her hand. 'I know. I've got all the press cuttings of you.'

She looked up at him. It had never occurred to her that Charlie took pride in what she did. Not trusting her voice, the lump filling her throat, she pressed her hand to her mouth, making the words come. 'The work I did at headquarters brought kudos to the university. It opened up big opportunities for criminological research for staff and PhD students at the School of Psychology. It attracted funding, new students and now . . .' She bowed her head, her hair falling around her face.

He was at her side. 'Kate, Kate. It will work out, you'll see.'

'It won't, Charlie.' She sobbed. 'I've resigned from UCU. I've let down two people I really . . .' Not looking at him, she brushed her face with her hands.

He got up, walked across the kitchen, returning almost immediately. 'Here,' he said quietly. She took the paper towel, pressed it to her face. 'You'll find a way to resolve it,' he said.

'There isn't one. The chief was angry. I was angry. I accept he has a point about following orders but I find that difficult because although I'm involved in police work, I'm not part of the force.' She took several breaths. 'None of that matters now. There's no going back for me.'

He reached out his hand to hers, gave it a squeeze. 'Let's stick with the here and now. You need to eat.'

She watched him get up and walk across the kitchen and start organising the food. She leant her head on her hand, staring unseeing out of the window, her head crowded with images of the day: David Lockman looking defeated, Watts and Corrigan shocked and disbelieving, the chief puce-faced. A plate arrived in front of her. She looked down at it. Eggy-bread. It was something Charlie would make for her when she was very young, when her mother either didn't have time to make anything or decided she didn't want to bother. Hanson knew better than most that neglect was not exclusive to homes marked by lack of money and personal limitation. It hid itself in comfortable, middle-class, professional homes like that of her childhood. She looked up at Charlie. No wonder he'd left all those years ago. She would have done the same if she'd been able to. She'd had to wait until a university place provided her escape.

'Thank you.'

She wasn't hungry but she'd eat it because Charlie had made

it for her. Two mouthfuls in, she realized she was ravenous. Within minutes, the plate was empty.

Charlie drew up a chair next to her and sat. 'How was that?'

'Lovely.' The doorbell rang. She looked at him aghast, watched as he got up from his chair. 'That's Maisie. She's forgotten her key. She mustn't see me upset, Charlie . . .'

'It isn't Maisie. I said I'd pick her up at nine.' He left the kitchen, heading for the front door. She listened to it open, heard male voices, one of them deep. She stood, pushed back her hair as Watts and Corrigan came into the kitchen. They looked serious.

She got straight to it. 'I owe you both an apology. I thought I'd found a way of . . .' She put her hands over her face, breathed Corrigan's cologne as he came to her, felt his hands on her arms, heard his voice in her ear.

'Every word you said to the chief is fine with us, because we know *you*. We're with you, Red.' She leant against him, listening to his voice resonating in her ear as he and Watts outlined for Charlie what had occurred earlier at headquarters.

'Don't get the idea you're free of us, doc,' said Watts. 'Me and Corrigan still need you on this case.'

'I don't have access to headquarters any longer and the chief would be furious if he found out I was still going there and you've only just got your promotion, so getting on the wrong side of him isn't a good idea . . .'

'We'll see you here or at the university.' Watts gave her an impatient look. 'Come on! Buck up. We've got work to do. Starting tomorrow it's business as usual. Psychologically speaking.'

Her colleagues had left. Charlie had brought Maisie home and she was now in bed. Hanson was in pyjamas and robe, staring at the television screen, too tired to go upstairs. She was forcing herself off the sofa when Charlie came into the room. 'Don't go, Kate. There's something I need to say. I know you're having a hard time right now, but I can't leave things the way they were between us when I was here a few days ago. What I said about living here still stands. I can't do that, but I'll still come over to see you and Maisie as I always have, stay over if that's OK with you? Nothing's changed. I want to spend as much time as I can with you both. There's a lot of years I need to make up for, if you'll let me.' There was a short silence. 'How are you feeling?'

'Like an overemotional idiot.'

They both stood. He came to her, kissed her on the forehead. Feeling another wave of emotion building, Hanson turned and headed for the door.

TWENTY-TWO

Head down, shoulders hunched, Archie Fenton hurried through early-morning freezing fog. He knew the police were looking for him so he'd kept away from this whole area. He'd managed to persuade one or two people he knew to let him kip on their sofas for a few nights but he'd run out of acquaintances and had no friends. Last night had been bloody grim. He hadn't gone to a shelter, fearing that his whereabouts might be reported to the police. He'd huddled on some wasteland next to a fire but when that burned low and a couple of dodgy geezers turned up, he'd left and gone to a local church place for the rest of the night. It was either that or freeze to death. Chucking-out time was seven o'clock that morning. On his uppers as he was, he managed a thin smile. Once he had what he'd come back here for, things would be safer for him.

With quick glances to right and left he veered off the pavement and followed the path up to the house. He took his key from his pocket and pushed it into the lock, his hand so cold he couldn't turn it. Sending quick looks over his shoulders he tried again, then again. It didn't budge. Realisation hit him. That bastard of a landlord had changed the lock.

Pulling out the key, he hurried along the narrow alley between the two houses to the back door and tried the key again. Same story. He stood, arms hanging at his sides, staring at the ground floor windows. All locked tight. Going to one of them, he cupped his hands either side of his face and looked inside. It was just as he'd left it. He went to the door and listened. Nothing. Chill sweat broke out onto his head, swept over his neck. He couldn't stick another night outside but there was a more important reason to get inside. If he didn't, if he couldn't collect the laptop, if the police got hold of it, he'd have more trouble than he'd ever had. His eyes scoured hard-as-iron earth and weeds. A few quick steps and he was back at the door, a brick in his hand. He hefted it, gave the small glass pane next to the door handle a tentative tap.

It sounded like a whip-crack in the sleeping street. The glass stayed intact. He let the brick fall from his hand, backed away until he made contact with next-door's wall. He slid down it, his hands clasping his head and stared at the brick lying among weeds. For all he knew, the landlord could have wired up some kind of alarm inside this rattrap. It could bring the police here any minute.

Light-headed now, he got up, hurried down the alley and back to the road. There was nobody about at this hour. He had to have money. He had big expectations of what was on the laptop he'd left inside that house but he had to get his hands on a few quid right now. There was one person he could put pressure on, but did he dare show his face there? He rummaged in his pockets. The few coins he found were proof if he needed any that his life had hit the buffers.

He started walking. If the police found what was inside that dump of a house, who knows what they might get from it? Ten years ago, he'd seen plenty of goings on at Marlow Gardens, had seen that posh car leave, and then he'd gone up to the first floor, seen Harrington's apartment door slightly open. He'd gone inside, had wanted to vomit but had the sense to get control and help himself. Not that any of it had done him much good back then, once the police got involved. Pulling up his collar, he trudged on. Now the law had given him a second chance. He was about to collect.

The young woman from the agency tapped on the office door, opened it and leant inside. 'Coffee, Mr Dobbs?'

He looked up, giving her a wide smile. 'Thank you, Juanita. Very kind.'

She withdrew, closed the door and headed across the reception area to make it. Five minutes later, she was back, tapping the door, opening it. The white smile was back. 'Mr Dobbs, sorry to disturb, but a . . . gentleman has just arrived and he wants to see you.'

Dobbs frowned. 'Who is he? What's his name?'

'He wouldn't say.' She waited. 'What shall I tell him?'

Dobbs came around the desk, hands smoothing his hair. 'Leave it to me. I'll sort it out.'

He followed her out of his office into the main reception and stopped dead, his eyes on the unkempt figure. 'Juanita, how about you take your lunch break?'

She frowned at him. 'Lunch? It's only half eleven and—'

'*Now.*'

She fetched her coat and bag, gave Dobbs a look, the man a wide berth and headed to the door and out. Dobbs watched her disappear from view, put the closed sign on the door then turned, his face reddening. 'What the hell are *you* doing here.' He stopped, his mouth turning downwards. 'You look like a bloody tramp and you smell as bad.'

'I've got more important worries than that,' said Fenton. 'I need money.'

'So?'

'So, you've got plenty and I want some of it. Just to tide me over, like.'

Dobbs stared at him, his eyes narrowing. 'You're in trouble.'

'Yeah. The landlord's changed the locks on my place and some of my things are still inside the house . . .'

'That's your problem. I don't give a damn.'

'You should because I know all about you and if I don't get hold of a few quid today, you'll be in worse trouble than I am.' He glanced around the spacious premises. 'Doing well, are we?'

Dobbs' eyes narrowed. 'You listen to me. I don't know you anymore and that's how it's going to stay. If you've got some misguided idea that I owe you anything because you used to work here, you've got it all wrong.'

Fenton walked slowly away from him and sat on the receptionist's chair, looking up at him. 'That the way you see it? You listen to me, sunshine. I need money. I need somewhere to be for a few nights so I won't freeze to bloody death and you owe me.'

Dobbs stared at him, the area around his mouth turning white. 'Don't you threaten me,' he whispered. 'That would be the biggest mistake you'll ever make.'

'Look at it this way,' said Fenton. 'I'm an old colleague who's having a cash flow problem and you're giving me a temporary helping hand.' He sauntered across the office to look out of the window. 'Looks like your girl is on her way back.' He turned. 'Your type, is she?' Dobbs' eyes narrowed. He said nothing.

'What's it to be, then? A bit of money up front to tide me over?' His eyes moved over photographs on a clear Perspex display board. He tapped one of them. 'And maybe you can find me a bed for a night or two? Something "well-appointed"?'

'Get out,' hissed Dobbs. 'I don't owe you a damn thing.'

Fenton shook his head, tut-tutted. 'Leonard, you have got a short memory. You and me share knowledge. If the police pick me up, I'll tell them what we both know.'

'. . . Wait here.'

Dobbs turned on his heel and headed for his office. The door opened and the receptionist came inside. She frowned at Fenton. 'Is Mr Dobbs attending to you?'

'I would say so and thanks for asking.'

Dobbs reappeared, an envelope held close to his side. 'OK, sir. Thanks for coming in to report problems with your heating. I'll get onto it as soon as you've left.' Pressing the envelope into Fenton's hand, he gripped his arm and propelled him to the door, lowering his voice. 'Don't show your face here again, ever, you hear me?'

'I'll ring you.'

The door closed on Fenton. He walked away, feeling Dobbs' eyes following him. At the corner, out of sight, he tore open the envelope. Ten new-looking twenty-pound notes, plus a key. He read the label attached to it. It was a place a stone's throw away. He shoved the envelope into his pocket and glanced across the road at Marlow Gardens Apartments. His face changed. If that was the last place on earth, he'd rather sleep rough. He looked away from it and headed in the direction of the address on the key Dobbs had given him. He hadn't got much to lose but Dobbs was a different kettle of fish altogether. In his case, there was a hell of a lot he wanted to hang onto. Aware of voices nearby, the convivial clink of glass on glass, he glanced inside the pub he was passing and stopped. He was still chilled but now he had money. Time for a small one. A little stiffener.

Watts nodded into UCU's phone, making brief notes. 'What time was this? Right. Leave it with us.' He looked up as Corrigan came through the door. 'Yeah, we do have an interest in him. Thanks for letting us know.' He put down the phone. 'That was police local to Fenton's place. A neighbour coming home from his night shift reported hearing noises round the back early this morning and somebody legging it who he thinks was Fenton.'

'Have the local cops attended?' asked Corrigan.

'No.'

'I'll get over there. Take a look.'

Watts pecked out details of the call on the desktop, a pointless exercise as far as he was concerned but if he didn't log it he'd have Admin on his back. 'I'll come as well. We'll park-'n'-walk because Fenton might turn up and spot us. When we do get hold of him, I want to know where he's been this last week-plus and why he hopped it. As if we can't guess. I've got a call to make before we leave.'

Leaving Watts' vehicle in a side road, they walked to Fenton's house. Watts pounded the door with his fist. It was opened by a smart-looking man of about his own age. The landlord. 'Thanks for coming, Mr Groves.'

'It's the least I could do, detective inspector. When I got your call, I was a little surprised. I hadn't expected the police to be interested, particularly somebody of rank and—' his eyes went to Corrigan – 'two of you. I'm very impressed—'

'Where's Fenton?' The landlord's face hardened. 'I haven't seen him for days but take my word, it was him who tried to get in here early this morning. He does nothing but complain and when I—'

'Why didn't he let himself in?'

'When I came here a couple of days ago, all his things were gone. It was obvious he'd done a flit to avoid paying his rent. He owes me two months as it is, so I had the locks changed.'

Gesturing at them to follow, he went along the hall and into the room Watts and Corrigan had been inside a while ago. It was freezing. Watts walked to a scattering of burger cartons, nudging one or two with his toe.

'That's all he left,' said Groves.

'Leave us to it. We'll shut the front door when we've finished.'

Groves looked at him then at Corrigan. 'I think it might be best if I stayed. I'm planning to pursue Fenton for unpaid rent.' He took a phone from his pocket. 'I'd like to take a few pictures to record the decoration in progress, plus the poor state Fenton left the place in.'

Corrigan took his arm and steered him towards the door and out to the hall. 'Sure you do, sir, but right now it's best if you wait in your vehicle and we do our job real quick, so you can have the place to yourself. How's that suit you?'

Watts heard Groves' querulous voice, followed by the sound of the front door closing. He grinned as Corrigan returned. 'I like what you call your "down-home" style. I wish I had one.' He looked around the room. 'Groves never busted a gut in the furnishing and décor department, did he?'

'Hardly liveable, if you ask me,' said Corrigan, surveying the almost empty room. 'I'll check the upper floor.' He headed for the stairs and was back within a minute. 'One bed up there and that's it. The other bedroom is empty and the bathroom is Staph Central.'

Watts pulled a face. 'Fenton was no oil painting ten years ago but it looks like he's a right dirty bastard now.' He walked slowly around the room, eyes fixed on the bare boards. 'He was taking a risk coming back here. For all he knew we could've had it staked out.'

'You said the neighbour reported hearing sounds that Fenton was trying to break in?'

Watts nodded, eyes still fixed on the floor. 'Yeah. Looks like he had second thoughts and hopped it. What I want to know is why he took the risk of coming here and trying to get inside.'

Corrigan looked around. 'This place is virtually empty of furniture so what was the payoff that was worth the risk?'

'Time to get methodical, Corrigan.'

Watts stood with his back to one of the long walls, stepped forward and took several regular paces across the room, his footfalls echoing round the room. On his third turn, halfway across, the sound of the footfalls changed. He stopped, tapping his foot several times. 'What do you think?'

'Sounds hollow.' Corrigan came and looked down, pointing. 'See the edge of that floorboard, there? It's ragged.' He walked to the paint tins and decorating tools they'd seen before, reaching for one of the tools there and brought it back to where Watts was standing. He crouched and applied the tool to the floorboard's edge. A couple of back and forth movements and it rose clear of the one next to it. Corrigan gave it a sharp tug. It came up with hardly any resistance. Taking a Maglite from his inside pocket, he switched it on and aimed the small, powerful beam inside the small void. 'Whatever it is has to be down here.' Pulling up another floorboard he reached down and brought out a large package wrapped in a piece of paint-spattered cloth. Watts went onto his haunches as Corrigan removed it, revealing a laptop.

Watts took it from him. 'This has to be what Fenton came back for. My guess is, it's full of his Naughty Nuns and Bouncy Housewives.' He gave the outside a quick examination. 'He's had this for a while. It's an old model. Maybe he was writing his memoirs.' He opened it. 'Look, there's something on the keyboard.' Watts watched Corrigan take the small blister pack of oval yellow tablets and walk to the window with it. 'What do you think, Corrigan? Any ideas?'

After a short pause, Corrigan nodded. 'Yep. It's imprinted with a C and 2½. It's Cialis.'

'Who's See-Alice when she's at home?'

'It's a brand name for Tadalafil.' He looked up at Watts who was waiting for more. 'It's for erectile dysfunction.'

'Never had you in that category, Corrigan.'

Walking back to him, Corrigan grinned, unfazed. 'I recognize it from some narcotics training I did back home with the FBI. This one has a nickname: "the weekend pill".'

'Oh-ah?'

'The same effect as Viagra but it lasts thirty-six hours.'

'Blimey, that would be some party.' His eyes moved to the gap in the floor. 'Anything else under there?'

Handing Watts the tablets, Corrigan lowered his head to the narrow opening in the floor and applied the Maglite again. 'Nope. Can't see anything.'

Watts looked around. 'The cold in here's getting to me. Time we went.' He raised the laptop. 'And this is going straight to Forensics, along with Fenton's happy pills.'

TWENTY-THREE

Hanson was staring out of the window. She was on her light timetable for the remainder of the week, thanks to the VC, although she was starting to suspect that a return to full days was what she needed. She watched student stragglers walking across the campus then glanced at her desk calendar. Friday. By next Monday everything would be back to . . . normal. What had she been thinking that evening when she had phoned David Lockman for the first time? She bowed her head, pushing her fingers through her hair. She'd achieved nothing. *Except trashing my career, probably.*

'Kate? . . . *Kate?*'

She looked up. Crystal was standing in the doorway of the adjoining room. 'Sorry, Crystal. I was miles away.' She looked away from the sympathy on her young assistant's face.

'Lieutenant Corrigan just rang. He'll be here in about ten minutes.'

'Thank you.'

Hanson waited for Crystal to return to her room then sat back, closed her eyes and breathed steadily, in and out. Opening her eyes, she let her gaze drift over familiar features and objects of the room, accepting them . . . resisting negative associations . . .

She came upright. *For God's sake! If I carry on with that, I'll go mad.* Dragging the Harrington file from her briefcase, she dropped it onto the desk where it landed with a muffled thump. Seeing it lying there brought the lump back to her throat. *Snap out of it.* She opened it at the first page and did the same with her notebook. Within two minutes she was immersed in the case, cross-referencing facts against her own notes, highlighting the latter in red. A familiar knock at the door and she looked up. Corrigan's face appeared around the door.

'You busy, Red?'

'Yes and no.'

He came into the room. 'How about we make the next few minutes a "no"?'

She grinned. 'Go on, then. What are you up to?'

He came and sat on the edge of her desk, looking down at her. 'Saying hi to you.'

'Hi. Next?'

'I've come bearing news.'

'Tell me and make it the good kind.'

'We think we know where Archie Fenton is. Or was, a day or so ago.' He told her about Fenton's attempt to get inside his rented house, the visit with Watts earlier that morning and the finding of Fenton's laptop.

She stared up at him. 'Any ideas as to what's on it?'

'That's a can't-say, right now. We don't have a password so Forensics have it but they're under pressure so it's waiting in line to be examined.' He leant towards her, one eyebrow raised. 'Speaking of examining . . .'

'Stop that and tell me what you know about it.'

'If Fenton bought or stole it when it was pretty new, we're hoping it's gonna show his full "My Life Interest in Porn" story and possibly a whole lot of other stuff that might be of interest to our case.'

'Are you thinking it might hold a connection to Della Harrington's murder?'

'All's possible,' he said.

'But how could it be relevant to her murder? I know Watts is dragging his feet, but we accept that it wasn't a sexual homicide.'

'Yep, but it's potential information. There's more.' She waited. 'When Watts opened it, guess what was between the screen and the keys?' She waited. 'Cialis tabs.'

She stared up at him. 'You know what that means, Corrigan. Fenton is porn-addicted and, like all addicts, he's built up a tolerance . . . he needs those tabs to heighten the pornographic experience.'

He grinned down at her. 'Atta-girl.'

She frowned. 'I hope I'm not wrong about the motivation behind the Harrington murder.' She looked up at him. 'What if I am? What if it was about sex?'

He leant closer, traced his finger slowly down her forehead, her nose to her mouth. 'Come on, Red. What's with the self-doubt? So, you had a row with the chief. You're still on this case with us.' He stood. 'I better go. We'll let you know as soon as we get the forensics report on the laptop.'

She watched him go and the door slowly close on him. Sighing, rotating her shoulders, she went back to what she had been doing. An hour later all she had were two persistent questions. One: Steffan Coultard described the operatic rehearsal which was arranged for the evening of the murder as an important one. So why hadn't Della showered and changed clothes after her run earlier that day, in anticipation of his arrival? Two: why had Karen Forster's name held some kind of resonance for David Lockman? She shook her head. He hadn't been able to explain it so it was unlikely she could come up with an answer. She closed the notebook and pushed it away. 'I'm chasing shadows. I need to get out. Get away.' She fetched her coat. There was only an hour before Julian arrived for a tutorial.

'I'm going out, Crystal. I won't be long.'

Reaching the massive hospital, a relatively new feature on the local landscape, she parked, hurried inside and was immediately overcome by the spectacle of its size, its high ceiling. A nearby voice said, 'May I help you?' She turned to a casually dressed man, the badge on his sweater indicating that he was a visitor guide.

'I'm here to see a patient named Steffan Coultard.' He led her to a screen where he tapped in the name. 'He's in a room on the first floor. Are you a relative?'

Hanson berated herself for failing to anticipate this potential difficulty. 'No . . . I work at police headquarters.'

'Do you have identification?'

She pictured it the last time she'd seen it on the chief's desk. 'No. I don't.'

He gave her a sympathetic look. 'I doubt you'll be allowed in to see the patient without it.'

She spoke quickly. 'Staff caring for Mr Coultard will have notes detailing the reason he was brought in here. Those notes include two names: Detective Inspector Bernard Watts and Lieutenant Joseph Corrigan. They're the officers I work with.'

The guide gave her a steady look. 'Wait here.'

He went to a nearby phone and spoke into it, giving Hanson several glances. He hung up. 'Take the lift to the first floor. A nurse will be waiting for you.'

Hanson took one of the lifts. Stepping out she saw a nurse come towards her. 'I'm here to see Steffan Coultard. How is he?' she asked as they walked towards Coultard's room.

'He's still very poorly. He lost a lot of blood.' He opened the door and Hanson went inside. 'Don't tire him. I'll be back in five minutes to show you out.'

Hanson went inside the low-lit room, the only sound the steady bleep of some kind of monitor. She looked at Coultard's face. It was waxen, deathly pale. Below it, his neck was heavily bandaged. 'Mr Coultard?' He stirred. His eyes fluttered and opened. 'Kate Hanson here. Remember me?' She thought she saw a hint of recognition. 'Mr Coultard, I'm only allowed five minutes with you so I need to ask you just two questions.' No response. If he was able to comprehend what she said, he probably had no voice with which to reply. Something else she'd failed to factor in to this visit. 'Do you know why Della wasn't ready to go with you to rehearsal that evening?' His eyes opened. He frowned. She took it as a possible no. Her next question was more challenging. 'Mr Coultard? Why did you do this to yourself?' His eyes opened again and fixed on hers for a couple of seconds then drifted away.

The door opened and the nurse came inside. 'Your five minutes is up.'

Hanson stepped away from the bed. 'As far as you're aware, has Mr Coultard indicated a reason for doing what he did?'

'He was in no condition to do that. Our job right now is attending to his physical needs. We haven't asked any questions.' He indicated the door. 'Please.'

Hanson came into her room and threw her handbag across it. She was angry at herself for thinking that a man with a serious throat injury would be able to tell her anything and dispirited because she'd felt like an outsider with no authority or role when asked for identification. They still didn't know if what Coultard had done was an act of hopelessness or one borne of guilt for murdering Della Harrington. Closing down the line of thinking, she turned at a knock on her door as it opened.

'Hi, Kate.' It was Julian, here for his tutorial.

'Hi,' she said. 'Have a seat while I get my act together.' She opened a desk drawer, took out his student file and read the last page. 'How's your data-gathering progressing on the psychological impact of property crime?'

'I'm still searching records for more cases but I'm already seeing some interesting victim responses, ranging from, "that's life these days", to references to an inability to leave the house. As soon as it's finished and analysed, I'll let you have it.'

'I'll look forward to it.'

Removing notes and books from his bag, he looked up at her. 'One of the names I saw just before I left got my attention because I'd heard Watts and Corrigan mention it: Andrea Jones.'

Hanson's head came up. 'Della Harrington's sister?'

'The very same.'

'In what context, exactly?'

'Her house was broken into.'

Hanson stared at him. 'Do you have a date?' He looked through a list of details. 'Here it is. Property entered between the hours of eight and ten p.m. on the 8th November, 2006.'

An hour later, Hanson was absorbing the sitting room's stylish mix of furnishings, her eyes on Andrea Jones sitting across from her. 'I'm hardly likely to forget the break-in,' said Jones. 'Not because it scared me, but because it was the day before my sister was murdered. I reported it to the local police. They came straight away, dusted for fingerprints but they weren't hopeful of finding who did it. They came again, a week later and advised me on how to improve security here, which I did and that was the end of it.'

'Had anything similar happened before or since?'

'No.'

'Was much taken?' asked Hanson.

'No, although it was obvious whoever got in here did a thorough job of searching the house.'

'It was left in a mess?'

Jones shook her head. 'I'd been home about half an hour before I noticed anything amiss. I went upstairs and that's when I noticed one or two things slightly out of place. One of my wardrobe doors was slightly open, the clothes on hangers had been pushed to one side. Like Della, I like order. I wouldn't have left them like that. That's when I called the police.'

'Tell me exactly what was stolen,' said Hanson.

'Not much, given that whoever did it searched the whole place.' She itemized the items on her fingers. 'A carriage clock, a pearl necklace, not real by the way, and about thirty pounds which I kept in a jar in my kitchen. That's it.'

'Anything electrical or electronic?'

Jones shook her head. 'No. The television wasn't taken. I've never had a computer. I tend to do everything on my phone.'

Hanson's spirits dipped. When she'd learned of the burglary from Julian and its proximity to the Harrington murder, she'd hoped it might provide a lead. 'Does the name Romily Petersen mean anything to you?'

Jones frowned. 'No. Who is she?'

'She was a friend of your sister's.'

'Oh.' She looked up at Hanson. 'Are you making any progress on my sister's case?' It was a question often asked by relatives and friends of a victim. One that Hanson struggled with if there was little to report.

'We're working hard on it. Doing all we can.' Seeing the downhearted expression on Jones' face, Hanson leant forward, covered Jones' hand with her own. She pressed it lightly. 'We won't stop. I promise.'

TWENTY-FOUR

Watts tapped the door of Hanson's room later that afternoon, opened it and looked inside. 'Alright, doc?' She looked up from her desk. 'Fine.'

'How's it going?'

'Just getting organized for Monday when I'm back to my full timetable. Want some coffee?'

'Thanks, no. I've come to take you out. Get yourself organized. We're going to see how the search of Coultard's place is progressing.' Grabbing her coat, she followed him out of her room, down the stairs and out to the Range Rover.

Thirty minutes later, they got out into searing cold and the noise from a small digger scraping topsoil from Coultard's front garden, the whole of it screened from view. Hanson glanced at one or two people standing on the other side of the road, arms folded, their faces solemn. 'Are there neighbour problems?'

'We've talked to them. They're just fed up of looking out at the thick trees around Coultard's house. They've asked us to take them down. I've told them we can't. Come and have a look at the rear garden.'

They walked along the side of the house, Hanson picking up voices. Coming into the garden she could see that the digger had already done its work here. Watts walked over to one of the forensic officers, took some printouts from him and brought them back to Hanson. 'Have a look at these.' He pointed to several heavily shaded areas. 'See? They're having to check all of these dark areas.' He pointed to a different area. 'This lot here has been done. Turned out to be a load of buried bricks, old water pipes and remains of footings.' He pointed across Coultard's garden to the properties either side. 'These houses were built in the seventies on land previously occupied by an old manor house and outbuildings. A lot of what they're finding are remains of that. Not the sort we were hoping for.'

Hanson's attention had been drawn to one area of activity

towards the far end of the garden. She pointed. 'What's going on there?'

'Not a lot so far.'

She looked up at him. 'Have you questioned Coultard's neighbours about his life here?'

'Corrigan has. The people living either side, and in the houses facing have all said the same: Coultard kept himself to himself. They hardly know him. One couple living opposite have told us that they've occasionally seen him with young women during the time he's lived here. As far as they're concerned, they've never seen anybody who looked like she might be his wife.'

Hanson counted the officers working here, added those she had seen when they arrived, plus the digger and its operator. 'This is costing,' she said.

'You're right and you can imagine how thrilled the chief is, but it has to be done.' A shout drifted over to them from the end of the garden. 'Come on.'

They walked the extensive lawn to the back fence of the property. 'Got something?' Watts asked.

An officer in coveralls looked up at them from an area of garden showing signs of deep excavation. 'Give us a few minutes.'

Watts nodded, turned and looked back at the large house. 'A big place for a single bloke,' he said.

'Coultard wanted to be private. Not overlooked.'

'And not being overlooked, who knows what he was up to that we don't yet know about.'

'DI Watts?'

He turned to an officer pointing at the excavation, two more officers resting on shovels, their breath coming in clouds. One of them spoke. 'Nothing. Just more bricks.'

Watts waved his large hand and they walked back the way they'd come and got into his vehicle.

'What now?' asked Hanson.

'I'll drop you off and get back to headquarters.' His phone buzzed. He dug in his pocket. 'I'm waiting for a call from Forensics about Fenton's laptop.' He lifted his phone, listened. 'On my way,' he said, starting the vehicle. 'You're coming with me, doc.'

'I can't.'

'Yes, you can. The chief's out for the day.'

On arrival at headquarters, they went directly to the forensic lab where Corrigan was waiting. 'What do you know?' asked Watts.

'There's plenty on Fenton's laptop, mostly photographs.'

They looked up to see a white-coated officer walking through the large lab towards them. 'Looks like we're in business,' said Corrigan. The officer laid an inch-thick stack of photographs on the table in front of them. 'There's more being processed. There are indications of a couple of hefty documents having been saved then deleted, one of several thousand words but that's all I can tell you right now.' He left them to it. Corrigan and Watts spread the photographs on the large lab table. They almost covered it. Hanson moved along, letting her eyes drift over them, her colleagues doing the same. Most of the shots were of young women naked and in various poses.

She broke the silence. 'This is bad.'

'I'll tell you something else,' said Watts. He pointed at specific prints. 'See that one? And that? And that one over there? I recognize them. They're the three young women Dobbs was messing around with in exchange for them keeping a roof over their heads.' He moved the photographs around. 'See that? Hanson looked to where he was pointing to one of a young female face just visible over the shoulder of a male, his back to the camera, his pale hair pristine. 'Dawn Wilson and guess who's with him.'

'Leonard Dobbs,' she said.

'All these are dated from the last decade or so. We've got him, doc.'

'Dobbs and Fenton had to be together on this,' said Hanson. She reached for another of the photographs. 'This one concerns me. The female in it looks unconscious. Or worse.'

Corrigan took it from her. 'This was downloaded. Fenton's been into porn for years so he knows his way around, including the dark web. We find him and we've got a prime witness to what he and Dobbs were up to, plus Dobbs' possible role in the Harrington murder.'

'We've had no sightings of Fenton in the last twenty-four hours since he tried to break into his old flat,' said Watts. 'But we know where Dobbs is.' He reached for a nearby phone, dialled and waited. 'Leonard Dobbs?' He gazed at Hanson and Corrigan and nodded. 'That's right. We want to talk to you again.' He listened some more. 'Yeah, yeah, you're busy. So are we. Bring your lawyer with you. Now.' He replaced the phone. 'He's on his way, sounding like he's not got a care in the world. We know different.'

Hanson was preoccupied with what the forensic officer had told them earlier about the traces left on the laptop: two documents, hefty, several thousand words. 'Is Archie Fenton somebody you think would be into a lot of word processing?'

Watts looked at her. 'Fenton's somebody who's got a passing acquaintance with the alphabet. I can see your train of thought. I'm expecting it's stuff he downloaded.'

'Given your description of him, I doubt Fenton's much of a reader.' Seeing one of the officers pull on his coat and head towards the door, she raised her hand to him. '*Wait.*' She turned to her colleagues. 'I'll get a lift back to the university, then go over to Dobbs' business premises.'

'For?' asked Watts.

'I won't know till I get there.'

Hanson pushed open the door of the letting agency and went inside. A young woman looked up from some speedy word processing. 'Can I help you?'

'My name is Kate Hanson and I'm part of a current police investigation in this area.'

'Sorry, if it's Mr Dobbs you want to talk to, you've missed him. He left half an hour ago. Hanson placed a photograph next to her on the desk. 'I'd like you to take a look at this man.' She watched as the woman did so. 'Have you seen him?'

'. . . Yes.'

'You're sure?'

'He looked older, scruffier, but I'm sure it's him.'

'When and where did you see him?' asked Hanson.

'He was in here a couple of days ago.'

'Tell me all you remember about him.'

The young woman wrinkled her nose. 'I thought he was a homeless person. I couldn't believe it when Mr Dobbs came and spoke to him. He obviously knew him.' She shuddered. 'I can tell you, as soon as he left I sprayed the place with this.' She held up a small perfume bottle.

'Do you have any idea why he came here?'

'I can make a guess.' She leant on her forearms. 'Mr Dobbs left him here and went into his office. When he came out he had an envelope in his hand, sort of down by his side.' She pointed to the photograph. 'He gave *him* the envelope. If you ask me, there was money in it. There was something else.' Hanson watched as the young woman got up from the desk and walked to a glass screen on which were mounted details of properties for rent. She pointed to a space. 'There was a studio apartment right there. Last week, Mr Dobbs told me that it had been unlet for weeks. He told me to push it to anybody who came in looking for a small place. Next thing I know, after that man came in, he's telling me to take the details down.'

'Do you still have them?'

The woman opened a drawer in her desk, took them out and handed them to Hanson. 'I can see why he couldn't shift it. Who'd want to live in one room like that? Easy to keep clean, though. Not that that would bother him, the one you're looking for, if you get my drift.'

'I need to take these details with me,' said Hanson.

She shrugged. 'Makes no difference to me. I'm temporary. I've got a different job starting Monday which suits me. It's dead boring here.'

Hanson left Dobbs' premises and in ten minutes she had located the address. It looked like a hasty conversion of one-time factory premises. She went inside. The apartment she wanted was on the ground floor. She went to it, knocked and waited, rock music thump and a baby's fretting drifting down from an upper floor. Getting no response, she knocked again. 'Mr Fenton?' She banged the door with her fist. 'Mr Fenton, open the door or I start talking to you through it, which your neighbours might find very interesting.'

Silence, followed by the sound of a safety chain being put on. The door opened a centimetre and a bloodshot eye regarded her through the narrow space. 'Whoever you are, clear off.'

'Let me in.' She raised her phone. 'Let me in *now*, or I ring the police.' The door banged shut. She stared at it, heard the safety chain being removed. It opened. She pushed it wider, walked inside. The place was minimally furnished and not overly warm but it didn't smell too bad. She glanced at Fenton. His hair looked damp. Obviously, he was taking advantage of the apartment's amenities. He was now fashioning a roll-up, not looking at her. 'Whatever you're after, I don't want it and whatever you think I've got, you're wrong. Shut the door on your way out.'

'Not until you tell me about photographs you took of young women at Marlow Gardens.' He stopped what he was doing, looked up at her. 'I don't know what you're on about.' Now, she saw the cut just below his right eye, the surrounding skin bruised, his lower lip split. 'What happened to your face?'

'Nothing that's anybody else's business.' He lit the roll-up and drew on it. She took out her phone and tapped UCU's number. Julian answered. 'Hi,' she said. 'Are they busy?'

'Yes, they're upstairs with Leonard Dobbs.'

'Thanks, Julian.'

She cut the call. 'Mr Fenton, if you're in fear of someone . . .'

'What gives you that idea?'

'The state of your face, for a start. You're living here courtesy of Leonard Dobbs,' she said. He tensed, not looking at her. 'Dobbs is with the police.'

'Oh, yeah? What's that to me?'

'I thought it might make you feel safer, knowing he isn't close by. How did you persuade him to give you this place? And money?' Fenton said nothing. 'You're playing a dangerous game, Mr Fenton. My advice is that you go voluntarily to police headquarters.'

'Oh, yeah? Thanks for that. Now feel free to fuck off.'

'I think you know something about Della Harrington's murder.'

'Don't know what you're on about.'

She gazed at him. 'You were in that building on the day she was killed.'

'Not all of it, and so what? I worked there.'

'You were there from three o'clock, or that's what you told my colleagues.' She walked towards him. 'What have you got on Leonard Dobbs? What is it you know about him?' She waited. 'Come on, Mr Fenton. Of all the people who were at that building on that day, *you* probably knew most about the people living there and those visiting, such as Leonard Dobbs, Steffan Coultard, Wayne Chatterton.' Hearing the last name, his face darkened. She nodded. 'Oh, yes. Mr Chatterton has told us about your interest in females' clothing.'

Fenton's face filled with rage. 'If you believe Chatterton, you and the police are bigger fools than I thought. Instead of harassing me, you should be looking at that Coultard.'

'Why?'

'Because he's dodgy. Always hanging about, creeping around. He had a thing for that Harrington woman.' He came closer. 'I was there the day he found her, remember? In case you and your police cronies have forgot, he was inside her apartment before I got there. When he come out of it, he looked the same as when he went in. When I went in there, I wanted to puke. You'd do well to look at him, before you start throwing accusations at me. Now get out!'

'Not until you tell me what you know about Della Harrington. Or what you think you know.' He said nothing, his face still angry. She went to the window and looked out. From here she could see a corner of the Marlow Gardens Apartment building. Turning to face Fenton she said, 'Or have I got it wrong in thinking of you as an informant . . .'

'Yes, you have.'

'When in fact you had a central role in Harrington's death?'

His face drained. He went to the door, opened it. '*Out.* I've got nothing to say to you or anybody else about her.' Hanson walked past him and through the door. It banged shut on her.

She left the building, her head filled with thoughts about the case, one of them of Fenton as killer. She had just spent several minutes with him. She had said things to him which had made him surly, angry even. In that small space she had turned her back on him. Angry as she knew he was, she hadn't felt fearful. She walked on, head down. Her instinct was telling her that whoever killed Della Harrington had been angry, raging. Having killed her, he'd switched his attention to displaying her and searching the apartment. Which suggested that his anger had quickly evaporated. The question was, why, if Della Harrington induced such anger, such rage, was he able to get control of himself so quickly? Was it because he knew she was silenced?

She thought of one or two professionals she'd known over the years who believed they'd built up trust with violent individuals, only to pay for that belief with their lives. Confident as she had felt inside that apartment, she wasn't about to rule out Fenton, or any of the other persons of interest who had surfaced during this investigation. She slowed to a stop. She'd asked Watts about Fenton's language abilities. Having met him, she was struggling with the idea that he had either the ability to create large documents on his laptop or the motivation to acquire any. She frowned. Maybe that raised questions about the laptop itself.

TWENTY-FIVE

I n an upstairs interview room at headquarters, Watts and Corrigan were waiting, their eyes on Dobbs. Watts pointed at features of a photograph on the table in front of him. 'That is *you*. *That* is a teenager named Dawn Wilson who's been missing for several years.'

Dobbs' lawyer gave a vehement headshake. 'You can't make accusations against my client on the basis of a partial rear view of a male's head.' She reached for the photograph, her eyes moving slowly over it. 'There are no distinguishing features on this male's back. You need more than this.'

'This photo speaks for itself.'

'Actually, it doesn't,' she snapped.

'It's fake!' shouted Dobbs, glaring at both officers. 'Photoshopped. I never heard of a Dawn Wilson. I know what you're doing. You're setting me up.'

'Keep your voice down,' said Watts. 'You don't know when to give up, do you? You're already on bail, charged with coercing young females into sex in exchange for payment of their rent. We're about to add another: coercion of a young woman to participate in the production of pornographic images.'

Dobbs looked at the ceiling. 'And I'm telling you, whoever that is in the photograph, it isn't me.'

Watts eyed him. 'The hair looks just like yours. Same colour. Same style.' He turned to Dobbs' lawyer. 'We think your client poses a risk to several young females, more specifically to those whose identity we know about.'

She closed her file. 'If you're planning to keep him here, think again. We've already agreed bail restrictions, that photograph changes nothing and my client is leaving with me.'

She stood and Dobbs did the same. As they reached the door, he turned, sending Watts and Corrigan a smirk.

Fenton gazed out of his window and across to Marlow Gardens. Scarcely three o'clock but almost dark. Just like it was that day.

He turned his attention to people hurrying past not far from his window. Well-dressed, most of them. Some with briefcases. His lips compressed as he watched them. Alright for some. They wouldn't look so smug if they had no work, no home. He was about to leave the window when one of the passers-by caught his eye. Dobbs. The cops must have let him go. Which was handy because the money he'd got from him wouldn't last for ever. He pulled out his phone, selected a number from a very short list, listened to it ring then cut the call. What if it was a set-up? What if the bastard had done some kind of deal with the police? He rubbed his whiskers. Dobbs might have told them about him asking for money. He frowned. It's what Dobbs owed him but the police wouldn't see it like that. They'd call it blackmail. He might end up inside. He tapped his phone again, listened as his call rang out. Immediately it was picked up, Fenton spoke. 'It's me. That first payment we talked about? I want it.' He listened, his face darkening. 'Don't you cop an attitude with me, mate. I could do you a lot of damage and you know it. I know what I saw that day and you're going to have to pay.' He listened as the voice flowed into his ear. 'Listen, mate, you've got a way with words but none of it means nothing to me. I'll be seeing you very soon about the money.' He cut the call.

Hanson's phone rang. She reached for it. It was Corrigan. 'Hi. How's things?'

She stared out at the frigid campus. 'Fine. How did it go with Dobbs?'

'He's still admitting nothing, despite the photograph. We had to let him go.' There was a brief silence between them. 'Tell me how you're really doing,' he asked.

'Like I said, I'm fine.' She imagined his face, guessing that he wasn't convinced.

'OK, I'll call you later,' he said.

She put down her phone, her eyes drifting over the Harrington case file and her own notes. Returning to her desk, she turned several pages of notes, eyes moving steadily over her own writing. She closed the small, black book. It was time for the task she'd decided on, earlier in the day. She stood, lifted her briefcase onto the desk and began to fill it with everything related to the Della

Harrington murder. When it was done, she stared down at all of the data tightly wedged inside it. She would give it to her colleagues next time she saw them. She knew now that she couldn't work unofficially with UCU. Since the scene with the chief, the last couple of days had shown her that she couldn't be on the outside of UCU yet still involved. She was an all or nothing kind of person. Not necessarily a good thing but that's how it was. She was out of UCU. This case was no longer hers. It belonged to her colleagues. Time to move on.

She turned to the desktop and began word processing a plan for a lecture the following week. It was one she'd given many times but she'd decided on a revamp. Her fingers flew over the keys. Hitting a final full stop, she sent the document to the printer, hearing it whir inside Crystal's room. Halfway to the door to fetch it, she stopped, turned and came back to the desk. Reaching for her briefcase she pulled it open, lifted out the case file and the black notebook. She sat, turning its pages. Within a few seconds she was looking at what she'd written of David Lockman's recall of Karen Forster's name during their meeting the other day. She gazed down at the few short words he had said at the time. Why would he remember Karen Forster? She shook her head. Strictly speaking, he hadn't. Her name had merely caught his attention. Had he heard it during the original investigation? It was possible that it had reminded him of someone entirely unconnected to the Harrington case. Hanson thought back to her and Watts' visit to the pleasant, heavily pregnant woman and the arrival home of her irritated husband. She closed her eyes. She needed to keep focused on the future and stop responding when-ever a thought about the case came into her head. If David Lockman was unable to say why Forster's name meant something to him, what chance did she have of identifying any relevance it might have? She took some deep breaths. Crystal was taking a few days' leave. The building was quiet. Hanson was relieved to be alone. She still couldn't trust herself to talk about what had happened at headquarters, if she was asked. And she would be asked. The groves of academe were a tinderbox of gossip. Chilled, she walked to the radiator, put her hand on it, felt its heat.

Returning to her desk, she sat, hands gripped together. She'd spent a sleepless night going over the scene at headquarters. Now she was thinking that maybe the chief had a point. She had chosen not to be bound by his rules but they were his and he ran headquarters. She put her hands over her face. She'd created one hell of a mess. And the worst part of it was that she hadn't achieved anything except make her colleagues' lives difficult. She'd spent twenty minutes with the VC earlier. He had listened as she told him exactly what had happened at headquarters and her resignation from UCU. Kindly as always, he'd commiserated, sounding upbeat. Although nothing had been said, she knew there would be repercussions from this change to her professional life. The VC had hinted of his regret that she would no longer have involvement in the real and current work of the force. She had got his oblique reference to the benefits her work with the police brought to her students and her department. She hadn't responded. She knew that her future work here would now increasingly rely on research projects she set up, when what she wanted was hands-on investigative work. Her thinking spun on. At worst, she could find another job. But that might have implications for Maisie's student place here, if she herself was working some distance away. An even more perturbing thought occurred to her: if she was working several miles from home, might Kevin try to encourage Maisie to live with him on the basis of convenience for Maisie's academic progress? *Stop. Get a hold of yourself.*

A quick application of a tissue to her eyes and she pushed her notebook back inside her briefcase. Now wasn't the time to think about the future. She had to deal with those parts of her life which had felt stable but were unravelling. She thought of Corrigan. They had barely begun. Despite her two colleagues wanting her to continue working with them, she wouldn't. 'What's wrong with me?' she whispered. She already knew the answer. She wanted whatever she wanted on her terms. Corrigan would attest to that.

She looked down at the case file on her desk, two words written on its cover in her own bold, black print. Not just words. A name: Della Harrington. She opened it. All the facts were here. She turned pages, halted by a red asterisk she'd added very early in the investigation, a reminder to ask Julian to do something. A loose end. One she could do something about right now. She reached for her phone, tapped his number.

'Hello, Kate.'

He sounded subdued. She guessed he was at headquarters, in which case he would know what had happened. 'I need you to do something for me, Julian.' She waited, imagining him grabbing something to write with.

'Fire away,' he said.

'There was a request in one of the original investigation files for some phone call searches but no indication that they were carried out.'

'I remember. You want me to action them?'

'Please.'

'Cool. I've never done that kind of search. Remind me of the names.'

'Leonard Dobbs, Archie Fenton, David Lockman and Steffan Coultard.' She listened to the rattle of computer keys. She glanced at her watch. He was back. 'All done, Kate. I've requested CSP searches which means a full examination of the records of all the communication service providers. I'll let you know what I get. Not sure, but it could take a while . . . Where are you?'

'At the university. Let me have the results in a text and I'll add them to the file data.'

'Will do.'

She ended the call and went back to the file. Halfway through, she came across a thick envelope. She opened it, let the crime scene photographs spill onto the desk, seeing yet again how truly awful Della Harrington's death had been, saw the various elements that contributed to it: the savage blow to her head, the evidence of post-mortem piquerism on each arm, the shocking way she'd been left for crime workers to stare at, record, measure and comment on. Della Harrington's killer was no sadist. Corrigan had now accepted it. Watts was still hanging onto it as a possibility, in the absence of an alternative explanation as to why Della Harrington had had to die.

She looked away to the window and the campus trees, some leafless, some hanging in there, in the midst of them a tall, dark fir. There had to be a different kind of meaning within that scene in Harrington's apartment. A different kind of killer. One who purposely set out to portray himself as sexually perverted. For what reason?

She went into Crystal's room, switched on the kettle then on to the window to look out at the campus. Even at this late stage of the year it looked – what had Maisie said? 'Totally awesome'. Maisie the mathematician, who didn't have a lot of time for lyricism. She was right. Hanson let her eyes roam over Chancellor's Court and on to the far section of the Aston Webb Building just visible. She loved it all. Which was just as well. She'd be spending most of her time here from now on. That is, if she stayed. She poured boiling water onto instant coffee granules and sat on the edge of Crystal's desk.

A voice drifted into the room. 'Kate? You around?'

'In here.'

Julian opened the door of Crystal's room and came inside. 'An officer on reception gave me this as I was leaving.' He put down the bulky parcel.

She looked at her name on it, followed by headquarters' address, crossed through. 'Thanks, Julian. Coffee?'

'No, I'm off to the computer lab, now. See you.'

Her office door closed on him and she went back to her desk, relieved that he'd made no reference to what had occurred at headquarters. She trusted Julian but she wasn't ready to talk to anybody. She checked the time. She'd been here two hours, hadn't achieved much of anything. 'Go home,' she told herself.

TWENTY-SIX

Charlie's car was on the drive when she arrived home. Hurrying up to the front door, she let herself in. 'Charlie?' He came into the hall and she went to him, put her arms around him.

'Hey. What's all this?'

She separated from him. 'It's OK. I'm just glad you're here.' They walked into the kitchen which was warm and smelled good. 'You made dinner?'

'Of course. Part of our hospitality exchange.'

'You know you don't have to do that,' she said. 'Is Maisie home?'

'Yes. It looked like it might snow, so I picked her and Chelsey up from school. Tea?'

'Mm . . . please.'

He got busy with kettle and mugs. 'Have you and the chief made it up?'

'No.' Hearing feet on the stairs, she said, 'Don't say anything in front of Maisie.' She got up and went into the hall. 'Hello, Chelsey.' She got a subdued look. 'Would you like to stay for dinner?'

'No, thanks. I have to go.'

Leaving them in the hall, Hanson returned to the kitchen. Two minutes later, Maisie came in. 'Is Chelsey OK?'

Maisie dropped onto a chair. 'Fine.'

Hanson eyed her. 'You've had a row.'

'No, we haven't.' She gave Hanson a mutinous look. 'She's going to the park later with Issy and a couple of other girls from school.'

Charlie looked at her. 'You weren't invited?'

Maisie jumped up and headed for the door. 'Ask Mom why I'm not going!'

He looked at Hanson. 'I walked straight into that. Sorry.'

'Don't worry about it. In a day or so it'll be replaced by something else.'

* * *

Hanson reached for her phone. It told her it was one-thirty a.m. It felt like she'd been lying there for ever, searching for sleep. Throwing back the duvet, she dragged her robe off the bed, headed for the door and downstairs. Reaching the hall, she saw a glimmer of light coming from her study. Going inside to turn it off, she saw the package Julian had delivered to her from headquarters lying on the desk where she'd left it, unopened. Taking scissors from her desk drawer, she cut through the sturdy brown wrapping and sealing tape. Pulling out its contents, she looked down at it, bemused. She lifted the plain cover, seeing lines of handwriting. She turned pages. There had to be hundreds, all handwritten. She took it into the sitting room, sat in a corner of the sofa and began to read.

Forty minutes later, she stopped, went to her study, searched the wrapping paper, looking for an indication of who had sent it to her. There was nothing. Back to the sitting room, she picked up what she'd been reading and fanned its many pages. Between the last two was a single sheet of paper. A letter from Andrea Jones: *Dear Professor Hanson, you were so kind when you came the other day that I wanted you to see this. I want you to know how clever, how talented my lovely sister was.*

Hanson looked down at the unpublished novel. Della's own story of a working life that was unfulfilling, a personal life that was secret and family members whom she protected from the truth. Della's truth. She shook her head. If she'd thought about it at all, Hanson might have assumed that the secrecy it related and the difficulties it caused for those involved were a thing of the past. Apparently not. She ran her hand over it, hoping that writing it had given Della some peace of mind. Now she understood Della's attendance at literary events. She rested her head, imagining Della queuing to meet published authors, breathlessly telling them of her own writing, her own hopes for the future, and David Lockman encouraging her, writing: 'To Della, do your own thing', then promptly forgetting her as he moved onto the next person in the queue. But Della hadn't forgotten the thrill of meeting him, had taken the bookmark and his used coffee cup, kept them as a reminder of that meeting and that, like him, she wanted to be an author. Months later, someone had killed her and David Lockman's small, forgotten kindness had cost him his family and a decade of his life.

Hanson pushed the manuscript away. If Della had felt able to tell her own truth to her family, if she had been able to tell them about whom she loved, she might never have felt the drive to write it. If she hadn't had that drive, David Lockman would still have his family and be unaware of her existence.

If, if, if.

'Maisie? *Maisie. Get up!*'

Maisie lifted her head and gazed through sleep-heavy eyes and tumbling curls to her mother at the door of her room. 'Wha's going on?'

'We're *late*. It's eight-thirty. Get up.'

Hanson's footsteps faded and Maisie flopped down. '. . . Fi'e minutes.'

Hanson came into the kitchen, searching for her phone as Charlie carried granola to the table. 'Have this before you go anywhere.'

She looked at it then around the kitchen. 'I don't have time. I have to drop Maisie off . . . Where *is* she.' She headed through the door. '*Maisie*. Come on!' Reappearing, she looked around the kitchen. 'Where's my damn . . .' She picked up a ringtone, saw Charlie, leaning against the worktop, his phone raised. She tracked her phone to where it was hiding under a newspaper. 'Thanks, Charlie.'

'I'll drop Maisie to school,' he said as Maisie came through the door, dressed, hair still chaotic.'

'Thanks, Grandpa. Mom, what happened?'

'I didn't get to sleep until around four a.m. You work it out. I'll phone the school and let them know that you'll be late. What lesson will you miss?'

Her response was indistinct through the mouthful of granola. 'Double English. No need to rush, Grandpa.'

Arriving on campus, Hanson rushed up to her room. She had three lectures to deliver, interspersed with admin. Dropping her things onto the old armchair she went to her desk, switched on the desktop. She went across the room to gather journals, brought them to the table, now on a mission to find criminological research directions she might encourage her new PhD students to take on. She had listed five when her phone rang.

'Blast.' She looked at its screen. It was Julian. She reached for it. 'Hi.'

'Hi, Kate. Got the results of the four phone searches you wanted. Ready?'

She reached for a pen. 'Read them to me.' She listened, wrote, listened again and stopped. 'Are you sure?'

'I followed the search steps, so yes. Why?'

'Nothing. Thanks Julian.'

She ended the call, staring down at the information he'd given her. It couldn't be. There had to be another explanation. She gave it some thought. If there was, for the life of her she didn't know what it might be. She heard a soft knock on her door. She was expecting one of her students who was struggling with stats. Putting Julian's results into a drawer, she went to open the door.

Throughout the day, Hanson had been busy but also preoccupied, searching her head wanting an explanation for Julian's data search which didn't – couldn't – make sense. She went into Crystal's room, this time to make real, strong coffee. During this investigation someone had said that coffee helped with thinking. She took the large cup to her desk and sat, her hands around it. She opened the desk drawer, took out the results, looked at them yet again. They still made no sense. She drank her coffee, searching for possibilities. Julian had seemed confident that he'd not made an error but was it possible he had? Last night, when she'd read what Andrea Jones had sent her, she'd thought she'd found some clarity, some . . . She came upright, spilling coffee on the desk. It wasn't just Julian's result which was bothering her. There was something else pushing at her. It was a name which was no longer relevant in 2006. Her head was reeling. She rummaged in her briefcase, brought out a photograph of Della Harrington's death scene, stared at it, let it fall onto the desk. Now she understood it. Because she knew exactly what it was. A pastiche. A mock-up. A fake by someone who needed to portray himself as a sadistic killer to conceal the real reason why Della Harrington had to die. She seized her phone, selected a number, waited for Watts' voice. It came into her ear, gruff but warm.

'How you doing, doc? I was about to give you a bell to see how you—'

'Is the chief there?' Before he could respond, she said, 'Forget it. I'm coming in.'

TWENTY-SEVEN

Her colleagues looked at each other then back at her. 'How sure are you?' asked Watts.

'I'm sure.'

Watts slowly shook his head. 'Before we act on this, I want all the detail, doc. We have to be sure. There's been too many blind alleys. I don't want us going down another.'

Hanson pointed to the crime scene photographs lying on the table. 'The original investigation accepted this portrayal of a sexual homicide, yes? After we'd worked the case for a while, we rejected it as a motive because aspects of it made no sense. The question was always, 'Why would a murderer who was not a sexual sadist, want the police to think he was?' She stopped, suddenly uncomfortable. 'I need you to understand why I arranged to meet David Lockman. What I wanted from him was a sense of why, how he had become caught up in this case. From what he told me, I suspected he might have been framed. The more I thought about it, the more likely it seemed to me that he had been lured to Marlow Gardens Apartments.' She reached for the small paperback she had brought with her, held it up. 'I've got a shelf full of true crime books like this one in my study at home. They can provide good insight into the thinking and the behaviour of murderers. I started looking through them, not sure what I was looking for. But as soon as I looked inside *this* book I thought I might be onto something. It's a factual account of a murder which I'd read years ago which had been bumping against the inside of my head whilst I was trying to work out why David Lockman had to be in the Jewellery Quarter that day. A few minutes of re-reading was all it took.'

Watts and Corrigan inclined their heads to look at the book now on the table. She turned it towards them.

'This murder occurred in Liverpool in the 1930s. Its two real-life characters were a middle-aged insurance agent and his wife. She was also the murder victim. The husband belonged to a local chess club. One evening, shortly before his wife's murder, he went to that club and was handed a telephone message, purportedly from a man wishing to discuss business with him. The message included an address on the other side of Liverpool. The husband set out the following winter's evening on public transport. He encountered significant difficulties in finding the address he had been given. Being a punctilious kind of person and also anxious to secure new business, he went to considerable efforts to locate it. He asked the tram driver, plus a local newsagent, plus several passers-by, even a police officer for help.' She paused. Both of her colleagues glanced at each other and she guessed they were seeing the parallels between this old case and the Harrington murder. 'The alibi presented by the husband raised a lot of questions, one being, why would the individual who left that phone message go to so much trouble to get that man to that area?' She leant towards them. 'His destination halfway across Liverpool was a misdirection. The home he had left that cold winter's evening held the solution to his wife's murder. Whilst the insurance agent was pursuing the non-existent address, his wife was alone in their terraced house. Inside that house was what would have been considered a sizeable amount of money for the time. Money the insurance agent had collected from his clients. *Someone* knew of the existence of that money. That someone got inside the house that evening whilst the husband was out, beat his wife to death and stole that money. The husband returned home and discovered his wife dead. He was arrested and sent to trial for murdering her. The prosecution's case was that his efforts to impress his presence onto people's memories as he searched for that non-existent address was intentionally deceptive. That they were his way of providing himself with an alibi away from that house during the time his wife was being killed. The police discovered that the call received at his club was made from a telephone box very close to his house. He was arrested for killing his wife, found guilty and sentenced to be hanged.'

'Poor guy,' said Corrigan. 'It's lucky the UK no longer puts felons to death.'

'He didn't hang. He was freed on appeal but died not long afterwards due to the impact of the case and the trial on his physical health, plus the incessant press coverage at the time.'

'Blimey, nothing changes does it?' said Watts.

'Actually, his guilt or innocence continues to be a source of contention even now. You could say it's still a cold case. My view, for what it's worth, is that the husband was lured away from his home by that phone call.' She patted the book. 'I know you've picked up the similarities with our case. It was this which led me to suggest to David Lockman that he'd been purposely lured by someone to the Jewellery Quarter and Marlow Gardens Apartments.'

'What did he say?' asked Watts.

'He thought it was laughable. His response to the idea that someone who knew him harboured sufficient animosity towards him to orchestrate such a plan was much the same.' She paused. 'You can see the dissimilarities with that old case but the central theme in both is a message, used as a lure to get someone to a specific place.'

Her two colleagues regarded her in silence. Watts was clearly choosing his words. 'Doc, you do know that what we're talking about here isn't evidence? Not so far as the law is concerned. Can you imagine the chief's response if me and Corrigan take to him what you've just told us as an explanation for Harrington's death?'

She reached into her bag and brought out the search information Julian had given her. She pushed it across the table to them. 'You might want to show him this, too.' She watched them read it. It didn't take long.

Corrigan sat up. '*Whoa*. This is crazy.'

Watts stared up at her. 'Are you sure this is right?'

'Julian is sure.'

Watts looked at it again, then up at the data that had accumulated on the Smartboard. 'You know I'm not often short of words . . . my money was always on Dobbs because he's a slippery, money-grabbing, sexually opportunistic, scheming bastard.' He looked up at Hanson. 'But *this* . . . it just about takes the biscuit.'

'How confident of your theory are you, Red?' asked Corrigan.

'Not one hundred percent, based solely on what I've told you. Like Watts just said, it's light on evidence. But I've got something that supplies motive.' She lifted the package onto the table. 'This is what tells us why Della Harrington had to die.' She pushed it across to them, watched their heads come together, waited while they read the first couple of pages. She pointed to it. 'This is the equivalent of the money inside that 1930s Liverpool house.

This explains why Della's killer went to her apartment. He knew the area. Once inside, he hit her, orchestrated the scene to look like a sexual homicide to deflect attention from the real stakes he was playing for.' She pointed to what they were reading. 'They were high. Thousands of pounds high. Like you said, a schemer. A tale spinner.'

'And nobody realized just how slippery he really is,' said Corrigan.

Watts regarded her. 'It took you long enough to put this lot together, doc, and you've got a criminal mind.'

'He's killed two women,' she said. 'The stakes are still high for him. As slick as he is, there's one thing I'm convinced of: he will admit nothing. He'll never confess.' She paused, looked at Watts. 'Like you said earlier, what we've got isn't hard evidence. In legal hands it's open to question, to second-guessing. *He* has to admit it. I'm going to be there when he does.'

'Forget it,' said Watts. 'The chief was livid about you going to see Lockman. Don't rile him again or we'll never get you back here.'

'This is a dangerous operator we have here,' said Corrigan. 'We need to be ultra-careful what we do now and you can't be part of that, Red.'

Hanson leant towards them, anxiety spiralling. 'If you approach him on the basis of what we have here, he'll take legal advice, find any way he can to get out from under all of it. He'll probably refuse to talk. You'll get one hell of a fight from him.' She looked down at what was lying on the table, then up at Watts. 'This is evidence of guilt only when it's looked at as a whole.'

She left the table, walked to the Smartboard and stood, her back to them. 'We have an advantage. We *know* him. He has a low opinion of women and he uses them. He's seen me. He probably thinks I'm easy to con.' She turned, pointed to words scripted in black above the window. 'Remember that?'

They looked up to the quote all three of them had insisted be written there following the successful completion of one of their first UCU cases. '"Let justice roll down." That's our reason for being here. Della Harrington and Romily Petersen are still waiting. He has to talk. It has to be me who gets him talking because he won't view me as any kind of threat.'

'If you've got a plan, tell me so that I can veto it,' said Watts.
'It involves me talking to David Lockman again. I'm no longer part of this unit or headquarters. We need him on side. We need to get him thinking and talking. I want to ask him again about the names in this case. I'll ask him if he's thought about my theory of a lure since I mentioned it to him. He might have something to say about that since I last saw him. I'm going to ring him now.' She picked up the desk phone, hesitated and replaced it. She brought out her phone, selected his number and waited, listening to it ring out.

She was about to end the call when it was picked up, his voice in her ear, a single, terse: 'Yes?'

She looked at her colleagues. 'This is Kate Hanson, Mr Lockman. Are you alright?'

There was a long pause. 'No. I'm not. My home was vandalized again yesterday. I've just spent two hours outside, removing graffiti.'

She mouthed his last word to her colleagues. 'I'm really sorry to hear that. Have you reported it?'

'What's the point? The police weren't able to do anything before, when the sundial came crashing through my window.' He sounded as if he hadn't slept in years.

'Maybe this isn't such a good time,' she said.

'Right now, I can't see a better one coming.'

'I was wondering, would you be willing to talk to me again?' She waited out the growing silence. 'Mr Lockman, I'm no longer part of the police investigation into Della Harrington's murder but my two colleagues are still working extremely hard on it. They think they may have a suspect. I won't name him, but if I meet with you, talk about the case a little more . . .' She heard him sigh.

'Professor Hanson, I've already told you all I know. I really can't see the point in us talking again.'

'I'll be honest with you, Mr Lockman. I don't know how you can help. All I know is that I have to give it another try.'

His voice came again. It sounded resigned. 'You say a place and when and I'll be there.'

'Thank you. Have you any objections to my coming to your home? I could come at say seven o'clock this evening, if that suits you?'

'Why not? People I don't even know seem to think they have
carte blanche to come here and wreck it so I've no objections to
you coming.' He gave his address.

'Thank you, Mr Lockman. I'm very grateful to you.'

She ended the call. She and her colleagues regarded each other
in silence. She reached for her coat. 'We'll see how it goes but
I think we might be on our way with this case.' They stood.
'Where are you two going?'

'We'll go and see a woman about a key,' said Watts.

Corrigan stood. 'Before we do, I'm going to talk to Forensics.
They've got a whole heap of gizmos up there. I want one of them.'

Several hours later, they were inside Watts' vehicle. 'We'll hang
on here for a bit, Corrigan.' He checked the time, looked out at
darkness and shook his head. 'We knew what he was and we let
him go.' He glanced at Corrigan, index finger against his top lip,
his eyes fixed straight ahead. Corrigan was no blatherer at the best
of times and this wasn't one of them. Chong called him 'the quiet
American'. He thought back over the case. Della Harrington, Karen
Forster and that nice woman, Josie Clark, the librarian who'd given
Hanson and him good coffee, all once living in an area where
they should have felt safe. They hadn't known that Archie Fenton
was a porn addict, that Coultard used sex workers. And then
there was Leonard Dobbs. Watts recalled what he'd first thought
on meeting him, with his hair, his BMW and his 'little place in
the country'. He'd initially summed up Dobbs as an irritating
git. Now they knew he was a lot more than that. He was a menace.
'It's time we moved closer to the house.'

They drove for a few minutes, houses becoming fewer and
further apart. Watts cut the engine and peered out at blackness.
After several minutes his eyes narrowed on distant lights. 'Ay-up,
Corrigan.'

'I see them.'

'Looks like we're in business.'

TWENTY-EIGHT

H anson parked her car and looked at the house in the middle of its spacious, expertly-lit gardens, her eyes moving from its thatched roof to its extensive ground floor. David Lockman's bestselling novel had been made into a film. It had made him a lot of money before his life fell apart. She noticed one or two faint swirls of colour still visible on white plaster. Red graffiti. She looked across the garden, eyes stopped by a sundial, its top missing. He'd obviously decided not to reinstall it after it crashed through his window. Probably just as well. She shook her head. He was still paying for his freedom. Bright light drew her attention back to the house. He was standing in the open doorway, his hand raised.

She got out of her car, fetched her bag from the boot, went through the small gate and up to the front door. 'Thank you, Mr Lockman. I really appreciate this.'

He smiled. 'Come on in. You had no trouble finding me?'

'No.'

'I had considered turning off the garden lights but you might not have found me at all and it would just be an invitation to the vandals if the place was all in darkness.'

She stepped inside and followed him across a wide hallway and into a large, homely kitchen. This was probably the family home where he had lived with his wife and children, while he still had them. He switched on the kettle and turned to her. She saw signs that he wasn't sleeping well.

'Please. Sit down,' he said. She went and sat at the solid wood table. He moved a heavy ceramic bowl to one side. 'Is it OK if we talk in here?' he asked. 'I'm sorry if I sounded ill-mannered when we spoke on the phone earlier. You caught me at a bad moment.'

'I understand. You seem to have a lot to cope with right now.'

'I've thought of moving away. I think about it every five minutes and change my mind as often.'

'Does this house hold a lot of memories?' she asked.

He looked at her, adrift. 'Oh, I see what you mean. No, this wasn't our family home for years. We bought it about six months before I was arrested.' He turned away, busied himself with the kettle and china cups. Listening to him, Hanson knew what a real tragedy it was that he'd come to this. He looked at her. 'I'm sorry. I haven't asked you what you'd like.'

'Nothing for me, thank you. I'm anxious to get to what brought me here. I'd like to tell you where my colleagues are in terms of their investigation.'

He came and sat opposite her. 'I'd really appreciate that.'

'They have three people they're very interested in for Della Harrington's murder. One is now a strong suspect but they're desperate to find anything which might prove it. Which is why I'm here.'

'I didn't realize the police were making progress,' he said. 'It's what I've been hoping for.'

'I can tell you in confidence that they're under considerable pressure, trying to obtain information to strengthen their case against that suspect. If they don't succeed, or not quickly enough, there could well be another victim.'

He stared at her. '*What*? . . . But that's . . . terrible.'

'That's why I had to see you again, Mr Lockman.' She reached into her bag and took out several A4 sheets. 'Will you try and help us?'

'Of course. What do you want me to do? Ask me anything and I'll do it.'

She unfolded the sheets. He looked down at the listed names. 'You'll remember this from last time we met?'

He nodded. 'Yes. I thought one of the names struck a chord.'

'Could you go through the list again and see if there's any other name which means something, anything to you?'

He took the pen she was offering. 'I didn't see anything else last time but I'll do my best.'

She sat back and watched as he went slowly down the list. Her eyes drifted to the red Aga across the kitchen then down to the floor and a narrow, coloured strip—

'That's the first page done. Sorry. There's nothing.' He continued on down the second to the end. He looked up at her.

'The name I noted before, Forster, still rings some kind of bell inside my head. As for the others—' he shrugged – 'there's only one: Leonard Dobbs.'

Hanson kept her face impassive. 'Any reason you can think of as to why those two names stand out?'

He shrugged, shook his head. 'Maybe the police at the time mentioned both of them. Who is this Dobbs?'

'He's an extremely unpleasant individual who preys on single females for sexual purposes.'

Lockman's head shot up. 'Really? Did the police know this at the time they arrested me?' She shook her head. He stared across at her. 'This Dobbs sounds like just the kind of person to have killed Della Harrington.' He patted his pockets. 'I have to contact my lawyer. Tell her.'

'Please, Mr Lockman, could you do that after I've left? I have some questions for you.'

He nodded. 'Sorry. I'm just keyed up at what you've told me.'

She pointed to a name on the list. 'You recognized the name of Karen Forster.'

He frowned at it. 'It caught my attention, yes.'

'How about I tell you what I know about her? It might help us both understand why her name resonates with you. Ten years ago, Karen Forster was a young woman who was a next-door neighbour of Della Harrington's. She shared her apartment with her boyfriend, Matthew, who worked as a doctor at one of the city's hospitals. She was actually the keyholder for the Harrington apartment. It was she who supplied the key which led to the discovery of the body.' Lockman's attention was total as Hanson continued. 'Karen loved her apartment but after the murder she and her boyfriend moved out.'

'Understandable,' he said.

'You were arrested and sent for trial. Karen played very little part in that. She was called to give her very limited evidence on a day you weren't in court. At the end of the trial you were sent to prison and eighteen months or so later she and her boyfriend got married.'

He sighed. 'Nice to know that some people's lives continued on happily.'

'I agree. What I don't see, Mr Lockman, is how you recognized her under her married name which she didn't take until you'd been inside for a long time.'

He looked down at the list then back to Hanson. 'I don't know. I just did what you said, looked at the list and . . . it leapt out. Maybe my lawyers mentioned it?'

'Maybe,' she said. 'And you think they might also have mentioned Leonard Dobbs to you?'

'It's very possible.'

'Possible yes,' said Hanson. 'But, in Karen Forster's case, I'd say very unlikely.'

He gazed at her, bemused. 'Why do you say that?'

'I can't think of a reason why your lawyer would mention Forster to you. And even less reason they would mention Dobbs who played no role in the original investigation.'

'I don't understand,' he said. 'I can't explain how I came to pick out those names but the fact is I did.'

'You were trying to be helpful.'

'Yes. I was.'

'Sometimes helpfulness can be a muddying of the waters. A distraction.' She saw him frown as she reached into her bag and took out another sheet, opened it and placed it on the table in front of him. 'Mr Lockman, can you help me some more by explaining this?' She pointed to the results Julian had obtained from his search of four individuals' phone records for the ninth of November, 2006, moving her finger down the short list to Lockman's name. 'See what it says here?' She pointed to two words: Zero Calls. She looked up at him. 'There were no calls to your house that day, no message instructing you to go to Marlow Gardens.' She sat back, they stared at each other and the meaning of the colourful scrap she'd seen on the floor close to the Aga clicked into place. 'Where's Archie Fenton . . .?'

The edge of the heavy wood table slammed against her diaphragm, forcing the air from her chest, leaving her incapable of breathing. He was across the table, dragging her onto it, his hands at her throat. Fighting to breathe, she looked into his soft, brown eyes, now flint, fixed on hers, blood thundering inside her ears as her hand scrabbled over notebook, pen, ceramic bowl. She grasped it, dragged it, hit him on the side of his head. He released her, the bowl fell to the floor and shattered. He was coming for her again when a large fist made contact with his jaw, sending him senseless to the floor. Corrigan had her by the shoulders, lifting her. Gasping, throat raw, she gazed down at Lockman lying among the ceramic shards, officers rushing him, Watts following, shaking and flexing his hand.

'What kept you?' she asked, once she had breath and a voice.

'Dodgy reception. They're subject to wireless interference.'

She reached inside her shirt. 'You didn't mention that,' she whispered, dropping the tiny black plastic device onto his palm. 'You also didn't tell me how uncomfortable those things are.'

Lockman was hauled to his feet, his face, his eyes vacant with shock, a reddened area on his jawline now visible. With an officer on either side holding his arms, he gazed straight ahead. In the silence Watts arrested him for the murders of Della Harrington and Romily Petersen. Hanson's eyes were on Lockman's face, watching as he gradually came to full awareness.

'I want my lawyer,' he whispered. 'But first, you have to hear me out. All I've achieved came through hard work. Nobody gave me a damn thing. I worked for it.'

'Della Harrington worked hard,' said Corrigan, not looking at him. 'You're right about not being given anything. She didn't give you her book. You killed her for it.'

'It wasn't a bloody book until I got it! *I* made it one. *Me*.'

A uniformed officer burst into the kitchen. 'Sarge? There's another one.'

Watts looked away from Lockman. 'Another what?'

'Another one he's killed.'

'That'll be Fenton,' said Hanson, pointing to the woven scrap on the floor, feeling Lockman's eyes on her as he was pulled towards the open door. She listened to his voice, loud now as Watts and the officers dragged him along the hall and out.

'*Wait*. You need to hear me out to understand why. I'm not a bad person.'

Watts' terse words to the officers drifted back to the kitchen. 'Watch him as you get him into the van. He's out of his tree.'

Hanson felt Corrigan's warm hand on her upper arm. 'The guy's crazy if he thinks he'll beat this.'

She shook her head. 'I doubt he'll satisfy the criteria for insanity.'

Watts had returned. 'Fenton's unconscious and half-frozen to death in an outbuilding. You're welcome to your opinion, doc, but right now Lockman's kicking off inside the van and screaming that nobody's listening to him. I'm with Corrigan where he's concerned.'

Hearing Fenton's name, Hanson said, 'Any progress on Dawn Wilson's whereabouts?'

'Just before we left we had a call. She's been traced to an address near London.'

'Don't tell me. I've had enough sad stories in the last twenty-four hours.'

'Right, then I won't tell you she's OK, married with two kids.' Hands thrust into his pockets he came and stood next to her. 'Alright?'

She nodded. He gave her a gentle nudge. 'Good work.' He turned, winked at Corrigan. 'I'm starting to think this psychology lark's got something going for it.'

TWENTY-NINE

L ate the next afternoon, Hanson was in the observation room, watching her colleagues as they faced Lockman who was now charged with the murders of Della Harrington, Romily Petersen and the attempted murder of Archie Fenton. They were having no problem getting Lockman to talk. In the last fifteen minutes he'd scarcely stopped.

'You do see that I had no choice? I asked Della to give me her manuscript. I said I'd take it to my publisher for her, but she wouldn't listen.'

'Probably because she guessed you were after it for yourself,' said Watts.

Lockman raised his hand, as though brushing away an irrelevant detail. 'She didn't know what she had. There was no chance she'd be able to do anything with it.' He stared at them. 'She knew nothing about publishing. What you need to understand is that Della would have hung onto what she'd written and that would have been it.' He pointed at the manuscript sitting on the table between them. 'It's basic, raw. It needed reworking.' He pointed to himself. '*I* did that. I took it apart, restructured it.'

'And passed it off as your own,' said Watts. 'There's a word for that.'

Lockman glared at him. 'You're not listening to me!' He moved his gaze to Corrigan. 'You look more the kind of person who has a modicum of literary understanding. Della Harrington produced an *outline* of a book, nothing more. *I* saw it's potential, reworked it into a bestseller. You must see that?'

'What I see is that you killed two women to get hold of it.'

Lockman was on his feet. 'With great art comes great sacrifice!' Hanson shook her head as she watched him being forced back onto his chair by two heavy-looking constables, his face flushed. 'It wouldn't have seen the light of day if it weren't for me. Look what I did with it.'

'I'm more interested in what you did to Archie Fenton.'

Lockman's face contorted. 'Collateral damage. He saw me leaving Della's apartment earlier that day and went up there. He'd guessed what had happened and contacted me. Tried to blackmail me. He'd have done it ten years ago but for me being sent to prison. Once the police started asking him questions again, he wanted his cut. He's a common, sleazy, little man and a villain. You should be focusing on him, not me. All I wanted to do was *create*. What I did was take a rough stone and smooth and burnish it into . . .'

Hanson stood, picked up her notebook, took one last look at David Lockman through the one-way glass, Watts' voice in her ears. 'Yeah, yeah. You're a prince.'

Lockman glared at him and then at Corrigan. 'Get Kate Hanson in here. She'd understand what it is I'm telling you.' Watts' gaze went to the glass then back to him. 'She's not here anymore. She's gone.'

That evening, in gathering shadow and silence they returned the case data to the lever arch files waiting on UCU's table. The door swung open and two officers came inside, loaded them onto a small trolley and left. Hanson gazed around the large room. It looked empty, done with. She felt Watts' eyes on her. 'That's the fourth time I've caught you looking at me. What is it? Have I got ink on my nose?'

He didn't smile. 'What are your plans, doc?'

'In ten minutes I'm going home.'

'You know what I mean.' He pointed to the scripted words on the wall above them. 'Justice, see? We'll never be out of a job here.'

She was about to respond that she was already out of UCU when the door opened and the chief walked in. This was the first time she'd seen him since she'd resigned. She kept her eyes on him as he came to the table. He didn't look directly at her. 'Good work. Fenton will need interviewing when he's fit enough. He's not the best witness material we could have but with what you've got on Lockman, he doesn't have to be. Pity about Coultard.' Hanson gazed out of the window. Coultard had died that morning. She heard the chief's voice again. 'I've spoken to Lockman's ex-wife. Nice woman. According to her he was a good husband

and father.' His tone changed to one of disbelief. 'He killed two people because he was ambitious?' He shook his head. 'It's going to cost him now.'

Hanson looked at him. 'Not as much as it cost Della Harrington and Romily Petersen.'

The chief turned and left without a word. She picked up her belongings. 'Bye, Watts.'

She and Corrigan walked to her car in silence. She dropped her briefcase into the boot and turned to him. 'Bye, Corrigan. Let me know how it goes here.'

He came close, freeing her hair from her collar. 'I will.'

She got into her car, looked up at him through the open door. 'See you.'

Watts turned from the window of UCU and let his eyes drift across the big room, in almost-darkness now. Everyone gone but him. He could ring Chong. See if she fancied going for something to eat. He walked to the big table, lifted his coat, put it on. No. Not tonight. At the door, he looked back, switched off the one remaining light and walked out.

Several hours later, Hanson took a deep breath and stretched in the wide, wide bed. She had come to it edgy. Now she was calm, rested. She looked up at him, propped on one arm, gazing down at her. 'What are you thinking?'

'I'm thinking we hit it clear out the park, Red.' He looked down at her. 'I see a real serious case of afterglow.'

She reached up, ran her hand over his chest then stretched again, eyes closed, letting the quiet of the room drift over her. In the silence, feeling him move, she looked up at him and burst into uncontrolled laughter, her hands covering her face. She wiped away tears. 'What *is* that?' Corrigan's face was grinning down at her from under a pale blue, knitted hat. He gave a small head-shake. The hat's two fluffy pom-poms shook, causing another wave of helpless laughter. She pointed at the hat and gasped, 'Don't tell me *that* is part of your sex repertoire.' She eyed it. 'Sorry to be picky but you do realize, it's too small?'

He nodded, provoking more pom-pom jiggles. He took it off, pressed it into her hand. 'I bought it for you.'

Her hand folded around the soft wool. 'For me? I don't understand.'

'I've been thinking.' He took it and gently pulled it over her hair, looked down at her, his head on one side. 'Cute.'

'What else are you thinking?'

'I'm planning a trip home at the end of the year, probably in the fall. I want you to come with me. I want to show you where I'm from. I want you to see Quincy Market and the Common. I want to follow the Freedom Trail with you, drive up to Salem, get spooked, have chowder and fish-shaped crackers, then back to Boston for dinner at Papa Razzi in the Back Bay which is kind of American-posh but real casual . . .'

'Corrigan, *stop.*'

He leant over her, looking down and into her face. 'I can't do that. I want you to meet my folks.'

'Corrigan, we agreed, remember. No plans, no long-term expectations.'

He traced his fingertip around the edge of the hat then down her face to her mouth.

'Sure, I remember.'

ACKNOWLEDGEMENTS

As always, my grateful thanks go to my agent, Camilla Wray at Darley Anderson and to all at Severn House Publishers. A big thank you to two stalwart experts, Chief Inspector Keith Fackrell, West Midlands Police (Retired), and Dr Adrian Yoong, Consultant Pathologist, Birmingham, whose advice across several books is much appreciated. I also want to thank Detective Chief Inspector Chris Mallett, Homicide Team, West Midlands Police for his invaluable investigative insights. Further thanks are due to Dr Catherine Hamilton-Giachritsis, Reader in Clinical Psychology at the University of Bath for her guidance on the career paths of academics. Finally, belated thanks to Dr Jamie Pringle, Senior Lecturer in Geosciences at Keele University for his advice on the place of drone technology in the recovery of human remains whilst I was writing the previous book, *Something Evil Comes*.

As always, any errors or misunderstandings in the use of their generously given assistance are entirely mine. Thank you all.